a big name in erotic romance' *Dea*

'Some of the sexiest love scenes I h

'Nuclear-grade hot' *USA Today*

'Intoxicating and exhilarating' *F*

D1342391

04955275

*previously published under the pseudonym Bethany Kane

Since I Saw You
BETH KERY

headline
ETERNAL

First published in Great Britain in 2014 by HEADLINE ETERNAL
An imprint of HEADLINE PUBLISHING GROUP

Published by arrangement with Berkley Publishing Group,
A member of Penguin Group (USA) LLC,
A Penguin Random House Company.

1

Cataloguing in Publication Data is available from the British Library

ISBN 978 1 4722 1100 2

Offset in Adobe Garamond by Avon DataSet Ltd,
Bidford-on-Avon, Warwickshire

Printed and bound by CPI Group (UK) Ltd, Croydon, CR0 4YY

Headline's policy is to use papers that are natural, renewable and recyclable
products and made from wood grown in sustainable forests.
The logging and manufacturing processes are expected to conform to the
environmental regulations of the country of origin.

HEADLINE PUBLISHING GROUP
An Hachette UK Company
338 Euston Road
London NW1 3BH

www.headlineeternal.com
www.headline.co.uk
www.hachette.co.uk

Acknowledgments

My thanks go out to Leis Pederson, my very supportive editor, as well as Mahlet and Limecello for their beta read and extremely helpful and intelligent feedback. I'm so grateful that my unconscious mind came up with Kam Reardon, as he ended up being a favorite hero and a rich source of sexiness and humor. Lastly, as always, my eternal thanks to my husband, who is my number one fan and pillar of strength.

Chapter One

Lin Soong hurried down the sidewalk, her face coated in a thin layer of perspiration overlaid with an autumn mist. Damn this fog. There hadn't been an available taxi for blocks. She'd finally ended up just walking the three-quarters of a mile from Noble Tower to the restaurant. Her feet were killing her after a long day's work and rushing in heels. To make matters worse, her hair would be a disaster from the humidity. She imagined herself at ten or eleven years old and her grandmother standing over her, wielding a comb and a flatiron like a warrior's weapons.

"You got this hair from your mother," Grandmamma would say, her mouth grim as she dove into her straightening task. Lin had been left in little doubt as to what her grandmother thought of the potential threat of her mother's rebellious streak surfacing in Lin herself. According to Grandmamma, hair was something to be conquered and refined by smoothing and polish, just like everything else in life.

Lin plunged through the revolving doors of the restaurant and paused in the empty foyer, straining to calm her breathing and her throbbing heart. She despised feeling flustered, and this situation called for even more than her usual aplomb.

By the time she entered the crowded, elegant restaurant, she'd repinned her waving, curling hair and used a tissue to dry her damp face. She immediately spotted him sitting at the bar. He was impossible to miss. For a stretched few seconds, she just stared. A strange mixture of anxiety and excitement bubbled in her belly.

Why didn't Ian mention that his half brother looked so much like him?

She soaked in the image of him. He was very good-looking, even if that frown was a little off-putting. He wore a dark blue shirt, and the rich brown of a rugged suede jacket brought out the russet highlights in his hair. Kam Reardon didn't know it—and she'd never tell him—but she herself had picked out the clothing he wore. It'd been part of the mission Ian had assigned her to make his half brother presentable for a potentially lucrative business deal here in Chicago. Ian had suggested a new wardrobe for his trip to the States. Kam had grudgingly agreed after some skillful nudging on Ian's part, but insisted upon paying for everything. It'd been Lin who actually chose the items, however, and sent the articles to Aurore Manor in France. In fact, she'd been choosing and sending home furnishings to Aurore Manor—Kam's once grand home that had fallen into disrepair—as well.

It warmed her to see him wearing the garments, firsthand evidence that he'd considered the clothing suitable to his taste. Her clothing selection hadn't helped much in getting Kam to blend in, however. He was too large for the delicate chairs lined up at the supersleek, minimalist bar. He stuck out like a sore thumb in the trendy establishment, all bold, masculine lines and unrelenting angles.

No . . . not like a sore thumb, Lin amended. More like a lion that found itself in the midst of a herd of antelope. His utter stillness and watchful alertness seemed slightly ominous amidst the sea of idly chatting, well-heeled patrons.

Suddenly, she realized his gaze had locked on her from across the crowded dining area.

"*Bonsoir*, beautiful. We have your table waiting," a man with a mellow French-accented voice said.

Lin blinked and jerked her gaze off the man who was a stranger to her, and yet wasn't: her boss's infamous half brother, the wild man she'd been sent to tame.

She focused instead on Richard St. Claire's smiling face. Richard was a neighbor, good friend, and the manager of the restaurant where she stood, Savaur. He owned the world-renowned establishment with his partner, chef Emile Savaur. Lin was a regular here.

She returned Richard's greeting warmly as they hugged and he kissed her on the cheek. "Can you hold the table for just a moment, Richard? My dinner companion is waiting at the bar. I'd like to go and introduce myself," Lin said, turning as he began to remove her coat.

"Mr. Tall, Dark, and Scowling?" Richard muttered under his breath as he draped her coat elegantly over his forearm, looking amused. He noticed her surprised glance as she faced him again. How did Richard know her dinner companion was the man at the bar? "You mentioned you were having dinner with Noble's half brother on the phone when you made the reservations. I noticed the resemblance; who wouldn't? I can't wait to hear the full story behind this little scenario," Richard said with a mischievous glance in Kam's direction. "He's like Ian Noble posing as a Brazilian street fighter, but with the added bonus of having Lucien's seduce-like-the-devil eyes."

Lin stifled a laugh at the apt description. Richard was good friends with Lucien Lenault also, Kam and Ian's other half brother. He'd undoubtedly heard part, if not all, of Kam's story from Lucien. "He's actually cleaned up quite nicely," Lin murmured. "Not six months ago, the people from the village near where he lived thought him homeless and mad, when he's truly brilliant and extremely focused," she added, her head lowered. She smoothed her expression, acutely aware of Kam's sharp gaze still cast in her direction.

"He hardly seems like a vagrant, but he has been sitting at the bar, looking like he's been chewing nails for the past ten minutes. Victor doesn't know if he's scared to death of the man or in love with him," Richard said under his breath, referring to the bartender serving Kam. Indeed, Victor was surreptitiously studying the tower of whiskered, glowering brawn seated at the bar, with a mixture of wariness and stark admiration as he dried a glass.

Lin threw her friend a repressive, amused glance and walked over to meet Ian's brother. Kam was one of the few people seated at the teak bar, a half-full glass of beer in front of him.

"I'm so sorry for being late. Work was crazy, and there wasn't a single available cab to be found when I finally did get away. You must be Kam. I'd have recognized you anywhere," she said when she approached him, smiling in greeting. "Ian never told me how much you two resembled one another."

He turned slightly in his chair, giving her an unhurried once-over. She remained completely still beneath his perusal, her expression calm and impassive. Inwardly, she squirmed. Ian had also failed to warn her that Kam Reardon oozed raw sex appeal—not that Ian would ever say that about his brother.

Although it couldn't have been any more than a second that he studied her, it felt like minutes before he finally met her stare. She recognized the hard glint of male appreciation in his eye. A strange sensation rippled down her spine. Was it excitement? Or that uncommon brand of lust that strikes like lightning during a rare, uncommon rush of attraction? His face and form were similar to Ian's, although up close, there were notable differences: the nose was slightly larger, the skin swarthier, the mouth fuller, the hair not quite as dark as Ian's, with hints of russet in the thick waves. *Gorgeous* man-hair, Lin assessed. It had to have dozens of females longing to sink their fingers into it on a daily basis.

Ian would certainly never go into public with a day-and-a-half's growth of stubble on his jaw. Although Kam's clothing was suitable for the restaurant, it was far more casual than Ian's typical Savile Row suits. It was like seeing Ian in some kind of magical mirror—a shadowy, savage version of her debonair boss. Kam's silvery-gray eyes, with the defining black ring around the iris, were certainly strikingly unique, despite what Richard had said about them being similar to Lucien's.

Maybe it was more the effect they had on Lin that was singular.

"Ian probably never noticed our similarity," Kam replied. "He's never seen me without a full beard."

Another stark difference. Much like that of her grandmother, who had learned English in Hong Kong, Ian's accent was all crisp, cool control. Kam's French-accented, roughened voice struck her like a gentle, arousing abrasion along the skin of her neck and ear.

She put out her hand. "I'm Lin Soong. As you probably already know, I work for Ian. I can't tell you what a pleasure it is to finally meet you."

He took her hand but didn't shake it, merely grasped it and held on. His hand was large and warm, encompassing her own. The pad of his forefinger pressed lightly against her inner wrist.

"Does my brother make a habit of overworking minors?" he asked.

She flushed, the temporary trance inspired by his voice and touch fracturing. She knew she looked younger than her age, especially with her makeup faded from the mist and her hair curling around her face like a dark cloud. Besides, she *was* young for the position she held at Noble Enterprises as Ian's right-hand woman. She was used to the observation, although it typically didn't fluster her as much as it did at the moment.

"I'm hardly a minor. Ian seems to find me capable enough for all my duties," she said smoothly, arching her brows in a mild, amused remonstrance.

"No doubt." She blinked at the steel of certainty in his tone. His finger moved on her wrist, and she suddenly pulled her hand away, afraid he'd notice the leap in her pulse.

"Actually, I'm twenty-eight," she said.

"Isn't that young for the position you hold at Noble Enterprises? I've heard the stories from Ian and Lucien and Francesca. He can't seem to function without you," he said.

She flushed at the compliment. "You might say I was groomed for the role. My grandmother was the vice president of finance for Noble. She got me regular summer internships during college and graduate school."

"And one day you ended up in Ian's lap?" he asked, silvery-gray eyes gleaming with what appeared to be a mixture of humor and interest. "Does your grandmother still work for Ian?"

"No. She passed two years ago this Christmas."

Her breath stuck when he reached around her waist. Was he going to *touch* her? She jumped slightly when a chair leg made a scraping sound on the wood floor. She exhaled when she realized he was pulling back on the chair next to him so that she could sit.

"Our table is ready," she explained.

"I'd rather eat at the bar."

"Of course," she said, refusing to be flustered. She set down her briefcase in the seat next to her and reached for her chair. A frown creased his brow and he stood. "Thank you," she murmured, surprised when she realized he'd grudgingly stood to seat her. Maybe he wasn't so rough around the edges, after all.

"You're a cool one," he said as he sat back down next to her, his jean-covered knees brushing her hip and thigh.

"What do you mean?"

He shrugged slightly, his eyes gleaming as he fixed her with his stare. "I thought you'd take offense to sitting at the bar."

"Don't you mean you'd hoped I would?" she challenged quietly. She transferred her gaze to Victor when the bartender approached, speaking before Kam had a chance to refute her. "Victor often serves me at the bar when I stumble in after a long day's work. He takes good care of me," she said.

"And it's always a pleasure. The usual, Ms. Soong?" Victor asked.

"Yes, thank you. And will you please let Richard know he can give our table to someone else?"

Victor nodded, giving Kam a nervous, covetous glance before he walked away.

"Goodness, what did you do to that poor man?" Lin asked in a hushed tone, leaning her elbows against the bar and meeting Kam's gaze with amusement.

"Nothing. I asked him to give me a beer."

"That's all?" Lin asked doubtfully.

He shrugged unconcernedly. "Maybe not. Might have said something like, 'Forget all that crap and just give me a damn beer.'" He noticed her raised eyebrows. "He was trying to get me to buy some fancy drinks and two bites of food and a sprinkle on a plate."

"Imagine, him suggesting you eat and drink in a restaurant."

Much to her surprise, he grinned widely, white teeth flashing against his dark skin. "The guy's got balls, doesn't he?"

Lin forced herself to look away from the magnetic sight of Kam Reardon's smile. It was a tad devilish, no doubt, and full-out sexy, but there was also just a hint of shyness to him in that moment, as if his interest was unexpectedly piqued in meeting her. And like her, he hadn't been prepared for it. It was potent stuff. Perhaps she could forgive Ian for not giving her warning about his half brother, but surely his new wife, Francesca—as a fellow female—should have hinted at something that might prepare her for the impact of Kam.

"Most people who belly up to the bar expect a friendly chat with the bartender," she chided lightly.

"I'm not most people," he said, watching her as he also placed his elbows on the bar and leaned forward, matching her pose.

"Yes. I think we've established that," she murmured humorously, studying him with her chin brushing her shoulder. They sat close. Much closer than they would have if they'd been seated at a table. Their elbows touched lightly; their poses were intimate. Too much so for having just met. She instinctively glanced downward, taking in his crotch and strong, jean-covered thighs.

Heat flooded her cheeks. She fixed her gaze blindly on the glassware hanging behind the bar.

She silenced the voice in her head telling her to lean back and gain perspective. Lin Soong didn't hunch down over bars flirting with rugged, sexy men. His face fascinated her, though. She wanted to turn again and study it, the desire an almost magnetic pull on her attention. And . . . she could smell him. His scent was simple: soap and freshly showered male skin. No, it *should* have been simple, but was somehow light-headedly complex. Delicious.

"I wasn't trying to insult you by saying I'd rather eat at the bar," he said, referring to her earlier, subtle gibe that he'd intended to insult her. "I'm more comfortable here. I'm out of practice. I'm not used to places like this," he said, glancing around without moving his head.

"I'm sorry," she said, meaning it. With a sinking feeling, she thought of the schedule she had planned for him in the next few weeks. Ian had approved of it, but clearly Kam wouldn't. Perhaps it'd be best to ease him into things, maybe just tell him about each appointment a day or two in advance so that he didn't have time to dread them too much? "I wasn't trying to be pretentious by asking you to meet here. Even though Savaur might seem upscale, I consider it the opposite. It's almost like a second home for me. I'm good friends with the owners—they're neighbors of mine, in fact."

"Was that one of them who you were laughing with—presumably about me—when you walked in?"

Guilt swept through her. "We weren't *laughing* at you."

He arched his brows and gave her a bland look, as if to say it was all the same to him whether they were or they weren't. Lin had the distinct impression his impervious manner wasn't for show. He really must have built up a thick skin living like an outcast for all those years. She couldn't help but admire his nonchalance about what other people thought of him. It wasn't a thing she encountered much in this day and age. His concise observance mixed with his cool indifference and jaw-dropping good looks left her unsure of what to say.

"I'm sorry if I gave the impression I was laughing. I was—*am*, I mean—very eager to meet you." She cleared her throat. It suddenly struck her that they were speaking in hushed, intimate tones. She was relieved to see Victor appear with the menus. "May I order for you?" she asked Kam politely. She saw his flashing glance and knew she'd made another misstep.

"Which do you think? That I don't know how to place an order myself, or that I can't read?"

"Neither, of course. I was thinking of what you insinuated earlier about tiny servings. I promise you, I won't order two bites and a sprinkle on a plate. Emile Savaur knows how to feed a hungry Frenchman. He and Richard are Frenchmen as well, and more often than not, hungry ones."

She took his silence and slight shrug as agreement and ordered them both the steak au poivre.

"So Ian sent you to make me feel more comfortable for this experiment of his," Kam asked once Victor had walked away, his low, resonant voice amplifying the tickling sensation on her bare neck. Again, she experienced that heavy feeling in her lower belly and sex.

She blinked. What was wrong with her? This whole experience was bizarre. It was his similarity to Ian that was setting her off balance. She'd trained herself long ago to remain cool and professional with Ian Noble . . . even if in her deepest, secret self, her feelings for Ian were far from aloof. Only she knew that particular truth, however, although a couple of friends—namely, Richard St. Claire— seemed to have guessed it, much to her discomfort. She struggled to focus her errant thoughts. She would have defended herself better if she'd known how potentially volatile this situation would be.

"Is that what you call it? An experiment?" she asked crisply.

"I could come up with a more accurate description, but I'm not sure you'd like it."

She laughed softly, glancing around when Victor set a glass of claret on the bar in front of her, along with some ice water. She thanked Victor and took a sip of wine, glancing sideways at Kam as she set down her glass. "I hope you don't mind Ian suggesting that we meet. Work together."

His gaze dropped slowly over her face, neck, and lower. "Now that I see you, I'm kind of warming up to the idea."

She chuckled and shook her head, trying to shake off the spell again. Flirtation, she was used to. But who would have thought the alleged "wild man" of the French forest's subtle sexual advances would be so appealing? Who would have thought *she'd* respond to him on such a basic level? The way Francesca and Ian had described Kam, she thought he'd be some kind of brilliant social misfit. True, he was raw and primal, but he was hardly illiterate.

And those eyes packed a precise, powerful sexual wallop.

Of course there had never been any doubt that Kam was a genius. What he'd pulled off in that makeshift, underground lab in northern France was nothing short of revolutionary. The question at hand was whether Kam would do middling well with his brilliant invention or sow the seeds to create an empire. Ian believed he had the potential to do the latter. Ian's concern was that Kam would alienate every potential opportunity for capital and expansion on his climb up the ladder.

"Ian explained to me that you were doubtful about the idea of selling your biofeedback timepiece to the luxury watch industry. He thought I might be of some help in . . ."

"Making this whole ridiculous thing more palatable?" he murmured when she hesitated. She'd been trying to carefully choose her words. The truth was, Ian had taken her into his confidence, explaining that he hoped Lin could alleviate his brother's doubts about the advisability of selling his revolutionary medical timepiece to the high-end watch industry. Kam had already sold his patent to one of the pharmaceutical giants for millions of dollars, the contract calling for an exclusivity clause that prevented him from selling to other pharmaceutical companies. But there was no prohibition from selling to unrelated industries. Ian thought that one of the sophisticated, groundbreaking mechanisms Kam had invented—a biofeedback timepiece that could do everything from tell time, to send warnings for an impending heart attack, to signaling to a woman when she was likely ovulating—would also be a smash hit in the luxury watch business. Lin and Lucien happened to agree. It would give him the cash he needed to begin a groundbreaking company at some future date. The problem was Kam's condescending attitude about the industry.

To say the least.

Pair Kam's scorn about cutting a deal with one of the luxury watch companies along with his rough manners, and it was a recipe for a business disaster. Thus the reason Ian had called in Lin to smooth over Kam's jagged edges and present him in the best light possible to the interested buyers gathering in Chicago for a series of business dinners, presentations, and meetings.

Problem was, according to Ian, Kam would likely be insulted if he knew Ian had sent Lin to polish up a man who had once been considered an intimidating vagrant.

"Why do you find the idea of selling your invention to a high-end watch company ridiculous?" she asked.

"Look at me. I'm not interested in that world. I don't cater to fashion or rich bastards," he responded coldly, holding her stare. "It's a waste. At least in my dealings with the pharmaceutical companies, I shared the commonality of science. Medicine."

She considered him somberly before she responded.

"It makes sense. You hold degrees in both biology and engineering as well as a medical degree from the Imperial College London.

You received a highly esteemed scholarship to attend medical school there. I can understand how the world of luxury fashion might seem beneath your scholarly interests, but—"

She paused when he gave a harsh bark of laughter. "I'm no academic, either. I never finished my residency, and I don't have a license to practice. I'm not being highbrow by saying I don't want to work with the fashion industry." He took a swig of his beer and set the glass back on the counter with a thud. "I just think the whole business is a waste of time, no pun intended. No offense intended, either," he tagged on sheepishly with a flashing glance in her direction.

"None taken," Lin replied evenly. "Of course you have to feel comfortable with such a large business venture. I think you might be underestimating the business savvy and brilliance of some of the leaders of these companies. Watchmaking is an ancient art that has also been a forerunner in miraculous advances in technology."

"There isn't a damn thing those suits can teach me about watchmaking."

She absorbed his disdainful yet supremely confident manner. From what she'd learned from Ian, Kam wasn't bluffing. When it came to both mechanical devices and the biological rhythms of the human body, Kam Reardon was a veritable da Vinci.

"This could be a very lucrative venture for you," she reasoned.

He gave her a gleaming sideways glance, his eyes going warm as they wandered over her face. "How lucrative?"

"A hundred, possibly two hundred times more than the deal you cut with the pharmaceutical company for your device. Ian believes your invention deserves all the acknowledgment it can get. He wants you to have as much security as possible. This sale could give you even more working capital, a solid base for a future company."

Kam rolled his eyes and exhaled with a hiss. "Ian's got it all figured out, hasn't he? He's known we're related for less than a year and already he's pulling a big brother act on me."

Lin smiled. "I hadn't realized he was the elder of the two of you."

"By a year and a half. Lucien is the oldest of us all. Six weeks ahead of Ian," Kam said. She noticed him studying her face with a narrow-eyed gaze. Instinctively, she knew he wondered if Ian had told her about the background of their common heritage.

"Ian has explained to me about Trevor Gaines being his, Lucien's, and your biological father," she said without flinching.

"Did he also tell you that dear daddy was a fucked-up son of a bitch?" he asked with harsh flippancy, before he took a swallow of beer. *Too* flippant. She sensed the edge of anger beneath his unconcern this time. His description of Trevor Gaines was apt. The French aristocrat *had* been a sick SOB who got his thrills from impregnating as many women as he possibly could, whether by seduction, rape, or other unsavory means. Using those means, he'd gotten Lucien's, Ian's, and Kam's mothers pregnant in a close span of time. There had been other victims, too. The newly discovered knowledge had nearly sent Ian over the edge when he'd learned of it last year. This much she knew: Kam came by his bitterness toward his father honestly.

"He told me," she replied simply.

His tense expression relaxed somewhat when she offered no false platitudes in regard to the unthinkable crimes of the man who had created him.

"I'm having trouble finding uses for all the money I got with the pharmaceutical deal," he said, changing the subject. "What am I supposed to do with a hundred times that amount?"

"Ian and Lucien both seem to think the capital will help you to buy more advanced laboratories and equipment that will spur you on to more creative heights of invention. You could potentially create a lasting company that could revolutionize the watchmaking and medical biofeedback industries—not to mention people's everyday lives. You could provide thousands of jobs. Ian has a lot of faith in your brilliance, Kam. But in the end, if *you* can't think of anything you'd do with the capital from another sale, then this entire conversation is pointless."

His nostrils flared slightly as they faced off in the silence. Just beneath his obstinacy and wariness, she sensed he was listening.

"I've arranged meetings with three watch company representatives," Lin said, sitting back slightly so that Victor could arrange bowls of Emile's steaming, fragrant onion soup before them. "I can tell you with certainty that every one of my contacts is far from thinking it's a *waste of time*, as you put it. They're extremely interested in your product. Fascinated, in fact. They're all very eager to see a firsthand demonstration of your product."

"And to meet me," Kam muttered.

She met his stare calmly. "And to meet you, yes. Thank you, Victor," she said when the bartender handed her a black napkin. He knew the white ones left lint on her black skirts. She was in the process of smoothing the napkin over her thighs, when she glanced sideways.

Kam's gaze was on her lap. As if he'd noticed her sudden stillness, his stare flicked up to her face. The heat she saw in his eyes seemed to set a spark to her flesh. Excitement bubbled in her, the strength of her reaction surprising her. She couldn't deny it, this unexpected rush of lust.

It *was* because he looked so much like Ian that she was having this reaction. It must be that. The forbidden held the power to tantalize. God knew there was nothing more taboo than her boss. Ian Noble was the one thing she couldn't have . . . could *never* have. Even if he was the only man she'd ever loved, he was off-limits to her, now more than ever since Francesca Arno had entered his life.

But his newly discovered brother wasn't off-limits, Lin acknowledged as Kam's hot, gray-eyed stare lowered to her mouth and she felt her nipples tighten as if by magic. No, Kam Reardon appeared to be about as available as she wanted him to be.

Chapter Two

K am unglued his gaze from Lin Soong's mouth with effort.
She wasn't what he'd expected.

Not in the slightest.

He'd caught her scent as they talked, and his cock had appreciated it even more wholeheartedly than his brain. When she'd moved her hands over her lap, it'd been like mainlining lust into his blood. How could a woman's *hands* be so sexy? Watching her primly smooth the cloth napkin over her thighs had momentarily hypnotized him, not to mention made him go dry-mouthed. He couldn't help but imagine her touching herself while she was completely naked, shapely hands gliding over lithesome thighs . . . between them. She had the most flawless skin he'd ever seen. He'd touched her on purpose. He'd never done that before when just meeting a woman . . . He'd wanted to put his hands on her so much it was like a mandate.

He didn't need to guess that her skin would flow like silk beneath his discovering, hungry hand. She wasn't built like the women he usually favored—robust, voluptuous women who wouldn't quail at his demands in bed. No, she had a figure like an elegant wand, all compact, yet lush curves and graceful refinement. *Fiercely feminine* came to mind as an apt descriptor. Her effortless sense of chic defied description in any language he'd mastered. Her legs were long and shapely beneath the narrow skirt she wore. He hadn't realized it was possible for a person to possess such a slender waist. If it weren't for the suppleness of her movements and the sleek strength hinted at by her muscle tone, he'd worry he'd break her in bed.

Not that she would ever go to bed with him. That was just his cock spouting off, of course. Still, Kam was practical. He knew the game board had altered ever since he'd seen Lin walk into the restaurant; he just wasn't sure *how* it would change yet.

He was captivated by even the smallest of her gestures. She was utterly perfect with her clothes on. He could only imagine the raptures of her naked body. Did a woman as graceful and sophisticated as Lin Soong purr in bed, or did she hiss and bare those small white teeth?

He mentally cursed his uncontrollable thoughts, reaching for the loaf of warm, crusty bread that Victor had set before them in a basket.

What was Ian thinking, sending him a woman that was so gorgeous, she was almost otherworldly? Was Lin Soong the enticement to come around to Ian's way of thinking? Was Ian trying to prove to Kam there were indescribably worthwhile benefits to wealth and power? No wonder Ian grumbled that every chief executive officer and business mogul on the planet wanted to poach Lin Soong from him.

Too late, Kam realized he'd ravaged the bread with his rough hands. He glanced apologetically at Lin. Her face was still and calm as she watched him with large, dark eyes. Against his will, he imagined what it'd be like to have her look up at him with those eyes while his cock was harbored deep inside her, erupting.

"Sorry," he mumbled, taking a piece of the torn loaf for himself and leaving a mangled portion in the basket.

"No problem." She reached and ripped off a piece for herself, those hypnotizing white hands nearly as forceful as his had been. There was something sexy about her actions, knowing she didn't disdain the place where his fingers had been . . . his touch. Blood pulsed into his cock. He shifted in the uncomfortable chair, grimacing. She picked up her spoon and matter-of-factly dipped the edge of her bread in the fragrant broth. Unable to look away, he watched her insert the corner of the bread between her lips and bite. His cock swelled and twitched. He tamped down an almost uncontrollable urge to nip at that mouth. It was small, but her dark pink lips were lush and shapely.

Her nostrils flared slightly as she returned his stare and chewed her bread, her expression a strange combination of calm innocence and complete understanding of what he was thinking.

Which was ridiculous. A woman like her would take offense at his pornographic thoughts.

Wouldn't she?

"Should I explain what I have planned?" she asked in a low, melodious voice after she'd swallowed and tore off another piece of bread.

"Planned for what? The courtship of a bunch of rich stiffs who make status symbols for other rich stiffs that tell the rest of us peons loud and clear we're not a part of their club?" he asked, his voice unintentionally harsh as he again ripped his attention off Lin. He began to eat mechanically, grunting softly in acknowledgment at the first savory bite of soup. Lin had been right. Her friend knew how to cook.

"If anything, they'll be courting you, Kam."

He met her stare at the sound of her saying his name.

"Will *you* be there?"

She blinked. "At the meetings? Of course. I thought you knew that. Ian thought I could help. Is that all right?"

He shrugged. "I don't need any help. But seeing you again makes this whole thing interesting, at the very least."

Her eyes widened. He'd gotten to her. He waited, curious as to how she'd respond.

"I thought you'd prefer to settle in and spend time with Ian and Lucien for the next few days. I'm out of town, anyway. So we'll get things started on Thursday with two representatives from Gersbach," Lin began, her manner abruptly brisk and businesslike. So, she was going to ignore his overture. "I wanted you to meet with them first, let them set the stage for what we're dealing with here. As you probably know, Gersbach is the premier Swiss watchmaker. It's a large company, but it's still privately held by the Gersbach family. The family prefers doing business face-to-face. Otto Gersbach, the current chief executive officer, is carrying on the family tradition of sitting down with potential business partners, breaking bread together, really knowing one another on a personal basis."

"If he values personal business transactions, it's a wonder he doesn't take offense at the idea of me meeting with his competitors." He gave Lin a sideways glance and noticed her implacable features. "Oh, I see. He *doesn't* know," he added sardonically.

"I didn't tell him outright, no," she replied in an unruffled manner. She really was a cool one. He watched as she slipped the silver spoon between her lips. Her white, pearl-clad throat convulsed slightly as she swallowed. He mentally shouted at himself to look away. She was *too* cool to be making him so hot. The imbalance irritated him. Suddenly, the idea of him putting his rough hands all over her smooth body . . . of him sliding his big, aching cock into her sleek pussy, seemed about as likely as a balmy summer in Antarctica next year.

Still, a man could dream. When the fantasies were as hot as Lin inspired, he had no choice.

"But Otto likely suspects that he has competition for your product," she continued. "He's no fool."

He paused in eating as she set down her spoon, turned to the chair next to her and retrieved her slim leather briefcase. She lifted it to her lap and extracted something from the pocket, her actions precise and graceful. He stared at the black-and-white photo of a fit-looking man in his late fifties with graying blond hair. He was sitting at a table covered with papers and his thin lips were opened as if he had been photographed speaking.

"Otto Gersbach," Lin said. She placed another photograph on top of Otto. This one was of a good-looking, curvy blond woman in a business suit, walking through what appeared to be a large lobby. "And his daughter, Brigit. She'll be there tomorrow night as well."

"Where'd Ian hire you from? The CIA? These look like surveillance photos," he said, both amused and disgusted. He liked Ian and respected his brain, but Kam valued his privacy and freedom too much to condone spying. Just one more reason to tread very carefully in the carnivorous world of high finance and business—

"Ian values preparation," Lin said neutrally, interrupting his thoughts. "He likes to have every detail he possibly can available to him before he goes into a meeting."

"And you help him do that," Kam murmured, his narrowed gaze running over Lin's stunning face. What *was* Ian and Lin's relationship? He'd met Ian's wife—Francesca—on several occasions and liked her very much. He knew Ian was crazy about her. Other women didn't seem to exist for him with Francesca in the picture. The fact that Francesca was going to have his baby this winter cemented the idea in Kam's head that Lin and Ian definitely were not romantically involved. But what about *before* Francesca had come on the scene? Surely his half brother wouldn't have denied himself with this exquisite beauty efficiently meeting his every demand?

He let his spoon drop in the bowl with a loud *plink* at the thought.

"What lengths would you go to in the name of service to Ian?" he growled softly.

"What do you mean?" she asked, her smooth expression fracturing slightly. "Are you suggesting I'd do something illegal for my job?"

He tore apart a piece of bread and shot a pointed glance at the photos.

"Those photos were taken from a security feed at Noble Enterprises in public places. There's nothing illegal about them," she defended.

"How many photos of me did you review before you walked in here tonight?" he asked before he wolfed down several bites of soup.

"None, if you must know," she said, and he was glad to hear the anger in her voice. Good to know there was some passion behind that perfect face and body.

"You said you'd recognize me anywhere."

"Only because you look so much like Ian," she blurted out heatedly. He met her stare, a little shocked by her outburst. She inhaled slowly, seeming to try and calm herself, and Kam realized she'd been shocked, too. "Trust me, I never saw any photos of you. If I had, I . . ." She paused and looked away. "Why don't you tell me what's really got you so prickly?"

He gave a rough bark of laughter and shoved back his bowl of soup. "You want my whole life story?"

"No, just the reason you're so determined to dislike me," she replied without pause.

His gaze dropped over her white throat to the exposed skin of her upper chest, above the neckline of the fitted sweater she wore. The garment was streamlined and chic, but included a ruffle around the wrists that he found sexy—a concession to her femininity. Her breasts looked like they'd fill the palm of his hand perfectly, not too large, not too small. They thrust erotically from the plane of her chest, pert, firm, soft seeming. They rose as she inhaled. He met her startled stare.

Not *like* her? What gave her that impression?

Maybe it's because you know a woman like her would never give you

the time of day if it weren't for these unique circumstances. And you're
playing defense against that knowledge.

"I like you just fine," he said honestly, ignoring the voice in his head and refusing to censor the heat in his tone.

Her lush, unadorned lips trembled slightly. He couldn't take his eyes off them. She had to have the sexiest mouth he'd ever seen. He leaned in without conscious thought, a man who had caught the scent and was determined not to lose it.

"What do you mean by that? What if you *had* seen a photo of me?" he demanded quietly, their faces just inches apart.

"I would have been better prepared."

"Too late," he replied succinctly. He leaned closer still, her eyes drawing him in . . .

She blinked and started back. Victor had arrived with their entrees. The bartender flinched when he saw Kam's furious scowl for having interrupted at such a crucial moment.

He could tell Lin was flustered as she asked Victor for another glass of wine and swallowed some ice water. Feeling a little guilty for coming on so strong, he let her talk business as they ate the steak. She'd been right yet again. The meal was delicious and more than satisfying. So was listening to her smooth voice and watching her.

She ate with a combination of elegance and genuine hunger that fascinated him. He'd wondered at one point if she was studying his table manners, determining whether or not he'd make a fool of himself by grabbing his food with his hands or using the wrong fork at one of these stuffy business dinners. Her face was very hard to read, however, if lovely to look at. He realized he was taking pains to revert to his college and medical school years in London in an attempt to appear more civilized and refined. Irritation flooded him.

Lin had been sent here to make him more comfortable in this proposed venture, not judge his rustic ways. He hadn't adapted to polite society at his biological father's hypocritical urgings, he reminded himself, despite his mother's pleas for him to do so. He didn't change for any woman, either. His experience with Diana had proven that. He couldn't alter who he was.

He *wouldn't*.

"I understand from Ian that you appreciate art," Lin said after they'd both finished their meal and lingered over their drinks.

"I like looking at it. Some of it, anyway," he admitted gruffly. "I'm no aficionado like Ian or his grandparents. Don't get your hopes up."

"It doesn't matter. The Gersbachs aren't experts, either, just appreciative amateurs."

"So you figured this art showing of Francesca's at Lucien's new hotel would be an icebreaker for the Gersbach meeting? Something to talk about over dinner other than the weather and everything we don't have in common?" He shook his head.

"What?" she asked, her brows furrowing in bewilderment.

"You think of everything, don't you?" he asked.

"I like to take control of whatever is in my power to control. There are always plenty of elements that I can't control," she said, giving him a small smile and a significant glance, "so it'd be foolish on my part not to get a good handle on what I can."

"Elements like me, for instance?" he asked.

"I'd be a fool indeed if I thought I could control you," she murmured, holding his stare. For a few seconds, Kam forgot the topic. She cleared her throat and looked away.

"Do you want to know anything else about the dinner tomorrow night?"

"You already supplied me with Otto and Brigit's psychological profiles, including juicy details, like that Otto is a conservative control freak while Brigit is a little too *uncontrolled* with her love of men and scotch—something that infuriates Otto. I know their history, their hobbies, their politics, their favorite foods and vacation spots," he said dryly. In truth, he was impressed. She was everything he'd come to expect from Ian's references. He had the impression Lin

Soong's brain was like a vast warehouse filled with neat, meticulously kept files. All she had to do was mentally roll open an imaginary drawer and all the desired information she wanted was at her fingertips.

"I'm surprised you haven't told me exactly what they like in bed," he added, goading her a little.

Her dark eyebrows rose in amusement. Her expression was typically controlled, but her large eyes were compellingly expressive.

"That's something I wouldn't know," she replied evenly.

"What about Ian's preferences in that arena?" he prodded. "Are you familiar with those?"

Her gaze flashed to his at his impertinence, the whites of her eyes a striking contrast to the dark brown irises. "Absolutely not."

"Good," he said, unable to prevent a knowing, satisfied smile. She shook her head. She looked incredulous at his audacity . . . and slightly dazed.

"Presumptuous," she said in a hushed tone.

He wrapped her wrist with his hand, slipping his thumb beneath a ruffle onto her warm skin. If he knew anything, he knew how to read a woman's body. His own heartbeat escalated when he felt the rapid, strong throb of her pulse. He knew logically what it meant, but still his brain doubted.

"*Realistic.* Why deny it?" he said with much more confidence than he felt.

He was filled with an irrational urge to set Lin Soong off balance, to melt her cool exterior, to prove that beneath that crisp, efficient manner, she'd prove warm and supple beneath his touch.

He saw the column of her throat convulse as she swallowed. She twisted her wrist and slid her hand through his loose hold, her fingertips brushing against his palm.

"Why indeed?" she said so softly that he wondered for a second if he'd heard her correctly. Those two words and that whispering caress against calloused skin made the hair on his forearms stand on end. Part of him still doubted what was happening—not really believing a woman like Lin would ever want him—until she encircled his thick thumb with her elegant fingers and squeezed.

For some damn reason, it was the most erotic caress he'd ever experienced. His cock swelled painfully.

She glanced at his half-full glass. "We could stay here and finish our drinks," she said, her lustrous eyes bewitching him. "Or we could go to my place."

His eyebrows went up in wry disbelief. "It's a good beer, but *really*? Compared to option number two?"

She laughed softly. "I'm glad we're in agreement on at least one thing," she murmured. She met his gaze frankly. "This is probably not a very good idea," she said in a hushed tone, and he sensed her anxiety twining with lust.

He studied the sublime line of her jaw and the curve of her mouth.

"Maybe. But it's the *only* idea in my head at the moment," he admitted gruffly. For a moment, she just stared. Then she nodded once—*done*—reminding him of a woman who had just made a business decision and wouldn't back down now. The spike of irritation he experienced wasn't enough to lessen his intense interest, let alone cause even a flicker in his arousal. In the periphery of his awareness, he saw Victor set the check on the bar. His hand slid out and grabbed the leather portfolio, beating Lin by a hairsbreadth.

"Let me. Ian would insist," she said anxiously as he pulled the folder out of her reach.

"Ian isn't here. I am."

When she didn't reply, he reached for his wallet with a sense of grim satisfaction. Her submission in this wasn't much.

But it was something.

She unlocked the front door and held it open for him to enter. He hadn't tried to touch her during the foggy cab ride through the city.

They hadn't spoken, just sat in silence as the tension and anticipation mounted until it almost felt unbearable to her.

He was slightly taller than Ian, Lin realized dazedly. Ian had been to her place several times over the years in order to drop something off or for a working dinner, both when the condo had still belonged to her grandmother and after she had died. She knew precisely where her boss's dark head hit the doorframe, and she thought Kam surpassed that imaginary measuring mark by a fraction of an inch.

He met her stare as he crossed the threshold. Her consciousness felt fogged by a glass and a half of wine and a rush of unexpected, potent lust.

She couldn't believe she was doing this.

She saw his nostrils flare slightly as he approached—a predator's stalk. A thrill of excitement went through her as she guessed what he was about to do. He swept down and captured her mouth with his. Firm, warm lips moved over hers, not forcefully, necessarily, but with unapologetic hunger, shaping her flesh to his own, learning it, owning it. He placed one hand on her jaw and penetrated her lips. She gasped at the impact of his taste and heat.

"I've been wanting to do that since I first laid eyes on you," he said roughly next to her lips a moment later. "Your mouth is downright indecent." He pulled her closer to him so that he could close the door. He shut and locked it, his piercing stare never leaving her face. Her sex clenched tight at the sensation of his large, lean, solid body pressed against her own.

"Use that mouth right now," he demanded hoarsely. "Use it to tell me you want me."

"You really need me to tell you that?" she asked, touching his face experimentally. She liked the sensation of his whiskers abrading her fingertips so well, she opened her other hand along his jaw.

"I think it'd help to make this whole night seem a little more believable," he muttered, leaning down and nipping at her lips with his. She joined him in a barely restrained, blistering kiss.

"Go on," he said in a gravelly voice after a mind-hazing moment.

"I want you. I *must*, to be doing something so crazy," she whispered, meeting his stare and arching her back, rubbing her breasts against his ribs. He growled appreciatively and ducked his head, greedily taking her lower lip between his scraping teeth. A hand came up and cupped her left breast, squeezing it firmly, molding her flesh to his, testing her texture. She moaned as liquid heat rushed through her, the sharpness of her arousal a fresh cause for amazement. His groan sounded every bit as appreciative.

She'd never had a man sweep her into his arms before. Somehow, it didn't surprise her in the least that Kam did it without blinking an eye.

He was unknowingly stroking a narrow, sweet spot in her being without even trying. She wanted him just a little less than her next breath. She craved him just enough to relinquish her typical rigid control. That kind of desire left room for little else, let alone rational thought.

He held her stare as he carried her down the dim hallway.

"There," she said breathlessly, waving at the master bedroom suite.

He kicked lightly at the partially open door to widen it. She looked up at him as he set her at the foot of the bed, a thrilling combination of lust, wariness, anxiety, and electrical excitement beginning to simmer in her blood.

He couldn't take his eyes off her face. Later, he'd realize that if asked what her condominium looked like an hour after being there, he wouldn't be able to supply even a sketchy description. That's how rapt he was with Lin Soong. That lush, rosebud mouth was his to touch, lick . . . ravage, the smooth skin his to caress and kiss, the sweet, thrusting breasts his to drown in, to coax to a full response with his mouth, lips, and tongue . . .

. . . for a little while, anyway.

Without a word, he began to undress her, sweeping her coat off and tossing it carelessly on a chair, raising the thin sweater over her shoulders and head and discarding it on the mattress. His actions mussed her hair even further. He delved his fingers into the gathered mass at the back of her head, finding three long, smooth wooden hair sticks and removing them. He tossed them. The pins flew several feet where they landed with clicks on a bedside table, rolled and came to a rest. He never took his eyes off her. A midnight mass of hair whispered around her white shoulders. He clutched at it with both hands, burying his fingers in the curls. Gently, he arranged it around her back and upper arms.

"I've never seen an Asian woman with curly hair. It's beautiful," he muttered, distracted by the sensation of it coiling around his fingers. Her hair was a lighter weight than he would have thought considering the mass at the back of her head, but there was tons of it. The fragrance of the liberated tendrils reached his nose—fruit and flowers, musky and sensual. It whisked next to his calloused fingers, feeling like silk and air combined.

"It's not that common. The humidity makes it worse," she said huskily, staring up at him with a solemn, dark-eyed gaze.

His jaw tightened as he reached to unfasten her bra, the anticipation cutting at him. He could tell by her shape in the clinging bra she was going to be lovely. After he'd removed the bra, he just stared for a moment, lust and something sharp and unexpected tightening his throat and cock. When air finally escaped his lungs, it did so on a rough, uncontrollable groan.

"Lin," he said as he opened his hands along her rib cage, feeling the delicate lines of her carriage, her rapidly beating heart, her softness, her heat. He went lower, encircling her waist. He'd been right. He could nearly encompass her in his grasp. He scooted her farther up the bedcover and came down over her. Their mouths fused, hot and voracious from the first. He'd realized earlier that although her figure was slender and her features small, she was tall for a woman.

Their fit was ideal. He rested one hip on the bed, but she curved against him like a heat-seeking kitten, cupping his aching cock between her thighs. The evidence of her returned ardor inflamed him further.

He rolled on top of her, pressing her down into the mattress and ravening her mouth, suddenly too hungry to be polite.

"Ah God," she whispered when he raised his head a moment later and flexed, his straining cock pressing against the juncture of her thighs. She gyrated her hips, and he saw red. His lips found her cheek and her ear. He kissed the opening and she squirmed beneath him, gasping. He bit gently at the shell and brought her earlobe into his mouth, laving both skin and the smooth pearl inserted in the flesh, licking at the succulent contrast of smooth hardness and tender softness. The feeling of her sleek body writhing beneath him almost made him go berserk. Only his single-minded desire to taste more of her stopped him from driving into her then and there, from discovering firsthand if she was as soft and warm on the inside as she was on the surface.

Her neck was fragrant, her trapped cries delicious against his lips and gently scraping teeth. She craned her head up, trying to find his mouth again. Her hands moved frantically over his back, scooping his light jacket and the material of his shirt with them. He lifted his head and hissed when her fingernails scraped against bare skin and a shiver of sharp sensation rippled through him.

Their stares met briefly as he shifted on top of her, gathering her hands. He held her wrists and pressed them to the pillow above her head. He waited two heartbeats . . . three, but she didn't protest at his restraint.

Instead, she arched her back in an offering.

Lust tore at him, undeniable. Feral. She'd exceeded his expectations. Her breasts were mouthwateringly beautiful. They had the thrusting firmness of small breasts, but they *weren't* small. They were fleshy and ripe, and the way they stood out from her narrow, delicate rib cage drove him mad. He transferred her wrists to one hand and used the other to shape a breast, plumping the tender, extremely firm flesh.

"C'est si bon," he muttered before he went lower. Her skin was so flawless, so transparent, that he could see the delicate blue veins beneath it. He slipped a crown between his lips and laved the pebbled flesh against his tongue, drinking in her moans of pleasure, becoming drunk by her softness and scent, by her responsiveness. When he drew on her more forcefully, she bucked her hips and moaned her approval. Her pussy rubbed against his heavy erection, beckoning him . . . taunting.

He snarled in barely leashed restraint and secured his hold on her wrists. He transferred to her other sweet breast, keeping her immobile for his ravening mouth by cupping her rib cage with one hand and pressing her wrists down into the pillow. After he'd sucked and laved at her nipple until it grew tight and distended and her desperate cries told him how sensitive the flesh had become, he transferred his mouth to the sides of her heaving ribs.

"Please . . . Kam," she whispered frantically when he opened his mouth and scraped the skin covering her ribs. A shudder ran through her, delicate and delicious as the rest of her. His tongue ran over her skin, feeling the slight bumps his caresses had raised. He released his hold on her torso—it excited him how much of her trembling body he could hold with even one hand—and ran it over the mound between her thighs. She parted her legs immediately, and he looked into her face. Her cheeks were flushed, her pink mouth a parted invitation as she panted shallowly.

Fuck.

It was as much a curse as it was an order from the primitive part of his brain.

"You want it now, *ma petite minette*? You want it fast and hard?" he muttered roughly through clenched teeth.

"Please," she repeated, this time soundlessly.

He fell on her, ravaging her mouth. So sweet. So responsive. His hand moved, pulling up the edge of her skirt, fingers skimming across smooth, taut thighs partially covered in cool, smooth, clingy material. Arousal spiked through him and he lifted his head, staring downward. Jesus. She was wearing some kind of lacy, thigh-high stockings that were nearly as pale and soft as her skin. His cock lurched at the vision she made. Frenchmen were supposedly used to women in luxury lingerie, but the women Kam bedded usually weren't the type to wear such refined, feminine, frilly things—or to afford them, for that matter.

Spellbound, he moved his hand over her silk-covered mound. He felt her heat and jerked the pretty panties downward roughly. A groan scored his throat when he touched her. She was smooth here, too. Warm, sleek, and creamy. He dipped the ridge of his forefinger between shaved labia. Desire had softened and plumped her flesh. He leaned down and ate her aroused cries. She strained against him and writhed when he inserted a finger into her clasping vagina.

He lifted his head, his breath sounding ragged as he stimulated her and met her gaze. A primitive pulse pounded in his swollen cock, demanding he act. She was going to squeeze him until he didn't know his own name. She was going to wring him until he was an ecstatic, rutting savage.

Something hit him like a dull thud to the gut.

"I don't have a condom," he ground out, the harsh reality penetrating his rabid lust. He always brought condoms when he planned to be with a woman, but it wasn't part of his normal routine to carry one around. He was used to living in isolation in the country.

None of this—from the glittering city to these new clothes to this stunning woman beneath him who had been both what he expected and drastically different—remotely resembled his typical life.

She lifted her head slightly and glanced at the bedside table where he'd tossed the hairpins. "There," she said.

Caught between the choice of continuing to bind her wrists or remove his hand from her slippery, tight pussy, he let go of her wrists and strained toward the table, whipping open the small drawer. His hand moved over items in blind desperation.

"Merde," he muttered under his breath, forced to remove his hand from paradise in order to eventually achieve even more sublime raptures. He scooted up on the bed, peering into the drawer. He shoved aside a small bottle of lotion, a jar of lip emollient, a couple of elastic headbands, some pens, and what appeared to be several carefully dried and pressed purple lotus flowers inserted into a plastic sleeve. He finally spied an unopened box of condoms.

Her palm cupped his cock from below. She slid it along the shaft, as though testing his weight. He hissed and clamped his eyes closed as she closed her fingers around him, her touch even through his clothing thundering through him. He felt huge in her small, stroking hand, heavy . . . hurting.

He snarled and reached for the offending hand. The sweet one.

"I'm going to come in my pants if you keep that up," he uttered harshly. He focused on her face with effort. "Put your hand back above your head and keep it there, *mon petit chaton*. I'm not going to be exploding anywhere but deep inside you."

Lin tried to control her ragged breathing as she followed his instructions and placed her hands above her head, resting them on the pillow. She failed. Panting, she watched him as he impatiently shucked off his jacket and shirt. There was a good amount of dark hair on his chest, but it didn't hide smooth skin and flexing muscle. He came down on his hip on the bed and unfastened his jeans. She'd held his cock in her hand, felt his weight and heat throbbing against her sex.

Her heart began to race in her breast as adrenaline poured into her veins.

He unceremoniously jerked the jeans down his hips and over long, muscled hair-sprinkled thighs, his taut abdomen and powerful biceps flexing hard. His fingers hooked into the waistband of his boxer briefs and pulled them forward over his bulging genitals. He yanked downward.

His naked cock flipped onto his belly—desire-swollen, flagrant . . .

. . . indescribably beautiful.

Her lips parted. Her breath froze.

He ripped open the condom package and began to roll it down over his erection. She leaned up slightly to better see him, using her elbows to brace her, curious . . . hungry. The head was a succulence from which she couldn't unglue her gaze, a firm, flushed, and noticeably delineated crown to the long, thick staff. He cursed when the condom ran out with several inches to go to his testicles, covered by dark hair.

The prophylactic wasn't long enough.

"Is it okay?" he asked roughly, glancing up in her direction.

She nodded, unable to speak. It was like some pagan god of virility had landed in her bed, when before she'd witnessed only mortals.

He grunted softly at her permission. "Put your hands back," he prodded gently. While she followed his instructions, he lifted her skirt all the way to her waist. He rolled between her legs, and she opened her thighs to accommodate him. She bit her lip, anticipation cutting at her from the inside out, when he came down over her, bracing his body with a hand on the mattress. His other hand captured his suspended cock.

She exhaled the air she'd been holding in her lungs when he used the bulging head of his cock to rub between her labia, wetting the tip with her juices, stimulating her clit. She moaned and watched him as he stared between her thighs, moving his cock, finding her slit unerringly.

"Oh," she mumbled, shock and arousal flavoring her tone when he flexed firmly, working the fleshy cockhead into her. He paused, looking up at her, his jaw tight.

"You're tight. Try to relax," he said in a gravelly tone. "Spread your thighs apart farther and bend your knees a bit."

She moaned after she'd followed his instructions and his muscles contracted, pushing his cock farther into her. He stared at her face fixedly as he began to flex his hips, gently sawing the end of his cock back and forth in her slit.

"That's right," he muttered through a rigid jaw, his low, hoarse tone coaxing her . . . arousing. "You've got a tight little pussy, but you're going to let me in, aren't you?"

"Yes," she hissed at the same moment she flexed her hips upward determinedly. Her pussy stretched around his girth, her softness submitting to his pulsing, hard shaft.

He made a stifled sound like *archg* as his flesh slowly fused with hers.

It was both uncomfortable and headily arousing to hold him inside her. She clenched her teeth and flexed her hips up and down, stroking him, desperate to be filled. Completely. Kam made a harsh sound in his throat and used his hand to still her.

He met her stare, his teeth bared in a snarl as he held her steady and sunk in her to the balls. Her mouth fell open, and a shaky, disbelieving cry escaped her throat. He pressed closer still, smashing his balls against her outer sex, grinding. She'd never been so inundated, so full. The indirect pressure on her clit was wicked.

A light coating of sweat shone on his ridged, naked torso as he remained still with obvious effort. His gaze bore down into her.

"Is it too much?" he grated out.

"I'm going to come," she said, the shaky words spilling out of her a shock even to herself.

"Then do it," he rasped as he lifted slightly, exposing her outer flesh. He reached between her thighs and slid his finger between the smooth, slippery folds of her labia. He rubbed his fingertip against her clit with matter-of-fact mastery. She cried out and arched her back as orgasm shuddered through her, the ecstasy exponentially powerful with Kam planted deep in her flesh.

She heard his deep, primal growl as if from a distance. He continued to rub her for a moment. She was still coming—harsh shudders of bliss slashing through her—when he removed his hand. He folded her knees toward her shoulders and leaned down over her, using his body to fix her bent legs in place flush against her torso. He began to fuck while she still keened in climax.

For a few seconds, his demanding possession interrupted her bliss. It was too much, really, having him pound so high and hard inside her. It took her breath away. But then the friction caused by the swollen, defined cockhead rubbing previously untouched flesh began to mount. It was like he was building a fire in her.

She moaned and stared up at him helplessly. He looked down at her, his handsome face so rigid, his eyes so wild it was almost frightening, like truly being taken by a force of nature. His strokes became longer, even more forceful. She bared her teeth in the face of the intense pressure and mounting pleasure, groaning, and lifted her head off the pillow, glancing downward. The staff of his cock glistened with her juices as it moved like a piston in and out of her, his pelvis smacking against her briskly in an arousing, erotic rhythm that quickened by the second.

She fell back, gasping against the pillows. "Oh God, the condom." He was taking her so forcefully, so thoroughly, that the bottom rim of the rubber was coming down off his thick cock.

"I know it," he ground out in a strangled voice, never pausing his powerful thrusts. "It'll hold for as long as it takes. I won't last. Not in this sweet little pussy, I won't. I'm going to come."

She squeezed her eyelids tight at his harsh, erotic words. He slammed into her and circled his hips, once again overfilling her, grinding their sexes together. She screamed in excitement and felt his cock swell and jerk inside her. His shout was blistering. Raw. She lay back on the pillows, panting in sharp excitement and vague discomfort, watching him as he began to come. Every muscle in his lean, ripped body was contracted tight, rippling and jerking. Spellbound, she realized she'd been willingly depriving herself of his beauty. She reached for him, suddenly wild to caress and stroke what seemed like miles of smooth skin and delineated muscle. But he made a ragged sound and pushed down on her shins, stilling her action.

He rode her while he ejaculated. The intense friction made her eyes cross. She joined him in climax, too overwhelmed by his stark possession to stand outside the flames.

"Fuck. I can feel you coming," he groaned, sounding beyond miserable.

"No," she yelped when he withdrew.

It was like abruptly having ice water poured on her steaming skin, the deprivation of his flesh was so severe. He fell down on the mattress, panting, his pelvis cradling her hip, his damp cock throbbing on her thigh.

"I had to. The damn condom isn't going to stay put. I don't want to spill in you," he said at the same time that he slid his hand between her thighs. She cried out as her climax ramped up to its original potent blast as he rubbed her slick clit rapidly. Her eyes closed as she shook in pleasure.

"No, open them," he ordered roughly.

She lifted her heavy eyelids. Both of his hands resumed moving, and she realized he stimulated both of them at once.

It struck her as overwhelmingly intimate, to stare into his fierce gaze while they both shuddered in mutual pleasure . . .

. . . to stare into the familiar face of a virtual stranger.

Chapter Three

He sagged onto the bed next to her, his head falling into the pillow. As she lay there and felt his harsh breathing near her ear, slow and even, her body seemed to liquefy, melting into the mattress. He was warm and solid. Her drowsiness paradoxically alarmed her somehow.

She'd just had wild, impulsive sex with someone she'd just met. She could count using one finger the number of times she'd done that in her life—and that time on spring break during grad school didn't really count, given the uncustomary amount of tequila involved and the completely forgettable sexual encounter itself. She'd despised herself afterward for putting herself in that unsavory situation, vowing to never allow herself to lose control in that arena of her life again.

But tonight hadn't been some drunken encounter with a cocky yet fumbling college kid. This had been a lightning strike of desire with none other than Ian Noble's brother, the very man she was supposed to guide and soften for a potentially lucrative business deal. A deal that was certainly important to her boss, because Kam was family.

Ian.

A vision of Ian's laserlike, blue-eyed gaze and impenetrable expression flashed into her mind's eye. It set off a prickly feeling of anxiety that broke through her delicious lassitude. Realizing her hands were still above her head, she cautiously lowered them, glancing sideways at Kam all the while. Was he sleeping? His breathing had certainly become slow and even.

He reached up and grabbed one of her lowering hands. She started at his touch.

"I thought you were sleeping," she said softly, her voice thick with relaxation.

"I'm awake."

She turned her head fully and saw his stare on her. He certainly was. His facial muscles looked relaxed in comparison to how rigid they'd been when he'd been inside her—pounding, pulsing, demanding—but his gaze was sharp and alert. He kept her hand in his grasp and moved it to her waist, his arm draping her.

"You may have fried half my brain cells just now, but I don't want to sleep. Not yet," he muttered thickly in his rough, French-accented voice. Her heart throbbed back to life. Had there been a thread of suggestiveness in his tone? He moved the pad of his thumb over her wrist in a gentle quest. "I wanted you so much, I never got a chance to appreciate you. I was too busy combusting."

She swallowed, feeling the weight of her pearls on her Adam's apple.

"I certainly felt appreciated," she assured.

A smile flickered across his lips as he continued to touch her wrist. "Still, it was hardly a savoring experience. More like a gorge-fest."

She returned his grin, warmed by the laughter in his eyes. The pad of his thumb moved subtly on her wrist.

"Are you feeling my pulse? When you touch me there?" she murmured. Their faces were only inches apart. She could clearly see the black ring that surrounded his irises and flecks of midnight in the silvery-gray of his eyes. His eyelashes were surprisingly thick for a man, further highlighting his magnetic gaze.

"Yes."

"You're using your knowledge of biology, the same knowledge you used to make your biofeedback mechanisms, in order to read me?"

"The human body has a language all its own," he said, still feathering her pulse with his thumb. "It's usually more honest than the kind that comes out of a person's mouth."

"What's my body telling you right now?" she whispered, unable to stop herself from asking.

His gaze moved slowly down over her chest. She felt his stare on her breasts like a touch. She shifted restlessly an inch or two, increasing her contact with his body. Her shoulder pressed against a dense pectoral muscle. She inhaled deeply, making her breasts rise. Her nipples tightened beneath his weighty stare.

"The leap in your pulse along with the increase in your muscle tension could mean anxiety. Or it could mean you're heating again." He glanced up into her face and caught the burn in her cheeks. His gaze had grown heavy-lidded, somehow both satiated and aroused at once. *Heating again.* How aptly put. "In combination with the rest of the signs," he said with a quick glance at her erect nipples, "I'd opt for the latter, though. Am I right?"

She licked at her lower lip nervously. "I think it might mean both anxiety and . . . the other thing."

He released her wrist and cupped her waist, his large, warm hand and long fingers stretching from back to belly.

"What are you anxious about?" he growled softly.

"I don't think Ian would approve of this, for one."

His nostrils flared slightly. "He sent you to me, didn't he? What right has he got to complain if we like each other? What's it got to do with him?"

"You know it's not that simple," she chastised.

A frown pulled at his mouth. "Right. Let's consider what Ian would want in this situation, by all means."

He released her suddenly and rolled off the bed. She started at his abruptness—not to mention his simmering sarcasm—but then immediately became distracted by the image of him almost entirely naked, save for his jeans and underwear bunched around thighs that were long and solid as young oaks. Hadn't Ian told her that Kam had built a sophisticated workout area in his underground home that took into account his intuitive understanding of the subtle mechanisms and physics of the human body? Ian was supremely in shape, but had wryly told Lin after he'd joined Kam in one of his workouts that he practically hadn't been able to move for three days afterward.

Kam's back was beautiful—all lean, defined muscle, a narrow waist that angled up to broad shoulders. He had more color in his skin than Ian, a swarthy gilt. There didn't appear to be an ounce of fat anywhere. Lin supposed he wouldn't have had much of a chance to acquire any, living a solitary, meager existence for so many years in the country. Arousal flickered in her sex at the vision of him carelessly jerking his underwear over his ass. The skin there was as smooth as his back, the buttocks powerful, round, very . . .

. . . grab-worthy.

She'd been *mad* to follow his demand and keep her hands out of the action.

"Bathroom?" he asked gruffly, breaking the settling spell of lust . . . and disappointment.

"Oh, there," she pointed at a door to the right.

He came around the foot of her bed. He hadn't buttoned his fly. As he walked, his hand cupped his exposed cock from below, sliding off the condom. He wasn't as rock hard as he had been earlier, but his penis was still beautiful—shapely and slightly distended from his body.

Heat rushed through her, as powerful and stunning as it had been the first time. When he disappeared behind the bathroom door, she blinked and looked around her bedroom as if seeing her surroundings for the first time that night. She glanced anxiously at the closed bathroom door. Was he pulling himself together in there? Washing and fastening his clothing? She didn't want to be sprawled on the bed with her skirt shoved up around her waist, her thighs spread, vulnerable and exposed when he returned. She sat up and dove for her sweater. When the door to the bathroom abruptly opened again, she hastily pressed the silk knit over her breasts, feeling like she'd been caught red-handed.

He stepped across the threshold, pausing when he saw her. A shadow of disgust—or was it disappointment?—crossed his bold features. He readjusted his jeans and fleetly fastened his pants, his ridged abdomen flexing. He *hadn't* been pulling himself together in there. She watched helplessly as he stalked across the room and grabbed his wadded shirt and jacket off the floor.

"Are you . . . are you going?" she asked.

"Looks as if," he said shortly, untangling his clothing.

"I didn't mean you . . . that is . . . I'm sorry," she fumbled. Why didn't she know what she wanted in this situation? It was as if she couldn't interpret her own desires anymore. Maybe it was best if he did go. Surely she'd regret her impulsive behavior. She rarely went to bed with men and *never* at the first meeting, which was no great shock. No one had worse luck with men than Lin; she must hold a world record for her number of abysmal first and only dates. But her judgment was especially lacking in Kam's case. First of all, he *wasn't* a date. He'd been a work assignment. Secondly, he was Ian's brother, for God's sake. Lin was always fastidious about keeping the boundaries intact between her work and her personal life. Not that she *had* much of a personal life outside of work and Ian, but . . .

Surely she'd also regret seeing Kam Reardon walk away in that moment as well.

You were right before. I was heating up. *I shouldn't have brought up Ian. That's not for us to think about now.*

"What I don't get," Kam said as he drew on his shirt, taut muscles flexing in a jerky, impatient motion, "is the limit."

"The limit?" Lin asked slowly, his words interrupting the flow of her mental rehearsal for talking him into staying. His flashing, furious gaze made her pull the sweater tighter over her naked torso.

"Yeah. Weren't you up for working overtime?"

It took a moment for his meaning to settle in. When it did, hurt and fury flooded her.

"How dare you say something like that to me! This," she glanced back at the mussed bed, "had nothing to do with work."

"Really? Nothing to do with Ian?" he bit out, shoving his arms into the sleeves of his jacket so forcefully she heard the seam protest with a ripping sound. "Everyone is always saying you'd do anything for him."

"No," she exclaimed, standing. She couldn't believe he'd just said that. But then a thought occurred to her, and she paused in her heated defense. Her uncharacteristic behavior tonight *did* relate to Ian, didn't it? To her secret, buried feelings for him? Too late, she realized Kam had noticed her sudden distraction.

"Did Ian ask you sleep with me? Soften me up a little? Make the stubborn country relation a bit more malleable? Palatable?" he demanded quietly, taking a step toward her.

"No! Of course not. You realize you're practically calling me a *prostitute*, don't you?" she almost shouted, anger and disbelief and confusion twining and beginning to roar in her blood. "Is that what you think? That Ian sends me out to sleep with his business associates? His *family members*?"

His features darkened. "Of course I don't think you're a prostitute. What I do think is that you're a woman who would do just about anything for her job. For her boss. Everyone in the family is always going on about how loyal you are to him."

Her mouth fell open in shock. *Oh my God*. She'd been so idiotic. How could she have *ever* thought this rough, savage jerk was attractive? He didn't even vaguely resemble the men she usually favored, but her libido just *had* to be appeased, didn't it? This was the stupidest mistake she'd ever made.

She drew herself up to her full height, refusing to be cowed by the fact that she was standing half-dressed in front of such a complete, astronomical son of a bitch. He'd just burned her to her very core, and then had the nerve to call her a whore and Ian's bowing minion in one fell swoop. She'd *let* him burn her.

"Get the hell out of my house," she said quietly.

A strange expression broke over his face, as if her response had been disappointing, but also precisely what he'd expected of her.

She was almost as furious with herself as she was at Kam Reardon for giving a good goddamn one way or another *what* the bastard thought. He stalked out of the room without a backward glance, his backbone as stiff as hers. She still stood in the exact same position when she heard the front door close with a brisk click.

It slowly settled on her like a creeping chill that Kam wasn't the only person who was disappointed in her behavior tonight. She'd let herself down. She'd never before backed down or failed at an assignment Ian had given her. There was a first time for everything, though. She'd have to break the truth to Ian.

There was no way in hell she was going to work with his insolent brother.

Morning sunlight poured into Ian's corner office when she entered it three days later. She was jumpy from nerves, but knew she looked calm on the surface. It had taken a lot of energy to stifle her anxiety over what had occurred with Kam, but she'd had several days focusing on business in New York to do it. She'd carefully constructed a lie for why she couldn't work with Kam, but her story seemed full of holes. Surely Ian, of all people, would never believe it.

Maybe she wouldn't have to convince him after all, she reasoned as she approached Ian's desk. She'd spoken to Ian last evening before her flight back to Chicago. Their discussion had been a practical rundown of her meetings in New York. Ian had only mentioned Kam in regard to his personal visits with family. Nevertheless, Kam might have told Ian in the interim what had happened between them Monday night. Perhaps Kam had already suggested he was the one who didn't want to work with Lin?

Not knowing the lay of the land only amplified her barely restrained anxiety.

As usual, Ian sat behind his massive carved hardwood desk, talking to someone on his earpiece, his fingers moving fleetly over a keyboard placed in front of him. Despite his multitasking, his blue eyes met hers as she handed him the latest numbers from Tyake, one of his subsidiaries. She immediately recognized the glance of significance at a chair before his desk, her heart sinking a little. He wanted her to wait.

Residual anger, hurt, and humiliation crowded her consciousness when she considered the possibility of Kam spilling the dirty details to Ian. How could she have been so stupid? Her impulsivity shocked her to the core. She sunk into one of the upholstered chairs before his desk, a nauseating feeling of dread rising in her belly.

"We'll wait and see how the Nikkei opens tonight and go from there," Ian was saying, glancing over the contents of the file she'd handed him. Lin had known who was on the other end of line almost immediately by their topic. His typing fingers paused as he signed off from his conversation with Alexandra Horowitz, one of his vice presidents.

He pulled off his earpiece.

"Good morning," she greeted him with false, brisk cheerfulness.

"It is one, isn't it?" he commented quietly, glancing toward the floor-to-ceiling windows. The brilliant sunlight turned his usually cobalt eyes into gleaming slits of sky blue. "Francesca has that showing tonight. She'll be pleased weather won't stand as an excuse for people not to come."

"She must be very excited."

Ian's brother Lucien and his wife Elise had opened a sophisticated boutique hotel and restaurant in the Prairie Avenue district several months ago, where Elise also worked as the executive chef. Francesca had been so inspired by the elegant brick structure where Lucien had situated the hotel that she'd completed a collection of some of Chicago's architectural vintage classics, buildings evocative of a different era and graceful lifestyle. Lin had arranged for the Gersbach meeting with Kam to take place at the reception for Francesca's showing, with dinner to follow at Frais, Elise's new restaurant.

"Francesca has sketched for this collection, isn't that right?" Lin hedged, hoping to avoid the inevitable topic of Kam for another few seconds.

"Yes," Ian said wryly. "It's been hard for her, being put off the paints while she's pregnant. I'm betting she'll be covering herself with the stuff once the baby is born."

There it was, that far-off look Ian got in his eyes whenever he spoke of Francesca. It pained her far less today than it had in the past. Lin recalled vividly the first time she'd ever seen that expression—so different from Ian's typical brutally sharp focus. It'd made her jealous to see it, she admitted, but there had also been a strange feeling of happiness going through her as well, witnessing such a determinedly lonely man finally lose himself thoroughly in thinking of another. She'd long ago accepted he'd never look that way for her. The pain had become a distant ache that bothered her less and less with each passing day.

"Francesca would deserve it," Lin said with a smile. "How difficult for her, to have to abstain from something so entwined with her existence. I'm glad she's found some alternatives, though. Francesca is nothing if not resourceful." She arched her eyebrows and gave him a small smile. "I'm assuming you got her a gift, something for her opening?" It was a little standing joke between them. Lin used to purchase all the gifts for the various women he used to see before Francesca. When Ian met Francesca, however, Francesca had understandably protested about his having Lin choose gifts for her. Ian had to take a crash course in buying personal, thoughtful gifts, and he'd come a long way.

"I'm sending flowers, and I got her a first-edition photography book on classical architecture she's been wanting from Lucien's shop," he said, referring to a vintage bookstore situated next to the Coffee Boutique in Lucien and Elise's hotel.

Her grin widened. "You're becoming an expert. The day is coming when you won't need me anymore."

His gaze sharpened on her. "Don't say that. You're one of my most prized assets. I can't exist without you. Or at least Noble Enterprises can't. Speaking of which, there's something I've been meaning to ask you."

Lin tensed. *Here it comes.* Had Kam spoken to him? "Yes?" she asked warily.

"Would you ever consider moving to London? For your job?"

The ensuing silence seemed to roar in her ears. "I . . . I don't know. Chicago has always been my home." She collapsed back into her chair, her mouth hanging open. "You're considering moving your home base to London?"

"I'm thinking about it," he said honestly. "You know Francesca is going to have the baby at Belford Hall," he said, referring to his grandparents' palatial estate.

"Yes. And I know your grandfather hasn't been in the best of health." She realized how hollow her voice sounded. In the back of her mind, she'd always known that Ian might choose to make Belford Hall his primary residence, but that day always seemed far in the future. She tried to give him a rallying smile despite a sinking feeling. "I can understand why you'd want to relocate to England to be nearer to both your grandparents. Besides, it'd be a lovely place for Francesca to recover after the baby is born."

"I'm considering it for a good chunk of time, anyway."

She willfully steadied herself. He said it would be a short period of time, but she could easily imagine the circumstances stretching into forever. "I can't expect everything to always remain the same," she said evenly. "That's the way of business. Things are always changing."

"You're more than just 'business,' Lin," Ian said, his eyebrows slanting. "That's why I brought it up. I want you to think about relocating. I'm sure we can come up with an arrangement that feels beneficial for you and isn't so life altering. We'll make a point to talk about it more next week?"

She nodded and gave him a reassuring smile, ignoring the snide voice in her head telling her *of course* she was nothing more than business to him. Her brain had always known that, even if her heart hadn't adequately learned the crucial lesson.

"Enough about that," Ian said gruffly. "We need to discuss Kam. How did it go the other night?"

"Fine," Lin said smoothly. "I was wondering, though, if maybe we should rethink the idea of my being Kam's guide through all of this?"

Ian sat forward in his chair, resting his elbows on the desk. "What's wrong? Did something happen the other night? Kam's been very closemouthed about it all, but then he is about a lot of things," Ian added wryly.

Palpable relief swept through her. *Kam didn't say anything.*

"It's just . . ." She stared out the windows at the pristine skyline of the city. Having never been substantial from the start, her carefully constructed lie completely evaporated beneath Ian's incisive stare. "I think you'd be the more ideal person, as his brother, to accompany him for these meetings. Don't you?"

"Not really, no. Kam needs someone to guide him, not take the spotlight off him. Besides, he'll be the first to tell me I'm being too heavy handed in dealing with matters that concern him. I can't tell you how many times he's told me since I've met him that it's his life, not mine—usually in much blunter terms. Your subtlety, your charm and manners are precisely what's called for. Next to you, he'll come off like royalty."

"You think far too much of my abilities," she muttered under her breath.

"I sincerely doubt that," Ian said, glancing at his watch. "At any rate, we can ask Kam what he thinks about the whole thing. He's due here any minute to get a tour of Noble. It's his first visit to the offices. Coraline went down to the lobby to get him."

Lin didn't have much time to get panicked. A knock sounded at the door.

"Ah, here he is," Ian said, standing.

A middle-aged, attractive brunette had been waiting for him in the lobby when he entered Noble Tower. She identified herself as Coraline Major and explained as they got on the elevator that she was one of Ian's administrative assistants.

"I thought Lin Soong was his assistant," Kam said as the elevator doors closed silently.

"Ms. Soong? Mr. Noble's secretary?" Coraline said, thin, plucked eyebrows arching high at the idea. Coraline waited discreetly while two young men in suits got off on the tenth floor. The door closed, leaving the two of them alone in the elevator. "Myself and three others are both Mr. Noble's and Ms. Soong's assistants. Ms. Soong is a Noble executive. She sits on Mr. Noble's advisory board and is considered by many his chief advisor. No one knows the company better, save Mr. Noble himself. She's worked here since she was just a teenager off and on. Even when she was still in high school, she used to come to the office sometimes and her grandmother would put her to work on the books and such. Ms. Soong has her grandmother's head for numbers. She's certainly every bit as elegant and graceful as Mrs. Lee was," Coraline recalled fondly.

"She was born and bred Noble, it sounds like."

"Precisely. Mr. Noble consults her on almost everything. Ian calls her his right hand. They work together exceptionally well."

A sudden, fierce wish went through Kam to return home to Aurore Manor, that familiar, brooding haunt of a home where he was free to do what he chose without overthinking everything, where he existed without the concern of offending. Not that the place was gloomy anymore. It'd been transformed under his hard physical labor, the massive cleaning Elise and Francesca had orchestrated with a platoon of maids, and the items that had arrived to refurnish the place. The shadows were being slowly vanquished, the darkness of Trevor Gaines evaporated by kind visitors, new hopes, organization, hard work, and streaming sunlight. It was becoming a home instead of a shell of a house. But more importantly, there was no one at Aurore to offend but his dog, Angus, and Angus was too good-natured of a beast to stay mad for long.

Phoebe Cane was caring for Angus in his absence, but he was suddenly quite certain his dog was as uncomfortable in Phoebe's house as Kam was in his luxury hotel room here in Chicago. After all, Kam himself had never been content in the confines of Phoebe's house for longer than it took to exchange pleasure. His dog would have one less reason for wanting to be there.

Coraline seemed to notice his scowl and thought it wise to change the subject.

"I can't get over how much you and Mr. Noble resemble one another," she said.

"If one more person tells me that, I'm going to grow back my beard as soon as nature allows it."

He was so preoccupied with a longing for home and considering what Coraline had said about Lin and Ian working so well together that he didn't notice he'd silenced Ian's assistant completely. Was this idealistic working relationship the reason Lin thought Ian would disapprove of her and Kam sleeping together? Perhaps Ian had to approve of everything in Lin's life since her life so closely intersected with his? And Lin had certainly pointed out that Ian would not give Kam the thumbs-up, brother status or no.

Kam couldn't say he'd be surprised in either case. He wasn't exactly in Lin's league. Still, the truth grated. It was best all around just to put Lin Soong out of his mind. He'd never really invited her in to begin with except in the peripheral sense.

He stalked off the elevator when the door opened at the top floor, temporarily forgetting his guide.

Lin was the first thing his gaze landed on in the large, sun-filled office when Coraline knocked and opened the door for him to enter. She sat on a chair before an enormous, elaborately carved desk, her chin over her shoulder, watching him warily with those large, dark eyes. She was a palette of black and sun-infused ivory skin, wearing an ebony dress with long sheer sleeves. Her long legs were crossed. He recalled explicitly how she'd looked Monday night with her skirt shucked up to her waist exposing lithesome, silky thighs and the sweetest pussy God had ever created—

He grimaced. So much for sweeping her out of his head.

He paused for a split second just inside the door, trying to interpret her expression, and failing. He hadn't overplayed the luster—or the appeal—of her eyes in his memories during the past few days. They drew a man in like a moth to dark flame. He yanked his stare off her and automatically took Ian's hand when he extended it.

"Welcome," Ian greeted warmly. "I hope you found us all right."

"It's kind of hard to miss," Kam said dryly. Noble Tower was one of the most impressive of the high-rises along the river. He understood that his brother's new headquarters had already become an iconic symbol of the city.

"Can we get you anything? Coffee? Breakfast?" Ian asked.

"No. I had breakfast at Lucien and Elise's." Coraline took this as her signal to go and exited silently. Ian waved him over to the pair of chairs where Lin sat.

"I wish you'd reconsider staying with us at the penthouse. Francesca was on me about it after you left last night," Ian said. "I understand from Lucien that Elise is giving him just as hard of a time because you're not staying with them, either."

"I'm used to being alone," Kam replied shortly, even though the last thing he felt was alone in his hotel room. More like a cooped-up lab rat.

"Lin and I were just discussing the meeting with the Gersbachs tonight," Ian said as he went behind his desk. Kam lowered to the chair next to Lin. He gave a sideways glance and caught her staring. Her gaze immediately jumped off him like a skipped rock. Her dress was loose and shapeless, like an oversized man's shirt, but made of draping, soft silk. Unfortunately for him and his overactive libido, it was also cut just above her knees, leaving a few inches of thigh and her lower legs exposed. To add to his misfortune, she also wore a pair of spiked heels with inch-thick straps that buckled around her ankles. The vision of the black leather against her slender, elegant ankles sent an electrical jolt through him. *Fuck* if it didn't make him think of tightening leather restraints around those sexy ankles— straps that had nothing to do with luxury footwear—of Lin bound and helpless, writhing and moaning in pleasure beneath his mouth and hands—

Ian interrupted Kam's uncontrollable pornographic thoughts. "Lin seems to be of the opinion that you might be more comfortable with me there instead of her tonight."

"Is she?" Kam asked, giving Lin a glance. He wasn't shocked, precisely, but he was irritated. As he stared at her, however, a different feeling crept into his awareness: curiosity. Her throat looked exceptionally white and flawless next to her dark, upswept hair and the dress. It tightened as she swallowed.

"I just think a family member might ease things for you more than I can," she said, her low, honey-smooth voice at odds with the delicate, quick flutter of the pulse at her throat.

"So you're not up to it," Kam said. "Funny, you seemed up for the challenge the other night."

Her gaze flashed to meet his, and this time he clearly sensed her anger flowing toward him like a cold, clear stream. "I didn't say I wasn't up for it," she said.

"Then why are you trying to pawn me off onto Ian?"

"It's not a matter of . . ." She faded off when she looked at Ian and noticed his curious stare, as if Ian, too, had wondered the same question. So . . . Lin definitely hadn't revealed to her boss any of the dirty details of Monday night. He'd wondered. Was that because she was worried about her job or because she was personally embarrassed about having had sex with him? He noticed the delicate stain of pink on her cheeks and decided on the latter. Her lush, rosebud mouth flattened.

"It was just a suggestion on my part, that's all. Ian is on more familiar terms with the Gersbachs," she said evenly.

Kam slouched back in the chair. "If you aren't up for doing it, that's fine by me. The whole thing is a joke, so it hardly matters to me who's in on the laugh."

Her head swung around at that. "Who is going to be laughing? And at *what*?"

"Presumably the Gersbachs at my rustic ways, isn't that what you and Ian are worried about?" he replied without pause. "But don't worry, I'm sure I'll get a good laugh out of the whole thing as well."

"Do you often think people are laughing at you?" she asked with quiet sarcasm. "That's called paranoia, Kam. No one is laughing at you, or is *going* to be laughing at you. You think far too much of yourself if you think you affect other people so much."

She started back slightly when he laughed. Kam's burst of amusement faded and was replaced by guilt when he saw how stunned Lin looked by his impulsive reaction. He knew it'd been rude, but her depiction of him had given him a sudden bird's-eye view of himself—a bitter, paranoid loner who was more comfortable with his dog than with most people. The vision had struck him as apt, sad, and strangely comical as well.

"I get it," Lin said, recovering from his harsh bark of laughter and turning away from him dismissively. "It's easy to stand on the sidelines and jeer."

Irritation spiked through him. A movement broke his focus on Lin, briefly fracturing his attention. Ian sat behind his desk, a very untypical expression of rapt bemusement on his face as he watched the two of them.

"If you don't think I'm going to be a source of amusement in all these meetings you have planned, why are you backing out of them?" Kam demanded of Lin.

"I don't appreciate your disdain for the proceedings," she said, picking at an invisible piece of lint on her dress and sweeping it away. "You're determined to ruin the whole thing without even really trying. It's an insult to all the preparation I've done."

"At least I was willing to show up tonight. More than you can say."

"So you actually *want* me there?" she demanded, giving him a sideways glare.

"I figure you're the best bet I have."

Her nostrils flared slightly as they faced off in the silence.

"I couldn't have said it better myself," Ian said. Both Lin and he turned to look at him.

"Yeah. I'm still here," Ian said drolly under his breath.

"Fine," Lin said abruptly, as if Ian had never interrupted. Kam blinked when she practically hurled herself out of the chair, her actions rapid yet graceful, controlled but somehow aggressive as well. Ian seemed as cowed into silence as Kam was as they both watched her grab a pad of paper and pen off Ian's desk and lean over to write in a slashing scrawl. Kam saw that the sexy shirtdress was slightly longer in the back than the front, but still gave him a tantalizing view of slender calves. In her bent-over position, he could see the outline of her shapely, taut ass through draping fabric. It twitched ever so slightly as she wrote.

She ripped the piece of paper off the pad with a vicious swipe.

"Meet me at this address at noon. Bring your credit card," she said, handing Kam the slip of paper. She turned to Ian and flipped her hand open in a succinct demand. "If you're finished with the Tyake numbers, I need them back."

Ian handed her the file wordlessly. They both watched Lin sweep out of the office.

"I've never seen her this way," Ian said a moment after his office door shut briskly behind Lin. He stared at Kam looking a little sideswiped. "What in the world did you say to her when you two met?"

"Nothing," Kam said laconically as he stood. He noticed Ian's skeptical glance. "I just told her I thought she took her job way too seriously."

"You told *Lin Soong* that?"

"Yeah," Kam muttered under his breath as he walked over to study the view. "I didn't realize at the time it was a dead-on poke at the hornet's nest."

Chapter Four

She circled the tailor's podium like a sleek cat on the prowl, examining every detail of the tailor and his assistant's work, occasionally calling out adjustments she wanted.

"No, the sleeve is too short," Lin said.

Kam glowered at her display of cool efficiency in the mirror, but she was impervious. He felt very much like an elephant in the center ring as the tailors poked and prodded at him. He'd purposefully goaded Lin into guiding him through the next few weeks. He'd realized too late she'd issued a return challenge when he saw that the address she'd given him was a high-end men's haberdasher. Knowing what a big deal he'd made in Ian's office, it was too late to back down. Now that he stood here with one man kneeling before him and another poking at his arm and back, however, he wished he'd turned tail and run while he had the chance.

The assistant's hand brushed against his balls as he measured his inseam.

"*Merde,*" Kam muttered heatedly. The young tailor's assistant's hand jerked back guiltily. "Watch where you put that tape measure!"

"I'm sorry, sir."

The boy looked too anxious to continue. Kam glanced up in the mirror and noticed the amusement in Lin's expression.

"You'd better get on with it," she said from behind them. "We have three more suits to go plus a tuxedo."

"Can't they just go by the measurements from this one?" Kam demanded.

"Each suit is slightly different in the cut."

"Why so many?"

"We have more than just the meeting with the Gersbachs. I told you that Monday night. There are other parties interested in your product. I have other meetings lined up for you," Lin said, her focus returning to watching Mr. Marnier's actions. "And I want you to be perfect for each one. Besides, it's not as if you won't need the suits for future business."

He snorted in derision. Still, he couldn't pull his gaze off her face. Or her legs. Or her *anything*, really. A man could make a meal out of looking at her. He couldn't deny his appreciation at being granted access to look his fill. She glanced up and met his stare in the mirror. He went rigid in awareness and was suddenly glad Junior had stopped poking around his privates.

"You are bound to be disappointed," he told her point-blank. His gaze sunk over her lithe body. "I'm not the perfect one in this scenario."

Her nostrils flared slightly as their gazes clung. "It's a relative term," she replied softly. "I meant to perfect what you already are."

"You make me sound like I'm a doll you're trying to make pretty for tea. It'll never work."

Her chin tilted up in a subtle dare. "We'll see."

Her heart leapt an hour later when he caught her elbow on the way out of the store. She honestly couldn't say if it did so in panic or in acute anticipation.

"Where are you running off to so fast?" Kam asked when Lin glanced over her shoulder as she finished buttoning her coat.

"I have a thing called a job."

He rolled his eyes. "Yes, I think we established that the other night."

He grabbed her elbow again, when she turned irritably and started out the door.

"Why are you so prickly about my job?" she hissed over her shoulder. Immediately, she felt guilty. *She* was the one who was so prickly about her job today . . . about what Ian had told her about relocating to London . . . about Kam's insinuations about her doing anything for her work . . . about *everything*.

"Because I don't like being one of your job duties," he replied in a hushed tone, glancing around the luxurious store. A man holding up two ties looked their way, obviously hearing their tense hisses. Kam nodded to the sunny street and sidewalk and followed Lin out the revolving door.

"I told you. Monday night was *not* a job duty. Not the end of it, anyway," she said succinctly when they faced off on the sidewalk. "Monday night *was* a mistake. And everything we do together from here on out? *Definitely* work, and tedious work at that," she added with a hard glare. She started to walk away.

He cursed in French under his breath. "I'm sorry," he called out baldly.

She halted abruptly and glanced back at him, her mouth falling open in surprise.

"I'm sorry for suggesting that you were acting on Ian's orders to have sex with me to soften me up," he said in a muted tone, glancing from side to side to make sure no one was in hearing distance. "I wasn't thinking straight at the time."

"I'll say you weren't. You were acting like a bully."

His eyes flared with anger, but then he briefly closed them and inhaled.

"You're right. I deserve that," he said stiffly.

Her gaze narrowed as she stepped toward him. "It would have been one thing if you were just being an oaf. But you were being intentionally rude. You were *trying* to be hurtful. Why?"

He blinked, grinding his jaw, looking like he was "chewing metal" as Richard had put it. "When I saw you getting dressed that night when I came out of the bathroom, I realized you were done with me," he suddenly bit out.

Her expression went flat. A tingling sensation swept along her limbs. A car horn beeped loudly as traffic passed, but it barely penetrated Lin's awareness.

"It suddenly hit me how truly unlikely it would be that a woman like you would have initiated something with me," Kam said.

"So you accused me of going to bed with you on Ian's orders?" she clarified quietly.

He shrugged and glanced uncomfortably out at the street. "I knew I was wrong almost the second I walked out your door. But if I hadn't fully guessed how wrong I was then, I would have this morning."

Lin took another step closer. For the first time since they'd slept together she looked straight into his eyes. He noticed and glanced down at her. She thought she really did see regret mixing with irritation in the light-infused, silvery depths. She got the distinct impression the frustration she witnessed was with himself. "What do you mean?" she asked. "What happened this morning?"

"Ian seemed genuinely put off by your . . . presentation in his office earlier. There's no way in hell he could have asked you to tango with me purposefully," Kam scoffed. "If he had, he wouldn't have seemed so stunned by the way you acted. He seemed completely out of the loop for once in his life."

"*Tango* with you?" she clarified, amused despite her determination to keep him at arm's length.

"Face it. I set you off balance," he said, leaning down slightly, a small smile tilting his lips.

She blinked, unsteadied yet again. "Your cockiness is *epic*," she said in mixed amazement and irritation, forgetting momentarily that he'd just admitted point-blank a weakness to her. He'd been as vulnerable as she had been after they'd had sex.

"Only if it works," she thought she heard him mutter under his breath in a thick accent. "Will you have lunch with me?" he asked, his gaze sinking slowly to her mouth in a familiar way that she recognized from the other night. Heat rushed through her, testing her straining defenses.

"I told myself I was going to steer clear of you, Kam."

"Why?" he asked, taking a step closer, so that the placket of his open shirt brushed against her coat. She found herself staring up into those magnetic eyes. She was nearly as close as she had been Monday night when they lay side by side, both of them turned inside out by thunderous climaxes. "I apologized, didn't I?" he reminded her quietly. "I know when I make a mistake. Or are you one to hold a grudge?"

"No, it's not that. I appreciate your apology," she admitted. "It's just . . . you're trouble."

"As a rule?" he murmured. "Or for you in particular?"

She hesitated. "Both, I think."

"Best news I've had all day."

Something hitched in her chest when she saw the smile in his eyes.

"At least have lunch with me. It's boring in that hotel room all alone."

"You said you wanted to be alone. You've lived in isolation for almost all of your adult life," she reminded him.

"But always with something to do. I don't like being bored."

"There's a fantastic workout facility at the Trump Tower hotel."

"I already used it today."

"You could take a tour of the city. Or I could plan a tour for you at a Noble Enterprises manufacturing plant."

"Ian is going to take me out to a plant next week to show me around. We planned it today during the tour downtown. But if you know of any other technology or telecommunication sector companies I might visit while I'm here, I'd be interested," Kam said, surprising her. He leaned in and said with mock confidentiality, "And you don't even have to hold my hand during the tours if you don't want to."

"Kam, I'm not trying to patronize you. I'm trying to help."

"I know that, and you will," he said so earnestly he took her off guard. "But what I want to do right now is take you to lunch. Please?" he prodded, probably sensing her crumbling resistance.

She hesitated.

"I don't want Ian to know. Or Francesca. Or anyone," she stated finally.

"About today?"

"I haven't done anything regrettable today with you, except for lose my temper in Ian's office." *Not yet, you haven't,* a knowing voice in her head sneered. She suppressed it with effort. "I meant I don't want you making Monday night public."

"Because Ian is your boss?"

"Because I don't want him to know," she repeated.

He shrugged in that insouciant way of his. "Fine. It makes no difference to me. Ian isn't my concern. Not at the moment, he isn't."

She hesitated but then noticed his small smile. A thrill prickled through her. That grin was piratical, yes, and daring, but there it was . . . that hint of shyness. She *shouldn't*, but that smile told her she *would*.

"I have a feeling I'm going to regret this," she said in a hushed tone.

"Sometimes the risk is the only thing that makes something worthwhile."

Before she could respond, he'd taken her hand in his and was leading her to the curb to hail a cab.

"I read about it in a travel magazine while I was at school in London and always wanted to come," Kam said by way of explanation when they pulled up to a restaurant and Lin stared out the window in amazement. She glanced around curiously when Kam held the cab door open for her and helped her alight onto the sidewalk. They were in the midst of an established North Side neighborhood. Kids played in the schoolyard across the way. Neat brick row houses lined the street for blocks.

"Lou's Ribs and Pizza," she read the sign in the window. The building looked like it'd gone through its share of years and renovations. It was a hodgepodge of materials from different eras.

"You've never been here?" Kam said as he walked ahead of her and opened the door.

"No," Lin admitted. She followed him into a surprisingly crowded bar and eating area. A jukebox played a muted pop classic, and people chatted at booths and tables. Everyone's conversation automatically went up in volume when someone turned on a blender behind the bar, as if the crowd was accustomed to the sound. "It's doing a good business for weekday lunch. How in the world did you know about a neighborhood place like this?"

"I told you, I read about it when I was in college. It's known for ribs and deep-dish pizza and incredible milk shakes. It's been around forever. Frank Sinatra used to come here with his buddies. It's crowded today because there's a Cubs game at three. You grew up in Chicago and never heard of Lou's?"

She shrugged apologetically. "I guess it took a Frenchman to introduce me to something in my own hometown. Besides, my grandmother was a vegetarian. She was very selective about where we ate."

"You're more used to places like Savaur or one of Lucien's restaurants, but it wouldn't hurt you to step out a little." A flicker of irritation went through her at his smug certainty, but she quashed it as she glanced around at the homey restaurant. Maybe he was right. Maybe she should expand the boundaries of her world a little.

A stocky woman wearing an apron over stretchy polyester pants approached them. "We're full at the moment. Give me fifteen minutes?"

"What about those two?" Kam asked, pointing at two empty stools at the bar. The woman looked doubtfully at Lin's high heels and lightweight tailored coat, then more appreciatively at Kam. Again, Lin had chosen Kam's clothing: a pair of jeans, a white shirt that set off swarthy skin, and a rugged gray overshirt that doubled as a jacket for the pleasantly cool fall weather. He fit in here. The waitress's glance told her clearly she did not.

"They're yours if you want them," the woman conceded with a shrug.

Lin smiled at Kam and nodded. He took her coat and hung it on a coat rack at the front of the bar.

"Belly up to the bar yet again," he said quietly when he returned and sat next to her, leaning his elbows on the scarred, yet gleaming walnut bar.

Lin glanced away, unsure what to say to that. She was strangely happy to be there with Kam in the bustling restaurant, but she was torn by that happiness. He'd been very rude to her Monday night, but she'd believed his apology. She'd actually been touched by his admission of vulnerability. That wasn't what was bothering her.

"You mentioned earlier that Ian was upset by what happened in his office this morning?" she asked with forced casualness.

"Not upset. No," Kam said, his gaze running over her face. She schooled her features into a neutral expression. "He was more surprised. I've only seen Ian riled a few times. Even when he got shot, Ian was calm," Kam mused, referring to a horrifying event that had occurred earlier this year when Ian's cousin Gerard Sinoit betrayed Ian and shot him in the shoulder. Kam had saved Ian and Francesca on that occasion. "He was just put-off, " Kam explained presently. "I got the impression he's not used to seeing you rattled."

"I wasn't rattled. I was . . ."

"Pissed off and good," he finished for her.

"Thank you," Lin said to the bartender when he set down two ice waters and a menu before them. "What did Ian say, exactly?"

Kam didn't reply immediately, just took a sip of ice water and idly watched the bartender making a milk shake behind the bar. The machine made a discordant *clunk, clunk, clunk* sound.

"He was a bit shocked at the idea that I told you that you take your job too seriously. According to Ian—and to a few other people I've talked to—Lin Soong and her work are practically synonymous."

She sat back. "You were talking to other people about me?"

"Not anything major. People talk," he said impassively.

"Especially when you ask," she returned wryly.

"Nobody has explained one thing. Why does a gorgeous, single woman bury herself in her work to the exclusion of almost everything else?" he asked, watching her with a sidelong stare.

"Why don't you tell me why a good-looking, brilliant man with the potential to do anything he wants in life lives holed up in an underground laboratory for years?" She picked up her menu and studied it, but he continued to look at her. She knew he did because her cheeks heated beneath his steady gaze. He leaned closer.

"Maybe Francesca and Elise and some of the people at Noble have it all wrong. You *do* appear to be secretive," he mused, choosing to ignore her question. Like it had in the restaurant on Monday night, his low, confidential growl caused the tiny hairs on her neck and ear to prickle in awareness. "Maybe you do have a man stashed away somewhere, someone you carefully hide from Ian."

She dropped her menu to the bar with a slapping sound. "Why would I do that?"

"You tell me."

She shot him a glare and really tried to read the menu this time instead of just pretending she was. "For your information, I've introduced several men to Ian over the years. Francesca has even met a few of my dates."

"Several, huh? Nothing sticks?"

She was glad that the round, harried-looking bartender chose that moment to come and get their order. She ordered a salad, ignoring Kam's frown of disapproval. He ordered a small stuffed pizza, a large chocolate shake, and a rib dinner.

"Hungry, are you?" she asked, chin in her hand, watching him as the bartender walked away. He placed his elbow on the bar next to hers. A prickle of awareness went through her at the feeling of him pressing lightly against her. The fabric of the shirt she'd purchased for him was thick and hardy, a stark contrast to the sheer, insubstantial fabric of her dress's sleeve.

"I had to order all the specialties since you were being such a spoilsport and ordered a salad."

"I like to eat light for lunch. You'll regret not doing the same when you're served Elise's food tonight at Frais and don't have room for it. Your sister-in-law is a fabulous chef."

"You don't have to tell me that. I just had one of her breakfasts this morning." He took a swallow of ice water. "And she's cooked for us at Aurore Manor when she and Lucien were visiting. I won't regret a damn thing about ordering this food, though. And don't think I'm sharing any of my ribs and pizza."

"Fine with me," she said with determined unconcern. He rolled his eyes.

"All right," he said with an air of being strong-armed, his gaze dipping to her mouth. "I'll share."

She smiled. Why did she always feel that shift in her lower belly and sex when his stare sunk to her mouth like that? It was like he could stroke the very deepest pit of her being with his eyes. The lighting in the bar probably didn't change much from day to night given the three solitary windows all the way at the front. In the dimness, Kam strongly resembled Ian. Was that the real reason for that delicious sensation? Somehow, she didn't think so.

A question wormed its way into her entrancement.

"Do *you*?" she asked quietly. His brows quirked slightly in puzzlement, so she clarified. "Have a woman back in France, I mean? Someone special?"

"I wouldn't have had sex with you last Monday night if there was someone special."

"That's good to know," she said, her gaze dropping at the mention of them having sex. It sounded illicit and exciting murmured in Kam's rough, accented voice. Not to mention how him speaking the words caused graphic snippets of erotic memories to flash across her brain.

You want it now, ma petite minette? *You want it fast and hard?*

"Good to know I have a smattering of basic morality, you mean?" he asked.

"*You* aside, Kam," she said, recovering from the charged memory. "It's a good thing for any woman in this situation to hear."

There was a loud metallic grinding sound from behind the bar and the bartender cursed. Kam winced slightly, but neither of them broke their stare.

"Ian never talked to you about it?" Kam asked.

"About what?"

"About me . . . and women."

Now she was confused. "I thought you said there wasn't anyone."

"Not anyone special."

She blinked. "Oh, I see. There are *women,* in the plural sense. The *non*-special variety. What does Ian know about it?"

His expression went blank. "Nothing."

She gave an exasperated sigh. "Then what would he have to tell me if he knew nothing? He stayed with you on several occasions at Aurore. Aren't you suggesting he knew something about your comings and goings?" She flushed. *Comings* and goings. Every word she used with him seemed to take on a sexual tinge.

The bartender was now cursing in subdued tones while the woman who had come to seat them barked instructions at him. Kam's impassive expression didn't give.

"Okay, so we're not going to talk about it," she said.

He sighed in a beleaguered fashion. "No, it's not that. Just . . . excuse me for a moment."

"Okay." Was he irritated at her probing? Maybe he was going to use the men's room. She sat forward curiously when instead of walking toward the rear of the establishment where the restrooms were located, he calmly walked around the bar. The waitress immediately noticed his tall, formidable and uninvited form behind the bar, but the bartender kept wrestling with and poking at a countertop shake freezer and blender, cursing. Kam thumped the bartender on the shoulder.

"Do you mind?" he asked, pointing at the machine.

"Be my guest," the bemused-looking bartender said after a second, stepping aside.

Kam had caught the attention of everyone sitting at the bar now, not just Lin. He stepped up to the machine and opened a utility cover. For a moment, he just studied the whole unit. Lin had the impression he was absorbing the machine somehow. It was a little how she felt whenever he looked at her with his laserlike stare that seemed to see more than just the surface, like he was examining her component parts and analyzing how they all worked together. She couldn't say precisely what he did next, but if she had to describe it, she'd say he flipped one thing, twisted another, and jerked a third: one, two, three, quick as counting up to something good.

He turned on a switch and the blender made the familiar monotonous roar Lin had heard sporadically when they first entered.

"I hadn't even noticed it was broken. That was nice of you to fix it," Lin said in amazement when he sat down again next to her at the bar a moment later, waving off the bartender's profuse thanks with a look of vague discomfort on his face.

"Not really," he said, his mouth curled in a self-derisive expression. "I wanted my milk shake."

"That's not it," she said quietly after studying him closely for several seconds. "It bothered you. Having something out of joint . . . broken in your vicinity. Didn't it?"

He frowned, not replying for a moment.

"I can't stand to be around a machine that doesn't work. It's like they call out to me. Scream at me. It's been that way for as long as I can remember."

She recalled him reading her body the other night with his touch. "And with human beings? Is it the same? Is that why you studied medicine?"

"Human beings, animals . . . anything that isn't humming the way it should. Anything broken won't let me rest. If something is out of rhythm, I hear it. Feel it. It puts me out of joint, too."

"That's fascinating," she said softly. Strange that such a rugged, bold man could feel the delicacies of the universe so acutely.

"Why didn't you finish your residency after graduating?" Lin wondered as the bartender put place settings, Lin's salad, and Kam's milk shake in front of them.

"My mother got ill."

"She lived at Aurore Manor, didn't she?" Lin asked.

He nodded. "She worked there. She grew up in an orphanage in Dublin. After she signed up for a maid employment service, she was transferred to Aurore from Ireland. I think she considered herself a temporary Irish visitor until the day she died, even though she lived in northern France for twenty-seven years of her life. She never really mastered the French language, even after all that time," he explained with a small smile.

She watched as he lifted the long silver spoon from his shake and ladled some of the thick, white liquid between his lips. He slipped it out. The frost on the chilled spoon vanished in a second by the heat of his mouth. She blinked, mesmerized by the sight. "My father seduced her when she was nineteen," Kam continued bluntly, "got her pregnant with me, and probably never said a dozen words to her between then and the time he died."

Lin took a sip of water. He'd sounded brutally honest about his father's crimes. What a strange, lonely existence Kam Reardon must have lived growing up on the grounds of his twisted father's home.

"But Trevor Gaines spoke to you," she said softly after a moment, studying his profile. "He taught you what he knew about machines and computers and watches."

"Yeah. He spoke to me. He *allowed* me to live on the estate and eat his food and work my ass off for him. When I was eight, I begged him to send me to the public school in the village. He permitted it because he thought the basic knowledge of mathematics might make me a better assistant in his laboratory, and he didn't have the interest in teaching me myself. When I got older, I bargained with the knowledge of how to improve a couple of his inventions. He sent me to college in exchange for the information, and then resented me ever after for surpassing his mechanical abilities. I guess all that makes him Father of the Year," Kam said with a dark sideways glance.

She inhaled slowly, trying to dissipate the ache in her chest. "I'm sorry, Kam. Was . . . it better getting that grudging attention from him? Or would you have rather been like Lucien and Ian?"

"Lucien and Ian were better off shot of him altogether. Best thing Gaines ever did for them, ignoring them the way he did," Kam muttered viciously. He inhaled when he noticed her startled expression.

Not wanting to say something when words would never suffice *or* make him think she couldn't handle what he'd said, she picked up her fork and mixed her dressing onto her salad. Neither of them spoke for a charged moment.

"Living in the vicinity of Trevor Gaines was like living near a perpetually broken machine," he said in a subdued tone after a pause, staring straight ahead. "It almost drove me mad to be near him, like living with a relentless *clunk* and *bang*, a grinding on my bones, just from his damn presence. At one point, he requested that I live up at the manor with him. My mother insisted I go—she lived in some kind of dreamworld when it came to him and me—so I went. He had me dressed up like Little Lord Fauntleroy and tried to teach me to be a gentleman," Kam recalled with simmering sarcasm. "But I knew who he really was. *What* he really was. Who better than me, after what he'd done to my mother? Filthy fucking hypocrite," he seethed under his breath. "I finally lost it and told him what he could do with his social graces. No," he concluded darkly. "Ian and Lucien were lucky to never have laid eyes on the bastard."

Lin didn't flinch at his sudden flash of savageness. His snarl faded slowly as he seemed to come to himself. They both watched in silence as the bartender set the remainder of Kam's meal in front of him.

"Sorry," he said dully after the bartender left.

"You don't have to apologize. There's nothing shocking about your anger toward him. It's very understandable."

"Are you worried about tonight?" he asked warily after several silent moments of eating.

She glanced aside, surprised. "No. Are you worried?"

He swallowed and shook his head.

"Just be yourself, Kam," she said quietly.

"I thought that was what you were trying to help me avoid," he said before he took a swift bite of fork-tender ribs.

"You're wrong. I wouldn't want you to be anything but yourself." She searched for a way to ease his anxiety, grabbing on a thread of advice. "Just talk to people like you do me," she suggested.

A strange expression came over his rugged features. He set down his fork and knife and took a swallow of ice water.

"What?" Lin asked warily.

He leaned closer until their mouths were only inches apart.

"We're screwed," he said, his warm breath brushing her lips.

"What do you mean?"

"I hardly talk to people as a rule. At least not for the past few years."

"And?" she whispered cautiously, caught in the gleam of his shadowed eyes.

"I've said more words to you in the past twenty-four hours than I have to people I've known my whole life. I don't have to think about talking to you. It just . . . happens."

"Oh," she said, flustered. She stared at the fork in her hand, wondering how it had gotten there. What was it even *used* for? She set it down abruptly, grasping for the thread of rational thought.

"Well then . . . just listen," she suggested breathlessly. She looked up into his somber face. "Listen to the Gersbachs like you do the rest of the world, absorb their intentions, feel their rhythms. Don't feel any pressure to perform. That's not what this is about. Observe them tonight, and afterward, you can tell me all your impressions. You'll put it into words then."

"So I get you afterward? To myself?"

Her pulse began to throb at her throat as she stared at his mouth. She hadn't prepared for him saying that. She was wide-open to him. His gaze was fixed on her throat. She instinctively pressed her hand to her neck, but he stopped her by wrapping his hand around her wrist. Her breath froze and then burned in her lungs as she watched him slowly raise her hand to his mouth and place a single kiss on her palm. It was a simple gesture, and yet mind-bogglingly complex. Her sex clenched tight at the sensation of his pressing, firm lips and the hint of his heat behind them.

"I'll think about it," she whispered shakily when their gazes met again.

The hint of a smile pulled at his lips. She couldn't make a logical decision with his knowing eyes seeing straight through her and his kiss still burning her palm. She had the uncomfortable impression that while she was unsure of how tonight would end, Kam was one hundred percent positive.

Chapter Five

Lin ended up having a wonderful time at lunch, finally letting Kam talk her into sampling his ribs and pizza. He'd been right. The food was delicious. They'd lingered over it until Lin regretfully said she needed to get back to work. Since he'd expressed interest in touring other businesses, she made a phone call on the cab ride downtown and got Kam in for a tour and executive meeting with both Schnell Industries, a young and promising technology company; and Alltell, a major wireless telecommunications company.

"Are you interested in acquiring wireless technology that could make your watch into an organizer and communications device?" she asked him while they were in the cab.

"Thinking about it," Kam said vaguely.

"Because that's a fantastic idea," she enthused. She sat back in the seat, and was considering all the innovative possibilities for Kam's watch, when she noticed him eyeing her closely.

"You must be very excited, having a groundbreaking product like this. I could really get behind your watch, Kam," she said sincerely.

"Could you?" he asked. Lin blinked when she sensed the intensity behind his quiet question.

She finished with work early and returned to her condominium, where she decided to practice a new dance routine that had proved challenging for her. Traditional Chinese dance emphasized exquisite control of movement. It was a sort of moving meditation for her, an exercise that helped her find her center, her peace . . . her control.

Something told her that her control would be in short measure tonight.

She ignored the volatile thought and for a while was able to lose herself in the fluid rhythm of the dance. Afterward, she showered and retrieved two potential dresses for dinner from her closet. As she came out of her walk-in closet, she heard her doorbell ring. She draped the dresses over her arm and hurriedly tightened her robe. After checking who it was through the peephole, she swung open the door.

"Hi," she greeted Richard St. Claire, smiling. "What are you doing home at this hour?" she asked, knowing he was usually working at the restaurant at this time.

"I'm coming down with something. Emile told me to get home and to bed before I spread things to the customers," Richard croaked, pointing to his chest. "Can I borrow your humidifier? My chest is killing me every time I cough."

"You sound like you're about to get laryngitis, too," she said, alarmed. "Have you been to the doctor?"

He shook his head. "I don't have a fever. I just need some rest."

"Follow me," she said, bustling back to her bedroom. She tossed the two dresses on the foot of the bed and entered her bathroom. When she came out a moment later carrying her humidifier, Richard was looking at the dresses. "Going out tonight?" he asked.

"Yes. To Frais," Lin said, handing him the humidifier.

"Traitor."

"Elise and Lucien are practically family, just like you and Emile are," she chastised him fondly. "Besides, Otto Gersbach is a health nut. Doesn't touch alcohol, and just between you and me, would prefer to dine at restaurants that don't serve it when his daughter is with him.

"Ah," Richard said, nodding in understanding. He knew that Elise's restaurant catered to individuals with a history of substance abuse and their friends and family, taking away the element of alcohol, yet still providing everything else an epicure might desire in a luxury dining experience. "The things you learn about Noble's business associates would stun the man on the street, Lin. Speaking of which, how did things go on Monday night?" Richard asked. He gave her a give-me-a-break glance when she feigned confusion. "With the sexy Brazilian street fighter?"

She picked up the dresses. "Very well, I think. It *was* just work, you know . . . Ian's brother," she reminded him when she noticed his amused expression. "I have a business dinner again tonight with him, in fact."

"Uh-huh," Richard murmured doubtfully.

She shot him a cool glance. On the inside, however, her heart began to throb in her chest. She had tried not to be conspicuous in leaving Savaur the other night with Kam, but Richard didn't miss much. He might have noticed they got in a cab together. Still, that didn't mean anything necessarily. They might have been sharing a cab.

"He really does look an awful lot like Ian," Richard said too casually.

"Yes, he does," she admitted, going to a mirror over her dresser and holding up one dress and then the other. "Although he couldn't be more different."

"So being around him isn't . . . difficult for you?"

She knew what Richard was hinting at, but she didn't want to discuss it. Richard and Emile were both smart, observant men. She'd never admitted point-blank to either one of them that she had a "thing" for her boss, but they suspected. She ritualistically refused to talk about it with either of them, so why would things be different tonight?

"No," she replied. "Kam is a unique, shall we say *challenging* personality, but nothing I can't handle."

"You're certain?"

"Absolutely," she replied, meeting his eyes calmly in the mirror.

Richard studied her face soberly for a second before he shrugged. "You're a locked chamber when it comes to some things, Lin."

"I have no reason to lock anything away. Not on this topic," she lied.

"So socializing with a man who looks so much like Ian Noble is a simple, easy thing for you, eh?"

As easy as sin.

She suppressed the automatic thought and held up the two dresses. "Which one?" she asked.

"Is this some kind of riddle for me to answer my own question?"

She gave him an exasperated glance, and he laughed. Richard considered the two dresses with the air of an expert. He said the name of the designer of the black-and-white dress, as if the choice was obvious. It was a tuxedolike halter cocktail dress with a high neck that left her arms, upper back and shoulders bare. A curved cutout in the front also left a good portion of her legs exposed. It was a structured, geometric design, but the dress was also fiercely sexy.

"Don't you think it's too . . . *much*?" she asked doubtfully, examining the dress critically.

"*You* tell me which one," was Richard's arch reply.

She held up the decidedly more demure dress with frothy skirt and a high waist and collar.

"Interesting," Richard mused as he started to leave, carrying the humidifier.

"Be sure to drink lots of liquids. I'll check in on you later. And the dress is *not* interesting," she couldn't stop herself from calling after him. "It's a perfectly *uninteresting* dress."

"That was what was interesting about you picking it," he said before he walked out the door.

* * *

Francesca immediately greeted her when she walked into the small ballroom. Lucien's staff had converted it into a studio to display her artwork.

"Hi! You're one of the first to get here. Or maybe you're one of the only to come," Francesca added worriedly under her breath, before she gave Lin a hug and a kiss on the cheek and Lin reciprocated.

"Don't be silly. Loads of people will come. You got that wonderful mention in the *Chicago Tribune* last Sunday in the arts section. I just came early to be sure I was here before everyone else. You look beautiful," Lin said. The vibrant green color did wonderful things for Ian's wife's rose-gold hair and dark eyes. The cut of the dress subtly emphasized Francesca's pregnant state rather than disguising it. Francesca was in the fifth month of her pregnancy, and she looked radiant. Strangely enough, considering Lin's secret feelings for Ian, she'd never been painfully jealous of Francesca. Perhaps that was simply because the vibrant, fresh, and singularly talented young woman was difficult not to like. Lin's feelings toward Francesca Noble had deepened from cautious amiability to respect and caring. She understood why Ian was so captivated by his wife. Besides, how could she profess to genuine feelings for Ian and not be glad for his obvious peace and happiness?

"Thanks," Francesca said earnestly. "I haven't had a showing in almost a year. I'm very nervous."

"I'm excited to see your work. I'm sure it'll be amazing," Lin said, glancing around the mostly empty ballroom. Some of Francesca's framed sketches had been mounted on the walls, but some were displayed on erected panels throughout the room.

"I hope so. I'm a little nervous about the different medium. Let's go and check your wrap," she suggested, waving toward the far corner of the room.

"*Wow.* What a dress," Francesca said a few seconds later when Lin removed her wrap. "You always manage to look like you just walked off the runway, but *this* . . . very sexy," Francesca praised with a grin.

Feeling uncommonly self-conscious, Lin handed her wrap to the smiling coat check girl. What had made her choose the halter tuxedo dress, after all? Her back, shoulders, and arms suddenly felt overexposed, the bare skin prickly and sensitive.

"I can't wait until I can wear a dress like that again," Francesca said touching the slight bulge of her stomach.

"You could wear it now," Lin said, meaning it. "You've hardly gained a pound beyond the baby's weight."

"Yeah. Like I could pull off that number," Francesca said, looking at Lin's dress and laughing. A spark of sudden interest flew into her eyes and she took a step toward Lin. "We have to talk about what you think of Kam. Ian hinted that things must have become . . . *interesting* when you two met the other night."

An alarm began ringing in Lin's brain. "*Interesting*? What did Ian mean by that?"

Francesca opened her mouth to reply, looked over Lin's shoulder and checked herself. "Hi," she called in greeting. "Here's Lin. She looks amazing, doesn't she?"

The prickling of awareness on her bare shoulders and back amplified. She turned around. Lucien and Kam stood just behind her, their heights similar, two formidable, extremely handsome men. Kam's stare dropped fleetingly over her. She couldn't quite interpret his rigid expression, but his eyes were like gleaming quicksilver in the mask of his face.

"They delivered the suit all right?" she asked him. He just nodded once, his stare on her unflinching.

Hungry?

"It . . . it looks great," she stammered. It was a monumental understatement. Kam was devastating in the well-cut black suit with crisp white dress shirt and royal blue tie.

"How did the tour at Schnell go this afternoon?" she asked.

"Good. Jim was great," he said, referring to the vice president who had met with Kam as a favor to Lin. "Thank you again for setting it up for me."

"It was my pleasure," she said.

Kam was clean-shaven for once and his dark, russet-tinted hair was neatly groomed and combed back in thick waves. He'd told her his mother was Irish. Were those reddish highlights the Irish influence in him burning through the swarthy Gallic? It was like she'd never seen him before.

"Lucien," she said, realizing she'd been staring at Kam. She stepped forward to exchange a kiss of greeting with Ian's older brother.

"Hello. Francesca is right. You look incredible," Lucien greeted her in his low, fluid, French-accented voice.

"Thank you." She stepped back and experienced an awkward moment. Shouldn't she greet Kam in a similar fashion? He was Ian's brother as well, after all. Fortunately, she was spared having to decide. She saw the Gersbachs enter the ballroom along with a dozen or so other attendees.

"There they are," she said in a muted tone, leaning her head subtly toward the door. Francesca nodded in understanding. Lin took Kam's hand and started to lead him toward the father and daughter. It was easy to touch him when her excuse was guiding him to a business interaction.

That's what she told herself, anyway, as she tried to ignore the feeling of his large, warm hand tightening around her own and her heartbeat began a steady throb in her ears.

He heard Lin greeting the Gersbachs and introducing them, but he wasn't really listening. Even though he wasn't looking at Lin, the vision of her still burned in his mind's eye. She usually wore her hair up. The only time he'd seen it down was when they'd been in bed together. Then, it'd been a waving, curling, tumbling delight that fell to her mid back. Tonight, she wore it down, but it had been straightened. Without the curls and waves, it fell in a straight, fluid line almost to her waist. It was drop-dead sexy. As Lucien and he had approached her, the silky curtain of it brushed her naked back, the vision disrupting rational thought.

She'd turned, and it was like silk whisking against silk. He was suddenly overcome with a brutal, primal need to be inside her once again, pounding inside all that soft, sleek glory, straining to build a crashing crescendo in the harmonious orchestra that was Lin. A pulse began to throb in his temple and his cock at once as he'd met her stare.

How inappropriate could he be? He really was going to ruin this whole fucking night.

". . . he just arrived on Monday. Isn't that right, Kam?"

He blinked and the present moment plummeted into his awareness jarringly.

"Yes," he said, realizing that Otto Gersbach's hand was extended. He shook it and mumbled something that was mostly unintelligible except for the word *pleasure*. He did the same when he was introduced to Brigit Gersbach. Brigit stared at him with wide blue eyes like he was part of the exhibit. Kam glanced uncomfortably sideways at Lin, looking for a cue as to what he should do or say next. Her hand looped around his elbow, and it suddenly didn't matter.

"I can't tell you what a pleasure this is for us to meet you as well," Otto was gushing in crisp, Swiss-accented English. "Brigit was very busy with the advertising campaign for the holidays, but she insisted upon accompanying me in order to meet the genius who created such a revolutionary mechanism. Even now, I can't quite grasp what you've managed to accomplish."

Kam resisted an urge to shrug and just held Otto's stare.

"He's modest," Brigit said in mock-confidential tone to Lin. "The brilliant ones often are."

"He's unconventional, that much is true. Don't try to pigeonhole him if you truly want to draw his character," Lin said, smiling warmly up at Kam.

"Do you?" Kam asked Lin, looking down at her upturned face.

She blinked, taken off guard by his question. "Do I what?"

"Want to draw my character?"

"Of course she does. Everyone knows Lin has a talent for seeing straight to the heart," Otto joked. "She can see to the rotten core of a person in two seconds flat during a business deal. It's one of the many reasons Ian guards her like a personal treasure."

"Fortunately I see no rotten cores here tonight," Lin replied.

Her manner was easy, polished, and businesslike, but Kam took heart from her light touch on his arm. A waiter approached carrying sparkling fruit juice and carbonated water. "Shall we take in Francesca's exhibit?" Lin invited when they'd all taken a flute.

"Absolutely. Such a talented young woman . . ." Otto was saying. Kam tuned him out as the four of them began the circuit around the room. He was forced to break contact with Lin as they moved about. He was too distracted by her to be anxious about meeting the Gersbachs. He was caught up in the spell of Lin's lithesome bare arms and sexy long legs. His senses were always extremely sharp, but tonight they seemed exponentially sensitive. He was entranced by the sound of her melodious voice and the nearly silent swish of hair on both her bare skin and the fabric of her dress. He managed several responses to the Gersbachs, a decent amount of which were longer than two words. It wasn't that hard, given his honest admiration of Francesca's sketches and Lin's effortless, yet warm and genuine skill for social conversation.

Even though he'd been forced to allow her to drop her hand from his arm, he touched her whenever he got the chance, subtly and outside of anyone's notice. He'd brush her waist or bare shoulder, silently urging her to a more ideal spot in which to see the artwork. Significantly, she never gave him a quelling glance when he first did it, so he continued.

As they moved throughout the exhibit, more and more people started to stream into the room. Many of them took different paths than the Gersbachs, Lin, and Kam.

Several people were already gathered in front of one of the larger sketches when they reached it. Otto and Brigit maneuvered for a view. Kam reached out and spread his hand on the tight curve of Lin's hip, urging her in front of him. He was tall enough to see the sketch over her head, but he wasn't looking. Not really. He dared to put his other hand on her hip, encircling her. She went very still in his hold. He just *felt* her for a stretched second, absorbed her refined energy, the sensation of her feminine hips and the delicious fragrance from her hair. A tickling, arousing buzz started on the root of his cock. He resisted a strong urge to press himself against the tight, round curve of her ass. Somehow he knew that, for that brief moment, she was as hyperfocused on him as he was her.

From the corner of his vision, he noticed a familiar form coming around the corner. He dropped his hands from Lin, recognizing Lucien walking next to Francesca.

They finished the circuit and approached Francesca, the Gersbachs and Lin giving their warm praise and impressions of the exhibit.

"And you, Kam?" Francesca asked after a moment. "You haven't said much. Worried about offending your sister-in-law?"

"You know me well enough by now to realize if I wanted to offend, I would have by now," Kam mumbled. He blinked when Brigit Gersbach gave a loud laugh, as if he'd been joking. "I enjoyed it," he told Francesca. "No reason I wouldn't. Your attention to the tiniest detail is amazing, and yet it only adds to the overall impression of harmony."

"Not unlike a quality timepiece, no?" Brigit asked him, looping her arm around his elbow, staring up at him with a brilliant smile. There was something jarring about her voice. He looked down at her in bemusement. Lin cleared her throat, and he suspected he might have been wincing.

"Speaking of time," Lin said brightly, checking her delicate diamond watch. "Shall we go into dinner?"

"Absolutely," Otto said briskly. "I have pages of questions for you," he told Kam, drawing him away from his clinging daughter.

Kam glanced back warily at Lin. She seemed to notice his resigned suffering, her humorous glance encouraging him to bear it out. She'd said he could have her to himself afterward. Or at least she'd said she'd think about it.

He was having trouble thinking about anything else.

Kam seated Lin when they were led to a table at Elise's chic restaurant, and then took the chair next to her. Brigit and Otto sat across from them. Lin noticed that Brigit appeared to be slightly annoyed by Kam's indifference toward her. Lin wasn't immune to the other woman's disappointment. Neither Ian nor she should have worried about Kam ruining anything with his disdain for luxury and fashion. If anything, his tendency to say little in combination with his penetrating, intelligent gaze and stunning good looks gave the impression of an aloof prince. The quieter and cooler he was, the more Otto, and especially Brigit, seemed determined to draw him out.

Otto wasted no time in beginning to question Kam about his invention, digging in even before they'd ordered drinks. Lin listened with interest, although she understood only a portion of the technical terms the Gersbachs and Kam used. Even with what little she comprehended, she was fascinated. According to Otto, the brilliance of Kam's invention was not only the minuscule size of the data chip, but his ability to use the delicate clockwork of the watch to enhance the mechanism. As Kam spoke, she slowly realized it was as if he'd needed a surrogate for his device and found the perfect mechanical organism in the escapements of a timepiece.

"It's as if your invention should have been there all along, and we watchmakers were blind to the absence until now," Otto enthused.

Kam's explanations were short, but always to the point. He gave Lin a quicker and more valuable explanation of his own invention than anything she'd been able to glean so far from journal articles or patent drawings. His ability to concisely verbalize a complicated process was a valuable marketing commodity, Lin noted, filing away the information for future use.

It wasn't just what Kam said or how he said it that fascinated her. She was highly aware of his long, strong thighs just inches away from her own. He rested his left hand on the thigh closest to her, moving it back and forth in a rubbing gesture every once in a while as he spoke or listened. She thought initially it was a nervous habit that only she could see from her position next to him. After a while, however, she altered her opinion. Kam really didn't appear to be all that nervous. Instead, he seemed uncomfortable, yet forbearing, as if he were impatient to be elsewhere. It was highly distracting watching his large hand move so subtly over his thigh. His other hand rested on the white tablecloth. He possessed extremely masculine, capable-looking hands with several visible veins and blunt-tipped fingers that he drummed or tapped every once in a while against the white cloth. She recalled how they'd felt encasing her hips out there in the ballroom, warm and all encompassing.

The memory of him encircling her torso and moving her so effortlessly up the length of her bed on Monday night blazed into her consciousness. He could manipulate her into any position he chose so negligently. She'd never really thought about it before— perhaps because she'd never slept with a man as powerful as Kam— but it was arousing to know that he could maneuver her weight with such ease to optimize her pleasure. His.

Theirs.

She took a long draw on her ice water. Kam drummed his fingertips lightly on the tablecloth, and her clit tingled in response. He'd used those fingertips to take her to heaven Monday night, rubbing and sliding and vibrating her so masterfully until . . .

"Now I have a question for you, Otto."

Lin came back fully to the moment at the sound of Kam's frank declaration.

"Of course," Otto said earnestly. "Anything."

"Why don't you have a line of watches that the average person can actually afford to own?"

Lin's heart paused in her chest. She glanced anxiously across the table at Brigit's frozen expression.

"We come from a long tradition of innovative, premier watch-making," Otto said, recovering before his daughter. "We employ the most talented engineers in the world and utilize the highest-quality components and materials. Gersbach is always pushing the envelope of the technology, giving our customers not only a luxury timepiece, but the most exclusive one in the market."

Kam nodded thoughtfully. Lin forced herself not to start when he abruptly lifted his hand off his thigh and subtly moved it the two or three inches to settle on hers. He squeezed. The front cutout of her cocktail dress left her knees and a few inches of thigh exposed, but when she'd sat, the dress had ridden up a few inches. His hand enclosed a stretch of silk-covered skin. He continued talking as if nothing had happened. His heat emanated easily through the super sheer fabric of her silk thigh-highs. Lin just sat there stiffly, trying to rein in her scattered thoughts and slow her racing heart.

"You just said a moment ago that my invention would revolutionize the way people took care of themselves. With the constant feedback the mechanism can provide, people will know when they are in a medical crisis or when they need to make a doctor's appointment. They will automatically change their habits to become healthier when they see firsthand, in a split second, how a behavior is affecting their heart or their blood pressure or their stress response," Kam said as he picked up his fork. "Is it your belief that only the wealthy deserve to possess such technology?"

Lin hastened to say something that would smooth over his bluntness. Kam squeezed her thigh again gently. She was stunned to realize *he* was reassuring *her*. Her mouth clamped shut.

"I don't think it's up to me to decide something like that," Otto sidestepped gracefully. "I run a company and provide a certain product to a defined market."

Kam nodded. "You're right. I'll have to make similar decisions for my own product, and who has access to it is a major one."

Otto glanced uncertainly at his daughter, who seemed even more ruffled than him.

"Well, I suppose that's what this meeting is all about," Lin said, unable to keep quiet a moment longer. "Gathering information so that decisions and plans can be made." She made a toast and successfully turned the conversation while they ate to lighter, although still-relevant topics. At some point during the main course, Kam returned his hand to his own lap, but she was still highly self-conscious of the warm, tingling patch of skin on her thigh where it had rested.

By the time coffee and dessert came around, she realized she'd been foolish for feeling the need to bail Kam out of a crisis. He clearly was not uncomfortable with what he'd asked, and why should he be? If the issue of availability of his product to the majority of people was important to him, then clearly it was relevant for discussion. She wasn't here to make sure he sold his products to the Gersbachs or any of the representatives from luxury watchmakers, but to assist him while he explored whether this was a transaction he wanted to undertake or not.

Elise arrived at their table during dessert, pleasantly distracting Lin from her concerns. They all thanked her for the wonderful meal.

Lucien's wife wore her chef's smock, her lovely face radiant either from the heat of the kitchen or good spirits or both. After repeating a request for Kam to stay with Lucien and her, and being politely refused yet again, she shrugged good-naturedly, clearly recognizing a losing battle.

"He doesn't even want to stay at our hotel, why should he want to stay with us at our home?" Elise jabbed Kam fondly, grinning at Lin.

"Oh . . . that's *my* fault," Lin blurted guiltily. "I thought he might be more comfortable near Noble Tower."

Elise waved her hand with matter-of-fact elegance. "Nonsense. I was just teasing him. Kam knows it. He's not comfortable in most places in the city." Lin glanced at Kam, worried Elise's frankness had embarrassed him. Instead, Kam wore a sheepish grin. Lin really should talk to Lucien's irrepressible wife about her handling of Kam sometime.

Elise beamed at the entire table in with that patentable Elise charm. "But we'll get Kam wherever he wants to go eventually," she told Brigit with a confidential, significant nod. She winked at Otto Gersbach. Otto blinked as if targeted by a stun gun. "Because he's brilliant, but more importantly, he's family. And family is very important to us," Elise said simply, blessing them with one last smile before she bid them good night.

Otto muttered unintelligibly under his breath after Elise left them; the only phrase Lin caught was *that charming, golden ray of sunshine*. Lin was having trouble disguising her smile. So was Kam, she noticed when they shared a glance of amusement. By the time they finished their dessert, Lin was feeling much more at ease.

"The showing must be over. There's Lucien, Ian, and Francesca," Kam observed for Lin's ears only as the waiter returned with their receipt for the bill. Lin had already noticed the subtle shift in the atmosphere, and knew Ian had entered the room. The energy of a place always amplified when he arrived. She'd been keyed in to Ian's movements, his desires . . . his very presence for so long now. Of course she sensed it not only in herself, but also in others around her. A youngish-looking man standing at the periphery of the restaurant aimed a camera at Ian, who was escorting Francesca to their table. Lucien grabbed his wrist swiftly, forcing the camera downward. Lin saw Lucien utter a few quiet words to the would-be photographer, and the young man blanched. He walked out of the restaurant of his own volition. She gave a tiny sigh of relief. Lucien was an accomplished pro at keeping his patrons' experience private and comfortable while they were in his establishments.

She felt Kam's gaze on her profile and met his stare. "You don't miss much when it comes to Ian, do you?" he said, his gaze piercing, his voice a low rumble.

"It's my job."

His eyebrows went up in an expression that might have been interpreted as politely interested or subtly sarcastic. Lin couldn't say which. "Do you need to go and speak with him?" he asked.

Lin Soong and her work are practically synonymous.

His question had made his statement from earlier today spring into her brain.

"No," she replied in a hushed, non-carrying voice, her eyebrows raised in a subtle challenge. "I'm done with work for the day."

His nostrils flared slightly. His gaze dropped to her mouth, and Lin felt that familiar dip below her navel. It felt so strange to experience that familiar awareness of Ian across a crowded room and yet at the same time to feel a distance from it. It was hard to focus on the everyday with the exciting novelty of Kam so close.

"I think we'll be making our way back to our hotel," Otto said. "All I can think about is bed after that delicious meal."

Lin started guiltily, realizing too late she'd been staring at Kam, and he'd been staring back with that hot gleam in his eyes.

"I look forward to seeing a demonstration of your mechanism, Kam," Otto said as he set his napkin on the table.

"I was wondering if you'd be willing to let me see Gersbach's operations and facilities in return?" Kam said, making Lin blink in surprise.

"I'd be delighted to give you a tour myself," Brigit interrupted, leaning forward and catching Kam's gaze. "And you must stay with us at our home."

"We *both* would be delighted to have you," Otto clarified. "Brigit and I are returning home at the end of next week. When do you think you might be able to visit us in Switzerland?"

"There are still quite a few things that I need to settle here," he glanced at Lin. "And we're still in the process of setting up a demonstration, right? We have to program for a test subject."

"I'm working on that part," Lin assured. By "subject," Kam meant someone from whom they could gather baseline physiological data to import to Kam's chip. His invention included the technology that personalized the device for every individual owner's unique body. "But we're set up for the demonstration at Noble Enterprises next Wednesday," Lin said, reminding Otto of the schedule she'd provided his assistant.

"I'm still in the process of creating a reliable protocol for each individual watch owner so that they can gather their baseline physiological data themselves," Kam explained.

Otto nodded. "I understand. For the pharmaceutical companies, there are qualified professionals built in to the process that can gather the data. But I've studied the outline you've done for self-administration during the data-gathering phase, and I have complete faith that we can integrate successfully. It's an entirely safe, nonintrusive procedure that anyone who can read can learn to do."

Kam nodded. "I agree. But given the fact that a full instructional protocol hasn't been written yet, I'll do the data gathering for the demonstration."

Otto gave Kam a sharp, blue-eyed stare. "I sense your reservations about a deal with us. I'll be unconventionally frank with you. I want your invention for Gersbach at all costs. It's the most innovative, exciting thing to happen to watchmaking in centuries. The idea of the watch being a tool to tell the date and time is going to become an antiquated concept, thanks to your genius. I will not allow Gersbach to go the way of the dodo. The ball is in your court. If you have specific demands for your product, please assume that I will do whatever I can to meet them. I'm sure that we can come to some sort of compromise that will leave both of us very, very happy."

Brigit couldn't hide her surprise at her father's words, and Lin understood why. Otto hadn't even seen Kam's mechanism firsthand yet. Otto Gersbach was not known for being so forthright, or for being so willing to waver from the conservative path of Gersbach tradition.

Lin gave Kam a private, barely repressed smile of triumph as they rose to leave the restaurant a moment later. His lips quirked at her show of enthusiasm.

They paused in the entryway of the hotel to say good-bye to the Gersbachs. Otto had hired a driver for their visit. He pulled up in a sleek black sedan.

"Will we give you a ride back to the hotel?" Brigit asked Kam hopefully as she grasped his forearm. They'd established during dinner that the Gersbachs were staying at the same hotel as Kam, much to Brigit's apparent approval.

"No, thank you," Kam replied. "I need a word with Lin. I'll catch a cab."

Brigit didn't look very pleased, but had no choice but to drop her hand. Lin felt her evening bag vibrate and glanced at her phone as the Gersbachs entered the car. She slipped the phone back into her purse and turned to Kam when the sedan rounded a corner and was out of sight. He lightly brushed his hand over her bare upper arm, and she shivered.

"You're cold," he growled softly, taking a step closer to her and putting his other hand on her, chafing the pebbled skin on both her arms lightly.

"No, I'm not," she said honestly. It was a warm fall night. It hadn't been the night air coming in through the doors when the Gersbachs exited that had made her shiver, but rather his touch. "Kam, I wish you would have told me and Ian about the real reason you weren't interested in the luxury watch companies. If you want your watch to be accessible to most people, I can understand that. Do you want to go through with the rest of the meetings?"

"Yes," he said, with much more conviction than she would have expected, given his prior reservations.

"But—"

"I want to continue," he said firmly, stroking her bare arms again. "I have my reasons."

She hesitated, looking up at him. "Well, if you want to, of course. If anything, it's a good experience for you, talking shop with premier watchmakers and businesspeople."

"Exactly."

"You were certainly a hit with Otto. And definitely with Brigit," she said, giving him an amused, knowing glance at the last.

"You had warned me that one of Brigit's 'hobbies' was man hunting," he reminded her. "At least I wasn't surprised."

"You still seemed a little dumbfounded by her boldness a few times, not that most men wouldn't be," Lin chuckled. "I think she might have stepped up her game a bit even past her normal activity to be so obvious in front of her father. I'd definitely watch out for her."

"Are you saying that for my sake? Or yours?"

"For yours, of course." His fingertips glided across the sensitive patch of skin at the back of her shoulders, and again she shivered.

"I can't get over how soft you are," he said bluntly, his brows quirked as if he really was a little disbelieving of the evidence his fingertips sent to his brain.

Her smile faded as she looked up at him. For a few full seconds, neither of them spoke, although she read the message in his eyes like a bold neon sign.

"Ian texted me," she said in a hushed voice after a moment, kidding herself by bringing up mundane topics, trying to ignore the blatant, unapologetic lust in Kam's gaze. "He asked if we'd meet them in the Coffee Boutique for an after-dinner drink in a half hour or so," she said, referring to the extremely popular European-style coffeehouse and bakery inside Lucien's hotel.

He stiffened. "I thought you said you were done with work for the night."

"I did, but it wouldn't hurt, would it? Ian and Lucien are just curious about how things went with the Gersbachs. They're your family, Kam," she added when his frown grew fierce. "They care about you."

"You said you'd think about it."

She froze. She knew exactly what he was talking about, of course. Heat rushed into her cheeks despite her chilled skin. She'd told him she'd think about whether he'd have her to himself after the Gersbach dinner. His thumb moved, caressing her right arm. His touch amplified her trembling.

"What about Ian?" she asked.

"Hang Ian."

She gave him a repressive glance.

"All right. We'll meet with them," he growled. "But I'll give him a half hour tops. And afterward, you're mine. In the meantime . . . we still have a little while together."

She swallowed thickly when his deep, rough voice dropped in volume, sounding more intimate. Sexy. Something flickered inside her, like a match being struck at her very core. She avoided his piercing stare. Or maybe she was avoiding studying her own motives. She hadn't agreed to come with him later tonight, but she hadn't said no, either. The sexual awareness they'd had of each other all day and night was electrical. She longed to allow the spark to ignite. Still, her doubts lingered. Her motives for lusting after Kam Reardon were not rational.

Nor were they pure.

"We do have a lot to discuss after tonight," she continued, studying his silk tie, trying her best to keep up the lie, and failing miserably. "And I still need to brief you about our weekend meeting with Jason Klinf, the CEO of Klinf Inc.," she rambled on stupidly. His hands tightened on her arms. She shivered again and swallowed. Her throat had gone very dry.

"I don't give a fuck about Jason Klinf." For some reason, his raw language struck her as honest, slicing through her façade like a hot knife through butter. He drew her closer, so that the front of her just whispered against his length, the tips of her breasts brushing against his lapels. Her nipples drew so tight at the gesture that she nearly whimpered. Liquid heat surged from her core.

"I . . . I left my wrap in the cloakroom. I just realized," she said in a choked voice. She dared to meet his eyes. "Just give me a moment while I go get it?"

His eyelids narrowed, making his eyes into gleaming crescents of silvery light. Her blood began to pulse like a beacon at her neck.

She turned, and the doorman opened the door for her to reenter the hotel.

Her gaze automatically went to the entrance of Frais in the distance as she hastened through the luxurious lobby. Francesca, Elise, and Lucien were in there.

Ian.

She walked down a hallway that led in the opposite direction, her breath escalated far past what it should be given her activity level. The ballroom door was shut, the room desolate and the lights dimmed when she entered. She felt breathless as she opened the cloakroom. Why was her heart racing so fast?

She found a switch just inside the door. Light flooded the narrow, long room. Her wrap was the only garment remaining after the showing. She passed a rack of hangers and a wooden shelf with dozens of compartments in it for hats or gloves. She had just removed her wrap, when there was a click and the closet plunged into opaque blackness.

"Shhh. It's me," a voice said when she gasped.

"Kam?" she whispered, recognizing his familiar, rough growl.

"Yes."

She started at the sound of the door clicking shut. She heard the metallic snick of a lock. Her pounding heartbeat became a roar. They were alone together in the darkness. Her nipples chafed and prickled against the tight fabric of her dress.

"What are you doing?" she demanded, finding her voice.

His hands enclosed her shoulders, gentle but firm.

"You know what I'm doing," he replied, his knowing tone sending a thrill through her.

His hands moved over the naked skin of her back, gliding and kneading. A shaky moan escaped her throat when he pushed her against him at the same time he stepped forward. She bumped against a solid surface from behind. She was sandwiched between a storage cabinet and Kam, the fronts of their bodies sealed tight. He was long and hard, all hungry, primal male in the darkness. His hand captured a fistful of her loose hair at the nape. He tugged gently, tilting back her head.

"Here?" she whispered shakily, but she was still clinging on to her lie by asking the one-word question. She'd guessed his intention earlier when he'd said: *In the meantime . . . we still have a little while together.* She'd seen that look in his eyes when she'd said she was going for her wrap. Somehow, some way, they'd made an illicit, nonverbal pact in those seconds, although she'd doubted at the time she was correctly interpreting his boldness. Her wantonness. Who could really believe they would go to such extreme ends for sexual gratification? Now the undeniable truth was pressed against her, his hands

moving over her greedily, her fragile lie turning to mist next to his male heat.

She trembled uncontrollably when he nipped insistently at her mouth and she opened for him.

"Here," he assured succinctly.

Chapter Six

His warm, fragrant breath brushed over her sensitive lips in the pitch-black room. "You've been driving me crazy all day and night. I won't wait another second to taste you. All of you."

He seized her mouth with his own. His tongue penetrated her lips. That sinking sensation she felt every time he looked at her struck, but this time, it was exponential; a stark, thrilling plunge straight into lust. Heat swept through her like a flash fire. She dropped her wrap and clutch purse heedlessly and reached for him, grasping his shoulder and twisting her fingers in his gorgeous, thick hair. It was like setting a spark to carefully laid timber. She hadn't realized until that moment how her desire had been building all night . . . all day, ever since he'd entered Ian's office this morning and pinned her with his stare. She kissed him back, starved for his taste, begging him without words to take possession, to sweep aside her uncertainties and make her forget everything but this heat.

He moved his hands to her hips and lifted. Her bottom plunked down on the top of the cabinet. His kiss never faltered. He ate her tiny cry of surprise and her subsequent whimpers of arousal. His hands moved over her, bold and hungry, kneading her hips and ass, shaping her flesh to his palms. She parted her thighs willingly, using them to bracket his hips and bring him closer. Working feverishly, she loosened his tie, her fingers finding the buttons of his shirt. She unfastened the top three before she grew impatient and plunged her hand into the opening. The heat of him, the feeling of his smooth, thick skin and the springy hair on his chest, only amplified her lust.

She pulsed her hips forward on the smooth surface of the cabinet, bumping her crotch against his. She moaned into his mouth. He was a full, delightful package against her straining flesh. She recalled the stark beauty of his cock from that night they'd been together. She ground against him at the same moment that she found a nipple with her fingertip and flicked it gently with a nail.

His cock leapt against her spread pussy, and even through the fabric of their clothing, she felt his heat. He broke their kiss and hissed against her lips. He reached for the clasp of her dress at the back of her neck. Their soughing breath and the pound of her heart mingled in her ears as he deliberately lowered the dress over her breasts. He cupped her from below. He gave a low growl and his body responded just as appreciatively. She wasn't wearing a bra. His thumbs feathered both nipples, and she gasped as pleasure shook her.

Then he was gone, his big, warm hands, his solid body, his addictive taste. Everything.

"Kam?" she asked shakily, disoriented by his abrupt absence.

The light switched on. Her breath caught. He stood just inside the closed door, his hand still on the switch, looking back at her. He came toward her, his gaze scorching.

"Damned if I'm going to miss out on seeing that," he said, nodding at her partial nudity and splayed thighs. He knocked aside a couple of hangers above her head, and then reached for her hands. He guided them to the metal coatrack just above her head.

"Hold on tight," he said, giving her a swift, grim glance. "And don't let go. Do you understand?"

Her lungs weren't working properly. She couldn't speak, so she nodded and gripped onto the metal bar. Kam slid his hands beneath her dress and grasped her ass. He lifted and used his forearms to peel back her dress. When he set her back on the cabinet, her dress was bunched up around her hips. She looked down when he just stared fixedly between her thighs. A tiny triangle of black silk barely covered her outer sex. He opened his hand along her silk thigh-highs. It looked large and dark and masculine next her pale skin and feminine lingerie.

"I can't stop thinking about your pussy," he muttered, his jaw tight. A shaky cry fell past her lips as she watched him bend at the waist while, in one swipe, he used his hands to part her thighs wider. He grabbed her hips. She gripped onto the rack and stared ahead in sightless wonder as he pressed his face against her outer sex and nuzzled her labia. He tongued her through the thin fabric of her panties, his tongue warm and wet, pressing insistently against her sex lips, providing a relentless, delightful . . . forbidden pressure against her clit. He tightened his hold on her hips and ass, pulsing her hips forward against his rigid tongue.

She bit her lip as she resisted an overpowering urge to sink her fingers into his hair and pull him closer to her. He made a harsh sound in his throat and abruptly slid his hand along her hip, inserting his finger beneath her panties and lifting the fabric just an inch or two sideways over her pussy.

His tongue swept between her labia, slipping between the folds. She gasped sharply, the sensation of naked, wet flesh sliding and pressing against her naked clit growing exponentially powerful following the separation by fabric.

"Ah God . . . Kam," she moaned, one of her hands releasing from the bar, automatically wanting to press him to her. He lifted his head slightly.

"Keep your hands on the bar," he said, as if he had eyes in the back of his head and knew precisely what she'd been about to do.

She suppressed a groan and did what he demanded. Her reward was to have his tongue burrowing again in her outer sex, rubbing and agitating her clit. His mouth closed over her, his lips applying a firm pressure. His tongue continued to torment her . . . to delight her. When he applied a gentle suction, she barely stopped herself from screaming. She pulled down experimentally on the bar, but the construction was secure, the metal rod unyielding. She firmed her hold and used it to shift her hips, pressing her pussy against the heaven of his mouth and rigid tongue, earning more pressure and pleasure. He'd transformed her into a greedy wanton, and part of her was liberated.

Free.

He tightened his hold on her hips as he continued to eat her and she writhed against him. Her clit sizzled. She longed to ignite. She grew so frantic, perhaps he grew weary of having to hold her steady for his tongue.

Smack.

He'd popped her bottom with his palm.

Lin stilled, feeling the sting on her ass. She looked down in amazement and saw him looking up at her, his eyes hot, his lower mouth slick with her juices. He was so beautiful, her core clenched tight in instinctive craving.

"Keep still and take your pleasure, *mon petit chaton*," he ordered gruffly.

She nodded, panting raggedly. No one had ever swatted her before. She had the impression no man would ever dare. Not that it hurt. It stung, though, like a sexy, tactile tattoo. She swore she could feel his handprint burning on the side of her right buttock. His gaze sunk down over her face and latched onto her heaving breasts.

"Such perfect breasts. Touch them," he demanded suddenly, his nostrils flaring as he looked at her face again.

She lowered her hands from the rod and skimmed her fingers beneath her breasts. He tracked her actions with his gaze, his steady stare making her shift her hips, tempting him back to the center of her heat. She cradled each mound and lifted, plucking at the nipples with thumb and forefinger.

"Squeeze them," he said harshly. "That's right," he muttered when she complied and molded the firm flesh to her palm. "Keep that up. Don't stop."

He jerked her panties down to her ankles, and then whisked them over her heels. He leaned down over her again, tilting his head. Lin moaned in overwhelming anticipation as she watched him use his fingers to gently pinch the bottom of her labia together. He tilted his head and looked up at her as he slid his tongue down into the pocket he'd formed, slipping the tip against her clit. He moved it, rubbing her, applying a firm pressure. She gave a restrained groan and pinched at her nipples, cresting, all the while aware of his hot eyes watching her. His red tongue plunged and thrust into the juicy pocket of flesh, lewd and insistent. Her clit went from a sizzle to a mind-blowing burn.

A moment later, she clutched onto the metal bar and quaked in climax.

As she shuddered in orgasm, he released his gentle pinch on her labia and used just his mouth. He covered her outer sex with his lips, the insistent suction he applied making her eyes go wide in shock and her tremors amplify. It was almost impossible to muffle her cries as ecstasy blasted through her.

He lifted his head as her trembling waned. Watching her face, he thrust a thick forefinger into her drenched channel. Another wave of orgasm hit her. He grunted, a snarl shaping his mouth.

"Come here," he said, reaching for her waist.

A fresh wave of excitement tinged with wariness went through her. She wasn't afraid of him in the slightest, but he was one hundred percent primal male in that moment, savage in his intent. A woman would be crazy not to feel pure excitement and a hint of anxiety upon seeing the wild light in Kam's eyes as he lifted her into his arms and set her high heels back on the floor. He swooped down and kissed her like a bird of prey claiming its meal before he turned her. Her eyes sprung wide when he bent his knees and pressed his cock to her backside.

Oh my. They had unleashed a tempest.

He pushed aside her hair and pressed his mouth against her neck; she stumbled slightly in her heels, not because he was pushing her, but because another wave of heat and excitement had gone through her at his kiss, making her dizzy. He steadied her, pressing her more firmly back against the solid length of his body.

"Slip off your heels," he muttered next to her ear before he sealed his mouth to it, sending a delicious ripple of sensation through her.

Kam grunted when she followed his order and her body slid a good four inches down his.

"The angle isn't ideal with us standing. Not with the way I want you right now." Lin swallowed thickly at the heat in his tone. She didn't have to be a brilliant engineer like Kam to realize the obvious. He was too tall and the cabinet too high for her to lean over for optimal positioning. His lips moved firmly and hungrily. He bit gently at the skin just below her hairline, and she shivered in his arms. "Can you go on your hands and knees on the floor with your wrap under you?" he coaxed.

For a split second, she pictured what was about to happen. Liquid heat surged through her at the raw eroticism of the image.

"Yes," she whispered.

He helped her spread her wrap. He held one of her hands, steadying her when she went to her knees in the dim closet. She sensed him pull back slightly, halting her.

"What if I tear your hosiery?" he asked.

"I'll take them off if need be. Afterward," she added, meeting his stare, her gaze solemn.

His nostrils flared slightly. He nodded. She raised her dress to her waist.

She was in a dim, unfamiliar cloakroom in a hotel, positioning herself to be fucked while her boss and his family enjoyed their elegant meal just down the hall. The illicit, exciting sound of Kam's zipper lowering pierced her awareness, and all thoughts of Ian evaporated.

She looked over her shoulder anxiously. He was shucking off his new trousers, and much to her surprise, he didn't just shove them or his boxer briefs down to his thighs. No, he whisked them all the way down and stepped out of him. He retrieved something from his pocket, his pants draped in front of him. He tossed the pants onto the cabinet. She stared, her mouth going dry. His cock sprung from his body at a nearly perpendicular angle, poking out from the bottom opening of the placket of his dress shirt. From her vantage point, it looked fearsome and flagrant. Beautiful.

He grasped his heavy erection from below, stepping behind her. He caught her staring as he rolled on a condom—this one actually fit. Had he bought a new box since their tryst the other night? Had he guessed something like this would happen?

Didn't you? A voice in Lin's head asked. *No,* she immediately answered. *Not like this. Not like this crazy, impulsive moment.*

Their gazes held for a heart-stopping second.

Then he lowered to the floor behind her.

He saw her watching him as he rolled on a condom, and a fierce stab of need went through him, a feral mandate to mate. Her dark eyes were somber and achingly lovely, her pale skin a stunning contrast next to the black of her dress, her ass round and compact. Her taste still lingered on his tongue, taunting him. His cock swelled tight as he lowered, heaven within his reach.

He knew what to expect after Monday night and used a finger, and then two, to ready her, his lust mounting to rabid levels all the while. Her pussy was a man's dream come true, especially when accompanied with Lin's choked whimpers and gasps of arousal. She clung to even the relatively slender invaders of his fingers like a sweet, sucking mouth.

His cock lurched. Best not to think about Lin and sucking mouths right now.

He slid out his fingers and replaced them with the tip of his cock. "Shhh," he soothed as he pulsed into her pussy and she gave a muffled moan. She clamped him like a vise, but her heat and abundant juices welcomed. Tortured. Lust raged in him. Jesus. *I'm not going to last any longer than I did that first night,* he realized incredulously. He flexed forward, accepting his fate. Relishing in it. Clutching one tight buttock, he watched as he sawed his hips and penetrated her more and more with each pass. Finally, he gripped both buttocks and pulled her against him, his balls grinding against her outer tissues.

She made a high-pitched, strangled sound. He could only imagine how it must feel for her. He was near to bursting with lust himself, she was so compact and small . . . supple and sleek . . .

"You're so fucking perfect," he growled before he began to thrust.

After a few moments of pounding into her and hearing their body's frantic mating rhythm and Lin's arousing whimpers and hums of pleasure, he stared at the back of the cloakroom. The sensation of her bobbing hips, strong counterthrusts, and the tight, unrelenting clasp of her pussy were more than enough to make him come. Watching the whole thing made it twice as excruciating. God, she was a fast, scorching ticket to heaven. Even if he was hell bound for rutting like a slavering savage on this exquisite, elegant woman, he'd arrive at the gates like a charging locomotive.

He jerked up her hips and ass and drove into her. *"C'est si bon,"* he hissed in pleasure as he fucked her at the divine new angle. He paused after a moment and grimaced at the halt of the intense friction. "Put your shoulders and head down on the cloak, baby. That's right," he praised, once again enthralled by the vision of her. Holding her hips up to his raging cock, he withdrew up and sunk into her again and again, his actions deliberate.

Perhaps a little ruthless.

Distantly, he became aware that he was likely putting too much pressure on her knees, but it felt *so* damn good. His only saving grace was hearing her sharp cry and feeling her muscular walls squeeze his driving cock as she climaxed a moment later. Her warmth rushed around him.

He saw red.

He rose to his feet, crouching over her. By lifting her hips to his thrusting cock and controlling her weight with his straining arm and legs muscles, he took some of the pressure off her knees while creating an optimal friction. He let go, fucking her in a frenzy of blind lust. The sound of their slapping skin outpaced his heartbeat in his ears. Nothing could have stopped him in that moment. He grasped for nirvana, taking one last savage thrust.

He crashed into her, holding tight. Orgasm hit, brutal and blistering, sparing neither of them. He wasn't sure later if he'd continued to move, fucking her as he ejaculated, or if he'd been frozen in a rushing overdose of pleasure.

He only knew that as his orgy of need quieted, and his lust was appeased, regret began to worm its way into his awareness.

She kept her head lowered a minute later when he stood and helped her to her feet, the long, dark drape of her hair hiding her face. She started to turn away and lift her dress up over her breasts, but he stopped her.

"Lin?"

She didn't move, her beautiful, thrusting bare breasts still rising and falling irregularly following their shared storm of lust. He used his free hand to push back her silky hair so he could see her face. She jerked her head away, but not before he saw what she tried to hide. Two tracks of tears shone on her flushed cheeks. Dread swept through him.

"Did I hurt you?"

"No." She swiped at the dampness and turned, finishing pulling up her dress. "Of course you didn't hurt me. You must have . . . realized how much . . . I liked it," she faltered.

It alarmed him, the strained quality of her voice. She was typically so controlled. True, she'd lost her temper with him this morning—deservedly so—but this break in her armor was much more alarming. He put his hands on her shoulders and turned her to face him.

"What is it? What's wrong?" he demanded, sounding harsher than he intended, out of concern. He wouldn't apologize for taking her under these circumstances. In his opinion, it was a natural conclusion to all the heat they'd been generating all day, as normal a progression as a storm breaking after the buildup of a hot, sultry day. But he did feel guilty for how forcefully he'd made love to her . . . how savagely . . .

"I just had sex with you on the cloakroom floor of a hotel—"

"There's no one around—"

"With my boss dining just down the hallway," she finished without pause. His mouth snapped shut. She stared up at him wildly. Desperately. He couldn't say which. One thing was for certain: He'd run up against her walls again.

He dropped his hands. "So. Here we are. Back to Ian."

She turned abruptly and began fastening the collar of her dress around her neck. She found her discarded panties. Unable to think of anything else to say to make her feel better, he removed the condom, found a place to dispose of it and grabbed his discarded clothing. The atmosphere in the small cloakroom seemed to take on a heavy, stifling weight as they both gathered themselves. Their separation and silence seemed especially glaring following their raw, uninhibited joining just now. It seemed a little bizarre that they'd both been frantically in the grips of lust only moments ago. He finished dressing first, seething as he watched her smooth her hair and apply some lipstick from her purse, her back turned to him the whole time.

She finally turned and met his stare calmly. His irritation mounted, but then disappeared in an instant when he looked down over her.

"Damn it. Your knees," he muttered. Her delicate hosiery hadn't torn, but the color of it was so sheer that he could see the skin of her knees was red and abraded.

Merde. *You rode her like a fucking animal.*

"I'm going home," she said quietly. His eyes widened with alarm as he studied her impassive, beautiful face. Her cheeks were still flushed from arousal and orgasm, but her skin looked especially pale beneath it. "Will you please tell Ian, Lucien, and Francesca that I felt a little unwell?"

"But—"

"Tell them. Please. I can't show up looking like this."

"I'm sorry about your . . ." He glanced down at her knees, regret swamping him. "I tried to take the pressure off them by standing, but—"

"I *know* you did," she said. "I'm not blaming you. It's my fault. I'm the one who let it happen."

He made a disbelieving sound at that. "You make it sound like you agreed to a crime. We didn't commit murder together," he added darkly.

She closed her eyes. He flinched inwardly, seeing her discomposure. "You don't understand. I don't do things like this."

"You obviously do now," he said before he could stop himself. "Why is that such a problem?" She shot him an anxious glance and draped her wrap over her shoulders, covering herself.

"Lin, wait—" he called out when she moved past him. She unlocked the door. "We still need to talk."

"I know. We still need to discuss the details of the Klinf meeting this weekend. I also need you to tell me all that you require for the first demonstration of your device for the Gersbachs. I'll call," she said.

And she was gone.

For several seconds, he just stared blindly up at the ceiling, replaying the last half hour of his life and trying to make sense of it, with not a modicum of success. They'd gone from combustible lust to uncontrollable, wild, blistering sex to Lin saying the only thing they had to discuss was business.

"C'est vraiment des conneries," he cursed bitterly before he stalked out of the cloakroom and slammed the door shut with a loud bang.

The Coffee Boutique was hopping with customers when he arrived. He understood from Lucien that while Elise's heralded new restaurant was the soul of their hotel, the coffeehouse was the heart of the thriving microcommunity. It was the comfortable living room of the luxurious establishment, a place where travelers, locals, and tourists alike lounged on deep couches and chairs and sipped premium coffees that had been individually prepared with chicory-roasted beans. They devoured mouthwatering confections made by Elise's pastry chef. Some of the patrons read books and magazines they'd bought at the attached bookstore that specialized in first editions, rare books, and antiquities. Lucien must have spent about what Kam survived off of annually on the two space-age coffee makers behind the bar.

Not that Kam was focused on any of these niceties. His purpose was single-minded as he stalked into the energetic room. He saw Lucien exiting the coffee bar at the same time he was entering. He gave Kam a bland look as they met, and paused.

"What happened to you?" Lucien asked.

"What?" Kam demanded sourly.

"You look like you're about to kick someone's ass. And your

shirttail is hanging out," Lucien added calmly under his breath as several patrons passed them.

"Merde," Kam muttered, shoving his shirt down into his pants. He never wanted to dress like this to begin with. He wouldn't be trussed up in this damn suit if it weren't for Lin.

"Did something happen with Gersbach?" Lucien asked.

"No. It went well with the Gersbachs."

"Was Lin pleased?" Lucien asked, glancing in the direction of the lobby as if in search of her.

"What, my opinion isn't good enough?" Kam growled.

Lucien's eyes narrowed on him. "Trying to pick a fight?" he asked levelly, gray eyes as cool and sharp as a driving ice pick. "Pick a better target. I've got too much work to do at the moment. If you still feel like a spar tomorrow, give me a call and we'll go a couple rounds at the gym."

Kam rolled his eyes in mounting frustration when Lucien walked past him. His eldest brother was intimidating and tough, but it was his control that was already growing legendary in Kam's mind.

He'd apologize to Lucien for his rudeness tomorrow. Tonight, he was done being a polite, powdered good boy. Lucien was right. He did feel like kicking someone's ass just for the satisfaction of hearing his victim thump to the floor.

"Lin didn't feel well and had to leave," Kam said to Ian without any preamble when he approached the seating area where Ian and Francesca lounged. "She wanted me to tell you."

"Oh no," Francesca said, concerned. "Was she all right to go home by herself?"

"She seemed to think so."

Francesca glanced at Ian with arched brows at Kam's curt reply. She cleared her throat and stood. "If you two will just excuse me for a moment? I've decided that the baby's favorite room is going to be the bathroom, as much time as he wants me to spend in there."

"Have a seat," Ian said quietly when Francesca walked away, nodding at the chair across from him.

Kam gave his brother a sidelong glare. "I'm not really in the mood for—"

"Sit down, Kam," Ian repeated more succinctly.

"I said I'm not in the mood," Kam repeated through a clenched jaw. "I'm not in the mood for any of this crap," he said, waving in a frustrated manner around the luxurious, crowded coffeehouse.

Ian stood, his mouth set in a hard line. "Will you just sit down and talk to me for five minutes? Is it really that hard?"

"No, it's not that *hard*," Kam snarled. "I just don't want to fucking *do* it." Ian glanced aside and Kam noticed several people looking their way. They'd both raised their voices.

"Just for a moment?" Ian persisted in a level but determined tone. "Please?"

Kam sat, feeling cornered. He didn't feel like being still. He had a wild urge to go back to the gym at his hotel and punish his body with a rigorous workout, or maybe go running for miles and miles on the lakefront—

"Did something happen with the Gersbachs?" Ian began, brows slanted dangerously.

"No."

"Everything seemed to be going well. Francesca said everyone seemed mellow during the showing. From the little I glimpsed as you left the restaurant, I'd say Otto looked pleased. I thought you seemed all right as well. Lin certainly seemed happy. She must have gotten sick soon after that."

Kam just stared at his brother, all signs of irritation gone from his face, all traces of *anything* vanished. Ian looked down at the coffee table between them and idly began flipping a sugar packet with his long fingers.

"I'm going to try to be careful about saying this, Kam. I hope you understand that I'm coming from a . . . sensitive place?" Kam didn't reply, but he grew tenser in his chair. "Lin isn't just an invaluable member of my staff. She's a very good friend. I've known her since she was seventeen years old, you know."

It wasn't really a question, so Kam still didn't reply.

"Lin hasn't been all that fortunate with the men she's dated in the past."

He sensed the electrical thread in Ian's seemingly neutral comment. He leaned forward in his chair. "What's that supposed to mean?" he asked, gaze narrowing.

"Just that. Very few men seem to have the ability to appreciate her character. Her refinements. Her sensitivities."

"You make her sound like some kind of inbred show poodle," Kam stated bluntly. He glanced impatiently around the confines of the coffeehouse, despising walls at that moment. "She's a lot hardier than you make her out to be. Maybe you don't know her all that well."

"And you do?" Ian challenged, his quiet voice like steel. "Because I'd hate to see you put Lin in the same category as say . . . some of those *hardy* women you kept company with at Aurore, for instance."

Kam's gaze zoomed to meet his brother's. Ian's stare didn't waver.

"Don't get all holier-than-thou with me," Kam seethed, shocked and infuriated at Ian's reference. His brother had accidentally walked in on Kam engaging in the midst of some spontaneous recreation with two women last summer at Aurore. Ian had been circumspect enough not to mention the uncomfortable moment. That he brought it up now in association with Lin pissed off Kam royally. "Don't try to convince me you led a monk's existence before you met Francesca, because that's just offensive. And Lin doesn't have *anything, whatsoever* to do with that situation," he emphasized by aggressively tapping his fingertips on the tabletop.

Ian's gaze narrowed. Kam glared back. Finally, Ian exhaled.

"I'm glad to hear it," he said frankly.

Kam took his fisted hand off the table. *Merde.* He really didn't want to fight with Ian. But dammit, why did he have to be so smug at times?

Because he usually knows exactly what he's talking about, that's why. He's never given me bad advice before, and for whatever fucked-up reason, he seems to actually care.

And if he were in Ian's shoes, wouldn't he think of warning a guy like himself away from Lin? It was just common sense, wasn't it? A woman like Lin would never find much worth for a man like Kam except for sex, and after tonight, she probably was second-guessing even that.

Kam heaved a sigh as well, feeling defeated, but not by Ian. The mounting tension between them had broken, although Kam wasn't sure exactly why.

"Don't bring Lin into this. It's my fault. I'm the one that's struggling with being here . . . this whole damn thing," he mumbled, sinking back in his chair. "I'm a fish out of water."

"If this particular line of business is unsuited to you, Kam, that's something we can deal with," Ian said quietly. "I don't want that to be your sole focus here. This is your first visit to the States—to the city where Lucien and I have made our homes. Let's make *that* the focus."

Kam transferred his gaze to Francesca as she approached the table, giving him a bright smile. He tried to smile back, but his muscles twisted uncooperatively. He suspected he grimaced instead. "Why don't you come to the penthouse right now for a cup of tea or something," Ian said.

"Wonderful idea," Francesca said, hearing the last as she arrived.

"Come on," Ian urged. "We'll have a talk. About whatever you want," he added when he saw Kam's hesitance. He certainly didn't want to have any more incendiary conversations about Lin or Kam's sex life. "It's a beautiful night. We can turn on the fire pit up on the deck and sit under the stars."

He gave Ian a sheepish glance, feeling doubly guilty about his outburst. Ian had guessed he'd reached his limit for crowds and civilized conversation and confinement. He really did read Kam well for having only known him nine months.

"Make that tea a bourbon and you've got a deal," Kam mumbled, standing.

Did Kam think Lucien, Ian, and him would end up bosom brothers, the idealistic family featured in make-believe and television sitcoms? Not a chance. Not with their common screwed-up origins.

Still, there must have been a whisper of a promise of *something* that had enticed him out of his solitude and brought him to Chicago, he admitted to himself with dark amusement.

He trailed Ian and Francesca, who walked arm in arm, out of the bustling coffeehouse. Francesca paused abruptly, making Ian halt in turn. She extended her free hand to Kam with a warm smile. He hesitated a second before he took it, managing to return her smile this time without frowning. Or at least he hoped so.

Chapter Seven

The next morning, Lin methodically briefed Ian on how things had gone with the Gersbach meeting. Ian listened intently as he sat at his desk and she sat in her usual chair before it. She must have reinforced her defenses as she slept last night, because she felt back on track today . . . steadier. In the morning light, what had happened in that cloakroom with Kam seemed like an incredible dream—an exciting, forbidden dream, yes, but also a foreign one, as if she'd somehow tapped into someone else's brain.

It was fortunate, this morning-light distance, because last night, she'd feared becoming completely unwound. The feeling was not entirely unfamiliar to her, a mild version of the numbness that settled upon her when she finally understood that her father and mother had left for Taiwan, leaving her behind for good.

"Why hasn't Kam mentioned before that he's uncomfortable with only a small portion of the population having his product?" Ian asked.

"You probably know the answer to that better than I do," Lin replied.

"I'm not so sure about that," Ian said slowly, studying her face.

"Your brother thinks a lot of things, Ian. The problem is getting him to reveal them. One has to either wait for the right opportunity for something to come out or pry the details out of him, and good luck with that," she added wryly.

Ian's smile was nearly imperceptible to someone unfamiliar with him. Lin immediately recognized it. "I have a feeling you might be more skilled at decoding Kam than any of us. Do you think it's worthwhile to even continue with these meetings, given his preference for his product?"

"He says he wants to continue. He wouldn't tell me why, exactly, except to agree that it was good experience." She hesitated.

"But? Why do you think he's doing it? You know I value your opinion," Ian said intently.

"At first, I thought Kam was nervous about these meetings because he felt out of place, like an outsider. Awkward."

"Not to mention being completely derisive of the industry," Ian added, a smile tickling his mouth again.

"Right," Lin agreed.

"But now? You've changed your mind about where he stands?"

She met Ian's stare. "Kam might feel uncomfortable in formal social situations, but I don't think it's his biggest concern. If your brother were curious about something, he'd find a way to get answers. And he *is* curious," she assured with a significant glance. "It's like . . . he's on a scouting mission or something. He's getting the lay of the land."

"You make it sound like he's planning a battle," Ian said wryly.

"Not a battle, no. But he's planning something."

"What?"

Lin shrugged. "His future company? His life?" she replied uncertainly, saying the first things that came to mind. "Circumstances outside of his control have always kept Kam from doing that in a proactive sense. Trevor Gaines's neglect and emotional abuse, his mother's illness, lack of financial security. For the first time in his life, he's got this amazing product, millions of dollars, supportive people. If I were him, I'd relish taking control and constructing the exact future I wanted, wouldn't you?"

"No doubt."

She told Ian about Kam's request for her to set up tours for him of telecommunications-sector companies in the city. "He's brewing on possible alternative purposes for his invention, immersing himself in the industry, wetting his feet in a way he couldn't living in isolation," she explained. "It might make him uncomfortable to do it, but he's not the type of man to back down from a challenge because of his lack of social graces. It's seems very odd to say it, but he genuinely doesn't care what other people think of him. He's never admitted it, but I think he's curious about the premier watchmakers, despite his disdain for luxury. I don't think he'd suffer these meetings with them for any other reason."

Ian took a moment to absorb her information. "I think you're right," he murmured thoughtfully after a moment. "I guessed right away Kam was a very complex individual. He makes the world believe he's this social misfit, when really he's more complicated than his inventions. Do you like him?"

His unexpected question made her blink. "Yes," she admitted honestly before she could engineer a lie. "He's a puzzle at times, but I like that about him. He's extremely original. He never ceases to surprise."

"You seemed less thrilled with him yesterday, here in the office," Ian observed dryly.

She glanced away from his lancing blue-eyed stare. "As you know, Kam can also be a bit . . ."

"Stubborn? Arrogant? Contemptuous?"

Lin cleared her throat. "Yes, all of those things."

Ian nodded and leaned back in his chair. "Don't worry. You're not telling me anything I don't know. He nearly goaded me into a fistfight last night at the Coffee Boutique."

"What?" Lin asked, alarmed. Was this a result of what had happened in the cloakroom, or more accurately, her leaving without Kam? *"You?"*

"I know. It's been like that since I first met Kam. He has the ability to rile me like no other," Ian said before shaking his head in bemusement. "He really knows how to push some buttons."

Against her will, the vision of Kam's tongue burrowing between her labia as he looked up at her with that hot, quicksilver stare flooded her consciousness. Heat rushed through her at the graphic memory . . . at having such a charged, lascivious memory *period*, sitting here in front of Ian. Was her morning "distance" really so short-lived? For a few charged seconds, she couldn't draw breath into her lungs.

"Something must have upset him after the Gersbachs left, since as you mentioned, everything went so glowingly well at the meeting," Ian said.

"I suppose, yes," she said, struggling to keep her voice even and her expression impassive. "I can't imagine what."

"You can't?"

She shook her head, holding his stare, all expression carefully ironed out of her face. It took a monumental effort on her part.

"Because I got the impression he was very irritated by your leaving," Ian said.

"Really?" Lin asked uneasily.

"Yes. He seemed concerned about you and annoyed by your absence."

She couldn't stop her blush. She felt like a bug under the microscope of Ian's piercing stare. Suddenly, she couldn't take it anymore. She stood abruptly.

"Lin?" Ian asked sharply, sitting forward in his chair. "Is Kam making you uncomfortable? Is he being . . . inappropriate in any way?"

"No," she blurted out. "He's not." *I'm the one who is being inappropriate by lusting after him because he resembles you,* she thought wildly.

"Would you rather not continue to work with him?" Ian demanded.

She stood there, wavering in her heels, unsure of how to reply. This was her chance to back out. Ian could ask another Noble executive to support Kam during his stay in Chicago. Kam wouldn't like that, though. She just knew it. He may have his own personal motives for agreeing to these meetings, but they *did* still make him uncomfortable. It would be unfair to toss him to someone else just because they couldn't keep their hands off each other.

"I want to keep working with him," she said.

"You're sure," Ian prompted.

"Absolutely."

"All right then."

A flash of guilt went through her at his quiet show of complete confidence. Ian respected her decisions. She'd earned that respect from him. She prayed she wasn't throwing his hard-earned trust to the wolves with this thing between her and Kam.

Whatever this *thing* was.

"Since we're on the subject of Kam's discomfort, he came to the penthouse with Francesca and me last night. Two things Francesca was able to . . . 'pry out of him,' as you put it, is that he's very uncomfortable at the hotel, the other is that he misses his dog."

"His dog?" Lin asked incredulously.

Ian nodded, his amusement easily read in his gleaming eyes. "Yes. Angus. Kam seems to imagine that Angus is a vicious guard dog, but in reality, Angus is a sweet golden retriever that doesn't know an enemy and was happy to be a lapdog for Elise and Francesca whenever they visited Aurore. Angus also has the distinction of being Kam's first and longest-standing test subject for his biofeedback timepiece. While we were at Aurore, Angus wore one of the most sophisticated, technologically advanced watches in the world around her left front leg. Even while Kam looked like the wild man of the Aurore Woods and forgot to eat because he'd get so caught up in his inventions, he kept Angus clean, extremely well-groomed, and gave her better food than he ever consumed himself. *Yes*." Ian added when he saw Lin's eyes widen in amazement. "The fierce Angus is a girl."

Lin burst into choked laughter.

Well, she had said Kam never ceased to surprise, hadn't she? Ian uncharacteristically joined her, chuckling quietly. The idea of scowling, primal Kam behaving so fussily about a dog that he imagined to be as intimidating as him was too priceless.

She was glad Ian had revealed this tidbit about his brother. The information made her less anxious about their next meeting, something she'd been dreading after her second instance of impulsive, rampant promiscuity with him last night.

A *little* less anxious, anyway.

It did her heart good to see Ian laugh. He really was fond of Kam, she realized in wonderment as their mirth faded. She'd guessed it before by his actions, but seeing his full-out smile as he recalled his brother's idiosyncrasies really brought it home.

"There's an available furnished apartment in my building," Ian continued. "I've discovered the owner is agreeable to renting it out on a week-to-week basis until he gets a permanent lease. He's also all right with a well-trained dog, so . . ."

"You'd like Kam to move there and have arrangements made for Angus to come to Chicago?" Lin finished for him. "Kam is interested?"

"Yes. He gave me a check last night for two weeks' rent and I've had it delivered to the owner. The staff at the building has the keys ready for him at the front desk. Let's stock up the place for him with food, any appliances he might need, and dog food, I suppose. I thought we could surprise him with Angus," Ian said, picking up a piece of paper and handing it to her. "Here's the address in my building, along with the name of the woman watching Angus in France. I don't have her number, but she lives in the village. It's tiny, so it shouldn't be too hard to find and contact her," Ian said, opening his laptop and tapping out his password.

"I'll have one of the administrative assistants see to the details," she assured, glancing at the paper he'd handed her and turning to go. "Oh, and it's Friday, so I have dance practice. I'll have to be out of here by five," she reminded him. It was the only day of the week she routinely left the office before eight or nine in the evening, and that often was true for weekends as well. Too often.

"I remember," he said, and by the distracted tone of his voice, Lin knew he was already absorbed by whatever he was studying on his computer screen. She had long ago become used to Ian's ability to shut everything out as he focused, including her.

At five that evening Lin headed for the door, her packed briefcase on her shoulder. Her gaze lingered on the phone on her desk. She paused.

She'd been telling herself to call Kam, but had managed to put it off for one reason or another. They had a lot of details that needed to be addressed for the Klinf meeting for Saturday and the Gersbach demonstration of his mechanism, plus she'd scheduled another facility tour for him with one of Noble's technology suppliers early next week. Now the day was done, and she still hadn't called.

Had she been half hoping he'd be the one to call, or even show up at Noble Enterprises wanting to speak with her?

She sighed irritably and exited her office. On the way out, she passed Maria Chase's desk and heard her talking rapidly in French. Among the four administrative assistants that worked for both Ian and Lin, they covered the gamut of the majority of languages spoken on the globe. Lin's French was spotty, but she recognized enough of what Maria said to slow in front of the admin's desk, listening. Maria noticed her and smiled as she signed off and hung up.

"You were able to find the woman who is watching Kam's dog?" Lin asked.

"Yes. I made arrangements with her," Maria said, holding up a pad of paper with neatly written details on it. "I was about to call and arrange for a courier service to pick up the dog and take it to the airport."

"Can you fill me in on the all the details?" Lin asked impulsively. For some reason she very much wanted to see Kam's reaction when he realized his dog had become an international traveler and was there to make him feel a little more at home in Chicago.

Kam glowered at the doorman, the unlikely guard for Lin's luxurious, supermodern high-rise. The middle-aged man puffed out his skinny, concave chest.

"I'm sorry, sir. Those are the rules. I can't let up anyone up onto the resident floors unless the owner gives permission. Ms. Soong isn't even home. She's never home at this time of day, anyway," he said, his patronizing manner amplifying Kam's annoyance. Kam checked his watch.

"It's going on seven. How late does she work?"

The doorman rolled his eyes. "You obviously don't know Ms. Soong very well."

He leaned forward menacingly. "Listen you puffed-up little—"

"Hello," a man said next to him in a French-accented, stuffy-sounding voice.

Kam glanced aside distractedly and did a double take, recognizing the face smiling back at him.

"Richard St. Claire," the dark-haired man said, ending with a nasty-sounding cough. He transferred an obviously used, crumpled tissue to his left hand and extended his right for a handshake. Before Kam had a chance to give him a *you've got to be kidding me* glance,

Richard's face quivered as though a sudden pain had come over him. He turned and sneezed loudly.

"Damn flu," he mumbled hoarsely, wiping his nose.

"You really shouldn't be out of bed, Mr. St. Claire," the doorman said disapprovingly.

"I know, but I had to run out for some Tylenol." He focused watery eyes on Kam.

"You're the guy from the restaurant the other night. Lin's friend," Kam said.

"That's right. I assume you're looking for her?"

"Yeah. I'll try her office," Kam said, starting to move past Richard.

"You won't find her there, either."

Kam glanced back.

"It's Friday. The one and only day Lin ever leaves Noble Enterprises before eight," Richard said.

"And where would she be then?" Kam asked with sarcastic politeness when Richard didn't continue, just studied him with a smug smile.

"If I tell you, you won't do something to make me regret it, will you?"

"Do I look like someone who is out to cause trouble?"

Richard's gaze dropped over him, a glint of admiration in his eyes. "That's exactly what you look like." He sighed when he noticed Kam's frown. "But I suppose I can use the excuse of a fever if Lin calls me on it. Besides, she could use a little trouble in her life," Kam thought he heard him mutter under his breath. "She's at the Community Arts Center on Dearborn and Astor. Two blocks west of here. She goes for dance lessons every Friday. Main auditorium."

"*Merci,*" Kam muttered.

"*Je t'en prie,*" he heard Richard croak amusedly behind him as Kam stalked to the glass door.

When he entered the community center a few minutes later, the entry hall was empty. He found Lin by following the music he heard in the distance—a methodical composition of plucked string instruments, flutes, and gongs. He opened a door and let it shut quietly behind him when he saw the movement on the stage, pausing just inside the threshold.

Lin was the center spoke in a wheel of five other dancers. He knew her immediately, not just from appearance. He recognized her harmony: that smooth, supple, exquisitely controlled movement of her body. All of the dancers typified control, but none more elegantly, nor with such apparent ease, than Lin. That ease was an illusion, Kam realized as he slowly walked down a flight of steps, mesmerized by the dance. The amount of muscular control and balance required for the movements and postures would fell a trained athlete.

All of the dancers, including Lin, wore everyday workout attire for the practice—body-hugging cotton pants, shorts, and T-shirts. Their only concession to a costume was a sort of jacket of purple silk that included sleeves that extended several feet past the dancers' hands. Every time they moved in unison, they did so in perfect synchrony. Not only their limbs were identical in movement, but also the twirling and twitching of the long sleeves. The overall effect was hypnotic.

He came to a halt fifteen or so feet before the stage. The house-lights in the auditorium weren't on, so he was cast in shadow. Still, he knew the moment when Lin became aware of him. Her dark eyes fixed on him as she continued the dance without pause, her gestures and movements incredibly precise, so graceful . . .

. . . so fucking sexy, it blew him away, but not in any way he'd ever before experienced.

As the center of the moving wheel, Lin was the only one who occasionally danced separately from the others, then blended seamlessly with their movements as the dance progressed. She wore only a pair of form-fitting black shorts and a cropped white T-shirt along with the long costume sleeves. Her feet were naked, a living poetry of graceful movement and strength. He couldn't take his eyes off her pale belly and gliding, shifting hips. It called to mind the strength and precision of her counterthrusts to his when he was inside her.

A pleasant tingling sensation started in his lower spine and transferred to his cock, swelling the flesh. He couldn't unglue his gaze from her.

Her hair was pulled back from her face in the front, but the rest was unrestrained. With her back to him, she slowly arched her spine until her long hair hung like a drape less than a foot from the stage, her arms weaving a spell. She made eye contact in the impossible position.

His flesh tingled like an electrical charge had gone through it.

She was like a carefully controlled conduit of pure sexuality. Just being in her vicinity made the hair on his arms stand on end and his blood race.

The last plucked note sounded, and Lin gracefully lowered a long leg and her extended arms. The women all relaxed their poses and began chatting to one another, some of them walking over to gym bags, the spell of the dance dissipating.

But not vanishing, Kam thought as he watched Lin walk toward him. She shucked off the long-sleeve jacket and agilely leapt off the stage.

"Hello," she said.

"Hi," he returned. He suddenly felt very hulking and clumsy next to her sleek, contained beauty. For a few charged seconds, they just looked at one another, but then she glanced away. The hint of shyness in her manner fascinated him.

"How . . . how did you find me?"

"I went to your condominium looking for you, and someone pointed me in this direction."

"Who?" she asked.

He shrugged. "Someone who thought I should find you, I guess."

"I didn't realize such a person existed."

"Besides me, you mean?"

Her small smile fell at that. He noticed her pulse fluttering at her throat. Acting purely on instinct, he reached out and placed his hand on her neck. He closed his eyes briefly, focusing on the vibrant pulse of her strong heart.

She was so beautiful. Inside and out. Only true beauty could dance to the heartbeat of the universe so effortlessly. He opened his eyes. She looked up at him slowly, and again, he felt himself stir.

"I'm sorry. About last night. It seems I'm doomed to keep screwing up and then apologizing to you for behaving like an animal," he muttered.

He felt her throat constrict as she swallowed.

"You're not alone in this, Kam."

He studied her still features searchingly. "Why can't I stop wanting you?" he muttered. Her pulse leapt beneath his fingers like a tiny, trapped creature.

"Why can't I stop wanting you as well?" she whispered, her desperation and longing an echo of his tone.

He found himself staring at her mouth, his nostrils flaring to catch her scent.

"Let me get my things and we'll walk back to my place," she said.

He just stood there. His anticipation was just beginning to build, and yet it had already cut him to the quick.

They entered her condominium, and Lin led him to her living room. "Why don't you make yourself comfortable. I'm just going to take a quick shower. Can I get you anything to drink?"

He just shook his head, feeling awkward yet again in the midst of her luxurious living room with her formal manner. He wanted to tell her not to shower—he'd rather taste the efforts of her dance on her smooth skin—but maybe she hadn't even asked him back to her place for sex.

She left him. He listened for a second to the bathroom door

closing and pictured her peeling off her tight workout clothing. Again—he experienced that delicious ripple of sensation along the shaft of his cock. His body had never been more finely attuned to a woman, his cock never more sensitive to every nuance of her movement. He heard the shower turn on. She'd be naked now, jets of warm water beating against her smooth skin.

He removed his coat impatiently. The living room was like Lin herself: effortlessly elegant, expensive looking, and more comfortable than he would have thought at first glance, he conceded as he slouched down on a deep, soft couch. His gaze narrowed on the luxurious, raw silk, taupe-colored curtains with sheers on the windows. They were the precise ones Ian had recommended Kam buy for Aurore Manor for a majority of the downstairs windows. Removing the mildewed, heavy velvet curtains that had obliterated sunlight and replacing them with the sheer curtains and lightweight silk panes had made a world of difference. That, and the simple changes of new paint and a hard cleaning had altered the mood of the manor almost immediately. The decrepit mansion had been transformed into a home, and he had Lin's impeccable taste, in large part, to thank for that.

Of course Ian hadn't been the one to expertly choose those curtains or the sophisticated, yet comfortable, furnishings and bedclothes for the bedrooms. Lin had. Kam had realized that almost immediately after observing how Ian operated. She'd never even seen Aurore, she'd never even met Kam, and yet she'd clothed both his house and his body in a way that innately appealed to him.

Why can't I stop wanting it, too?

We'll walk back to my place.

The memory of Lin saying those words as she watched him with liquid brown eyes scored his consciousness. Was he supposed to have read them as an invitation? His body had considered it as such, but his mind continued to doubt.

He cursed quietly, stood and walked down the hallway toward

her bedroom. His interpretation didn't really matter. Staying away from her was an utter impossibility.

As he neared the closed bathroom door, he heard the water shut off and the glass door of the shower click open. He rapped softly before he put his hand on the knob.

Almost the second he opened the door and saw her standing in the shower, he knew she wasn't surprised. She'd been waiting for him to come—or at least some part of her had. She stood very still, her beautiful body sheened with moisture, water droplets clinging on her bare breasts and thighs. He'd never seen her completely naked. His body hardened in a second, aching. He stepped toward her, vaguely realizing that the spell she'd woven as he watched her dance had fallen upon him again in full strength. How she did it was a mystery, but he was beyond wondering.

He was only feeling.

He reached for one of the towels on the rack without looking away from the vision of her. As he approached, she stepped out of the shower to meet him. He partially wrapped her in the towel, holding her stare as he lightly chafed her supple back and buttocks and thighs, drying her. She felt small in his hold, firm and feminine. His hand opened over a stretch of shower-warmed, moist back and lowered over her ass.

The towel dropped from his hands at the same moment that he palmed her bottom and hips, lifting her against him and pressing her tight.

It was as if they'd practiced this dance before. She saw the flash in his gray eyes, and he was lifting her to him in one fluid, muscular movement. His mouth covered hers. His tongue penetrated and stroked, wet, firm, and demanding. Lin kissed him back, every bit as greedy as he was, every bit as hot. She gripped onto his shoulders, and he turned, leaving the bathroom and taking her with him. Once he'd cleared the door, she wrapped her legs around his middle, her bottom resting below his belt. His erection was trapped against his clothing, slanting upward toward his right jeans pocket. She circled her hips, grinding against it, loving the vibration of his rough groan of appreciation into her mouth.

He set her on the edge of her bed and broke their kiss. Holding her stare, he reached for her hand and placed it on his cock. For a lung-burning few seconds, he just kept his hand pressed to hers, and then his hand dropped away. She bit her lip to stifle a moan as her fingers and palm mapped out his contours. He began to unfasten his belt as she stroked his solid length more rapidly through his clothing. It aroused her exquisitely, the weight of him, the shape. Leaning forward, she pressed her mouth to his jeans, gently biting at the hard column of his erection.

"Oh oui, encore," he grated out. *Yes, again.* She gave him what he wanted, liking his rough groan. He shoved down his jeans. She grew impatient to feel him naked in her clasping hand and immediately reached for the waistband of his boxer briefs.

"Ah" popped out of her throat as she freed his tumescent cock. He felt very warm . . . hot even. Feverish. She fisted him, her thumb and fingers not quite able to meet around his pulsing shaft. She regretfully released him momentarily while Kam rapidly shucked off his pants and underwear. Then he was standing before her again, his cock standing at rigid attention, hers to touch and pleasure.

She lifted the heavy weight of it and brushed the swollen, bulbous head against her cheek experimentally. Oh, he was soft as warm silk and yet so hard. He hissed and sunk his fingers into her upswept hair, loosening some of it so that it fell down her back and shoulders. A thumb slid under her chin and he pressed up.

She looked up at his face.

"Take me in your mouth. Please."

It was both a demand and a ragged plea. She was more than eager to comply.

Chapter Eight

Using her hand, she pulled him down toward her mouth, licking at the smooth, fleshy head and tasting his flavor before she inserted him between her lips. His rough growl seemed to vibrate from his flesh to hers, thrilling her. She pulsed her head, her rigid lips sliding onto the thick, veined shaft. When she pulled back, she moaned in excitement at the sensation of sliding her lips across the defined ridge of the head. His whole cock was beautiful to her, but the swollen cockhead was exquisite—fleshy, succulent, mouthwatering. She slid down his shaft again, pausing to pulse him back and forth an inch with firm strokes until his hands tightened on her skull and he groaned. She pulled back, slapping her tongue against the fat head playfully before she sunk down on him again.

He was a mouthful, but she was hungry. So hungry. Her jaw began to ache from clamping him so tight.

"That's right," he grated out from above her. "I kept thinking about your mouth, but it's hotter and sweeter than I thought it would be. Are you trying to tell me how much you like this?" he added, his voice still rough as he watched her, but more sultry. Sexy.

She sucked him extra hard in reply, squeezing dense, delicious male flesh, letting him know without words just how *much* she liked this. He hissed a curse and abruptly reached down for her elbows, lifting her to her feet. She gasped when he popped out of her mouth due to their abrupt change of position. He urged her to turn and stand next to him, so that they both faced the bed. Opening his legs slightly, he firmed his stance. He lifted his glistening cock from below and held it at an upward angle, once again delving his fingers into her hair. She followed his urging, bending at the waist and immediately sucking him again into her mouth, the brief deprivation making her hungrier. He opened one hand on her back and swept it along spine, hip, and buttocks, as if he wanted to feel as much of her as he could while she gave him pleasure.

"Aw, Jesus. That's good," he moaned as she moved up and down on his shaft, her actions increasingly forceful and hungry. She placed her hand over his where he grasped his cock at the base. He relinquished his hold, and she wrapped her hand in his place. She'd pinned her hair onto her head for the shower with several clips, but thanks to their increasing excitement and Kam's delving fingers, long tendrils of hair now fell around her head, some of it impinging her progress as she sucked his cock deeper into her mouth.

"Here, I'll hold it for you," he muttered tensely from above her, brushing the hair off her face. He grasped the mass of it in one hand at the base of her skull, restraining it. She lifted her outside hand and gripped his hip to steady herself. She twisted her face slightly, sinking her lips over him at a slightly new angle. His cockhead brushed against her throat. She gagged slightly and retreated, but was back for more in a heartbeat. "Look at you," she heard him mutter roughly from above her.

Heat rushed through her at his words, a potent mixture of intense arousal and embarrassment, because he was looking at her as she devoured him. *Look at you, sucking me like a wild, sex-starved wanton. Who would have thought it of cool, contained Lin?* That was her imagination, of course. He'd never said that. She didn't know if that's what he truly intended, but her interpretation pleased her on some level. It also amplified her lust.

He tensed and thrust his hips forward slightly, his pose intensely virile and unashamedly male. He used his hold on her hair to guide her strokes, but he did so gently, increasing the pressure of her mouth on his cock but never forcing himself on her. She'd never performed fellatio like this—not that she'd done it more than a few times in her life. It was a very personal act, after all, and Lin had only had a couple of long-term relationships in which to practice it. On those other occasions, she'd been in bed with the man or kneeling before him. Kam was too tall for her to kneel, however. It was surprisingly comfortable, given their respective heights. With them both standing and her next to him, bent at the waist, the angle of penetration was ideal.

It was also shockingly arousing, and she loved the lascivious way he was rubbing her back, hips, and ass with his large hand.

She popped the fleshy round cockhead out of her mouth and bent farther, shifting her hand up the shaft and running her tongue over the root, wetting him. He grunted softly and she sensed his focused attention. When she reinserted his cock, she began to stroke the lubricated staff with her hand, pounding her fist forcefully in tandem with the movements of her sucking mouth. He groaned. She closed her eyes and lost herself in the primal rhythm, the feeling of desire infusing his flesh, engorging it, the clutching of his fingers in her hair as his excitement mounted . . .

She wanted nothing more in that moment than to feel him quiver in release, to squeeze his essence from his flesh, and blend his male strength with her own.

He cursed, piercing her tight focus. Then he was pulling his now-huge erection from her mouth and lifting her. He laid her on the bed and crawled on top of her. She lifted her lust-weighted eyelids with effort, watching as he straddled her hips with his knees and rose over her. He shifted his swollen penis until it thumped, heavy and moist, against her belly.

"I wanted to finish," she whispered.

"You think I don't know that?" he asked, his mouth quirking in amusement. "That was a definite one-way ticket, the way you were going at it." He reached with both hands and caressed her neck and then her shoulders. His cock seemed to burn the skin where it rested on it. She reached for it, but he halted her with a hand on her wrist. He pushed her arm against the pillow above her head. Her cheeks flushed hot.

"I want to see you come," she said, her stark admission surprising her a little.

His cock lurched on her belly. He seemed less surprised by her outburst than she was. "You will then. But not yet."

He watched her, as if assessing her reaction. Her nostrils flared slightly as he slowly moved her other hand to join its mate on the pillow. A bolt of excitement went through her. She ground her hips down onto the mattress, writhing, getting indirect friction on her simmering sex.

Kam's eyebrows went up in prurient interest. "You like to be restrained?"

"No." She bit her lip as molten heat surged in her sex. "I don't know."

"You mean you haven't let anyone do it before?"

She shook her head.

"Would you mind if I bound your wrists then? While I play with you? I'll free you anytime you like. Just say the word."

She swallowed with difficulty, suddenly going still when she noticed where Kam was lustfully staring. Her nipples had pulled into painfully hard points. Her body had certainly found his proposal arousing.

While I play with you . . .

"All right," she whispered.

He swung a long leg over her and clambered off the bed. She sorely missed his heat and hardness. She watched him remove his shoes and socks. He made short work of releasing the buttons on the white shirt he wore. Her breath caught as he whipped open the placket and she was gifted with the vision of flexing, ridged muscle and smooth, swarthy skin. His cock looked even more stark and flagrant jutting from his nude body. He retrieved a condom from his jeans pocket and lunged toward her bedside table. She turned her head, her line of vision directly on his suspended cock.

She moaned and reached. He captured her wrist.

He extricated something from her bedside table drawer and was crawling back on the bed again.

"You already almost made short work of me three times running. Give a man a chance," he murmured, his rough voice like a gentle fingernail going down her spine. He straddled her and gathered her wrists above her head again. She gave him a stunned glance. "You said I could restrain you."

She caught sight of something in his hand.

"With my headband?" she asked, realizing he'd removed the thick elastic headband from her drawer. She wore it, and others like it, to pull back her hair while she removed her makeup in the evening. She often forgot to remove it until she went to bed, and thus had a collection of them in her bedside table drawer.

He made a sound of preoccupied agreement as he twisted the band around both her wrists, restraining them. He gently pushed her hands against the pillows and sat back.

She watched, her mouth going dry as he just inspected her nude body for a moment with a long, glittering stare of male appreciation. He slipped a large hand beneath his heavy erection and stroked himself.

"*Kam,*" she whispered disbelievingly when arousal stabbed at her. It was unbelievably exciting to watch him touch himself. Her hips twisted on the bed, but he pressed down with his pelvis on her thighs, stilling her as he continued to slide his fist up and down his erection. He pressed the tip of the fleshy cockhead between her labia. Her eyes sprung wide at the erotic vision, her initial gasp becoming an incredulous, shaky moan. He stilled her shifting hips with an open hand at her hips.

"This pussy . . . I've been dreaming about it constantly," he said, sounding distracted. He began pulsing against her clit with his cock. "Do you shave because it makes you more sensitive?"

She just shook her head, too overwhelmed with pleasure to speak. It felt so good, to be stimulated so intimately with the very cockhead that made her mouth water. He looked up to her face when she didn't respond. A small, fond smile titled his mouth, the hot expression in his eyes leaving her even more breathless than she'd been.

"You do it because it's neater that way, right? Sleeker."

"I suppose," she gasped.

His smile widened slightly, then vanished when he looked back at his illicit task. "Look at that. Look how wet you're getting me.

Despite his words, she continued to watch his face. He looked utterly transfixed as he watched himself rub his cockhead against her clit. Eventually, she glanced down and saw how her juices made the ruddy tip shine. The pressure against her clit, the illicit slide and press of his most sensitive flesh against hers was delicious. She flexed her hips upward as much as she could, a choking sound rattling her throat.

He looked up at her face. "Could you come like this?" he rasped, continuing to manipulate his swollen flesh up and down a scant half inch, every once in a while pausing to stroke the heavy staff.

"Yes," she admitted shakily. Why deny it? Her clit was burning. She'd love nothing more than to ignite with the tip of his cock as the trigger.

"Hold still," he warned her darkly when he removed his restraining hand from her hip. She struggled to follow his instructions, even though she longed to push more firmly against the steely cockhead. He reached between her thighs.

"Oh," she gasped loudly when he inserted his thumb into her pussy.

"God, you're soaking," he mumbled, sounding both excited and gratified. The tip of his cock began outlining a tiny circle, pressing and bobbing against her clit. She simmered. Even the bottoms of her feet sizzled as they flexed helplessly. His thumb plunged in and out of her, amplifying the pressure on her clit. He grunted in arousal. Lin's entire body tightened. He began to thump his cock gently against her clit like a lewd drumbeat.

"Oh no," she mumbled, her head twisting on the pillow as she crested.

"Oh *yeah*," he disagreed as she broke in orgasm.

His body seemed to scream at him, the savage male in him pummeling at his consciousness as Kam watched her writhe against his hand and pulsing cock.

Take her. Sink into all that tight, sweet glory.

But the image of Lin experiencing rapture was even more compelling than the taunting voice. He nursed her through her climax, feeling the rush of her warm juices around his finger, her convulsing channel pulling at him. Desire lanced him. She looked so beautiful, her eyes closed, her face lightly glazed with perspiration, her breasts thrust upward, the nipples tight and hard. For a few seconds he protected himself against the image of her, clamping his eyelids shut. He grasped his cock hard, squeezing it into submission.

It didn't work—not really—because once she'd given one last gasp and sunk heavily onto the mattress, he fell on her like a ravenous animal. He nuzzled her belly and slid his tongue over satin-smooth skin. The harmonious beauty of her stunned him anew. Had he ever touched such an exquisite woman? He took a gentle bite at the side of her waist. He slid a delectable nipple into his mouth and laved the stiff crest briskly with his tongue. Using his hand, he molded the firm flesh, making it more pronounced for his mouth, licking and sucking and biting ever so gently at the responsive flesh. She bucked her hips up against him and moaned, giving him her approval. Finally lifting his mouth, he transferred to her other breast, but he didn't like leaving the first sweet crest at all. He continued to play with it as he hungrily sucked the other, tweaking the damp, erect flesh with his fingertips and shaping her breast to his palm.

Her sharp cries finally breached the thick haze of his lust. He lifted his head, staring at the erotic vision of Lin's firm, fleshy breasts flushed with desire, rising and falling so temptingly as she panted. His breath was coming fast and erratically, too. It was hard to think, with his cock feeling ponderous and aching between his thighs, his desire about to burst out of his very skin.

He shifted his knees slightly, kneeling over her, his gaze still glued to her heaving, thrusting breasts. He cradled them from below and lifted before letting go, entranced by the spring of firm flesh.

"Kam, *please*," she cried out sharply when he repeated the action, pausing to rub her nipples with his thumbs.

He focused on Lin's face. Her large, usually somber brown eyes were glazed with passion, her expression tight and wild. The vision of her transformed from a cool, calm professional into a hot-blooded, hungry woman scored his consciousness. She was an addictive substance, without a doubt.

He reached between her thighs, his fingers dipping into the evidence of her abundant arousal. He rubbed her clit firmly and soaked in her whimpers. His cock leapt a moment later when she held her breath and let it out on a shaky moan of climax. She twisted beneath him, her pelvis coming off the mattress as she pressed against him, shuddering in pleasure.

It was too much. He couldn't take any more. His cock couldn't. He grasped it and pumped, his intent single-minded. His rough moan strained his throat as he fell over the edge and began to ejaculate. Lin's cries of bliss fractured and turned to moans as ropes of white semen fell onto her heaving breasts and ribs. He couldn't stop it, the claws of pure pleasure clutching at him, ripping at him.

When he came back to himself, he was leaning down over her on his knees, one hand supporting himself on the upholstered headboard, the other still pumping his supersensitive cock. A few more thick drops of semen fell on Lin's nipple. For several seconds, he struggled to recover, the only sounds in the still room that of their combined soughing, erratic breaths. Their blended pants joined them somehow, the connection remaining even when both of them began to slow.

Lin lay there, completely undone, melted by blasting pleasure. Neither of them spoke when he finally moved, leaning back onto his knees. He rapidly unwound the band from her wrists, freeing her.

"I'll be right back," he said gruffly. She didn't have any strength to protest against his getting off the bed and walking toward the bathroom. He returned a moment later with a washcloth and a box of tissues. He tossed the tissues onto the bedside table and sat down next to her.

"That feels good," she murmured as he gently moved the warm, damp cloth over her skin.

"You're not mad at me?" he asked, his brow quirked upward as he attended to his task of carefully cleaning her right breast.

"Mad at you?" she asked, confused.

"For this," he clarified under his breath, nodding to his task of washing her.

"I'm not as much of a neat freak and perfectionist as everyone seems to think I am."

He glanced up and met her stare. "Funny."

"What?"

"I told Ian much the same thing."

For once, his reference to his brother didn't fracture her complete attention on him. "It was very erotic," she said in a hushed tone. "And I did tell you I wanted to watch you come."

Her core clenched yet again in desire when she saw his sheepish smile. She smiled back. The moment struck her as sublimely sweet, even more so because it was in direct contrast to Kam's typical raw, primal intensity.

After he'd cleaned her, he dried her with a few tissues. Then he came down next to her on the bed. The air against her damp, naked skin had chilled her, but Kam was like a cozy fire. She sighed in satisfaction when he rolled her into his arms and her cheek pressed against a dense pectoral muscle. She nestled her nose and lips in the crook of his shoulder and neck, thinking of how good it felt, how right the fit. He smoothed her hair back off her face and continued to stroke it.

"It's straight tonight. Your hair," she heard him say.

"It's dry outside."

"I can't decide how I like it better. Curly or straight."

She pressed her face to his chest and planted a kiss. She liked the sensation of crisp male hair and thick, smooth male skin against her lips. "I hate when it goes wild."

"Why? You look pretty with it curling around your face."

"Thank you," she murmured, stroking his biceps, wondrous at the density of the muscle, the curving shape. "I can hear your heart beat," she said after a moment of silence.

"What's it telling you?"

She listened carefully, taking his idle question seriously. She absorbed the strong, steady beat. "That you're a very healthy man who is quite content at the moment?"

"Are you asking me or telling me?" he asked, and she heard the smile in his voice.

"Telling you," she whispered, her mouth moving against his skin. She closed her eyes and purred when he kneaded the nape of her neck with his fingertips. "Who will you use for a test subject when you do a test of your biofeedback mechanism?"

"I don't know. What about you?"

Her eyes blinked open. "Do you think that would be a good idea?"

"Yes," he stated unequivocally.

"Well . . . if you need me . . ."

His low grunt as he leaned down to kiss the top of her head seemed to say, *Isn't that obvious?* She smiled. It was a nice, having him tell her he needed her even in such an indirect way.

"Did Ian tell you that I'm going to move into an apartment in his building?" Kam rumbled.

"Yes. We have things arranged so that you can move in tomorrow morning, if you like."

"I know, he told me. Will you come by in the afternoon?"

"I'll be working on a project that I have to get done before leaving town on Monday for a couple of nights in San Francisco," she murmured.

"Tomorrow is Saturday," he said disapprovingly. "Don't you ever take time off?"

"It's a special circumstance," she lied. She often worked on the weekend, although this really was an emergency situation. "I even had to ask some of the support staff to come in to help me finish. And then we have the dinner tomorrow night with Jason Klinf," she reminded him.

For some reason, it made her feel guilty when Kam chastised her for working too much, which was ridiculous. Somehow, her work had gotten all mixed up in her head with her feelings for Ian. Maybe that's why she was so sensitive talking about it to Kam. Maybe she *should* be ashamed of how dedicated she'd been in the past years to her work; how dedicated she'd been to a man who didn't return her feelings.

It really was pretty pitiful on her part, she realized irritably.

"It'll only take an hour or two to program the device for your body," he said. She lifted her head and gave him a doubtful glance. "If I tell you it's a work task, will that convince you?" he added dryly. "The Gersbach demonstration is on Wednesday, and you'll be out of town on Tuesday."

She thought there was a good chance Angus would arrive tomorrow afternoon and wanted to see his reaction to seeing the dog firsthand, so maybe Kam's proposition was a good thing.

"Okay, I suppose I could fit it in . . ."

She was distracted by the sound of Kam's stomach growling. She gave him an amused glance. He looked very appealing lying naked on her bed, his head on her pillow, his dark hair mussed and falling onto his forehead.

"You haven't eaten?" she asked him.

He shook his head, his sexy lips tilted in amusement. "You?"

"No. I was going to when I got home, but then . . ."

"You made a meal out of me instead," he muttered dryly. A flash of heat went through her at his reference and the erotic memory it evoked. "Can I take you to dinner somewhere?" he asked.

"Do you really want to get up and get dressed?"

"It depends." She gave him a querying glance. "On whether or not you're going to let me back in your bed after dinner. If not, I'd just as soon stay here and not forsake my claim."

She laughed. His brows quirked and he palmed her jaw, running his fingers gently over her smiling lips.

"You have a very gentle touch when you want to," she said, his fingertips moving along with her lips.

"Does that surprise you?"

Her smile faded as she considered him soberly.

"No," she said at last. "It doesn't surprise me in the least."

They cleaned up and dressed, then went downstairs. There was a nice restaurant in her building's lobby. When the host seated them at a cozy booth, Lin started to sit across from Kam. He grabbed her hand, however, and pulled her into the seat next to him. The host gave them a rather smug, patronizing grin, which Kam quelled immediately with a glare.

"Have you been dancing a long time?" he asked after they'd placed their orders and the waiter had left them alone.

"No. I just started it as a hobby four years ago."

He gave her a sideways glance that made her go warm. "You look like you were born doing it."

She smiled, flattered. "Thanks. My grandmother wouldn't have liked my learning traditional Chinese dance. She would have hated knowing about the Kung Fu classes I took several years back. That was both traditional *and* inelegant—or at least Grandmamma would have thought so," she said, and laughed. "I actually kept both hobbies from her in the last years of her life, which made me feel terrible. It was ballet Grandmamma encouraged. My mother, on the other hand, holds my Chinese dance hobby up to our family as a stellar accomplishment." She gave Kam a wry grin. "My *only* one, mind you, because I botch my Chinese, I don't work on my cooking enough, and worst of all, I'm still not married to a nice Chinese doctor."

Kam smiled. "Your mother and grandmother sound really different."

Lin rolled her eyes. "You have no idea." She looked over at him when he placed his hand on her thigh. She'd pulled on a pair of jeans and a sweater after they'd washed up earlier. She could feel the heat of his hand through the denim as he moved it up and down, squeezing lightly as if he was experimenting with the sensation of her flesh in jeans.

"Tell me then."

"Okay, I'll try," she said. His touch was distracting. It had the paradoxical effect of both lulling her and exciting her. "My grandparents and my mother were born in Hong Kong. For my grandparents, America truly was the promised land, and they totally embraced US culture when they immigrated. My grandmother especially was a very chic, modern woman. My mother never really seemed to assimilate here, though. My grandparents couldn't understand why she was so resentful and withdrawn. It was a constant thorn in my grandmother's side. She couldn't comprehend why mother felt so out of place, when Grandmamma militantly embraced it and loved the life she built for herself here."

"So obviously your grandmother wouldn't have condoned your participating in traditional Chinese dance or anything else Chinese."

"Oh no. Grandmamma wanted both a very westernized daughter and grandaughter. She got her way in my case."

"But not in your mother's?"

"No. Not in my mother's," Lin said, giving him a quick, sad smile.

"What happened between your mother and grandmother?" Kam asked.

"My mother rebelled against Grandmamma. She swung in the opposite direction, coming to despise Western ways and becoming extremely traditional. It was pretty confusing for me when I was little. We all lived in the same house together. My mother started insisting I speak Chinese, for instance, which I'd never learned, having been born here. She wanted to send me to a Chinese school and only eat Chinese food. It infuriated Grandmamma. Mother and Grandmamma officially went to war."

"And you were their battleground."

Lin blinked at his grim intensity. "Yes. That's a pretty apt description. Although probably misleading in one respect. I never resented my grandmother. We were always close, and had this natural connection from the very beginning. I think my mother might have felt like an outsider in that respect, which always makes me sad to consider. After my grandfather died, my parents decided to leave the States. Grandmamma saw my mother's choice as a betrayal." She paused as the waiter brought their drink orders. "It only made matters worse that they planned to live in Taiwan, near my father's family instead of near either of my grandparents' relatives. Grandmamma absolutely refused to let them take me. I was nine at the time. Grandmamma threatened to take my mother to court, although she must have been bluffing about her likelihood of winning custody."

"And so your parents agreed to leave you behind?" Kam asked, frowning.

She laughed softly. "You didn't know my grandmother. Ask Ian. She was a force to be reckoned with. Besides, it's common for Asians to want their children educated in the States, and so Grandmamma had that as her trump card. Even my traditional mother and father couldn't deny *that* was a desirable outcome."

They paused in talking when their waiter brought them their salads.

"Do you see your parents often?" Kam asked when they were alone again.

"Once a year. They never return here. Maybe there are too many bad memories for my mother." He gave her thigh a final squeeze and lifted his hand to begin eating. She sensed him studying her in the silence that followed.

"You miss them, don't you," he stated, rather than asked, after a moment.

"Yes," she said quietly, picking up her fork. "To this day, I don't think my mother understands how affected I was when they left. I don't wish I'd gone with them necessarily. I love my life here. It's just that my mom sort of looks at it in black-and-white terms. I'm an American, I live a similar lifestyle to Grandmamma's, so I must be a clone of Grandmamma. In her mind, I 'chose' Grandmamma and everything she represents over her." Lin sighed. "I didn't 'choose' anything."

"You were a little kid."

"Right. But I'm an adult now, and my mother carries on seeing Grandmamma instead of me. She disapproves of my choices and automatically assumes I disapprove of her and my father's," she reflected. She forked her salad. "I *don't*," she said, shrugging helplessly. "I just want them to be happy. But I can't seem to convince them—especially my mother—of that.

"Family, huh?" she said after a pause, feeling embarrassed when she realized how much she'd been going on about herself. It was strange, but even though Kam didn't talk a lot, he was very easy to talk *to*. "What about you? You mentioned not going back to your residency when your mother became ill," she said after she'd swallowed some salad. "You must have been close to her."

"I was. She was an easy woman to love."

She set down her salad fork slowly, studying his bold profile as he ate. "That's a lovely thing for a son to say about his mother."

He shrugged. "It's true."

"You must miss her," she said quietly.

"We were all each other had in the world."

"But now you have Lucien and Ian," she said quietly after a moment.

"There's no such thing as instant families, but yeah. I guess there's some truth to that." He gave her a flashing glance as he chewed.

"What?" she asked, sensing he wanted to say something.

"Ian is more family to you than he is to me," he said before taking a swig of ice water. "Your work is your life. That's what everyone says, anyway. Noble Enterprises became your family."

She blushed, looking away from his gleaming gray eyes, and picked up her fork again. "Ian is my boss," she stated unequivocally.

"He doesn't just think of you as just an employee. He told me so."

She felt his stare on her cheek and resisted an urge to squirm. "Really?" she asked, taking pains to keep her voice level. She took a bite of bread. "When was this?"

"Last night. When he was ever so delicately warning me I'd better tread carefully when it came to you."

Her fork fell against the bowl. She suddenly felt queasy.

"Please don't tell me that Ian realized what we were doing in that cloakroom," she muttered, horrified. "Did you tell him anything?" she asked, realizing too late she'd sounded accusatory.

"Do you think I would?" he demanded, scowling.

"If you didn't say anything to him, then why was he warning you about me?" Lin asked.

"He's not stupid," Kam muttered, holding her stare. "Although he can keep his holier-than-thou attitude to himself, if you ask me. You and I are grown-ups, free to do whatever we damn well please."

It brought to mind all their recent, extremely grown-up activities. Suddenly, she couldn't remember the topic of their conversation. His gaze sunk down over her, and as usual, she experienced that swooping sensation in her belly. Kam leaned in, his warm breath brushing across her parted lips. Their mouths touched. "If we want to spend time together, it's none of Ian's business."

Ian. Right, that's whom they were discussing.

"Spend time together?" she asked, her mouth twitching against his. "Is that a euphemism for having sex?"

"We're not having sex now. Unless you're interested?" he murmured, a devil's glint in his eyes. He nipped at her lower lip, his narrow-eyed, predatory stare on her mouth making her breathless.

They were halted in their flirtation and kissing by the waiter arriving with their entrees. Kam glanced up at the interruption, his expression fierce. The waiter's eyes widened in alarm. It seemed utterly impossible for Kam to even thinly disguise his wrath. The waiter served their food and escaped as quickly as he could.

"What?" he asked, his expression darkening even further when he saw Lin laughing under her breath.

She gave him an amused glance and patted his thigh. "Kam," she attempted gently, her palm lingering on jean-covered, dense muscle. "You do realize you scare people half to death the way you glower constantly, don't you? I get the impression people worry they might be knocked over by the force of your scowl."

"*What?*"

"See?" She pointed to his face. "Right there. Hurricane-force glare."

His gaze flickered down to where her fingers dug gently into his thigh. His expression went suddenly neutral, but she recognized that spark of male interest in his eyes.

"Does it scare you?" he murmured, the gruff quality of his voice making the little hairs on her nape stand on end.

"Sorry. No such luck."

"*Merde.* What am I supposed to do now?" he murmured, giving her a swift grin, which she returned.

She just watched him for a few seconds when he began to cut his chicken. She resisted a strong urge to run her hands across his broad shoulders. He looked very masculine and extremely appealing in the soft cotton white shirt she'd bought him, the color highlighting his dark skin and hair. She'd been surprisingly aroused when he'd restrained her wrists earlier, making her a captive to the pleasure he evoked so masterfully. But at the moment, she wanted nothing more than to put her hands all over his strong, virile body.

"I thought you were hungry," he said, turning toward her after he'd taken a swallow of water and noticed she wasn't eating.

She leaned forward abruptly and pressed her mouth to his. She'd never once in her entire life kissed a man in a restaurant. And this was no peck on the cheek. She shaped and molded his lips with her own, enjoying the firm succulence of them. She moaned softly into his mouth when he raised a hand and clutched her head at the same moment he sunk his tongue between her lips, claiming her completely. *Yes.* This is the response she'd been coaxing from him. So bold. So possessive. So Kam-like.

His mouth was still cold from the ice water he'd just drunk. She sought his heat just beneath the chilled veneer. He penetrated her with his tongue—back and forth, back and forth, a slow, suggestive slide. She felt his languorous, sexy kiss all the way to her core. Desire stabbed at her, the strength of it shocking her. She resisted a sudden, strong urge to touch herself to dull that sharp ache. No sooner did she have the inappropriate thought than Kam's hand was there, doing what she'd thought of doing to herself.

Doing it *better.*

Chapter Nine

like you in jeans," he said next to her lips as he rubbed her outer sex in an eye-crossing manner and examined her through heavy eyelids. "They show off your long legs and tight ass. And this"—he added, his lips rubbing against hers so seductively, his gaze sinking to where he stimulated her with strong fingers—"sweet little pussy."

"Kam." She'd meant it to be a remonstrance—he really shouldn't be touching her like this in public or saying such outrageous things—but instead, it came out as a shaky invitation. Wasn't this what she'd been asking for when she kissed him? His dirty talk in tandem with his stroking of her pussy aroused her.

A lot.

He moved his mouth and nuzzled her ear, making her shiver. "Eat some of your food," he said quietly. "Go on. I won't have you starving."

She glanced uneasily around the restaurant. It wasn't crowded, but she could see a couple dining at a table fifteen or so feet away. They seemed entirely unaware of Kam and her in the booth, but if they looked over, what would they see? Not much, probably. Just Kam nuzzling her, which wasn't the most scandalous thing on earth. The hanging tablecloth would disguise his movements between her legs.

"Eat," he ordered again next to her ear. She picked up her fork and took a bite. She was so focused on Kam's fingers on her pussy—rubbing and circling and pressing on her clit—that she couldn't have said what it was she ate. He used the thicker, stiffer material on the fly to his advantage, pressing against it, applying optimal pressure to her body. She registered none of what she saw in front of her. Every fiber of her awareness was targeted on him, and him alone.

"That's a girl," he murmured, nipping at the shell of her ear and making her shiver as she chewed. "I didn't get a chance to tell you how much I appreciated your mouth. Wet and sweet and so eager. You have no idea how much I wanted to come in it."

She flexed her hips against his ruthless fingers and bit off a moan. Who knew it could feel so good, even through her clothing?

"The first time I saw you," he continued ruthlessly, "I thought you were too delicate to like it fast and hot and furious," he murmured, taking her earlobe between his front teeth and scraping the sensitive flesh. "Too elegant. Too sophisticated. But you have a wild side, don't you, *mon petit chaton*?" he asked in that rough, deep voice in her ear. "Would you have liked it? For me to have erupted in your mouth?"

"Yes," she admitted; for how else was there to be with Kam but honest? She felt feverish, sitting there while he rubbed her and murmured outrageous, scintillating words into her ear. No one had ever talked dirty to her before, so she hadn't known she'd like it so much. He shifted his hand to the small of her back. She jumped slightly, glancing guiltily over at the other couple when his long forefinger burrowed beneath her low-riding jeans and underwear. He began to slide it in and out of the crack of her ass while he pushed her subtly forward with his palm, giving her more friction on her clit as he rubbed it firmly. His finger dipping between her ass cheeks struck her as intensely erotic, but also forbidden. Naughty. Electric.

Especially here, in a restaurant.

"That's what I thought," he said next to her ear. "You're all cool and crisp professional on the outside, but this"—he palmed her entire outer sex with his big hand in a starkly possessive gesture—"burns white hot. Keep eating," he instructed when she dropped her fork and her eyes sprung wide at his illicit words. She picked up her fork and slid some tender whitefish into her mouth, squeezing out the juices while her entire attention was on Kam's moving lips and the sound of his rough, accented voice. "Next time, you will swallow it," he assured her in a whisper that sent ripples of pleasure down her spine. "Every . . . last . . . drop."

She shuddered in excitement.

"Eat some more, or you'll be hungry later," he murmured. She blinked. She'd stopped eating and just stared, becoming increasingly dazed and fevered as he rubbed her. Mechanically, she took a few more bites. He slid his long finger deeper into the crack of her ass. She jumped and went still when he skimmed it against her asshole.

"Did you like being restrained while I played with you?" he murmured before kissing the opening of her ear and applying a slight suction that made her tremble uncontrollably.

"Kam . . . let's go. Please. This is crazy," she whispered shakily.

"Answer me," he murmured as he rubbed her asshole with his fingertip and pressed with his palm, amplifying the pressure on her burning clit even more. Lin glanced around nervously. The couple in viewing distance were gathering their coats in preparation to leave. She bit her lip. Her clit simmered. It was exciting, having him touch her in such an intimate way.

Oh no. She was going to come. *Here.*

"Lin," he prodded darkly, his warm breath on her damp skin increasing her shivers.

"Yes. *Yes*, I liked it," she said brokenly.

"Yes. And you looked so beautiful, letting me have my way with you. I think we'll go back upstairs now," he mused. "I want my cock in you."

"Yes. Yes," she chanted, relieved and excited at once. She dropped her fork on her plate, growing mindless with excitement.

"But you will come first."

Heat flooded her cheeks. She felt dizzy. His fingers were ruthless.

"I don't think I should—"

"But you will," he said, his tone brooking no argument. His entire arm began to move as he stimulated her pussy more forcefully. She cried out in stunned arousal, but fortunately the other couple had just walked away. She placed her palms flat down on the table, bracing herself, and she began to shake in orgasm.

"That's right. *That's* the real Lin," he muttered thickly in her ear as pleasure shot through her in heady waves. "Hot. Sexy. Risk taker."

She tried to whisper "no" but another shudder of pleasure blasted through her. She swallowed the word. Why deny it, when the truth of his words quivered in every cell of her body? Apparently she *was* a hot, sexy risk taker.

With Kam she was, anyway.

When they were on the elevator, he forced himself not to look at her. Something had happened to him while he'd sat there and watched her climax in that restaurant. Whatever it was, he wasn't sure he liked it. He felt strangely off kilter. Out of control.

Her image had been burned in his mind. He didn't need to look directly at her now to remind himself—her cheeks and lips had grown rosy as he'd stimulated her, her lustrous eyes had turned even shinier than usual with arousal. He knew he'd never forget the vision of Lin setting her palms flat on the table and coming against his hand. It had been the most potent vision of surrender he'd ever seen. It'd driven him half-crazy with need. He'd shouted at the waiter when he saw him, startling the man, and demanded the check.

He'd managed to shove some chicken in his mouth during the short wait, knowing he'd need the energy, because yet another storm was about to hit.

It made him feel uncomfortable, the magnitude of his lust, but he couldn't seem to control it. This wasn't something easily walked away from. *Lin* wasn't.

He took her keys from her as they got off the elevator, and then grasped her hand, leading her down the hallway, neither of them speaking. He was eager, so much so that it seemed ridiculous to disguise it. The door flung inward at his urging, banging against the wall. Then he was pulling Lin over the threshold and slamming it shut behind them. She gave a surprised whimper when he swept down on her and covered her mouth with his own.

A haze overcame his consciousness as he absorbed her taste and the sensation of her tongue dueling with his. His hands made a greedy worship of her taut curves. Then he was lifting her to him and striding to the bedroom for the second time that evening. Was it just her physical beauty that drove him wild? He wondered dazedly as he set her at the edge of her bed and whipped off her shoes. Maybe. He'd already admitted to himself he'd never made love to a more beautiful woman. He peeled her out of her clinging jeans, revealing the smooth, pale harbor of her belly, round hips, and shapely thighs. He jerked down her panties. She lay back on the bed, spreading her legs slightly. He hissed a curse.

Who was he kidding, trying to figure it out? A man didn't require logic to want *that,* he thought, staring hungrily at her pussy. Kam certainly didn't.

He could tell by the arousing vision of her flushed, damp-looking outer sex that she didn't need any preparation. He jerked down his clothing and sheathed his erection with a condom.

He rolled her hips back by pushing on her shins, keeping her pussy at the edge of the bed. Still standing, he arrowed his cock into her slit. She gave a sweet, soughing sigh as he penetrated her. *Mon*

Dieu, it was good. He watched her with a narrow focus, knowing the tension in her face and the excitement in her eyes mirrored his own blatant arousal. When he'd pushed into her to the hilt, her muscular walls squeezing him, he paused. She was too small for him.

She was too perfect.

"You're going to be sore tomorrow, aren't you?" he mumbled.

"Maybe," she whispered urgently, reaching for his shoulders. Her fingernails dug into his back muscles. "But I'm not now. It feels so good. *Fuck me*."

He exhaled roughly, her harsh whisper, so *not* like her and yet so completely Lin-like at once. The paradox of her, the sweetness, tore through him. "Oh baby, you're going to get it for that," he assured roughly.

He came down over her, his weight pinning her knees to her chest, his hands digging into the mattress. It was heaven.

"God," he grated out, withdrawing his cock and then driving back into the glory of her. Again, he pumped, and again, both of them immediately finding their rhythm, the slap of their skin coming faster and faster a driving drumbeat neither could deny. The mattress began to hop up and down beneath them, the bedsprings making a squeaky protest. It filled his ears along with the sound of their smacking skin and Lin's surprised gasps and whimpers of pleasure.

He was doing it again, taking her like she was a damn rodeo ride. He gritted his teeth at the thought, but he couldn't stop. Her pussy rode his cock, not the other way around. He was big and strong and he was on top, driving into her slender, sleek body, but it was he who was helpless in the face of this relentless frenzy of need. He fucked her like he thought the answers to the questions of the universe were just a quarter of an inch higher in her tight, clasping depths and he was straining closer with every pass; hungry, searching . . .

He lost all sense of time, only feeling her holding him like he'd never been embraced.

He flexed his hips forcefully, slapping their bodies together. A cry popped out of her throat, but then he felt that telltale rush of heat and her muscles clamping him, adding fuel to his flames. He transferred his hands to the backs of her thighs and pushed, sending her knees down next to her ears. She straightened her legs as he continued to pump, her feet above both of their heads, demonstrating her flexible, strong muscles to optimal effect. His eyes sprung wide in disbelieving pleasure at the new angle she granted him. He fucked blindly, a madly racing, vibrating mass of electric nerves and flesh, striving and pushing and feeling . . .

. . . and feeling *more*, until he roared as pleasure crashed into him. He pressed his face against the side of Lin's neck, burying his nose and lips in her fragrant skin.

"God, I want to be naked inside you," he grated out against her throat almost angrily as he pumped and emptied himself inside the condom. It seemed indescribably unfair—ridiculously wrong—in that moment that even the thinnest of barriers should come between him and this woman.

"Do you want to talk about our meeting with Jason Klinf?" Lin murmured later as they embraced under the covers, growing increasingly relaxed as Kam massaged her neck and scalp. He really had the most amazing hands.

"Not really."

Lin lifted her head off his chest. He gave her a heavy-lidded smirk and pulled her higher on his body. Using his hold on her head, he brought her to him. She melted against him, submitting to his drugging kiss.

"I think it'd be a good idea," she said breathlessly against his mouth a moment later. "Just some basics about Klinf and Jason himself?"

His right eyebrow quirked upward. "I told you. I don't like being your work duty."

"Then do you want another Noble employee for the job?"

His lazy, satiated expression hardened. "Not a chance."

She rolled her eyes in exasperation. "Then you've got to focus at least a little. Look, I'm not a fan of mixing business with pleasure, either. In fact, I'm going against all my principles doing this with you."

He shut his eyes. Despite his impassive expression, she sensed his frustration and regretted it. Still . . . this was her job, and Lin did things *right*. Or at least she always had in the past. The realization hit her that if she wasn't screwing Kam like a feline in heat every chance she got, she might be a lot more prepared for these upcoming meetings than she was.

She sighed with genuine regret and forced herself to move away from his deliciously warm, hard body. Kam's touch was a logic evaporator. His jaw tightened when she extricated herself from it, but he didn't say anything or move. Pulling the sheet up snugly over her breasts, she settled on the pillow next to where his head rested.

"Jason Klinf is a very cultured, sophisticated man," she began.

"*Hourra*. Just my type," Kam muttered under his breath.

Ignoring him, she launched into a brief overview of Klinf Inc., hitting some crucial industry highlights.

Kam didn't move from his pose. It was a little distracting, talking business with him lying there with his naked, sculpted torso exposed, one hand lying casually over his head on the pillow, his taut, ridged abdomen falling up and down ever so subtly as he breathed evenly. Despite his negligent pose, however, she had the distinct impression he was listening closely to her.

"Klinf started his company on his own?" Kam interrupted her at one point.

"Yes," she said pausing. "It's a boutique business, a much smaller company than either Gersbach or Stunde, the company we'll be meeting with next Thursday. You and Jason have some things in common, actually," she said diplomatically.

He turned his head on the pillow, meeting her stare. "Such as?" he asked, looking slightly suspicious.

She kept her expression calm. He seemed to catch her sleight of hand with miraculous accuracy. In truth, she was more anxious about the meeting with Klinf than anyone. She was worried Kam's raw honesty and Jason's smooth sophistication would not be a good combination. "Well, Jason is French like you, for one. He's also brilliant. Plus, you two are close in age. Jason is probably only three or four years older than you."

"You just told me that he's a darling of the fashion industry, a connoisseur of opera, wine, rare antiquities and women. Except for both being heterosexual, I don't see that we have a bit in common."

She gave him a repressive glance and continued. "Jason designs all his timepieces himself."

"You mean he's invented some novel technology? I've never heard—"

"No," Lin interrupted him. "I mean that he designs the exterior, creating stunning watches that women across the globe would kill for. Each watch is handmade and exquisitely detailed. His watches are probably the most sought-after—and expensive—timepieces in the market."

"You wear one."

Lin blinked when she absorbed the tone of his voice. It'd sounded like an accusation. She met his sleety stare and found herself blushing. She wouldn't have guessed that Kam had noticed the diamond Klinf watch she wore last night, although she suspected the Gersbachs would. She knew from experience, however, that Brigit herself owned a Klinf, so she hadn't felt uncomfortable wearing it for the meeting. Jason's fashionable luxury watches were almost like a different product from the Swiss-made timepieces, like comparing an exquisite bracelet to a Rolex.

"I do own one, yes," she conceded.

"So you're one of the few women on the planet who not only would 'kill' for a Klinf watch, you actually have the money to buy one?"

"I didn't buy it," she said before she could stop herself.

He sat up and turned onto his side, his elbow on the pillow, his head braced in his hand, his steady stare pinning her. Lin suddenly felt like the star witness who had just faltered. Kam was like the prosecutor going in for the kill.

"Jason Klinf gave you one of his priceless watches?" Kam asked evenly.

"Yes," she said, giving him a sharp glare for making her feel like she'd just admitted to a crime.

"Did you date him?" he probed.

Lin gave a frustrated sigh. "I did, yes—a few times—but that has nothing to do with him giving me a watch. He did it as a courtesy following a technology exchange deal he did with Noble enterprises a couple of years back. What?" she demanded when she saw the hint of disdain cross Kam's bold features.

"Nothing. It just figures he'd have to buy his technology from Ian. So who broke it off? Klinf or you?"

"Neither of us, really. It just sort of . . . faded away. It wasn't like a blazing-comet romance or something. I wasn't that interested, and Jason isn't the type to settle down or anything. It was just two single people passing some time together pleasantly while he was here in town."

"Did you sleep with him?"

"*No*. Not that it's any of your business."

"According to you, it's precisely my business," he said calmly.

"I never—"

"You said I should be as prepared as I possibly can be for these meetings," he interrupted. "Don't you think any former relationship between two of the players, sexual or otherwise, is relevant to the situation?"

Her mouth fell open but her words stuck in her throat.

"Just tell me this," Kam continued, taking advantage of her speechless state. "Is Jason Klinf one of the guys that Ian mentioned who you were unfortunate to have dated? One of the guys who didn't appreciate your refinements and sensitivities or sensibilities, or however the hell he put it."

"What?" she sputtered. "No, of course . . . Ian *said* that?"

"Yeah. He seems to think that you're like a piece of fine porcelain that we men trample all over in our blind, savage stupidity."

At first she just stared at him incredulously before the ridiculousness of what he was saying struck her. She burst into laughter. The familiar thundercloud expression darkened Kam's face.

"What are you laughing about?" he demanded.

She tried to stop giggling, but only snorted. His scowl was priceless. She brushed her hand over his jaw, heartened to see her caress lighten his expression ever so slightly.

"It's just hilarious. Why would Ian say something so strange to you?" she asked, repressing her mirth with effort.

Kam scooted closer to her. One second, they'd been apart, and the next his solid male body was close, skimming and brushing against tingling patches of her skin. His movement erased her erupting amusement like nothing else could.

"You think it's strange, do you?" he murmured, a warning glint in his eyes, his face just inches from hers. His big hand opened at her lower back and lowered to her ass. He pushed her closer yet with a precise flex of his arm. She zipped across the sheets and thudded against his solid length. He paused, squeezing her buttock. Desire rippled through her when she felt his obvious response to their pressing naked bodies.

"Yes. Don't you?" she asked, her chin tilting up to bring his mouth into striking distance of her own.

He held her stare and shook his head slowly. "I think Ian's got a point. You certainly turn me into an animal."

A smile flickered across her lips. "I don't think that's what Ian meant."

"He meant I should be careful with you," Kam said distractedly. Even though the light was dim, she sensed his gaze drop to where her breasts pressed against his chest. "But it's just so *fucking* hard when all I want to do is . . . fuck you hard," he muttered before he kissed her—hot and toe curling—and Lin gave up entirely on making sense of their conversation. He lifted his head slightly a moment later. "I want you again," he stated the obvious, which throbbed against her thigh. "I know you're probably sore. I'm sorry. I'll try to be civilized."

She closed her eyes and moaned softly as he shaped one of her breasts to his palm.

"I don't want you civilized," she whispered before she pressed her lips to his and lost herself in Kam's wild, fierce heat.

Kam awoke in the early morning hours. Rather than being disoriented like he had been almost every day when he woke up in his claustrophobic hotel room, he knew precisely where he was. The scent from Lin's hair combined with the unmistakable fragrance of sex lingering in the air had pleasantly warned him even before he'd opened his eyes.

He'd left the bedroom door open when he rushed Lin in here earlier, laid her on the bed and ravaged her. A light was on in the hallway, the distant glow sufficient for him to see Lin's face on the pillow next to him. For a few seconds, he just studied her sublime beauty cast in shadow and pale gold. He recalled in vivid detail their last joining. She'd been on top, her face tight with pleasure, her breasts heaving, her round hips gyrating in a graceful, precise rhythm that had left him sweating. He'd finally taken control, driving her down on him until her cries had grown frantic and she'd shuddered around him, her bliss driving him straight over the edge with her.

So much for going easy on her. He knew very well she was tender from his forceful lovemaking, but he couldn't seem to stop this frenzy of need.

He waited for the urge to leave her bed to settle on him, studying her peaceful expression the whole time. It finally dawned him that the impulse wasn't coming. Instead, he wanted to pull her against him and join her in the warm, secure cocoon of deep sleep.

He stiffened at the realization. The only woman he'd ever regularly spent the night with had been Diana. Even with Diana, however, he'd sometimes awakened in the middle of the night feeling claustrophobic. Suffocated. He'd controlled the impulse to flee, however, knowing it wasn't appropriate with the woman he loved.

The Kam Reardon who had first arrived in London for college at seventeen, the awkward, brutish young man, had vanished, replaced by a well-groomed and cosmopolitan, if occasionally taciturn, cardiology resident with a brilliant future. The nearly ten years he'd spent in London had altered him beyond recognition. Many of the quirky mannerisms he'd acquired at Aurore Manor had to be willfully abandoned, strangled out of existence, or at best controlled. His brooding, harsh moods morphed into reserved, aloof ones. He'd believed in the rightness of his self-discipline of his more idiosyncratic, loner mannerisms until the day Diana had found out about his parentage and bizarre, inglorious upbringing. He'd believed until the day she'd fabricated a lie for him to give as a cover story to their affluent "friends." Until he'd stubbornly shoved his ragged, shameful past into her and her friends' faces, publically humiliating her—or so Diana had claimed.

Until she'd left him. Or he'd sacrificed Diana to his pride and left her. Kam had never really figured out which.

After that catastrophe, he hadn't even bothered to rein in his instinct for isolation. He'd been entranced by Diana's elegance and sophistication, her beautiful body and a face that could make a man like him crazed, it was so beyond his experience. He'd been hypnotized into sacrificing his freedom.

It suddenly struck him that the more refined Kam had recently made a reappearance since coming to Chicago. Yes, his cosmopolitan impression was less consistent than it had once been, and probably a hell of a lot less convincing. But he'd definitely been donning the once-familiar role again.

He'd been doing it because of Lin, and for no other reason.

"Kam?" Lin murmured a minute later as he pulled on his pants, her sleep-roughened voice in the darkness causing goose bumps to rise on his neck and arms.

"Yeah. Sorry. Didn't mean to wake you. I thought I should go. I'm moving over to the apartment in the morning."

"I'll send a driver to the hotel who can help you transport all your things," Lin said in a hushed voice.

"It's okay," he assured, whipping on his shirt and buttoning it rapidly. "I can carry it all, no problem. I'll take a cab." He hesitated next to the bed, now fully dressed. Her low, melodious voice, graceful arms and soft-looking form beneath body-warmed covers pulled at his consciousness.

"I'll see you at two o'clock?" he said, reaching for his discarded jacket.

"What?"

"At the new apartment," he reminded her, determinedly looking away from the appealing vision of her. "You said you'd be my test subject."

"Oh. Right. Okay," she said sleepily.

"Ian told me that you have a workout facility for the managers at Noble. Do you use it?"

"Yes," Lin said, sounding a little puzzled.

"Can you use it sometime before you come to the apartment tomorrow? I'll send over a sensor and some instructions. I'll need to get your resting and exercise heart rate and your blood pressure. This part of the protocol is pretty straightforward. Just use the instructions and then bring the sensor with you when you come. I'll extract the information from it. I'll send over a quick questionnaire about your general medical history, too."

"Sure. I'll just do my workout before work."

"Good. I'll see you this afternoon then." He started for the door. "Kam?"

He paused. "Yeah."

"Thank you for a nice night."

For some reason, discomfort swamped him. He didn't know what to say. He almost walked out the door without a word, but instead found himself taking two long strides back to the bedside. He leaned down and kissed her, at first hard, and then lingering.

Which made it all that much harder to walk away a moment later.

"Did you hear anything back from the courier service we hired to pick up Angus from the airport?" Lin asked Maria the next day after she'd finished her workout. She carried the surprisingly small sensor that Kam had delivered to her in order to gather data. He'd been right; using it had been straightforward and easy.

"Yes. The 'goods' are supposed to arrive at O'Hare at two forty-five this afternoon. Given the check-in time and evening traffic, Angus should be downtown by four thirty or so," the administrative assistant told her, smiling. "I actually wish I could be there to see Mr. Reardon's surprise. I got the impression from Phoebe Cane, the woman who was watching Angus, that they have quite a relationship."

"Kam and his dog?" Lin murmured, distracted.

"Well, now that I think of it . . . them, too."

Lin blinked, her gaze sharpening on Maria where she sat at her desk. The small hairs on her nape seemed to stand on end. She walked toward the other woman.

"What do you mean?"

Maria chuckled and shook her head, as if to say, *It's nothing of consequence.* It suddenly felt as if she'd swallowed lead. Lin smiled congenially, even though her lips felt stiff.

"Are you suggesting that Kam and this Phoebe woman are an . . . item?"

"She certainly asked a lot of personal questions about Mr. Reardon for your typical dog watcher," Maria responded with a significant glance.

"Well it's not too surprising, I suppose." Lin attempted to make light of the matter. "Kam's a very good-looking man. He's bound to get a lot of attention from the women in that village."

"Right," Maria said, turning to her computer.

Lin wavered in her heels. Something in Maria's tone told her there was more to the story. "What sort of things did this Phoebe woman say?" Lin asked, despising herself for not being able to just walk away and dismiss the whole thing.

"Oh, the usual things like, whether or not Kam seemed to be enjoying his stay in the States, when he was returning, and if he missed Angus and Aurore Manor."

"Anything not so typical?"

"Well," said Maria, turning and putting her elbows on the desk and leaning toward Lin in a confidential, girl-talk manner. "She did mention that Angus was having trouble sleeping and had run away on several occasions. Then Ms. Cane made a comment like, 'Angus is just like her master. I can't keep him in my bed for more than an hour or two before he gets restless and is running for the countryside as well.'"

"Oh, yes, I see what you mean," Lin said with a small laugh before she walked to her office and shut the door.

For a stretched minute, she just stared out the floor-to-ceiling windows with her back pressed to the closed door, her brain vibrating with tidbits of memory and the knowledge Maria had just casually imparted. She heard Kam's voice in her head.

I wouldn't have had sex with you last night if there were someone special.

But how significant was that? Just because he spent a couple of hours a week in this woman's—Phoebe's—bed didn't imply she was his girlfriend.

Or that you are.

A blush of mortification heated her cheek at the thought. What was she, an eleventh grader? Of course she wasn't Kam's *girlfriend*. She was a mature woman who was sharing a private, extremely gratifying sexual relationship with a very attractive single man. Why was she getting so shaken up about the idea of discovering he had a bedmate in France?

She vividly recalled awakening in the early morning and seeing his tall, large form standing in the shadows as he hastily pulled on his clothes. His nighttime exit hadn't really bothered her all that much at the time, and whatever doubts had started to creep in were quickly silenced by his searing kiss before he left.

The realization that this was typical behavior for Kam, that he was known for not staying in a woman's bed far beyond what it took for the essentials, shouldn't have caused that jolt of icy anxiety to go through her.

It shouldn't have, but it did.

Lin pushed herself off the door and approached her desk, tossing the sensor on the blotter. She knew from years of experience of coping with unrequited feelings that there was one rational way to silence her anxieties: work. She put on her glasses and hunkered down behind her desk, a detailed financial report in front of her.

Much to her chagrin, it was harder for her to rein her mind in today than it had ever been on any occasion when she was heartsore over Ian.

Chapter Ten

K am opened the door to his new temporary apartment at two that afternoon.

"Hello," he said, his gaze lowering over her in a manner Lin was determined to ignore.

"Hi."

His head lowered. She felt herself panicking. His lips brushed hers. He smelled so good. For a few seconds, her lips responded to his kiss without her giving them permission to do so. Something snapped like a whip inside her.

She abruptly shoved an envelope that held the sensor and the completed medical information sheet into his hand and walked past him.

"Any problems with the sensor?" he asked after a pause, even though he sounded a bit puzzled.

"No, it was simple to use, just like you said," Lin replied airily.

During the past several hours, she'd forced her anxieties into neat storage at the corners of her consciousness. She'd open the containers and rifle through the difficult contents when she felt more in control of her emotions. But one of Kam's deep kisses could easily rattle something loose and cause some real damage as it bounced dangerously around her brain.

"This is a great place. And only three floors away from Ian and Francesca," she said, walking into the spacious, luxurious living room that was furnished with a pleasing combination of substantial Asian antiques and modern, comfortable couches and chairs. She turned when she reached the center of the room.

"Yeah. Francesca already asked me to the penthouse for lunch."

She arched her eyebrows and gave him a cautious glance. She knew he might quickly feel claustrophobic if family members pushed themselves on him too greatly. It wasn't that Kam didn't like his new family—Lin thought he had in fact grown very fond of them. He just wasn't a fan of frequent attention and chitchat.

"And did you go?" she asked.

He shrugged as if the answer would be obvious. "Have you ever tasted Mrs. Hanson's cooking?" he asked, referring to Ian's longtime housekeeper.

"Yes, it's fabulous. I never turn down an offer for Mrs. Hanson's meals, either. Did you get all your things transferred over from the hotel all right?" she asked, her manner perfectly friendly. Lin was an expert at unruffled amiability.

He nodded, his gaze narrowing on her. He followed her into the living room. From her peripheral vision, she'd noticed that he looked rugged and extremely appealing wearing a pair of faded jeans and a steel-blue button-down shirt that made his gray eyes look especially light in comparison. If only she'd known, she would have bought him uglier clothing, she thought, disguising her spike of irritation at his potent good looks.

"Yeah, and I have all my equipment set up," he said, pointing at small mechanical device with various wires and electrodes set up on the coffee table. As she watched, Kam extricated the sensor he'd given her and plugged it into the device. One of the wires connected to a laptop computer sitting on the couch. Another computer was turned on, but wasn't attached to the compact machine.

"Great. We should probably get started," she said. She removed her coat and draped it on a chair. "I have a few things I need to get done before I go home and dress for our meeting tonight."

She noticed his expression stiffen. "We have to get all dressed up again?"

"Yes. I haven't had a chance to tell you, but I was able to get tickets for opening night at the opera. Jason is so excited. The opening night festivities begin at six, but we aren't due to meet Jason until six thirty. *Otello* will follow. We'll have a late dinner afterward to discuss business. You'll have to wear the tux we got you."

His expression flattened. Unwanted guilt swooped through her. God, she was a bitch. She'd made the change of plans just an hour ago, knowing perfectly well Kam would be uncomfortable with the alteration. And why had she done it? Because she'd experienced some petty jealousy over the discovery of his French lover? Or was it because she'd come to understand that casual affairs were commonplace to him?

You need him off balance, she told herself fairly. He was getting to her more than she liked. Look at what she'd let him do to her in that restaurant last night. If she needed no other proof of her vulnerability when it came to him, it was that. And it wasn't as if she hadn't explained to Kam that they'd be engaging in some activities that he'd find vaguely uncomfortable. That's why she was there, after all, to alleviate his disquietude.

"Right. Tux. Opening night. Your old boyfriend. Sounds like a load of laughs," he mumbled, flipping a couple of switches on the sleek little mechanism on the table.

"Jason isn't my old boyfriend," she said. "It was a very casual affair. You know the type."

He glanced over at her, his dark brows scrunched together, a puzzled scowl on his face.

"What's wrong?" he demanded abruptly.

"Nothing," she said, returning his puzzlement with a warm smile. "Are you ready to get started?"

He opened his mouth to respond and seemed to think better of whatever he was going to say. He pushed one more button and straightened. "Yeah. If you are. You'll just have to take off your clothes."

She laughed. He quirked his eyebrows in a wry expression.

"You're not serious. Are you?" she asked, her voice ringing with shock when he just waited expectantly.

"Of course I am. I need to attach the electrodes at all your pulse points to gather baseline data."

For a few pregnant seconds she just stood there, her mouth hanging open, all of her easy indifference evaporated. Dread crept into her awareness. She had a vivid memory of him grasping her wrist at Savaur that first night and her subsequent fear that he'd been aware of her anxiety. Her excitement.

He would read her like an open book with his machine.

She was out of her mind for having agreed to this. Nothing could have been more anxiety provoking to her in that moment than the idea of Kam Reardon getting inside and rifling through her interior world. Her secrets.

"Why can't I apply the electrodes myself? Isn't that what you plan for owners' of the watches?"

"Yes, but we don't have a test protocol yet for teaching the customer how to gather the data. Either myself or a trained medical professional should do it in the meantime in order to get accurate information."

"Surely you can just do it with my clothes on," she protested weakly.

He gave her a dry glance and picked up on of the nodes from the table. "I held you for most of the night while we were both naked. We had sex—a lot of it—just hours ago. I can't believe you're shy about taking off your clothes in front of me."

"Well I am," she said defensively before she could stop herself. "Did all your other test subjects have to be in front of you naked?"

"No," he stated bluntly. "My human subjects wore a medical gown. But I don't have one here." He exhaled, frowning when he noticed her defensive stance. "Are you going to tell me what's bothering you, or not?" he repeated.

"Nothing is bothering me," she lied. She cast about for an out for this impossible scenario, but came up with nothing. She was supposed to be assisting him in this project that Ian had arranged for him, and gathering data for a product demonstration was a major part of that. What's more, she'd agreed to it yesterday. If she backed out now, it'd highlight her vulnerability all the more.

"Fine. But I'm leaving on my bra and underwear."

"I can work around the bra, but you'll have to take off your underwear."

She gasped in disbelief at his matter-of-fact reply. His expression went hard as he studied her. Too late, she realized she was tipping her hand.

"Wrap a towel around yourself if you want," he said, his mouth hard. She understood his annoyance. Where was her modesty, after all, when she'd been shaking in orgasm in a public place beneath the forbidden magic of his stroking hands? "Guest bath, first door to the left," he said pointing the hallway. "Towels are under the sink."

She strode down the hallway, her backbone erect. She tried to hold her head up just as high when she returned to the living room a moment later, but it was hard to be regal and aloof while clutching a towel around her naked body.

"Come over here," Kam requested distractedly when she stood awkwardly in the center of the room. As she approached him, something Kam had said to her in the past sprung into her mind against her will.

What lengths would you go to in the name of service to Ian?

Apparently, monumental ones, she thought bitterly as she

allowed Kam to seat her on the couch next to the computer. Except she wasn't doing this for Ian. She was doing it for herself; proving to herself that she could handle Kam without turning and running like a scared fool.

Her hair was down today. She started when he dragged his long fingers through it, drawing it away from her face. Shivers made a web work of sensation just beneath her skin. She backed away an inch or two.

"What are you doing?" she demanded.

He looked down at her from his standing position, his hands still in her hair. In her sitting position before him, her face was less than a foot from the zipper of his jeans.

"I have to apply electrodes to your temporal and facial arteries. I'm just brushing your hair away from your face. Is that okay?" he asked, looking fierce.

"Of course," she said, feeling flustered and hating it. "Is this going to hurt?" she asked anxiously when he picked up a small electrode with a wire attached to it.

"Not at all," he said. "I'm just reading your body, not doing anything intrusive. Just try to relax."

Lin swallowed thickly as he ran two calloused fingertips over her right temple, finding her pulse. He peeled the paper off the back of the electrode and pressed it to her skin, his actions rapid and knowing. *Just reading your body. Not doing anything intrusive.* Funny, it felt very intrusive to her. Well, not intrusive, exactly, but alarmingly . . . . . . personal. Intimate.

"I didn't realize I had a pulse there," she mumbled, worried she'd disrupt the electrode he'd just placed on the right side of her chin just a fraction of an inch above her jaw.

"You have them all over your body," Kam said, his manner distracted as he picked up another electrode. His finger slid against her neck, and she repressed a shiver. He gently pressed an electrode to the pulse he easily found there. "You have especially defined ones. That's why I thought you'd be a good test subject."

"I do?" she asked, her amazement temporarily dulling her anxiety. "You noticed that when we were . . . together?"

"Yeah. You show your emotions extremely well. Put out your arm like this," he instructed, extending his arm so that his palm was faced upward.

"I disagree," she said a little cantankerously, following his instructions. "I'm always told by business associates that I've got a great poker face. Ian values the fact that I always appear calm, no matter what happens." *In control,* she added in her head, mostly because she felt the opposite of in control at the moment. "It helps in stressful business interactions."

"I'm not talking about your facial expressions," he said, his first two fingers running over her upper arm. The skin on the underside of her arms felt very tender and sensitive. Kam found what he wanted and attached an electrode. He repeated the process on the inner side of her forearm, his long fingers trailing something that she realized was a vein before he found what he wanted. "I'm talking about your physiological responses," he continued. "The signs are there . . . if a person knows how to read them, that is."

He knew how to read them. No one better.

Her heart fluttered when he took her palm in both of his hands, gently probing her wrist. It felt good. Her sex responded to his touch, heat rushing through her. The realization that her body could betray her so easily—so wholeheartedly—left her mute. She watched him in silent anxiety as he attached the electrode to her inner wrist. He glanced up with quicksilver eyes and caught her staring.

"Can you stand?" he requested.

She stood, her legs feeling like rubber. Maybe he'd known they would feel that way, and so had asked if something so simple was a major maneuver. He knelt before her, and her alarm increased. The sure knowledge that he would be able to read her anxiety—her arousal?—like he would a document on a computer left her panicked.

But Lin wasn't in the habit of running away. She was trapped by her stubbornness.

She stifled a gasp when he opened his hand at the back of her knee, again gently probing with knowing fingertips. He must feel the bumps that rose on her skin caused by his touch. It was strange, experiencing his expertise, his easy knowledge of the human body. Most people would never think to describe Kam Reardon as subtle; his manner and sexuality were so primal. Observing this deft, complex side of his personality left her feeling even more vulnerable.

But Kam had graduated from medical school, hadn't he? Even though his mother's illness and death prevented him from finishing his cardiology residency, he would have gone through countless clinical rotations at hospitals, not to mention the fact that he'd recently managed a large-scale trial of his biofeedback mechanism at a college in France. He probably thought nothing of a subject getting some involuntary goose bumps on their skin while he applied equipment, right?

Did those subjects and patients get as damp between their thighs as Lin was right now, though? Extremely doubtful. Surely they didn't become bizarrely *both* aroused and panicked at the idea of being trapped and exposed to Kam's knowing eyes . . . of being unwillingly excited by his touch.

She closed her eyes and focused on her breathing, recalling in detail a complicated dance movement that required exquisite control and attention to detail. By the time Kam had finished attaching an electrode to her calf and then her foot, she had calmed a little.

"The watch with the mechanism in it will only be able to gather data at the wrist pulse," Lin said as he stood. "Why are you bothering to take information from all these pulse sites?"

"If I gather baseline data for your entire body, in addition to the other information you provided from the sensor and from the questionnaire, I'll be able to use a logarithm I created that will make an automatic correction for the data at the wrist. A huge amount of data is collapsed into one measuring device that can accurately predict what's going on in the body from basic readings of temperature, blood pressure, heart rate, galvanic skin response, and a whole lot of other things. In many ways, that mathematical formula is the true key to the entire device," he said distractedly. She just stared, a little stunned by his casual brilliance. She blinked when she realized he was studying a lot of squiggly lines on his computer screen intently. "You just did something. What did you do?"

"I don't know what you mean."

"You just did something to calm yourself," he said, switching his gaze from the computer to her face. "What?"

Was it her imagination, or did one of those moving lines on the screen jump at his question? "I just . . . pictured a difficult dance sequence."

He nodded as if her explanation made perfect sense. "That's good. Do you think you can do that when we demonstrate it to the watchmakers? Exhibit a relaxation response at will?"

She blinked, horror striking her in a wave. He gave a lopsided grin as if he'd read her mind. "You'll only have on the wrist mechanism. Every stitch of clothing in place. I told you we're just gathering baseline data for you today," he murmured, his accented, deep voice the equivalent of a caress on her cheek.

"I think I probably could," Lin said dubiously. If she could calm her responses while standing nearly naked here in front of Kam as he probed her most hidden, subtle responses, surely she could do so fully clothed with only a wrist sensor.

"Good," he picked up the last electrode. "I have to move aside the towel now."

He stood in front of the computer screen so she couldn't see it, but she was quite sure all those various lines spiked a mile high at his words.

"Where?" she asked, meaning where was he going to place this incendiary electrode.

He held her gaze and answered by placing his fingertips on his jeans just to the left of his fly. Her eyes sprung wide. Things looked very full in his crotch area. He wasn't as immune to touching her as he'd led her to believe.

"There's not a pulse point there, is there?" she asked shakily.

He dropped his hand. "An extremely important one, on the femoral artery."

She nodded, her mouth too dry to speak. Still clutching the towel between her breasts, she tried to move aside the fabric in as modest a fashion as possible, but the wires on her arm made her clumsy. Her sex was still tender and sensitive from their intense love-making last night, but in that moment, the slightly abraded sensation only served to excite her more, increasing the tingling, tight feeling.

"I've got it," he assured gruffly, crouching so that his face was at the level of her pelvis. Lin stared out the windows on to an azure, sun-infused Lake Michigan, but saw little. Her awareness was all being used up on attending to the feeling of Kam's hand sweeping aside the fabric of the towel, exposing her naked hip. A flap of material still hung over her genitals, but she felt cool air against her pussy.

Cold against hot.

He moved his fingers over that sensitive, naked patch of skin just to the side of her pussy, searching for the artery. A wave of dizziness struck her. Or was it lust? She had a sudden, vivid image of him moving aside the flap of the towel and dipping his tongue between her labia. She recalled in perfect detail how expert he'd been at that particular skill as well.

Arousal stabbed at her. She barely stopped herself from moaning.

"Lin."

She opened her clamped eyelids with effort. He looked up at her, his face just inches from her pussy. His nostrils flared slightly.

"Are you sore? From last night?"

"A little," she admitted through numb lips. Had he been reading her mind?

He nodded. "I'm sorry."

"I'm as much to blame as you are," she said in a hushed tone.

He blinked as if coming out of a trance.

"Maybe you should think of the dance," he said so quietly, she almost thought she'd imagined what he said. How mortifying. He *knew*. He knew that her body was zinging with arousal. She shut her eyes. He knew what he was doing to her. He wasn't catching her scent, was he? she thought with rising panic.

Think of the dance. Despite her vulnerability in that moment, she valued his advice. Disciplining her mind and body had never before failed her. She pictured herself taking the subtle, difficult poses, heard the music . . . lost herself to it. She knew the moment when he attached the electrode so near her naked sex, but she'd bought a little distance for herself with her focus. Even when she felt the fabric of the towel fall back in place, she continued to meditate on the dance.

"You can sit down on the couch now. They're all attached." She opened her eyes. Kam stood before her. He put his hand on her free arm, guiding her down to a sitting position, mindful of the attached wires. She self-consciously arranged the towel, making sure she was modestly covered.

"What do we do now?" she asked him when he sat down on the couch, a cushion and the two computers between them.

"I'm going to show you some images on the computer and then ask you a series of questions. All of these things are designed to evoke emotional and physiological responses. Don't try to control yourself for this part." He told her pointedly. "That's very important. I'm going to ask you to evoke a relaxation response later, which fortunately, you seem to have a talent for. But don't relax now. Don't think. Just react to the stimuli. Okay?"

Lin nodded. At least he wasn't going to be touching her during the process. That was something.

For the next forty-five minutes, he showed her a series of photographs and short videos that were clearly designed to evoke a range of emotions from anxiety to outrage to fondness to fear. Afterward, he asked her a number of questions, some of which were boring and mundane, and some of which did everything from embarrass her to make her laugh to cause her to blush. It was anxiety provoking, yes, but she recognized the universality of the stimuli. They were meant for any human test subject, not just her. That knowledge went a long way to calm her panic.

"Okay. We're done with that part," Kam said, tapping his fingers on the computer screen a few times. "Now I want you to do what you did before to calm yourself. Focus on the dance and relax while I take some readings."

"Okay," she said, wondering if she could do again what she'd reached out blindly to do during a panic. As it turned out, she could do it even easier without high anxiety edging her consciousness.

"Good. That's it," Kam said after a moment, sounding distracted. She opened her eyes. He tapped his fingers on the screen. "We're done."

"Really?" she asked gratefully, focusing on him where he sat at the end of the couch, one of the computers balanced on a muscular thigh. She could see some russet highlights glinting in his dark, waving hair. A loose lock had fallen onto his forehead. *Sexy as the devil.*

"Yes. It wasn't that bad, was it?" he asked, his gaze sliding over to her.

Lin repressed her genuine answer, which was, *about a hundred times worse than having all my wisdom teeth removed in one afternoon.* "I guess not," she said.

"Are you going to tell me now what got you so uptight before you came here today?"

His tone was so mild, it took a second for his words—his intention—to sink in. When they did, she felt the electrode at her throat give a little leap. He watched her calmly, waiting.

"Did you ask me that when I was unprepared just to get an anxiety response out of me? To *probe* me? That's an unethical use of your invention!" she accused.

Holding her gaze, he turned the computer in his lap. The computer was shut down. Lin blushed in embarrassment.

"Do you really think I need to use a machine to figure out that something was irritating you? I knew it two seconds after you walked in the door. Now are you going to tell me what's got your knickers in a twist or not? What the hell did I do?"

Her breath caught in her lungs and burned. Slowly, she exhaled, striving to get control of herself. She began to remove the electrodes methodically from her face, arm, and leg. "Nothing," she said quietly after a tense moment. "You didn't do anything but be yourself."

"Oh, that's helpful information. So you're pissed off at something I can't change?" he asked, his frown deepening, his eyes narrowing. "Can you at least tell me what this irredeemable character flaw is?"

Lin yanked at that incendiary wire that disappeared beneath the towel. She was free to go now. Instead, she met his fiery stare across the several feet that separated them. Didn't he deserve to know the truth? But if she told him the truth about how she'd found out private information about Phoebe Cane, she'd have to explain about Angus. She still wanted Angus's arrival to be special for him.

As she looked into his piercing eyes, she again experienced that familiar heavy, warm sensation in her lower belly. Things felt *very* damp between her thighs.

"It's not a horrible character flaw," she finally replied honestly. Suddenly, she felt tired. "And I'm not mad at you. Not anymore. I'm going to go change," she said wearily.

"Wait a second," Kam called when she stood. He sounded angry. "Don't just cut me off like that."

"I'm not cutting you off," she said levelly, clutching the towel between her breasts. "Look, I'm sorry. Just forget about it, okay?"

He didn't reply when she walked out of the room, but she could feel his stare boring into her back. Frustration set her teeth on edge. She didn't want to fight with him. She didn't want to feel so vulnerable where he was concerned.

The truth was, she just *wanted* him. Period.

She retreated to the bathroom to change, grabbing her underwear and letting the towel drop to the tile floor. The bathroom was quite large, featuring a massive antique carved wood mirror over the sink and countertop. Clutching her panties, Lin studied her reflection closely. Her cheeks were flushed and her eyes looked bright. Of course Kam had been reading her like an open book. It wasn't even possible to fool that sharp, quicksilver gaze of his.

She wasn't really surprised when he called her name and rapped once on the door.

"Yes?" she asked, frozen to the spot, every nerve in her body leaping to life.

The bathroom door clicked open. He met her gaze in the bathroom mirror, his expression hard and unreadable, his eyes gleaming. She felt pinned by his stare, unable to move. Unable to breathe. He stepped behind her. She was naked, save her bra. She felt the fabric of his shirt brush against her back and the fly of his jeans skim against the sensitive patch of skin at the very base of her spine. Hard, denim-covered thighs touched her bare ass.

He silently brushed her long hair over one shoulder, exposing the skin of her back. He slid one hand beneath her hair, settling his large hands on her naked shoulders. Her nipples prickled in awareness at his touch.

"I found out that you have a lover in France," she explained quietly. It hadn't been his touch that had popped the truth out of her lungs, but his scoring, inescapable gaze. His hands tightened slightly on her shoulders.

"What are you talking about?" he demanded after a stunned pause.

"Phoebe Cane. Isn't that her name?" Lin said in a hushed tone. "I realize I have no right to be angry about it. In fact, anything I felt when I first found out has faded now. You don't have anything to worry about. I just thought you deserved to know why I was acting . . ." She faded off, unable to find the right word for how she'd been acting, although *like a fool* popped into her brain after a second.

"Hold on," he growled, his nostrils flaring, his gaze narrowing on her through the mirror. "How do you know who Phoebe Cane is? Have you been talking to Ian about that time he walked in on us at Aurore?"

Lin blanched. "No. Of course not. Ian walked in on Phoebe and you?"

Kam's mouth went hard. Lin thought of turning around and studying his face, but his reflection seemed easier to face somehow. Not safe, just *safer*.

"Not on purpose," Kam eventually said. "And not just Phoebe and I. Phoebe and I . . . and one of her friends, Eloise," he admitted bluntly.

Heat rushed through her face and chest in the silence that followed. Wonderful. This was even worse than she'd suspected. "You have *two* lovers in France?" she asked after a moment. "You're . . . uh . . . involved in a ménage à trois?"

"No," he insisted with quiet scorn. "I'm not *involved* in anything. I only saw Eloise that one time. She was visiting Phoebe from Germany. They pounced on me at Aurore one night with a case of beer. They'd been out partying earlier, and I was some kind of girls-night-out bet. We were just having a good time. Ian accidentally interrupted us, and took it as proof that I'm a sex-starved degenerate. Like he lived his life like an altar boy before he met Francesca," he added derisively under his breath.

"I see," Lin said hollowly. "But Phoebe doesn't live far away. She's in the village, isn't that right?"

His face looked as hard as carved rock in the reflection in the mirror. His thumbs moved on her shoulders.

"Listen to me," he said quietly. "I am not involved in a relationship with Phoebe Cane. If you want me to profess to being celibate, I can't. But that doesn't mean I haven't been honest with you. Yes. Phoebe lives in the village, and we've been known to get together on and off over the years. We've also both seen other people. Neither one of us is perfect, but at least we're honest with each other about what we're doing."

"About the fact that you just want sex from each other," Lin said in a hushed voice.

His eyes glittered. "Yeah. About the fact that we just want sex from each other."

"She sounds very eager for you to return."

"Why in the hell have you been *talking* to her?" he demanded, an incredulous expression spreading on his features. "Don't tell me you've been doing more *research* for Ian."

"No. It's nothing like that. And I haven't been speaking with Phoebe, not directly. Maria, one of our admins, speaks French much better than I do," she said.

He did a small double take. Belatedly, she realized she was smiling. Could this situation be any odder? She was standing here nearly stark naked talking to Kam about his love affairs through a mirror. Strangely, she had no wild urge to cover herself. It was like a spell of honesty had come over her following her former unsuccessful subterfuge. There was something about Kam that just *inspired* honesty.

"We had a legitimate reason to get into contact with Phoebe," she said softly. "It has nothing to do with spying on you. It was Ian's idea, and his intentions were very good."

"Tell me," Kam demanded.

"No."

His eyebrows shot up at her firm refusal. Her small smile widened as a storm cloud crossed his bold features. "If it's got to do with Phoebe, it must have to do with Angus. There's no other good reason for you all to be contacting Phoebe. Is my dog all right?"

"As far as I know, Angus is doing very well." He gave her a fierce look that she perfectly read as *Well then, what's the problem?*

"It's a surprise. And you'll find out soon enough, so don't badger me to tell you." For a few taut seconds, his expression darkened. She raised her eyebrows in a cool challenge. Triumph soared through her when she saw his irritation melt. Her smugness was short lived, however. Her breath hitched when Kam's hands slid lower. Had she forgotten she was standing in front of him wearing only a bra? No, it wasn't that she'd forgotten. She'd been electrically aware of the fact the whole time. Being naked in front of him made her feel . . . not *comfortable* exactly. She was too excited for that. But it did feel *right*.

He molded her upper arms into his palms.

"So Phoebe isn't a serious thing," she said softly. "Has there ever been? Anyone serious?"

"Why?" he asked, his gaze dipping over her image in the mirror. Her nipples tightened into hard crests behind the fabric of her black silk bra.

"Because I'm curious about you," Lin replied without a trace of defensiveness. His stare flicked from her belly to her hips, lingering on her pussy, before it returned to her face. How did just one of his glances set a spark to her blood?

"There was a woman named Diana," he rasped. "In London. For almost four years."

"Did you love her?"

For a few seconds, she thought he wasn't going to respond.

"I thought I did. And she thought she loved me. Turned out, we were both in love with somebody that wasn't really there."

Lin nodded in silent understanding.

He stepped an inch closer so that she felt his hard torso through the fabric of his shirt and his fly bumped against her tailbone. She inhaled the smell of soap and male skin and something else.

Arousal.

"What about you?" he asked, his deep, rough voice a scraping caress on her neck.

"Have I ever been in love?" Lin clarified.

He nodded. Their gazes clung. He slid two fingers up the slope of her shoulder and pressed them gently against her thrumming pulse in a quiet challenge.

"Yes," she replied.

"And? What happened?"

"Nothing. Absolutely nothing," she whispered. "He was someone else's, never mine."

The words seemed to hang in the air between them. Her panties fell to the floor as she reached for his hand with both of hers. She lifted it from her pulse and pressed her mouth to his palm, holding his stare in the mirror the whole time. He flexed his hips ever so slightly, letting her feel his arousal at her gesture.

"Do you suppose this is some kind of magical, truth-telling mirror?" she asked him, smiling.

His hands drifted to the outside of her ribs. He moved them downward, detailing the shape of her waist and hips. She felt his cock stiffen against her skin, and a thrill went through her, the sure knowledge that she pleased him. He lowered his head and nuzzled her temple. "If it is, I've got nothing to hide," he said, his deep voice roughening the skin on her neck. One large hand swept between her thighs, cupping her sex. She exhaled shakily and tilted her head back on his chest. He met her stare.

"Can you say the same, Lin?" he rasped.

Chapter Eleven

He'd turned the tables on her so effortlessly.

"Oh," she sighed when he worked the ridge of his forefinger between her sex lips, rubbing and agitating the sensitive flesh there. She could tell from his easy glide she was very wet. All the arousal and tension she'd been experiencing since Kam had touched her body earlier as he gathered data erupted from a simmer to a burn.

"Answer me," he urged, even as the movements of his lips on her neck and his relentless finger made focus nearly impossible. He grabbed a bare buttock and squeezed it lasciviously, still stimulating her clit. "Is *this* what you want from me? What you need?"

She gasped when he released her ass cheek and spanked it firmly. Once. Twice. Her eyelids flew open. The smacking sound of flesh against flesh seemed to echo in her ears. He stared at her in the mirror, one hand buried between her thighs, the other cupping her ass. His cock had turned steel hard where it pressed against the base of her spine.

"If that's what you're offering. Yes," she replied.

He opened a hand on her belly and pushed her against him. "I'm offering, all right," he muttered before he bent and took a bite from her neck.

It was all he was offering. She knew this, but she didn't care. Not in that moment, she didn't. She gasped and shivered, instinctively squirming her body against his arousal. He cursed softly and swatted her ass again, the cracking sound exciting her further. She made a sound of misery when he lifted his hand from her pussy, but he shushed her quietly. He grabbed her wrists and placed her hands on the granite counter top.

"Bend over and stay still," he ordered darkly.

She took the position, watching him avidly in the large mirror as he bent down over her, continuing to sample the skin of her shoulders and back. His hands bracketed her hips, making a sensual circling motion. He scraped his teeth against her spine and cupped her bottom in both hands.

"Sweetest ass I've ever seen," he murmured distractedly. She moaned when he took a tender bite at the side of her ribs. He squeezed her bottom lewdly, ratcheting up her excitement. His hand shifted, cupping both ass cheeks at once from below, encompassing so much of her with his hold.

"Kam," she whimpered when he sent a long finger into her slit from behind. It felt wonderful. She wriggled her hips, trying to increase the stimulation. He dropped behind her. She couldn't see him in the mirror, but she felt his warm breath against a buttock. She gasped at the sensation of his whiskers abrading the tender skin of her ass, his firm lips pressing. He kissed and bit at the flesh exploring her, his manner somehow both gentle and greedy at once. She bit her lip, a moan vibrating in her throat. After making a quick meal of her ass, he stood again behind her and popped a buttock again with his free hand, sending a finger high into her slit. She made a surprised sound in her throat. Her muscles tightened around his thrusting finger.

"Look at me," he said.

Her gaze flew up to meet his in the mirror. *"Je te veux tellement."* She understood French better than she spoke it, but even if she hadn't comprehended his words, she would have seen the sharp truth in his blazing eyes. *I want you so much.*

He continued to finger-fuck her, this time more strenuously, his entire arm moving. Her mouth fell open when the wet sound of him moving in her flesh hit her ears.

"That's right. So wet. So tight." He lifted his free hand and spanked her bottom again. "Does that make you hotter?" he asked, almost as if to himself, as if he was running a little experiment. She bit her lower lip helplessly. He swatted her again. It didn't hurt, but it tingled and burned beneath his hand. And something about his deliberate spanks as he watched her left her speechless with arousal.

"You're not going to tell me with your mouth? It doesn't matter. I can feel the truth. Oh yeah," he muttered, sounding satisfied. "You're getting even wetter. Hotter." He spanked her again, pausing to shape a buttock to his big hand. "Nice and hot. Everywhere," he added thickly, his gaze dropping to her ass. "Little kitten likes a good spanking."

She quaked and moaned. One of his fingers slid between her labia, rubbing her slick clit. He spanked her again and she shut her eyes at the illicit, erotic beauty of him in the mirror.

Of them.

She suddenly felt his fingers slip beneath her bra strap, and it sprung open. Kam hastily shoved the bra down her arms. She tried to lift her hands to get the garment off her wrists, but he muttered, "Don't move. Just leave it."

He pushed closer suddenly, both of his hands firmly holding her hips in place. He pressed his thighs and crotch against her. She could clearly feel the outline of his erection pulsing against her lower back. He held her in place. It was a salacious pose, unapologetically so. He slid his hands up her nude body, keeping her pressed tight against his hard thighs and throbbing cock, and took both of her bare breasts in his hands.

"Lean up a few inches," he commanded. She straightened slightly, so that she was still bent at the waist and leaning over, but granting both of them a view in the mirror.

For a lung-burning moment, he massaged her breasts in his hands, pinching lightly at the nipples, his flagrant arousal resonating into her skin. She couldn't unglue her gaze from the vision of his big hands on her breasts, his skin so much darker than the pale globes he shaped and molded to his palms. Both of them watched his movements avidly. He squeezed both nipples between his thumb and forefinger, pinching them subtly, forcing them into further pronouncement. He lifted both breasts and jiggled the taut flesh, catching it again in his cupping hands. She made a wild, helpless sound in her throat. The next thing she knew, he was lifting her. She started in surprise.

"Wha—"

"Shh," he soothed. "Put your knees up on the counter and lean forward, that's right. Put your forearms against the mirror and brace yourself. It'll be okay. It's mounted securely, I checked it earlier because it's so large, and I was curious how they'd attached it. That thing isn't moving."

She did what he said. She hardly recognized the naked, wanton woman in the mirror. The reflection of her face was only inches away. Her skin looked dewy and flushed, her eyes enormous, her thrusting breasts heaving in excitement. Her eyes widened even more when she felt Kam part her buttocks and lean down.

"Oh my" spilled shakily out of her throat when he matter-of-factly spread her labia as well and slid his tongue onto her clit. Her expression tightened as if she were in pain, but it was the direct opposite. His agile tongue and firm lips conferred the most distilled form of pleasure. His depthless confidence was again in full evidence. He knew exactly what he was doing in this manner of lovemaking and wasn't afraid to show it. It was unprecedented in her experience. Nothing compared. Her clit sizzled beneath his agitating tongue. She no longer knew what she stared at in the mirror just inches from her face. Every nerve cell in her body was lit up with electricity, sparking and firing.

He spread her buttocks and outer sex wider, pressing more firmly to her. Again, she had that feeling of being split wide open beneath the onslaught of him, exposed . . .

. . . exquisitely desired.

His head moved back and forth as he lashed at her and simultaneously provided a firm, gentle suction. Her clit sizzled under his ruthless tongue. His obvious hunger battered at her awareness, unceasing and ruthless.

She cried out sharply moments later as orgasm slammed into her. He continued to eat her, his zeal never relenting. In fact, her pleasure seemed to amplify his ardor, as if he could actually swallow her bliss, and did so greedily.

Lin's head sagged beneath her bracing forearms, her ragged breathing causing a patch of appearing and disappearing vapor on the surface of the mirror. She was vaguely aware of Kam rising behind her, a giant, awesome male presence. His arms wrapped around her waist and he lifted her. She whimpered.

"Shhh, *mon petit chaton*," he soothed, even though his own voice was rough and thick with arousal. "Bend over the counter and brace yourself. I will have my pleasure of you now."

He swatted her bottom firmly, the swift spank like a miniature electric jolt to her satiated brain. She bent over the counter as he'd instructed, exposing her ass and pussy. She saw him fumbling with and jerking at his clothing behind her. *I will have my pleasure of you now*. Her sex clenched tight in excitement. He was going to push that beautiful, big cock into her, stretch her, make her take it all again and again . . .

He didn't fuck her immediately, however. Instead, he spanked her bottom several more times with a taut palm, creating arousing cracks to echo off the bathroom walls. Lin gasped, stunned at how the burn on her ass cheeks so quickly transferred to her clit, making it simmer in sympathy. She stared at Kam in the mirror, spellbound by the vision of his tight features as he squeezed an ass cheek and then spanked her again.

"Ooh" popped out of her throat. He glanced up at her with a white-hot gleam in his eyes. Holding her stare in the mirror, he swatted the underside of a buttock briskly, then paused to rub and soothe the punished flesh.

"Is this honest enough for you, Lin?"

"Yes," she hissed through clenched teeth.

"I'm going to show you more honesty," he assured. He reached around her and pumped several times at one of two bottles that sat side by side on the sink. She caught a whiff of a fruity scent and realized it was a hand lotion placed there to use following washing. Suddenly he was moving his hand back and forth between his legs. She went still, arousal spiking through just as hot and potent as it had before. He was rubbing the lotion on his cock, lubing it. She couldn't see the full image of him because her own body blocked it in the mirror.

He put a hand on her rib cage, halting her when she strained to watch him. She gave a frustrated cry. What sane woman wouldn't want to view such an exciting vision of Kam rubbing lubrication on his cock? He seemed determined to deny her the treat, however.

"Put your forearms on the counter and rest your forehead on top of them," he instructed gruffly. She hesitated, meeting his stare in the mirror. In that position, she would be fully denied the erotic image of him. It was the equivalent of blindfolding her. And what was he going to do? He'd lubricated himself with the lotion. Her heart began to pound very fast. He wasn't going to—

"I told you I would have my pleasure of you, and I will. But I know you said you were a little sore still," he murmured, low and seductive, interrupting her anxious excitement. Again, she saw his arm moving as he jacked himself slowly and deliberately while he watched her. She bit her lip to cut off a whimper. Why did those words arouse her so much? "Do you trust me?"

"Yes, but . . ."

"This isn't the kind of lubrication that should be used for that. I'm not going to do that. Not now," he added baldly, and she realized he'd read her anxiety about him putting his cock into her ass. Heat rushed into her cheeks. A small smile pulled at his lips, and Lin felt herself melting. *Oh no.* What was happening to her?

"Now, take the position," he dared quietly.

She lowered her head, but slowly, giving her time to see the slight snarl that pulled at his lips when she followed his instructions.

"You have the most incredible eyes," she heard him say before she placed her forehead on her forearm, blinding herself from him.

He spanked her bottom several times, making her skin prickle and heat. "Let's make this ass nice and hot," she heard him say thickly. He parted the cheeks and she felt the cool air tickle her wet pussy, perineum, and asshole. Her eyes sprung wide as she stared blindly down at the specks in the granite countertop. He grunted, low and harsh. Then he was swatting her again, this time getting at the tender, hidden skin deeper in the crack.

"Kam," she cried shakily, undone by the intimacy of what he was doing.

"Shhh, try to relax. I'm not going to hurt you, and you will be giving me so much pleasure. You'd like that, wouldn't you?"

"Yes," she assured fiercely. A shudder went through her when she felt his heavy, warm cock drop into the widened crack of her ass. She could feel the lubricated shaft pulse next to her sensitive asshole. She clamped her eyelids shut. How much more of this intensely intimate touching could she take? A whimper escaped her constricted lungs when he used his hands to bunch her buttocks around his burrowed cock. He flexed, his harsh groan of pleasure tearing right through her.

"Oh yeah, that's good," he grated out as he dragged his cock down through the valley of flesh he'd created between her buttocks. He immediately pushed it back again, the lotion providing an easy glide, until she felt his balls press tight against her lower bottom. For several tense moments, he thrust back and forth between the crack of her ass, squeezing her buttocks around his cock as he fucked her flesh in a pistonlike fashion. She didn't mean to make a sound—she was too busy focusing her entire attention on the illicit sensation of his fat cockhead burrowing up between her ass cheeks and rubbing against her spine—but apparently a shaky moan escaped from her throat. He paused, still clutching her buttocks around his cock.

"I know this can't be giving you any pleasure," he muttered, his voice sounding thick, his breathing erratic. "But it feels so good. I'm not trying to humiliate you, though. Do you want me to stop?"

"No," she said, biting her lip when she realized how emphatic she'd sounded. She squeezed her eyelids shut, suddenly glad he'd told her to put her head down. "It's not humiliating. It's . . ."

"What?" he demanded tautly, and she could easily imagine his intense expression in that moment, the one he got when he caught the whiff of something being withheld and went in for the kill.

"Turning me on."

He groaned gutturally at her shaky admission and immediately began plunging his cock between her squeezed buttocks again. His thrusts became more forceful and strident, the sound of his pelvis thumping against her ass synchronizing with Lin's heartbeat in her ears. Her pussy clamped tight, growing achy. Needy. She longed to feel him thrusting so eagerly into her sex . . . her mouth . . . anywhere. But it was a sweetness unlike anything she'd known before to have her body giving him such a hot, forbidden pleasure, to hear his feral grunts and moans. Even if she wasn't sharing in the sharpness of his bliss, she loved being a part of it . . .

. . . being used for it, but used willingly.

And she'd be lying if she said there was no direct pleasure in it for her. Especially as his excitement grew and his cock swelled even larger in the pocket of pressing flesh he'd formed for himself, she could intimately feel him rubbing against the sensitive, usually untouched flesh of her perineum and asshole. She was surprised at how many nerves were there, and found the stimulation very sharp and arousing. She made a desperate sound and cut it off by biting at her forearm.

"What? Do you like my cock rubbing against your asshole?" he rasped, never stopping in his rapid thrusting.

"Yes," she moaned.

"How could I have ever thought you were cold?" he grated out, sounding a little crazed. His pelvis popped against her bottom so hard, she lurched forward slightly, her forehead sliding off her arm. He jerked his hips back several inches, dragging his cockhead back to where it nestled at the top of her crack. He squeezed her buttocks so tight around his cock, she winced. "You're such a hot little thing," he muttered tensely, pulsing his hips back and forth rapidly just a fraction of an inch.

He shouted. Lin's eyes sprung wide at the sensation of warm semen shooting against the base of her spine. Kam's shout segued to a guttural growl as he continued to slide his cock in very short strokes back and forth between her buttocks.

He leaned forward toward her ear, still clutching her bottom as he ejaculated. "The next time, I'm going to be inside your little ass when I come. You won't be able to keep any secrets from me then, will you?"

Lin clenched her eyes shut, overwhelmed by the sound of his dark, intense declaration and the sensation of him still coming next to her spine, the warm fluid pooling at the top of her ass. Their heated exchange had been, by far, the most intimate, not to mention scalding, sexual experience she'd ever had. The truth alarmed her.

But unfortunately, that didn't make it any less true.

A moment later, she leaned up slightly and watched Kam in the mirror as he slid his cock out, still pinching her buttocks together with one strong hand. He reached with a long arm and snagged some tissues, mopping her dry before he released his snug hold on her. In the mirror, she could see his light eyes contrasted with his sex-flushed, perspiration-glazed features. His pants and underwear were gathered around his lower thighs. She remained still, allowing him to dampen a washcloth and clean his residue from her skin, but then she stood. What they'd done before—what she'd allowed him to do to her—had been outrageously illicit. His gentle cleaning of her felt no less personal, but also sweet. Poignant. It was unbearable somehow.

She hastily reached for the towel she'd dropped earlier. Her abrupt action seemed to startle him. She didn't meet his gaze until she'd covered herself.

"Why are you convinced that I'm keeping something from you?" she asked, coaching herself the entire time not to look down and gawk at the sight of his damp cock suspended between his thighs, firm and flushed despite his recent climax.

His mouth dropped open in surprise at her question. He seemed to gather himself after a moment and flung the washcloth he held in the sink. He jerked up his underwear.

"You're one of the most controlled people I've ever met," he answered bluntly. "But I still think you'd prefer to contain yourself with me even more than usual. Am I right? Are you? Keeping secrets?" he pressed, pulling up his jeans.

"What makes you say that?" she demanded, her voice going up a decibel. What precisely was he saying? How much did he really guess?

He glanced up from buttoning his fly. "Aside from the fact that you told me earlier you were keeping something from me about Phoebe?"

She bristled and turned to the sink, beginning to wash her hands. "You were the one keeping something from *me* about that."

"I told you. Phoebe and I are *not* an item. I thought you believed me before," he said, sounding slightly suspicious. In the mirror, she saw his dark eyebrows slant. Her discomfort ratcheted up a notch when she saw the dangerous glint in his eyes. "You *did* believe me. You're just saying this now to throw me off course."

She jumped when the house phone rang shrilly. He didn't move, just continued to study her furiously beneath a lowered brow.

"We should get that," Lin said levelly, drying off her hands. "It's probably the doorman calling about Angus."

"Angus?" he nearly shouted, nostrils flaring.

Lin neatly refolded the hand towel and rehung it. She turned to him. "Yes. Ian asked us to arrange to have Angus flown here to keep you company. That's my deep dark secret. Never mind, I'll go get the phone."

She walked past a dumbstruck Kam.

She couldn't keep this charade up much more. Her dishonesty with Kam seemed to cause something in her stomach to curdle.

But *was* she being dishonest? She was betraying no one in carrying on with Kam, except for perhaps herself. Ian didn't return her feelings; he didn't even know she had any beyond employer loyalty and friendship. Which brought up another crucial question.

How *did* she feel about Ian these days? It seemed impossible to focus on the question with Kam eclipsing almost her entire awareness.

Chapter Twelve

Lin had no sooner answered the phone when a brisk knock came at the door. She hung up and turned to Kam.

"The courier was already on the way up when the doorman called. Ian had warned him about Angus's arrival," she told him. "I'll just wait in the dining room," she said, since she was still wearing the towel she'd wrapped herself moments ago.

"I was wondering why all that dog food was in the pantry. I thought the previous owner had a dog," Kam said.

Lin just grinned and walked away.

Angus arrived like a furry rocket. As soon as the halter collar was released, she practically brought Kam to the floor with a tackle. He managed to calm her down sufficiently after a few rubs and pats to give the courier a healthy tip and shut the door. Then Angus's paws were up on his shoulders and she was giving his nose a tongue bath between excited barks.

Kam scolded her, laughing uncontrollably the whole time, turning his chin to avoid her tongue. When he opened them, he saw Lin standing in the living room, watching the joyful reunion with a sublime smile on her face.

"You've got good reason to look so smug," he muttered gruffly as he pushed Angus off him, giving the dog some hearty rubs and scratches. "I missed the beast."

"I'm not smug. I'm just glad that you're happy," Lin said, transferring her gaze to the golden retriever. "Hi, Angus. I'm Lin," she said, clapping her hands invitingly in front of her. "Did you have a good trip, girl? Are you happy to see Kam?"

Angus pranced over to her, pausing to spin in an excited circle. Lin laughed—a clear, uninhibited, sweet sound.

"She's a shameless showoff," Kam warned, but he couldn't keep the warmth out of his voice. He was glad to see his dog, no denying it. Angus wiggled around happily as Lin scratched and stroked her, and then bounded back over to Kam.

One thing about Angus, it was almost impossible to be aloof or reserved around her. People always seemed to show their true colors around Kam's rambunctious, friendly dog. She was usually frisky, but she was downright hyper after being penned up on a plane and then on the car ride downtown. He'd never heard Lin laugh so irrepressibly or smile so big as she petted and sported with his dog.

It was a damn appealing sight.

Seeing her carefree playfulness and happiness with Angus left Kam greedy for more of the uninhibited Lin. Why was she always so careful and reserved? Part of it had to do with her upbringing, he understood. Her grandmother had drilled contained, polished elegance into Lin from an early age. But there was something more to it, Kam was sure. She was cautious around *him*. The only time she wasn't holding back was when she abandoned herself to sensation and pleasure during sex.

That made him crave her surrender even more than he normally would. The memories of her submission to her desire earlier, of her admission of her arousal at giving *him* pleasure, even when it was denied to her, would undoubtedly plague him for years to come.

Angus served as a great icebreaker between them for a few minutes, but then the dog had gone and overdone it. While Angus and Lin tussled, the dog inadvertently tugged on the towel she wore. It slithered onto the carpet. Kam had a quick glimpse of shapely long limbs, thrusting breasts, and a pale, smooth belly before Lin scurried to retrieve the towel. She wrapped it around herself while Kam scolded Angus.

"Sorry about that," Kam said.

"It's okay. I need to get going, anyway. I need to check in on a friend before I start to get ready for tonight." He saw the color in her cheeks as she hurried out of the room to change.

"Bloody nuisance," Kam accused his dog as he fondly ruffled the hair on an unrepentant Angus's neck.

Lin returned a few minutes later wearing the black pants, high heels, and belted blouse she'd arrived in, looking so crisp, efficient, and untouchable that the memory of her perched naked up on the counter earlier, her eyes shining with lust in the mirror, seemed downright implausible to Kam. The only concession he had as she gave him his opera ticket and quick instructions on where they should meet was that laughter still clung to her lush, pink lips and shone in her dark eyes. Kam was about to breach the barrier and melt her reserve with a kiss—and damn her cool efficiency—when the doorbell rang again. It was Francesca, excited to see if Angus had arrived safely. Lin had made her escape while he made sure Angus didn't jump on his pregnant sister-in-law.

All he was left with was the promise that he'd see her again tonight.

Lin withdrew her gown from the closet and hung it on a hook, giving it a quick once-over. She hastily chose a pair of heels and a matching clutch from her walk-in, and set them on her dresser. She was headed toward the front door, when the doorbell rang.

"Hi! How are you feeling? I was just on my way out the door to go see if you needed anything," she told Richard when she saw him standing in the hallway. She stepped aside and waved for him to enter. "You look awful."

"Stop with the flattery," Richard croaked, reaching inside the box of tissues he carried. "I'm convinced I have a new form of the plague, but the doctor insists it's just the flu. How can a three-letter word equate to so much misery?"

Lin's face collapsed with sympathy. He really did look awful. She touched his forehead.

"You feel a little feverish. Have you taken something for it?"

"The entire pharmacy counter, it feels like."

"What you need is for someone to cook you a nice meal and wait on you hand and foot. Emile is too busy doing everything at the restaurant." She hesitated, thinking. She couldn't really afford to reschedule a meeting between Kam and Jason Klinf, but she doubted Kam would mind not going to the opera. "How about if I cancel my plans for tonight and cook up some hot-and-sour chicken soup— my mother's recipe? That'd cut through all that congestion."

Richard groaned. "I *love* that soup. But your mother's genius would be wasted on me. I can't taste a thing. That's very sweet of you, but nothing is going to help me but time. I just came over to get another box of tissues. I'm going through them by the gross." Lin nodded and waved him back to her bedroom. "So what *are* the plans for tonight?" Richard asked, plopping at the bottom of her bed while she retrieved several boxes of tissue from a closet in the bathroom.

"Opening night at the Civic," Lin said, returning with tissues in hand.

"Wonderful. *Otello*, isn't it? You'll have to tell me if that young tenor can pull it off. It's not an easy role. Ooh, and I *love* the dress," he said, nodding at the red evening gown she'd hung on her closet door in preparation. "You're going to knock them dead in that. *Who* are you going to be knocking dead, exactly?" he added as an afterthought.

"No one, I'm sure, but I'm attending with Jason Klinf and Kam. Kam Reardon," she fumbled the last stupidly. She looked up in time to see a sly grin spreading on Richard's face.

"So . . . you're wearing *that* for an evening with the prince of smooth and the big bad wolf," he said, glancing significantly at the dramatic red, floor-length gown. "Better watch yourself, Red. Sounds like there might be some fireworks tonight at the Civic."

"Don't be ridiculous," she scoffed, although privately she was thinking that Richard's description of Jason and Kam was pretty dead-on.

"Did Reardon find you last night? At your dance lesson?" Richard asked, opening one of the boxes of tissues.

"Yes, he— Wait, did *you* tell Kam where I was?" Lin interrupted herself.

Richard gave her a bland glance as he wiped his nose. "Of course. He's a hell of a gorgeous man. Can you blame me for wanting to live out a little fantasy through you?"

Lin rolled her eyes. "I'm sure Emile would appreciate that," she said drolly.

"He did appreciate it when I told him last night," Richard said with a shrug. "I'm just looking, that's no crime. So? Are you cursing me or thanking me for pointing Kam in your direction last night?"

"Maybe both," she mumbled.

Richard leaned forward with interest. "Why are you thanking me? Does it have anything to do with phenomenal sex?" She gave him an exasperated glance, feeling vulnerable. "It *does*!" Richard exclaimed, dark eyes sparking.

"Maybe it does," Lin admitted after a moment. It felt good to admit the truth to someone. Carrying around the secret of her smoking-hot sexual escapades with her boss's brother suddenly felt like too big of a burden to carry alone. "But amazing sex aside, part of me is still cursing you for directing Kam Reardon my way."

"So the sex *is* amazing?" Richard asked, latching on to that portion of her admission and refusing to let go. "I knew it would be. He's got that primal, raw, 'I'm gonna give it to you and you're gonna love every second and inch of it, baby' way about him, doesn't he?"

Lin rolled her eyes at the comical description uttered in Richard's French-accented voice.

"Amazing sex or not, it's wrong. I shouldn't be doing this," she said.

"Why not?" Richard demanded, looking scandalized. "You never indulge. A beautiful, smart, wealthy woman like you should have a different stud in your bed every night. But instead, you're always saving yourself for . . . *Oh*."

"What?" Lin asked, alarmed when Richard suddenly faded off and his expression fell.

"That's it. You think you shouldn't be fooling around with Kam because of his brother."

"Ian is my boss, Richard. You know it's not right to mix business and pleasure, and whether I like it or not, Kam was definitely a work assignment."

"That's *not* what I meant," Richard said significantly.

She checked her watch. "I really should get ready."

"Don't Lin. Don't put me off again," Richard said so gently that she glanced into his face, surprised. "I know you fancy yourself in love with Ian Noble."

For a second, she just stared. "What? What makes you think—"

"I've thought it for a while. So has Emile. There's no reason to deny it, sweetie. It's just me, your old friend. Don't cut yourself off. Sometimes it hurts to talk about this stuff, but it's better than keeping it all locked inside. That hurts even more in the end. Not to mention, it will make you lonelier. Emile and I have always said you're one of the loneliest women we know."

Tears burned her eyes for the next several seconds as she stared at her friend, aghast, emotion swelling in her throat. She didn't know what to say. She felt cornered. Miserable. Why did it feel like her world was crashing down around her? Ian was thinking about moving Noble Enterprises to London. She was confused about her job. She was perplexed by her life. And all she could think about was Kam—

"It's not like it matters" tore out of her throat harshly. "Nothing will ever come of it. It's just a stupid, hopeless infatuation."

"It's not stupid," Richard soothed, compassion filling his face. "And of course it matters. It's your feelings. There's little else *more* important." He paused, looking worried.

"What?" Lin whispered, noticing his sudden hesitance.

"It's just . . . has it ever occurred to you that the hopelessness of your feelings for Ian might have been one of the reasons you held on to the infatuation for so long?"

"What do you mean?"

Richard shrugged and gave her an apologetic glance. "An unrequited love sucks, but it certainly assures safety. I know how cautious you are in relationships. I know that it hurt you more than you ever let on when your parents left you here in the States and moved to Taiwan—"

"Oh, give me a break" burst out of her throat. "That was ages ago. Don't play psychoanalyst with me, Richard."

"And then your grandmother passed, and I know she was everything to you. I'm just saying that your fear of being abandoned by people you care about could make an impossible love pretty damn appealing. Face it. None of the men you ever date are going to match up. Take Jason Klinf, for instance, since we're on the topic and you went out with him a few times—"

"Jason is an inveterate womanizer, you know that. I'd just be another notch on his bedpost," Lin interrupted impatiently.

"So? He'd be another notch on yours, too. It goes both ways. My point is," Richard persisted when she gave a little disgusted groan, "his lechery for you aside, Jason also wanted you to work for him. He offered you a king's ransom to do it. But you wouldn't even consider the idea, not even for a second. No, you never wavered in your loyalty to Ian. Ian gets to exist on some kind of insurmountable pedestal, and you never have to worry about his rejecting you because he never knows how you feel."

"Or will *ever* know," Lin said with a pointed glance. She shut her eyes, pressing lightly on her burning eyelids. She was alarmed to feel her hand trembling.

"Do you think Ian would show you the same loyalty, Lin?"

She looked up slowly at the sound of his sober question. Richard winced at whatever he saw on her face.

"Aw, sweetie. I'm sorry," he groaned, standing.

"I'm not even sure how I *do* feel about Ian, despite all your confidence on the matter," she exclaimed. "I really can't think about all this right now. I have to get ready. I have to go—"

"To work," Richard finished. "I know. Work is the place where you make everything in your world right. I respect that. I adore *you*. Just forget what I said. Thanks for the tissues. I'd give you a hug, but I don't want to spread the plague, so I'll just say 'don't worry.' It's all going to work itself out. You'll see."

"Thanks. I have some homemade soup in the freezer. It's not the hot-and-sour, but it'll still be good for your throat," she said, leading him out of the room.

"Merci, ma poupée," Richard said gratefully when she handed him the container of soup in a plastic bag. "We'll talk more later, yes?"

Lin just nodded, sure her heart was on display in her eyes, and watched her friend leave the kitchen.

Kam resisted a nearly nonstop urge to rip at his shirt collar and give himself a little breathing room. Fucking tux. No wonder they called businessmen *stiffs*. These clothes were made for masochists, not men. Someone tapped him on the shoulder. He spun around and saw a startled-looking waiter. The thin-faced man hurriedly stilled his slightly tottering platter of champagne flutes.

"Might you be Mr. Kam Reardon?" the waiter asked when everything came to a rest.

"Yeah," Kam replied, his gaze skimming the elegantly clad crowd. They stood in the grand foyer of the Civic Opera House, people chatting, tippling champagne and eating hors d'oeuvres and fancy desserts. Lin had told him she'd meet him and Jason Klinf at the opening night party, so he'd reluctantly used his ticket to enter. It was now six forty, and Kam hadn't glimpsed a hair on Lin's gorgeous head, no matter how furiously he searched the crowd.

Even though he didn't particularly feel like talking business with Jason Klinf or attending a crowded opera, he'd been looking forward to seeing Lin again. Instead, he was standing here like a chump in a penguin suit at a stuffy formal event, and Lin was glaringly absent.

"That man over there"—the waiter said, nodding his head in a general direction of the black-and-white, cocktailing mass of partygoers—"requested that I come over and check if you were Reardon."

Kam's gaze landed on a tallish, debonair man in his thirties with short brown hair and an expectant expression standing at the edge of the crowd. "Why didn't *he* just ask me?" Kam asked bluntly.

The waiter looked offended. "I don't know," he said, his sallow cheeks flushing. "His name is Jason Klinf and . . . oh, here he comes." Kam nabbed a glass of champagne from the waiter before he made his escape, not because he liked champagne, but because he suddenly felt certain that a drink was imperative for survival of this evening.

"Mr. Reardon?" the elegantly dressed man said, approaching him with a smile and hand outstretched. "Jason Klinf. I can't tell you what a pleasure this is."

"Thanks," Kam said, shaking his hand. "I've heard a lot about you and your watches from Lin."

"I understand from Lin that this is your first time to the States. Are you enjoying yourself?"

Something caught Kam's eye. He stared. "Yeah," he said distractedly. "Enjoying myself immensely."

Jason looked politely confused and turned to see where Kam was staring. In a sea of black-and-white tuxes and monochrome dresses, Lin wore red. Jason and he weren't the only ones in the crowd gawking. The evening gown she wore had a plunging V neckline, leaving a mouthwatering, yet tasteful amount of her creamy, firm breasts exposed. Her hair was unpinned and fell in lush, sexy waves down her back and arms. She glided toward them instead of walked, her round hips moving in a mesmerizing, lust-inspiring sashay.

"Voulez-vous regarder ça!" Kam thought he heard Jason mutter under his breath. *Would you look at that!* Kam tore his gaze off the vision of Lin approaching long enough to throw the other man a repressive look. Klinf wasn't doing anything different than Kam and the majority of males in the ballroom were, but he found the other man's hot, covetous gaze on Lin especially offensive.

"I'm so sorry for keeping you waiting," Lin said breathlessly, glancing from Kam to Jason. "A good friend of mine is sick and I needed to make sure he's all right. Hello, Jason," she said warmly, accepting Jason's kiss of greeting on her cheek.

"Don't apologize for a thing," Jason murmured, not leaning back for a moment. "The result was more than worth the wait. You're stunning, as usual."

"Thank you," she said. Her smile wavered slightly and she hesitated when she transferred her gaze to Kam. With a slight jerk, as if she'd had to jumpstart her actions, she put her hand on Kam's arm and craned up to replicate the kiss of greeting Jason had given her.

"Kam," she murmured.

The fabric of the dress was cut out on her shoulders, leaving them bare. He touched her there, feeling exquisitely soft, cool skin. He turned his head, interrupting her intention to kiss his jaw. Her kiss landed on the corner of his lips, his on hers. Using his hold on her, he kept her in place for an additional second, sliding his lips against hers, aligning them. He felt the tiny puff of air that signaled her surprise, and then the slight give in her lips as she ever so briefly molded them against his. That tiny gesture on her part gratified him. It was a fleeting kiss, but it was far from being the typical dry peck of greeting. He was getting a little fed up with all this cloak-and-dagger business when it came to the fact that he and Lin were more than just business associates. As a result, he didn't regret Jason's slight scowl when they separated.

He didn't regret it a bit.

Lin stepped back. "Have you two had much of an opportunity to talk yet?" she asked, her voice smooth and melodious, even if a delicate pink hue was spreading on her cheeks.

"We had just introduced ourselves when you arrived," Jason said. "I've been looking forward to this meeting ever since I read your article in the *Journal of Electrical Engineering*," he told Kam. "Your invention is straight out of a science fiction novel."

"Oh, it's a very real—and brilliant—thing. Yes, thank you," Lin said when a waiter paused next to them with champagne. She started to reach, but Jason was already placing a flute in her hand. "Thank you," she said. "Yes, Kam programmed me today for a demonstration of his device, so I got a firsthand display of the reality of it all."

Klinf's dark brows went up in dry amusement. " 'Programmed' you, did he? That does sound interesting." Lin's smile faltered at Klinf's sly dig.

"What do you mean by that?" Kam asked quietly, holding Klinf's stare. Jason blinked disconcertedly.

"It *was* interesting," Lin said brightly, as if to erase Kam's glare. "I know I'm not an expert like the two of you, but it is starting to dawn on me how game changing Kam's invention really is."

"I do have questions about the practicality of the typical buyer of the watch being able to gather their own baseline readings. Do you really think it's possible, Reardon?"

Kam scowled and saw Lin shift uncomfortably in her high heels when he didn't immediately respond. He glanced at her face, guilt flickering through him at the hint of anxiety in her eyes.

"It's not complicated. If an individual can read at the fifth-grade level, and if they have access to a computer, we should be able to provide a protocol that's easily followed. There are several feedback mechanisms included, so a user will automatically be alerted if they are doing something wrong," Kam said.

Klinf smiled broadly. "I can't wait to see the demonstration. Especially since you've acquired the most lovely test subject," he added warmly, leaning in closer to Lin. Irritation tightened Kam's muscles when he saw Klinf's gaze lower to Lin's beautiful breasts. He opened his mouth to say something, but immediately closed it, his annoyance mounting. This was precisely one of the reasons why he didn't want to participate in this whole damn process. Kam despised pretending to be something he wasn't. If he said what he wanted to say—and do—in that moment, however, it would upset Lin.

Lin nodded in the direction of a distant archway. The crowd had begun to worm its way toward it. "It looks as if we're going in."

Kam frowned when Klinf was suddenly at Lin's side, taking her arm. *Slippery little eel*, he thought. Klinf certainly seemed more interested in flirting with Lin than he was with Kam's invention.

Not that Kam cared. He was in the habit of making quick but firm first impressions. There was no way in hell Jason Klinf was ever going to touch his device, let alone use it for his company.

Their seats were in the first row of a box on the mezzanine level. Lin paused before following Jason down the aisle.

"Perhaps you two would like to sit together so you can talk business before the opera begins?" she asked.

"Nonsense," Jason replied, grabbing her hand and pulling her after him. "We'll have plenty of time to talk at dinner. Nothing against you Reardon, but a beautiful woman next to me is a must for full appreciation of the opera."

Lin settled uneasily in her seat. What had gotten into Jason? Yes, he was typically a flirt, but usually more tastefully so. He seemed determined to insult Kam. His behavior confused her, given his former professed fascination and interest in Kam's invention. He'd certainly never woo Kam this way, she thought nervously, noticing Kam's expression as he came to sit on the other side of her; Jason would undoubtedly be felled by his scowl if he were bothering to glance in Kam's direction. Instead, he had leaned in to speak to her, his face just inches from her temple.

"How is Ian doing with fatherhood soon approaching?" he murmured.

"Oh, very well. He's very excited," Lin said, trying to speak loud enough to include Kam in the conversation and dilute Jason's intimate manner.

"I would have never thought I'd see the day when Ian Noble settled with one woman so happily," Jason continued, his voice volume very low. She glanced uneasily at Kam, but he was staring stonily out at the filling, gilded auditorium. As usual, she had the distinct impression he missed nothing about what was happening, however, despite Jason's clandestine manner. "Do you think it's possible now that Ian is finding so much contentment on the home front there might be the slightest opportunity that he'd loosen the reins on you, Lin?"

She blinked and turned to stare at Jason in amazement.

"What are you talking about?" she asked, her voice barely above a whisper.

"I was wondering if you would reconsider my offer about coming to work for Klinf. For me," he said, his dark eyes moving over her face.

She smiled stiffly. *Oh no.* She'd thought he was over this. "Thank you again for the offer, Jason, but my answer hasn't changed."

"But your situation has, surely?" He noticed her bewildered expression. "Ian won't be half so proprietary over you now that he's so involved with his wife and future child. And for you, surely the appeal of being at his beck and call every second of every day has dimmed as well."

It took her a moment to unfreeze her tongue. The icy hand that had seized her heart remained tight. She hated it, but some of the things Jason was saying now, and had said to her in the past, were not all that dissimilar to her own thoughts on the matter recently. Still, she'd never let Jason know that. "I'm a Noble executive. I hardly see how his having a wife and child affects my employment."

"Don't take offense, please," he implored quietly, grabbing her hand. Her head turned as she shot Kam a nervous glance. From her side vision, she saw his long legs tense and shift. "I just meant that loyalties often alter when such large changes occur in an employer's life," Jason continued near her ear. "Yes, even when the alterations are in his personal life. You're a practical woman. You must realize that."

She turned toward him briefly.

"I realize no such thing," she stated unequivocally. She pulled her hand away from his. What had gotten into him? She'd never seen Jason this way. Luckily, the lights dimmed and the audience hushed.

"We can speak more about it at the intermission," Jason whispered.

She opened her mouth to tell him there was nothing to discuss, but the orchestra began to play. She sat there, watching the stage unseeingly, feeling trapped between Jason's inexplicable crassness on one side and Kam's silent, smoldering intensity on the other.

She had never enjoyed the opera less, despite the superiority of the performance itself. Jason and Kam seemed as tense and dissatisfied as she felt as they stood in the crowded lobby at intermission, waiting for some drinks.

"And what do you think of Vasquez, Kam? Do you think he's adequate to the role?" Jason asked Kam pointedly, referring to the young South American tenor playing the part of Otello.

"He's good," Kam said with his typical laconism.

Lin had a sinking feeling when she noticed Jason's smirk. Kam's brief response had clearly been precisely what Jason expected from his pompous ideas of who Kam was. Why had she ever let Ian talk her into this? Beyond the fact of Jason's strange, competitive mood, it clearly had been a mistake. Kam was not enjoying himself any more than she was.

"I'm not so sure I can agree with such *eloquent* praise," Jason said drolly, taking their drinks from a waiter's tray and passing them around. "I'll admit to being a bit disappointed, given all the hype over Vasquez. Otello is one of the great acting challenges in opera. Vasquez has none of the flare and fire of Bardo, for instance, wouldn't you agree, Lin?"

"Bardo *blustered* his way through *Otello*," Kam said harshly. Jason looked at Kam in amazement, Lin with abrupt trepidation. "Vasquez has ten times his power vocally, and despite his supposed gaucheness, is much the subtler actor. If it came to a showdown of the two men, Vasquez would demolish that strutting peacock Bardo. Excuse me," Kam said so abruptly that Lin jumped. He turned and walked away.

Lin resisted an urge to laugh at Jason's slack jaw. Jason looked at her with his mouth still hanging open.

"Did I say something to offend him?"

"What do you think, Jason?" she snapped. When she saw his surprise at her outburst, she inhaled and calmed herself with effort. Kam had already cut down Jason to half his size, even if Jason didn't seem aware of his suddenly dwarfed stature. This night would not be made better by her further insulting one of Noble Enterprises' business associates. She just wished this event were over.

"He doesn't really like crowds," Lin said, attempting to be neutral despite her cool tone. "He probably just went to use the facilities or to get a breath of fresh air." She hoped what she'd said was true and that Kam hadn't just left the opera house for good. She wouldn't put it past him.

"He's an odd one, isn't he? If he didn't look so much like Ian, I'd never believe they were related."

Lin ignored the invitation to join in a sniping match about Kam. She sipped her champagne, thinking about the impatience on Kam's face when he'd soundly put Jason in his place just now and walked away. Kam thought she was wasting his time, and Lin had to agree with him in this instance.

"Speaking of crowds, can we find a private place to talk?" Jason interrupted her preoccupation. "We have a few minutes before the intermission is over."

Lin sighed. She didn't want to talk to Jason in private, but maybe she'd better just kill this idea he had of her working for him once and for all. Besides, there were a few other things she needed to clarify with him.

"All right. But only because I'd like to hear why you're being so rude to Kam." Jason blinked at her bluntness, but quickly recovered.

She followed him to a deserted alcove that led to a closed-off stairwell. Jason reached for her champagne glass and set it, along with his, on the marble column at the foot of the stairs. The sounds of the crowd were muted here. Lin stiffened when he placed his hands on her upper arms.

"Why are you acting so strangely tonight?" she demanded, her irritation with him undisguised.

"I'm sorry for upsetting you before the performance began," he said quietly. "But I think you know as well as I do that the Noble Enterprises of today is not the same company as it was yesterday."

"You're right," Lin said coolly. "It's more diverse and financially vibrant than it's ever been."

"Thanks to you, in large part," Jason said, rubbing his hands up and down her bare arms. "And what have you got to show for it, Lin?"

"Jason, I've said it before, and I'll say it again—hopefully for the last time. I'm flattered by the offer, but I'm not interested in working for Klinf. Now that's settled. Answer *my* question. Why are you being intentionally rude to Kam?"

His grip on her arm tightened. "Because of the two assets presented to me here tonight—Kam's admittedly brilliant invention, which I probably can't afford, in the endgame—and your beauty, talent, and expertise, I'd rather have you. Besides, if I play my cards right," he murmured, "I might be able to have both."

"What are you talking about?" she demanded, trying to step away from him. He pulled her toward him again, his grip unrelenting.

"You've been learning a lot about Reardon's device, haven't you? All that valuable firsthand experience? That's an asset all on its own."

Her disbelief at his audacity made her stop struggling for a moment. "You're deluding yourself if you think I can comprehend Kam's genius. Even if I could, I'd never divulge inside information to you."

"Does Ian allow you to hold private shares in Noble Enterprises?" Jason asked, switching tracks smoothly. "Don't bother to answer. I know he doesn't. He refuses to give anyone a single share of his hoard, not even to you, despite his professed loyalty to you and his supposed inability to do business without you."

"Noble is privately held," Lin hissed. "I've never asked Ian to buy shares."

"Because you know he wouldn't give you the opportunity." Lin flinched like he'd slapped her in the face, his blunt statement taking her off guard.

"Now that he has a wife and a child on the way," Jason continued relentlessly, "he's even less likely to release his tight grip on Noble.

It's a lost cause, Lin. All the time and sweat and tears you've put into that company, all your brilliance is being used by Noble to build an empire for his future family dynasty, and you'll be even more of an outsider," Jason murmured sadly. "If you come with me, I'll offer you not only a salary worthy of your talents, but I'll give you stock in Klinf. Up to ten percent, if you want it. We'll be true partners, not some hollow partnership like Noble is tossing out like leftover scraps to you. You'll epitomize the elegance and glamour of Klinf. The company will be stronger and more viable than ever with you by my side. *I* will be," he whispered hoarsely, his dark eyes glistening with a hard edge.

Lin saw it coming, but she still cringed when he leaned down to kiss her. She swung her chin aside, avoiding his descending mouth. *Could this evening be any more of a disaster?* She tried to break loose and stumbled in her high heels.

"Jason, let *go* of me," she insisted firmly. His mouth moved on her clamped jaw. She wrenched her arms from his hold, making a frustrated sound when he grabbed her again. He squeezed her arms painfully.

"I *mean* it. You're hurting me, damn it," she grated out.

She was seriously considering a particularly powerful form of the word *no* she'd learned in a Kung Fu class she'd taken. Something caught her attention first. From the corner of her eye, she saw a large hand tap Jason's shoulder twice. Jason lifted his head, an annoyed expression on his face.

"What the—" He loosened his hold on Lin to twist around when he was tapped again, harder. Lin's eyes sprung wide when she saw the thunderous expression on Kam's face. She instinctively stepped back, knowing a storm was about to break. Kam's fist struck Jason's jaw like a jet-fueled hammer. Jason's spin on his planted feet struck her dazed brain as bizarrely comical. He still had a slightly surprised look on his face when he crumpled to the floor.

Lin hurried over to him, kneeling to touch his temple. "Jason?" He was out cold. "Oh my god," she whispered, shock vibrating her bones. She checked his pulse in rising panic.

"He'll be fine," Kam said from above her, his tone derisive. "I punched him, I didn't kill him. Are you all right?"

She stared up at him. That thundercloud expression still tightened his features, but his gray eyes looked worried.

"I'm fine," she whispered. "I don't know what's come over Jason tonight."

Kam rolled his eyes. "I have a wild idea. I thought you said he wasn't interested? That guy is randy as a goat for you."

"I said *I* wasn't that interested. Besides, he just wants me for Klinf. He's just trying to seduce me so I'll work for him."

"I know, I heard," Kam said grimly. "But that doesn't mean he doesn't want you for his bed, too."

Jason started to regain consciousness, rolling his head and mumbling something in French she couldn't understand. Kam grabbed her hand and raised her so that she stood close to his tall form. He lightly brushed his hands across her upper arms, inspecting her. His gaze narrowed dangerously. Lin glanced down to see where he looked. Her skin was abraded and red from Jason's hard grip. Scowling, Kam used the toe of his shoe to prod Jason's shoulder. Jason opened his eyes and stared up at Kam woozily.

"Tu as mérite pire. Si tu mets encore la main sur elle, tu ne t'en sortira pas," Kam told him succinctly. Lin thought she understood, even with her rudimentary French. *You deserved worse. If you touch her again, you won't get off so easy.*

Jason looked understandably cowed even through his befuddlement. Kam started to pull her away.

"Wait," Lin said, catching up to his long-legged stride, her red gown streaming out behind her. "We can't just leave him there, can we?"

"He'll be up in a minute. If he's not, the janitors will pick him up with the rest of the trash after the performance," Kam muttered, his disdainful tone clearly signifying that any further discussion of Jason Klinf wasn't worthy of his time.

Lin considered what he'd said as they walked, and decided not to protest. Jason didn't deserve compassion. He'd been forcing himself on her and holding her despite her protests. Besides, her Kung Fu move on his open, unguarded stance would have definitely disabled him briefly as well.

Neither of them said anything else as Kam whisked her through the mostly empty mezzanine lobby, and then the completely abandoned grand foyer. The intermission was over. Not that Lin was vaguely interested in returning to their seats. Kam clearly agreed. She was breathless from their single-minded flight by the time Kam hailed a cab and they settled in the backseat.

"My place or yours?" he asked without preamble.

"Yours. *Angus*," she replied breathlessly without pause, reminding him of his newly arrived dog.

It had been one of the most complicated, confusing days she could remember. Her mind was a maelstrom. Answering Kam's loaded question was the simplest, surest decision she'd made in her life. She saw his grim expression soften slightly as he pinned her with his stare. He leaned forward to give the cabdriver the address. Lin could tell he'd liked her quick answer. She could tell he'd liked it a lot.

Chapter Thirteen

Angus treated them to an enthusiastic greeting, although she followed Kam's sharp order not to jump on Lin's evening gown.

"I should take her out," Kam said. "It won't take but a few minutes."

"Of course," Lin agreed.

Despite his proposed mission, he didn't move. "If you're worried about Ian's reaction to what happened with Klinf tonight, don't be. I'll explain. When he hears about how that moron was manhandling you, he'll understand."

"That's all right," Lin said quietly. "I'll tell him."

"One of us *will* tell him. Ian has a right to know what the man's really like if he does regular business with him."

"I agree."

She felt him studying her and examined her purse. "Will you tell him that Jason asked you to work for him?" Kam prodded.

Lin nodded, not looking up. "I didn't tell him when Jason asked me before, but I will this time."

"Why didn't you mention it to Ian before?"

Lin shrugged. She didn't want to tell Kam that Jason had asked her to work for him soon after Ian asked Francesca to marry him. Despite Richard St. Claire's accusation that she hadn't even considered Jason's offer, Lin *had* thought about it. A change in scenery would have helped her cope after seeing Ian so completely in love with another woman. She was glad now she'd never considered the offer too seriously. What a nightmare it would have been if she'd agreed to work with Jason.

"A lot of Ian's business associates try to . . ." She waved her hand in vague embarrassment.

"Poach you from him?" Kam prodded. "They know an asset when they see it." She glanced up in time to see his silvery-gray-eyed stare lowering over her. She repressed a shiver.

"I didn't want Ian to worry about it when he didn't need to," she said.

"Ian doesn't need to worry about you leaving Noble Enterprises because you never would?" Kam prompted.

She moved restlessly in her high heels, uncomfortable at the topic. How could she answer him when she wasn't sure of the answer herself? Jason's attempts at convincing her tonight had bothered her in part because there was some truth to what he'd said. Ian's life and priorities *had* changed since he'd met Francesca, and so would his business as a result. *She'd* changed. She wasn't sure where she belonged anymore.

"I didn't say that. Who knows what the future may bring?" she replied uneasily.

"Indeed."

"Why are you so curious?" Lin wondered suddenly.

"Curiosity is one of the palest of my emotions when it comes to you."

She felt her cheeks heating. Had he really just said that? He started to get Angus's leash but paused. "Speaking of *bolder* emotions," he said dryly, "I bought something for you today at this . . . unusual little boutique I found while I was walking Angus."

"You did? *Unusual*, you say?" Lin asked, the tension brought on by their former topic of conversation breaking. She smiled.

"Maybe it's not unusual. I haven't lived in a city for years, so what do I know? It was a nice surprise, though. At least it was for me. Maybe you won't think so."

"You *have* to show it to me now," she prodded softly. "I'm dying of curiosity."

His nostrils flared slightly as he regarded her, coming to a decision. "Okay."

He disappeared down the hallway. When he returned a moment later he carried a good-sized shopping bag. Her eyes widened when she saw the single black letter on the bag. It was a new boutique that had opened downtown. She'd read about it in *Chicago* magazine, but hadn't yet been there. The boutique specialized in luxurious lingerie, tasteful sex toys, and specially designed jewelry, some of it for everyday glamour, some of it with light bondage or other sexual practices in mind. The boutique might have a racy edge to it, but it carried the highest-quality merchandise and catered to an affluent clientele. Every time the owner was interviewed, he teasingly gave a different word from where the *E* was derived. So far, Lin had read *envy*, *exquisite*, and *erotic*. It had been a genius marketing ploy, because of course the mind automatically searched for other possible meanings.

She stared at Kam wide-eyed. "You just strolled into E while you were on a walk with Angus this afternoon, did you?" she asked, a smile pulling at her lips.

He arched his dark eyebrows in a droll expression. "You think that's odd?"

She shook her head and laughed softly. "I'm growing used to you. I'm beginning to think there's nothing you either *haven't* done or *wouldn't*, once you decided you wanted to. The way you told off Jason tonight when he was being so uppity about the opera. Your strolling into the hottest, most risqué boutique in the city; those and a thousand other things, will serve as my lessons to never be too cocky about *getting* you, Kam Reardon."

He gave her a one-sided grin and stepped toward her, holding out the bag. "I insinuated I didn't like opening night, which is true. Too crowded. But I actually *do* like the opera. I used to go in London pretty regularly."

"I figured. Did you used to go with Diana?" she asked, holding his gaze as she accepted the bag.

He nodded. "I think she was thrilled when she found something that I actually liked that suited her lifestyle."

"But you were just being honest about a discovered passion, weren't you?" Lin asked, studying his face. He shrugged. She smiled, loving his insouciance, his laconism . . . the fact that he was the most fascinating man she knew and yet hardly ever talked about himself. She loved him *period*.

"What's wrong?" Kam asked, his gaze narrowing on her.

Lin willed herself to recover from her automatic, incendiary thought. She hadn't meant she *loved* him loved him. Just that she adored his character. His honesty. His rugged good looks. And the way he made her scream in a frenzy of need in bed . . .

She cleared her throat and held up the bag.

"May I?"

"Please do," he replied.

She set the bag on an end table. The first thing she drew out was an exquisite black silk, short gown with lace at the breast. "Oh, it's gorgeous, thank you," she whispered, running her fingertips over the detailed lacework and held up the fluid, soft silk against her cheek. She glanced at Kam. He said nothing, but the look in his eyes and the small smile he wore made her heart beat faster.

She withdrew two packages tightly wrapped in tissue. "Just open the smaller one for now," Kam said gruffly. "The other one is just the hardware."

Her brows lifted at that. She fleetly unwrapped the package. "Oh," she murmured when she saw the four black leather straps with sturdy platinum buckles and small hoops and hooks attached. The cuffs were finely made and sturdy. Despite their obvious sexual intent, the bands were attractive—almost like edgy jewelry. She looked at Kam, her mouth hanging open, her pulse beginning to throb at her throat.

"They reminded me of when you were wearing those black leather high heels the other day," he explained quietly. She stared at him in blank incomprehension. "The ones with the thick leather strap that buckled around your ankles? In Ian's office? I was getting hard just looking at them. I was trying to figure out why the sight turned me on so much. It was something about the contrast. Thick leather against silk. You're so delicate, and your skin is flawless. I wouldn't have thought 'leather' for you, but there you have it," he finished a little sheepishly. "The boutique has a really talented artist—Jarvis Cooper—who hand makes all the jewelry, including the watches. I talked to him for a while and he showed me his workshop. When he showed me these, I thought of you."

She fingered one of the restraints, holding his gaze. He was telling her that for whatever reason, the thought of her in the leather restraints did it for him. "One for each of my ankles and wrists?" she asked.

He shrugged slightly. "We can just use the wrist cuffs until you're ready for the others—"

"I'm ready now," she whispered.

His mouth snapped closed. She saw his throat convulse as he swallowed.

She set down the cuffs and reached into the bag again. "You really went to town, didn't you?" she teased, lifting out another tissue-wrapped package.

"It was sort of one-stop shopping, especially for a visitor like me who wasn't planning for something like . . ."

She glanced over at him as she unwrapped what felt like a small box.

". . . you," Kam finished.

She tore her gaze off his face to look at what rested in the palm of her hand. This, she recognized. A small bullet vibrator. She owned a similar one. The thought of Kam using it on her, of watching what had formerly been a solitary, autoerotic experience, caused both her cheeks and sex to flush with heat. "You really were stocking up on the essentials, weren't you?" she said to hide her embarrassed excitement.

If her cheeks had warmed when she saw the vibrator, they flamed when she unwrapped a flogger with dozens of supple suede tails and a tightly wrapped leather handle.

"Don't be nervous," Kam said, his voice a quiet, arousing rasp near her ear. She hadn't realized he'd moved. He smoothed her hair behind her ears, his fingertips lowering to brush against her neck. She shivered. "I'm not *ever* going to hurt you. I'll awaken your nerves. I'll make you sting at worst, and the pleasure will trump it, every time. But anytime you tell me to stop, I will. Do you understand?"

She nodded and his lips brushed against her cheeks as if to absorb the heat.

"There's wine in the kitchen. Ian and Francesca sent some over," he said. "Why don't you go and pour yourself a glass while I take Angus out? That way, she won't bother us all night."

"Okay," she said, turning her face toward him. He leaned down and kissed her mouth.

She remained frozen to the spot for several seconds after the door closed with Kam and Angus on the other side of it. Finally she roused herself. In the kitchen, she decided against the wine and instead chose a bottle of water. She chugged down a third of it in seconds. Something about opening those intimate gifts in front of Kam, and then his melting kiss, had left her parched and . . .

. . . thirsty for sensation.

When Kam returned to the condo with Angus in tow, Lin was nowhere to be seen. A ripple of anxiety went through him. Had he scared her off with his purchase? He certainly hadn't thought so as he closely watched her reaction as she opened the packages, but maybe he'd been kidding himself.

"Lin?" he called.

"I'm back here," came her clear voice from the direction of the master bedroom suite.

He exhaled in relief. "I'll be there in a second."

Anticipation started to build in him as he finally loosened the restraining bow tie. He washed up in the bathroom. When he walked into the bedroom, he froze in the act of unfastening the second button on his shirt. Lin stood by the side of the four-poster bed. She wore not only the lace and silk black gown he'd bought her, but also a thick leather cuff on both wrists and ankles. His cock swelled tight in automatic appreciation.

She'd brushed her lustrous hair so that it fell in loose waves down her back and one shoulder. The gown fit her like it'd been made for her; the lace clinging tightly to her slender rib cage and emphasizing her thrusting breasts. The top curves of her breasts were left exposed, the firm, feminine flesh looking like a delectable, erotic feast. He'd been right. The vision of her lithesome, graceful limbs and pale, smooth skin contrasting with the thick leather cuffs acted like a shock to his system, tensing his muscles, making his blood flow fast and hot, readying him in an instant.

He walked toward her, his gaze unwavering. He whipped off his bow tie and tossed it in the direction of an armchair. She wore that sober, watchful expression that always killed him a little, her large, lustrous eyes drawing him in like magnets.

"You look like something out of a dream," he said.

A small smile curved her lips. "A good one, I hope."

"The best." He stepped forward and reached for one of her hands. He drew it out into an extended position. The skin on her inner arms was especially pale and vulnerable looking next to the thick cuff. He placed his hand beneath her elbow, lifting her arm, and lowered his head. He pressed her lips to the satiny patch of warm skin on the underside of her elbow, moving his head slightly, absorbing the exquisite softness of her skin. She gasped softly when he pressed the tip of his tongue to her fluttering pulse, tasting her.

"You're the most beautiful woman I've ever seen," he said, straightening. "I've never told you, but I think it every time I look at you."

Her small smile faded. It suddenly struck him how intense he'd sounded. He gave a small shrug and gently placed her hand back by her side. "I just thought you should know," he said, removing his tux jacket and hanging it on the corner of the chair.

"Thank you," she said somberly, watching him. He sat briefly, removing his shoes and socks. The skin of his chest, belly, and arms prickled beneath her stare a moment later when he hastily removed his dress shirt. He started to walk to her, but she met him halfway, her arms encircling his neck. He brought her against him, his hands opening at the small of her silk-covered back. She lifted her face, her lush mouth calling to him. Earlier when they'd talked and made love in front of the mirror, he'd never kissed her. That deprivation cut at him now, swelling his desire. He nipped at her pink lips briefly before he fell on her, kissing her deeply and thoroughly, drowning in her. God, he loved her mouth. She moaned and kissed him back with equal fervor, her supple body molding tight against him, the sensation of her firm breasts and hard, lace-covered nipples pressing against his bare chest, fevering him.

He lifted his head from the sweet heat of her mouth a moment later. He placed his open hands on either side of her jaw and met her dark-eyed stare.

"Can I restrain you to the bed?" he asked gruffly.

"Yes," she said without hesitation, but he noticed the flicker of anxiety in her eyes. He caressed her cheeks and forehead with his fingertips. "I am going to use your gifts on you," he said honestly. "But I'm not going to do anything until you're ready. We're both going to find out what you like and don't like, do you understand? You have to tell me."

"I understand. I'm not afraid," she whispered. He bent to kiss her mouth yet again, touched by her courage and honesty.

She'd placed the bag of things from E at the foot of the bed. He found the restraint straps and attached them to the four corner posters, gauging how much length he needed from Lin's height. "Come over here," he beckoned to her when he'd finished. He turned to her when she approached, smiling for reassurance. "I'm going to take off your pretty gown," he murmured, "and then you can lie down on your back. I want you to be comfortable."

She nodded, her big eyes glued to his face. He ran his hands along her soft shoulders, rolling back the thin straps. When he lowered the straps to her arms, anticipation cutting at him, she started to draw through her hands, assisting him.

"No," he said, meeting her stare. She slowly dropped her hands to her sides. "Give me this pleasure. I want to undress you. I want to control every move, because I want to own every gasp you make, every shiver, and every second of your pleasure. You may think that's selfish. Maybe it is, because I plan to guide you to heaven, and if I do my job, I will have found it, too. Do you understand?"

He felt a shudder go through her now and savored it.

"Yes. I understand," she said, her voice stronger than before.

He nodded his head and continued his precious mission, lowering the straps, revealing her ripe, succulent breasts, taut belly, and round hips. She wore no panties. His nostrils flared hungrily at the sight of her smooth labia tucked between pale, shapely thighs. As always, seeing her exposed had an almost cruel effect it was so sharp. His cock gave a vicious lurch against the confines of his boxer briefs and pants. The gown slipped down her legs to pool at her feet.

He took her hand and she stepped out of it, nude save the leather cuffs.

"Lie down on your back on the bed, but I want your head at the foot," he said quietly, pointing at the foot of the bed. He saw her eyes widen slightly at that, but she followed his direction nonetheless. When she'd taken the position, he methodically began to attach the straps to her leather cuffs, tightening the restraints and checking with her to make sure she was snug but comfortable.

When he finished binding her last ankle, he straightened and looked at her, taking a moment to fully appreciate her beauty. She lay naked with her legs spread and her arms outstretched toward the lower bedposts. He could easily see her pink pussy, the lush color and delicate shell-like shape of it so exquisite next to her pale, smooth thighs. The bed possessed a carved headboard but no footboard. Her dark hair lay in a cloud around her shoulders and head, strands of it falling off the end of the mattress. She was so stunning, so tempting, that it hurt him to look at her, but it was an ache he would never forsake.

The loveliest things of all were her eyes. He sensed a thread of anxiety in her gaze, but desire and trust trumped her uncertainty by far.

"You're sure you're comfortable?" he asked.

She nodded, her gaze never leaving his face. He put his hands on the mattress and started to join her on the bed. "Then let's begin, *mon petit chaton*," he whispered roughly.

* * *

A thrill of excitement and trepidation like she'd never known before went through her at Kam's words combined with the vision of him coming onto the bed on his hands and knees, lean, bulging muscles rippling, his manner reminding her more acutely than ever of a stalking predator. Perhaps he saw some of her anxiety after he'd straddled her body, because his brows quirked slightly as he watched her face. She wasn't afraid of him, she was just nervous about her reaction to being bound . . . to sacrificing control. Being completely restrained didn't frighten her—she believed Kam when he'd said he would stop their play at her request. It was just that she didn't know what to expect of herself. The anticipation and the anxiety had her drawn tight as a piano string.

"Shhh," he soothed, searching her face, even though she hadn't made a sound. He must have seen her nerves. "I'm just going to kiss you," he murmured. He lowered. She exhaled with an expulsion of pent-up tension at the sensation of his big, solid body pressing her down into the mattress. He leaned on one elbow, keeping his upper body weight off her, his long legs between her spread ones. His bare lower belly pressed against her mons, the pressure on her aroused sex feeling delicious.

And she *was* aroused despite her uncertainty. She had been ever since she'd buckled the leather straps around her ankles and wrists and felt their strangely erotic weight. *Prisoner. Slave.* The words had popped into her head at the vision of the thick black cuffs, both embarrassing and enticing her.

She looked into Kam's gleaming eyes as he brushed her hair off her temple and cradled her jaw in a possessive, prizing gesture. If she was a prisoner, it wasn't to him alone. She was ensnared by her own need, by this heady, singular desire for Kam. It was the sweetest trap, and one of her choosing.

He lowered slowly, his gaze fixed to her mouth. And yet it was her brow that he kissed. At his silent bidding, she closed her eyelids and let him kiss her there, her held breath burning in her lungs. He paid tribute to her temple, cheek and nose, his lips so firm and warm and patient, that by the time he landed on her sensitive lips, she gasped and trembled.

He kissed her for long, delicious minutes, his manner so deliberate, his intensity so great, that she found her tension melting, her sex turning to warm, sweet syrup beneath the pressure of his body. Her world became Kam and his deep, sensual kiss.

"Oh," she sighed when he plucked at her lips with a lazy hunger she loved. "That was nice."

He molded her moving lips to his. "Everything about you is perfect, but I could live on your mouth alone."

"I would never deprive you in such a way," she whispered, kissing him back feverishly.

"Because all of you is mine?" he asked gruffly, kissing her jaw and neck.

"Yes. Yes," she chanted mindlessly as he took one of her breasts into his palm and squeezed gently. Her breath caught in her lungs as he lowered, her anticipation sharp. She gasped when he took the sensitive crest into his mouth, sucking and laving the nipple with his stiff tongue. She moaned, her hips shifting instinctively, but between the restraints and Kam's weight, she was trapped . . . exactly where she wanted to be.

Suddenly he made a growling noise in his throat, a thrilling mixture of frustration and arousal. He scooted his knees up on the bed, kneeling over her. He placed his hands on the outsides of her breasts, pushing them together, his face between them, his growl vibrating into her flesh. He lifted his head and began kissing and licking both nipples at once. Lin whimpered not only at his rough, sweet treatment, but also at his intensity. "Your breasts make me crazy. I will turn your bottom red sometime for putting them on display in that dress tonight."

Her clit twanged in arousal. She moaned, feeling bereft of his weight on her pussy, even though his massaging palms and avid sucking on her nipples went a long way to make her forget.

"You didn't like the dress?" she asked shakily.

"No. I loved it," he corrected, his mouth lowering to her rib cage. He continued to shape her breasts to his palms as he kissed and scraped his teeth along her sides, causing her skin to roughen and ripples of pleasure to run through her. She found the vision of his masculine hands, molding and squeezing the captive flesh unbearably arousing. Lin pulled at her arm restraints, another jolt of excitement going through her at the stark evidence that she was bound, unable to escape the pleasure he gave her so knowingly.

"But you would punish me for it still?" she asked tremulously.

He lifted his head and speared her with his stare. She licked at the corner of her mouth nervously.

"Did you wear the dress because you knew I'd be forced to sit next to you all night and make small talk about business plans and the opera? Did you do it to torture me, knowing I could look, but not touch these?" he asked, squeezing her breasts in his hands.

"Of course not," she exclaimed. His stare didn't relent. "Maybe a little," she admitted after a moment.

"So you deserve a *little* punishment?"

Heat rushed through her pussy at the combination of his words and his small, sexy smile.

"Yes," she whispered, aroused by their exchange. "I deserve it."

He released her breasts and reached for the bag at the corner of the bed. She watched him take out both the bullet vibrator and the flogger, her breath becoming more erratic still. He removed the vibrator from the box and set it on the mattress. He came up over her on his hands and knees, and then gripped the leather handle of the flogger. Her heartbeat began to throb in her ears. She stared up at the awesome sight of him, her gaze sticking on the obvious shape of his erection pressing against the crotch of his black tuxedo pants.

He ran the suede lashes of the flogger along the sensitive skin at the side of her rib cage. She gasped. Her moist nipples ached.

"How does it feel?" he asked, watching her as he ran the tails over her belly.

Naughty. Exciting. "Good," she said shakily.

He moved back, kneeling between her spread thighs. He quickly, efficiently added some length to her ankle straps and then propped her hips up by sliding his knees and lower thighs behind her buttocks. Her ass was raised off the bed several inches, her pussy angled upward. She saw his small smile and knew he liked the position. Heat rushed through her when she realized how exposed her pussy was to him.

He picked up the flogger again, his free hand cradling her hip in a possessive gesture.

He ran the tails along her sides, causing goose bumps to rise along her skin. The little lashes glided just beneath her breasts and down to her belly and then skimmed her hip. She bit off a moan when he dragged the soft lashes over her pelvis, a stray lash licking over her labia.

"You're teasing me," she moaned.

"Just like you teased me all night. But this isn't teasing. I'm just warming up." Her hips wriggled on his thighs in acute arousal. He lifted the flogger and brought it down on her hip, the tails giving her a stinging caress.

"Oh."

"Bad or good?" he asked tautly.

"Good."

His nostrils flared. He lifted the lash again and brought it down on her belly. She gasped.

"Does it sting or does it hurt?" he asked, and she recognized that he wanted her honest answer. He was trying to read her.

"It doesn't hurt. It prickles and burns and—" she broke off when he brought down the lash on the side of her waist.

"What?" he demanded, sensually sliding the tails along the lower curves of her breasts.

"It feels exciting," she said in a choked voice.

He snarled. The next thing she knew, he was putting his hands on her hips and pulling her toward him at the same time he scooted under her farther. When she settled, his thighs were firmly under her and her bottom sat directly in his lap. Her mouth fell open at the sensation of his hard cock throbbing next to her ass, her spread pussy pressing tight against his waistband.

"There we go," he muttered thickly, sounding pleased. His gaze toured her naked, bound body with undisguised greed. "Now I've got you where I want you, spread out before me like a delicious feast."

Lin shifted her ass uncontrollably, wild at the sensation of his flagrant erection beneath her. She stilled and held her breath when he lifted the flogger.

Chapter Fourteen

The suede lashes fell on the tender skin of her inner thigh. Arousal shot through her, hot and forbidden. Instead of keeping her from squirming, she wriggled more, stimulating her spread sex and grinding against Kam's erection.

He gritted his teeth and brought down the flogger with more force than ever before on her hip. It made a whooshing noise as it flew through the air and landed with a burst of sensation. The lingering afterburn seemed to magically transfer to her clit, making it sizzle next to Kam's waistband.

"Ooh" popped out of her throat. She thrust her hips against him.

"Keep still," he warned, spreading his hand along the very top of her thigh and gripping her in place. She bit her lip, willing herself not to grind up against him, which is all she wanted to do at that moment. He watched her closely as he ran the suede tails over her ribs and then the lower part of her breasts. A moan broke free when one of the lashes accidentally tickled an erect nipple. He ran the flogger over her chest and shoulders and down the sides of her body. It was driving her mad.

"That's right. Keep very still. Focus on how it feels and tell me," he murmured.

She closed her eyes in an attempt to shut out the eroticism of what was happening to her. The vision only made her want to squirm against Kam more. "The tails feels soft. Exciting. When you . . . lash me, it sets the nerves on fire. It makes me crave . . ." she whispered.

The flogger landed on her hip. She gasped.

"More" popped out of her throat.

"Like this?" He lightly lashed at her belly, leaving her skin tingling.

"Yes." He brought the flogger down several more times on her hip, belly, thighs and the sides of her buttocks. It sensitized her skin, making it tingle and prickle like a dark caress, but what it did to her pussy was unprecedented. She'd never burned so greatly from an indirect touch. The experience was so much more intense than she'd ever imagined.

The tails struck with more force against her heaving rib cage. She instinctively arched her back, offering the tender flesh of her breasts to the lash. Kam made a rough noise in his throat.

"Open your eyes," he commanded roughly.

She opened her eyes and stared at Kam with wonder. His features looked as hard and strained as the rest of his beautiful body; his gaze was fierce, scoring her even more greatly than the flogger. "Do you want me to flog your pretty breasts?"

"Yes," she admitted. She was beginning to tremble. The anticipation was killing her. "So much."

"Oh oui, encore, mon petit chaton," he muttered. When Lin only blinked, made sluggish from lust, Kam interpreted. "Again, little kitten. Tell me what you want again," he said as he ran the suede tails over the globes of her breast, and finally over a peaking nipple. She whimpered and ground her sex against him. She couldn't stop it. The friction he was building in her was unbearable. He stilled her with a hand on her hip and a fiery glance.

"Use it on my breasts. Please."

His nostrils flared. "For being so sweet, you will get that and more."

Lin panted shallowly as she watched him pick up the little vibrator. "It will sting, but if you take it, I will reward you."

"Yes," she insisted. She arched her back as far as the restraints would allow it, thrusting her breasts up for the flogger, making her own flesh a sacrifice on the alter of desire. Beneath her ass, she felt Kam's cock leap viciously.

"So beautiful," he muttered. He brought down the flogger with a forceful flick, the tails stinging her breast. She moaned feverishly.

"Too much?" he asked, his sharp voice slicing through her haze. "If it isn't, ask for another."

"No. No. Another."

Again, that sweet, stinging lick of the tails. Her nipples pinched tight. It hurt, but the real pain came from sharp desire, not the flogger. Her chin came up, her head fell back on the mattress and her eyes closed. Her entire body stretched tight, her hips pulsing against the arousing sensation of Kam's erection, her spine curving as far as her restraints would allow it. She heard the tails flick in the air this time. This time, they gave her nipple a stinging kiss, and then another and another.

"Oh, God," she gasped, stretched on a rack of taut arousal.

"Look at you, giving yourself so completely. You are such a good girl," she heard Kam mutter in a thick accent. "So much sweeter than I ever imagined."

Her entire body jerked like she'd been electrified. She wasn't even sure what was happening to her. It took her vibrating brain a second to realize she was climaxing thunderously. Kam had turned on the vibrator and placed it next to her clit. For a wild moment, even her lungs seized in pleasure.

"Oh *God*," she gasped, her lungs finally unfreezing. "Oh Jesus," she keened between waves of crashing pleasure.

"Don't fight it. Let go," she heard Kam say.

She finally fell against the mattress, panting, still in the aftershock of searing pleasure. She moaned when she felt Kam's large, massaging hand move along her thighs, hips and arms.

"Still so tense," he said. "You are not finished yet."

He was speaking English, not French, but Lin's lust-scrambled brain was having difficulty in interpreting even that. Kam was moving, pulling his thighs out from beneath her. She gave a muffled protest at the loss of his hard muscles and throbbing cock. Then he was coming down between her spread legs again, his dark head a contrast to her pale thighs, his hands on her hips.

"Kam," she shouted in anguish at the sensation of his tongue swiping between her labia, gathering her juices. It might have been made of fire. Her hips bobbed uncontrollably, making his head rear back.

"Stay still," he said sharply. She moaned. What was happening to her? Just that single caress of his tongue on her clit had been almost unbearably exciting. He stilled her with his hands, holding her steady. "I know it hurts a little, baby. Try to endure it, and you will feel the pressure ease. Trust me."

She exhaled with effort, forcing her zinging, agitated nerves to calm. Kam began to tongue her again, more gently than he had in the past, his actions so deliberate her eyes crossed. She pulled at her wrist restraints, both hating her inability not to touch him and loving the feeling of security the bonds gave her. There was nowhere to go, nothing to do but lie there and submit to pleasure. As she surrendered, Kam's mouth became greedier. More forceful. Slowly, he built that crescendo in her flesh all over again.

Finally, he covered her with his mouth, demanding his due with his lashing tongue and an insistent suction, his head moving in a taut, firm twist between her thighs. She exploded in another powerful orgasm. This time, however, her entire body went lax as the shudders waned, all of her strain and tension melting away.

She blinked at the vision of Kam coming over her on his hands and knees. He looked truly awesome in that moment, a primal male, her female essence glistening on his chin and nose. He had her scent now. He wouldn't rest until he'd gotten his fill.

"How did you know?" she rasped, referring to her difficulty in relaxing her body following her first orgasm.

"You got so excited beneath the flogger, your climax wasn't sufficient to calm you. I could feel it in your rigid muscles, see it in your expression," he said, his narrowed gaze roving over her face and breasts hungrily. Despite the fact that he'd proved he could read her with subtle mastery before, the evidence of it still stunned her. He paused, kneeling over her supine body. His nostrils flared. He looked hungry as he looked down at her.

Very hungry.

"I had guessed you would be responsive," he growled softly. "But I had not dared to hope as greatly as all this. You're so lovely. But now you will have to put out the fire you started in me," he murmured, his eyes like crescents of gleaming silver.

"Yes. Whatever you want," she whispered heatedly.

He lifted his hand and pressed his thumb to her lower lip, his stare burning straight through her. "I will have your mouth since you are still sore from last night."

"No . . . I'm all right," she said in protest—she really wasn't all that sore anymore—but he silenced her by penetrating her lips with his thumb. He met her stare.

"I will have your mouth," he repeated. She sucked his thick thumb all the way into her mouth, her eyes speaking for her as she looked up at him.

Yes. Whatever you want.

And she meant it like she'd never meant it in her life. What was this throbbing, swelling feeling mounting in her, this unnamable need? Was it that he'd given her so much pleasure and she wanted to return it?

Yes, but it was more, Lin realized as he slid his thumb out of her sucking mouth, his hard mouth shaping into a slight snarl as she continued to pull on him, hard. She wanted to see pleasure tighten his face; she wanted to give her submission to him as a gift. She longed to do it because of the sweet, dark, secret place he'd taken her to just now, yes, but she would have craved it, no matter what had come first.

He came up on his knees over her, holding her stare as he began to unfasten his trousers.

A fever had come upon him, a trance of lust. He kept replaying it in his mind over and over, the vision of Lin strung as tight as a vibrating wire, back arched, hips flexed, head back, offering herself to the flogger. He had known she was incredibly responsive, but sensitivity and the capability for great passion did not equate to the ability for submission. That required courage, trust, and faith. Seeing that combination of all those things in her, witnessing that transformation, had cast a spell over him, sexual magic at its purest and most powerful.

He jerked down his pants impatiently, wincing slightly as he brushed his fingers against his rigid cock. Without thinking, he grabbed himself through his boxer briefs and hissed. It'd been a trial like he'd never endured, watching Lin as he flogged her gently, drowning in her sweet juices, burning but never igniting.

He was done with waiting.

He lifted his knee and hastily got off the bed, getting rid of his remaining clothing just as hastily. From the side of his vision, he saw Lin's head turn, feeling her stare on him like a touch. His cock dropped out of the confinement of his underwear, heavy and ponderous. God he ached. He fisted himself from below and stroked the length firmly, holding Lin's stare.

"I don't know what you're doing to me," he said. "You've taken root in my mind. I can't get you out of my head."

She blinked several times. So did Kam. His bald admission had shocked him a little, too. The feeling of vulnerability that came over him made him want to punish her a little . . . pleasure her a lot. He crawled back on the bed, kneeling over her, his knees near her armpits. He again took his aching cock into his hand. She looked up at him with somber dark eyes, and he felt himself pulse against his palm.

"You make it sound like you're angry about it," she said.

"No," he said. "You've left me spinning, that's all. Now you will have to face the consequences." He slid his knees apart on the silky duvet, lowering himself. He brushed the tip of his cock against her lips. Her tongue came out, red and wet, licking at the head.

"Oh, oui, encore," he demanded, watching her closely. *Again.* She ran the tip of her firm tongue over the slit, coaxing a drop of pre-ejaculate from the glans. Her quick tongue immediately swept it into her mouth. He grunted appreciatively, smiling down at her. "That's right, little kitten." he murmured. Unable to resist the bewitching target of her small smile, he fisted his shaft and pushed the thick head between her lips. She immediately clamped him hard, her cheeks hollowing out as she sucked. He made a strangled sound and pulsed back and forth between her lips with just the first several inches of his cock for several ecstatic seconds.

"You suck it like you really want it," he murmured, his nostrils flaring as he watched her. She nodded, twitching his cock as she did so, her lustrous eyes undoing him. He glanced up in rising arousal and frustration. The posters on the large bed were just out of the reach of his hands. He had nothing to use to support his upper body. Without balance, he risked hurting her if he went deeper, no matter how eager her hot mouth was.

She made a sound of thwarted longing when he willfully slid his cock out of the wet vacuum of her mouth. "A moment, baby," he said, going back on his haunches, his erection standing out from his body lewdly. He reached for her ankle restraints, giving her several inches of slack. He climbed off the bed and walked around to the foot. Her eyes widened slightly in surprise when he slid her entire body down the bed. Her head fell off the edge of the mattress.

"Oh," she whispered as if in understanding, her gaze fixing on his cock as she stared up.

"There you go," he murmured, enraptured by the vision of her craning for him. He fisted his shaft and arrowed the tip between her dark pink, parted lips. He flexed and grunted in pleasure as he slid along her tongue. Her tongue no longer rubbed on the sensitive underside of his cock in this position, but the eroticism of the position—not to mention her eager suction—more than made up for that. "That's so good." He placed his hands on the mattress, leaning over her, pulsing in and out of her sucking mouth. So quickly, so completely, she took him to heaven. Her hunger was a palpable thing. She sucked forcefully. He groaned when she took him deeper and he felt her satisfied hum vibrate into his flesh.

In this inspired position, he hovered over her bound, naked body while she took more and more of his cock into her mouth. It was highly distracting.

Carefully, mindful of her vulnerability, he reached for the discarded vibrator on the bed. He turned it on, still bracing himself with one hand, and reached for her pussy. She squealed onto his cock when he pushed the little bullet between her labia. She ducked her head forward, gobbling him even more greedily.

"Oh yeah," he muttered, his eyes rolling back in his head when he felt the tight ring of her throat squeezing the tip of his cock. He moved the vibrator, rewarding her. She gagged slightly and slid down over his shaft, but then she was almost immediately back for more. She swallowed him deep and fast, seemingly made frantic by the vibrator on her pussy. Her sex was pink and flushed, glistening with her juices, so vivid and flagrant next to her pale thighs. His mouth watered.

She gasped loudly when he slid his heavy erection out of her mouth. His cock protested as well, lurching angrily at the deprivation of her sucking mouth. But he couldn't resist her pussy. Putting his knees at the edge of the bed, he lowered over her.

"I just need a taste," he mumbled distractedly. He coated his tongue with her juices, only vaguely aware of her desperate cries. Her cream intoxicated him, her soft lips and the jewel of her reddened clitoris, which he polished with such care. His eyes sprung wide when he felt her lips capture the tip of his suspended cock. He groaned gutturally as she sucked him greedily into her mouth with a slurping sound. He had not wanted her to suck him while he hovered over her so precariously and she was restrained and helpless, but he couldn't deny her eager mouth. He firmed his hold, careful not to put too much weight or pressure on her. She sucked him deeper and he growled her name before he buried his nose in her sex, licking and consuming. He grew lost, surrounded by sensation, thrusting his hips back and forth, taking his fill of Lin.

It was true that he fucked her mouth in those tense moments of bliss, but he never forgot her vulnerability. Despite his restraint, he joined her in taut bliss, drowning in her juices and taking so much pleasure in her sweet mouth that it was as if they blended for a nirvanic moment, becoming one being that vibrated with a common pulse, fused together by fire.

He felt her scream vibrate into his cock and her hips buck in a frenzy. He laved her clit with a rigid tongue, feeling the tingle deep at the root of his cock that reminded him that heaven was short-lived for mortals.

It didn't really surprise him that they came simultaneously. He'd felt so joined with her, as if they were both controlled by the same brain for a precious moment. The same heart. It was a first for him, that feeling of deep communion during sex. He poured himself into her, thrusting shallowly, while she sucked and sucked like she was intent on turning him inside out. His mouth nursed her through her crisis, too, his tongue and lips coaxing another, and yet another shudder out of her body.

She continued to suck, wringing every last shiver of sensation out of him. He finally lifted his head, panting, utterly drained. He came up on his hands and knees, watching as he withdrew his cock from her mouth. Sliding his knees off the edge of the mattress, he took his lower body weight by standing on the carpet. He sunk his upper body onto the mattress next to her. He pressed his lips to her smooth hip, inhaling her exquisite scent as his body tried desperately to recover. She turned her head.

"Kam," she whispered next to his skin.

He clamped his eyelids tight when she pressed her lips to his hip in turn, her gentle kiss searing straight through him.

Twenty minutes later, Lin snuggled in Kam's embrace, his head on the pillow, her cheek pressed to his chest. Neither of them had said much as Kam had released her restraints and removed her cuffs, setting them on the bedside table. He'd peeled back the bedding and put out his arms, silently bidding her to him. Lin had gone gladly. It was like the hush following an unusually powerful storm, when the earth has been pummeled by Mother Nature. She lay in his arms, slowly recovering, but still cloaked by the powerful, scorching memory of the tempest they'd unleashed.

What exactly did one say to a man after an experience like that? It'd been eye-opening. Shocking. She had given him control, and in turn, he had showed her depths to her own soul she hadn't known existed. Had he meant to? Or was that just what any woman would experience when he restrained her and demanded she submit to pleasure?

"Are you all right?" he murmured after a moment, his large hand cupping and rubbing her shoulder.

"Yes," she whispered. She suddenly felt very small in his arms, overwhelmed by the intimacy of what had just occurred between them. She hid her face in his chest. It had probably not been all that of an uncommon experience for him. She was being foolish.

"Lin?" he asked quietly, his fingers brushing her jaw. Slowly, warily, she lifted her head. She met his stare for the first time since they'd quivered in fused ecstasy. His gaze ran over her face. His brows slanted.

"What is it?" he demanded.

She shook her head, unable to put these chaotic, new feelings into words. What had been happening to her ever since she'd walked into that restaurant and saw Kam sitting at that bar? She hardly recognized herself anymore.

"It was . . . unbelievable," she finally said inadequately.

His confusion faded as he stroked her cheek. "It was amazing. *You* are."

Then he was pulling her down to his mouth, and his kiss made her forget her anxiety.

For a moment.

When he finally sealed their kiss and studied her with quicksilver eyes, she found she couldn't take this feeling swelling in her breast anymore. She couldn't breathe.

"I'm just going to go wash up." She nodded toward a door she assumed was the suite's bathroom. He nodded and released his hold, but he wore a guarded look as he studied her face. She snagged her new nightgown on the way to the bathroom. She felt his stare on her naked back the whole way. After she'd washed and gathered herself, she returned to the bedroom now wearing the nightgown. Kam had turned down the bedside lamp to a dim setting. He lay propped up on the pillows, the sheet down around his hips, hair mussed, all lean, muscular, beautiful male.

"Do you want me to go?" she asked him quietly, sitting on the edge of the bed.

"No. I want you to take off that gown and get in here with me."

She arched her brows at his steadfastness. "For another hour or two?"

"Until morning," he said.

"Are you sure, Kam?"

"Of course I'm sure. Why do you say it like that?" he asked, scowling slightly.

She hesitated. "Something Phoebe Cane said to Maria gave the impression you don't like spending an entire night with a woman," Lin said, studying her hand on the dark blue silk duvet. "And then last night—"

"I was being stupid last night. I want you to stay," he said. Her gaze leapt to his face. He looked fierce and very beautiful to her.

"Okay," she whispered.

He took her hand and pulled, so that she slid up the duvet closer to him, still in a sitting position. He slipped the straps off her shoulders and lowered the gown over her breasts. He pushed the silk down into her lap and palmed her hips. She experienced that melting, heavy feeling in her lower belly. He not only turned her body into a syrupy mush with his touch, but her brain.

"I also want you to spend the rest of the weekend with me. Until Monday morning." One hand feathered up her rib cage. She inhaled sharply. He cupped a breast in his hand and ran the pad of his thumb over the nipple.

"I'm not sure those are fair tactics for convincing me," she said softly.

His gray eyes flickered up to meet hers. "I wasn't aware there were any rules."

"You would like that, wouldn't you?" she whispered when he lifted his other hand and cupped both her breasts at once. He finessed both nipples with his thumb and forefinger. She bit off a moan. Her breasts were still very sensitive, but the gentle pressure felt good. "No rules. No right or wrong. Only pleasure."

He paused in his caresses. "That's a problem?"

For a few seconds, she didn't respond, just studied his handsome, rugged features. His gaze narrowed as he peered at her closely.

"I thought it wasn't," she admitted shakily. "But as it turns out, I'm not built like you, Kam."

Her low voice, and all it implied, seemed to reverberate in her ears in the silence that followed. Slowly, he released her breasts. She missed his warmth. She missed it sorely.

"You mean you're not built for a casual affair?" he clarified.

She nodded, holding his gaze.

He seemed to consider. "So I would be a real bastard if I insisted you stay after you told me that?"

She smiled. "I don't know if you'd be a real bastard, but—"

He placed his hand along her jaw. "I'm not a bastard. Not when it comes to you. *Stay.*"

Her heart seemed to stall in her chest. *Not when it comes to you.*

"You're sure?" she asked, her voice sounding a little shaky.

He wrapped his arms around her and lifted her over his body. When she landed, she was next to him, her breasts pressed against the side of his chest. She stretched along his length. His mouth covered hers, firm and insistent. Her toes curled against the duvet as that delicious sensation unfurled and spread at her core like a flower made of heat. A dazed moment later, he sealed their kiss, laid her back against the pillows and leaned down over her.

"Do I look sure?" he asked.

She searched his face in the dim light. "You *do.*"

A small smile shaped his mouth. "You don't have to look so surprised. I wouldn't have asked if I wasn't serious about it. So you're mine until Monday?"

She smiled and nodded her head. For a heady few seconds, they just grinned at each other.

"So what are you going to tell Ian?"

She blinked, a sudden alarm sounding in her brain. "Tell Ian about what?"

"What's your excuse for skiving off that brunch meeting tomorrow? Ian mentioned something about it when we talked on Friday.

I remember, because he gave me quite a look when I told him he overworked you," Kam said, the hint of amusement in his tone saying loud and clear that he wasn't overly concerned by Ian's annoyance at his observance.

"He doesn't overwork me. I do it because I want to. And I don't think I need an excuse. I'll just call and cancel. Say something came up," she said, entranced by the warmth in Kam's eyes. She felt herself sinking. Flying. She didn't know which. She could so easily lose herself to this. To him. Did he realize that? He'd sounded so certain about telling her to stay after what she'd revealed to him, but that didn't mean he was feeling the same way as she was.

She immediately forced her thoughts away from figuring out precisely *what* she was feeling. It was too complicated, and too difficult, especially in the presence of Kam. He overwhelmed her senses and completely eradicated rational thought.

"You don't *think* you need to make up an excuse for canceling on work? Let me guess," he said, leaning down to kiss her neck, sliding his lips over her pulse. She sighed. He knew exactly where to kiss to get that reaction. "You've never called in and said you weren't coming in for personal, *selfish* reasons before."

He scraped his teeth against a patch of skin just behind her ear. A puff of air flew past her lips. "I've never had to before."

"No. You never *wanted* to," he corrected her, his voice muffled against her skin. His hand lowered, caressing a breast and feathering her belly. "But you want to for this?"

"Yes," she whispered, turning her head and seeking him out with her mouth. "Very much."

"That's what I wanted to hear," he growled softly, capturing her lips with his. He cupped her sex. She moaned against his mouth. He shifted, placing his mouth next to her ear.

"I'm saving this little pussy for tomorrow," he rumbled. "It's going to be all mine on the first day that Lin Soong ever plays hooky."

She laughed, shivering at the impact of his low, rough voice in her ear. "You don't have to wait, Kam. I'm fine."

"No," he said firmly, almost as if he was saying it to himself more than her. "I know how hard I rode you last night, again and again and again." She felt his cock leap against her as he repeated the word, and knew he was remembering their frantic, wild lovemaking last night just like she was. He swept her nightgown over her hips and down her legs. He reached behind him and the room was plunged into blackness.

Lin sighed in comfort and pleasure when he pulled her against him, spooning her, and she was surrounded by a wall of lean, hard muscle that resonated heat. She felt his cock throbbing against the lower curve of her ass. Despite being aroused by the sensation, a wave of lassitude overcame her. She was warm and content and satiated from phenomenal sex.

She was in Kam's arms.

"Lin?" Kam asked, his voice sounding thick with sleep.

She blinked open heavy eyelids.

"Yes?"

"Are you on birth control?"

"Yes. The pill," she murmured into the darkness.

Again, she felt his cock swell.

"If I swore to you that I typically religiously practice safe sex, and that I'm clean, could I—"

"Yes," she emphatically.

"You trust me that much?" he asked, sounding a little stunned.

"Well you are a doctor, after all," she said drolly. She laughed when she heard the indignant sound he made. "It's not just because of that. I don't believe you'd lie to me about something like that," she added softly, meaning it. "I can securely assure you, too. I had a doctor's appointment two months ago, and there hasn't been anyone since then."

He cupped her sex in that possessive manner of his.

"You just made me a very happy man," he said. She started to turn in his arms to make love, but he stopped her by kissing her shoulder. "Tomorrow," he said succinctly near her ear.

Her racing heart and Kam's throbbing erection made it extremely difficult for her to slide into sleep.

She swam in a cocoon of heavy, warm pleasure. A mouth pulled gently on her nipple, and she felt the sweet tug all the way to her core.

"Oh, that's nice," she muttered, her words slurred with sleep. She blinked open her heavy eyelids. The faded light of early morning glowed around the curtains. She lay on her back. Kam's shadow loomed over her. His body separated her thighs.

"Guess what?" he asked, his deep, accented voice causing her skin to roughen.

"What?" she whispered.

"It's tomorrow."

She snorted softly. "You've been waiting to say that, haven't you?"

"All blessed night. You have a lot of nerve, sleeping like a baby."

"You didn't?" she murmured in amazement, pushing her hair out of her eyes.

He pushed back her thighs. She gasped when he pushed a thick finger into her slit. "Not much. You think I could sleep when I've been craving to be naked inside you since I first saw you?" He removed his finger and she felt the moisture he brought with him against her thigh. He grunted in satisfaction. "You must have been having sweet dreams at least. You're nice and slick. Tight and soft. This is going to feel so good."

Excitement rippled through her at the sound of his illicit words in the near darkness. He shifted, bracing himself on one forearm, his other hand between his thighs. The head of his cock felt warm and hard, probing her slit, insisting upon entrance. She whimpered.

"That's right," he said thickly. "Open your thighs nice and wide. Let me in."

He flexed his hips, his cock stretching her, carving through her slowly, melting her flesh with his power and heat. She believed completely in that moment that he'd been up a good part of the night. His cock was huge and heavy with sustained arousal.

"Oh yeah, that's so good," he muttered. "You're so hot, baby. You're squeezing me so tight." He paused. She sensed his pitched alertness. "I can feel your heart beating inside you."

"Kam," she whispered, moved by the tinge of wonder in his voice. She ran her hands over his shoulders and chest, loving his hardness and strength. He began to rock her. She made a soughing sigh of surrender. He flexed his hips and seated his cock inside her completely.

"So tight but so wet," he hissed. "You're going to have a time of it keeping me out of this pussy."

"You'll have no fight from me. It feels so good," she whispered.

He withdrew and sunk back into her, a groan tearing at his throat. "Lin?"

"Yes?" she asked. It was hard to catch her breath with him throbbing so high inside her, filling her to the brim.

"When we made love before," he said gruffly. "It's never been like that for me. I thought you deserved to know. It's never felt like *this*." He stroked her again and groaned. She gasped, overwhelmed by sensation, stunned by what he was telling her.

"No. Not for me, either," she admitted shakily, her fingers digging into the dense muscle of his shoulders. He drove into her. Her head fell back on the pillow as she gasped.

He left her no choice. There was no guarding of her heart in this raw, honest place where he took her. She couldn't say no to the wild, fierce ride that was Kam.

Chapter Fifteen

She awoke later alone in the bed. She blinked several times, trying to figure out what it was that had awakened her. The memory of their early morning lovemaking lapped over her like a sensual, warm surf. She'd watched Kam fall into a deep, peaceful sleep afterward, unable to look away from his face. Finally, she'd roused herself from her trance to call Ian and apologize for not being able to attend the brunch meeting with a visiting CEO of one of Noble's subsidiaries. Then she'd finally joined Kam in a satisfied sleep.

Now he was gone. The bedroom door was closed. In the distance, she heard the sound of male voices. She sat up quickly, clutching the sheet to her breasts. The voices were similar in timbre and volume, but one was French accented, the other British. *Ian was here.* Her glance landed on her leather cuffs on the bedside table. Anxiety swept through her, which was ridiculous. Of course Ian wasn't coming back *here*. Kam would never let him. She leapt out of bed and approached the closed door. She tilted her head, trying to make out their words over her pounding heart.

". . . unfortunate what happened with Jason. I'd have never

guessed it of him, but some men will turn into idiots around a woman as beautiful as Lin," she thought she heard Ian say, the direction of his voice making her think he stood near the hallway in front of the foyer. "No wonder she wanted to take the day off to recover after something like that."

Kam spoke, but it was as if his back was turned in her direction. She heard her own name several times, and then he spoke vehemently in French.

"I understand," Ian said. "I'm only sorry I ever suggested the meeting. I would have done the same if I came upon someone holding Francesca against her will."

Lin's breath froze in her lungs. She pressed her ear to the door, but all she heard was silence. Ian had drawn a parallel between his protective feelings for Francesca and Kam's for her. Had Ian been opening a door for Kam to talk about her—Lin? If he was, Kam wasn't taking the bait. She was thankful.

"I stopped by to officially ask you to dinner on Monday night. Lucien and Elise are coming, and Mrs. Hanson is making roast beef and Yorkshire pudding. I'd ask Lin, but she's out of town for the night." Lin frowned. Ian certainly kept linking Kam and her together. How much did he really suspect about them? "And we're meeting for the demonstration of your device with Gersbach on Wednesday. Lin says you two are ready for that?" Ian continued.

"We're ready."

"Maybe tomorrow night, you can tell us all what you're really planning for your future," Ian said.

Lin's breath froze in her lungs at the unexpected comment. She pressed her ear closer to the door when Ian resumed in a more subdued tone. "Don't give me that look, Kam. I know you've been planning something all along for this business trip, and it wasn't that you ever expected to sell your patent to any of the luxury watch companies that Lin and I have arranged for you to meet."

"I haven't ruled anything out. I like Gersbach, and I look forward to meeting the people from Stunde," Kam said neutrally, foiling Ian's attempt to get him to open up. The two men continued talking, but they must have shifted positions, because their voices were more muffled and unintelligible.

By the time Kam rapped on the bathroom door five minutes later, Lin was drying off from a quick shower.

"Come in," she called, tucking the edge of the towel between her breasts.

They stared at each other for several seconds when he opened the door and stood in the entryway, one arm extended on the frame. He really was a sight to behold first thing in the morning.

"Hi," she said, stepping toward him and yanking her gaze off the thin trail of hair that bisected his ridged abdomen and disappeared below the low-riding waistband of his jeans. My, she had guessed his size perfectly. What Kam did to a pair of jeans would be considered illegal in some parts of the world. She yanked off the vision of him with effort. She noticed his flared nostrils and vaguely dissatisfied expression when she finally met his stare.

"What's wrong?" she asked.

"Damn Ian," he muttered. "I was hoping to wake you up myself and keep you in bed."

"You can't keep me in bed indefinitely," she teased him, a smile breaking through.

"Who says?" he asked, scowling at the same time he stepped toward her, his arms surrounding her. "Now let's just get rid of this," he murmured matter-of-factly. He tugged at her towel and it fell between them. "That's more like it." He pressed close against her naked, shower-warmed body. It felt decadently good. He hadn't showered yet. Ian's arrival must have got him out of bed, either that, or he'd gotten up to take Angus out. He smelled like soap and sex and man. Without thinking, she sunk her teeth gently into what was in front of her—a dense pectoral muscle covered in thick, smooth skin. She sampled his skin with her tongue and felt his cock twitch behind his jeans. His hands moved in her hair, releasing the restraining clip she'd put in it for her shower.

"Now that's *much* more like it," he growled, delving his fingers into the loose strands and tugging. Her head fell back and he swooped down, claiming her mouth. By the time he lifted his head a minute later, Kam's cock had stiffened next to her belly and Lin's flesh—to say nothing of her brain—had turned to warm goo.

"I'm going to make you into a complete hooky addict," he stated smugly as he nipped at her lips.

"You're off to a good start," she murmured, nibbling his mouth back hungrily as she spoke. "There's only one problem."

"There's *no* problem," he corrected, pulling her closer in his arms. She pulsed her hips against his cock. He hissed and bit at her a tad harder.

"I don't have any clothes here except for an evening dress," she reminded him.

"You won't need them."

"I will so. I'm not doing the walk of shame in my rumpled evening dress tomorrow morning. Plus, I told Ian when I called I'd get a few things to him by the end of the evening."

He lifted his head and arched his brows, looking down at her. "You are *not* going to work today."

"You can be awfully dictatorial for a man who lived alone for so long and had nobody to boss around. I feel a new kinship to Angus," she complained without any real heat. He gave her a bland look. "It's just a few things."

"You're a grown woman. When will you learn to live a little? There's more to life than work, little kitten," he coaxed, running his firm lips along her cheek and temple.

"There's an important memo I need to draft."

He lifted his head and scowled.

"At the very least, I have to check a few e-mails this morning and answer them."

"You can use my computer for that, but after that, you're done with work," he said, his hands running over her back, massaging her . . . influencing her. He knew precisely what he was doing, she admitted as her flesh softened and warmed even further under his touch. "And you're only going to need one set of clothes, because otherwise, I'll want you naked," he murmured near her temple. He undoubtedly felt her shivers of pleasure beneath his stroking hands at the sound of his rough voice in her ear. "I'll shower in the other bathroom and run out right now to one of the stores on Michigan Avenue. I'll get you some dog-walking clothes."

"Dog-walking clothes?" Lin asked, her eyes drifting closed under the influence of his big, rubbing hands moving so deftly on her muscles.

"Yeah. Casual, easy, weekend clothes—the kind I hardly ever see you wear. You'll need something for when we take breaks and take Angus for walks." She blinked her eyes open, his hot stare telling her precisely what they'd be *taking breaks* from. He kissed the end of her nose and then her mouth, lingering for a moment to penetrate her lips ever so briefly with his tongue, sampling her.

"Well?" he prompted as he backed up, his gaze lowering over her naked body.

"Well what?" she asked, made stupid by the way he looked at her with such heat.

"My computer is out in the living room. Do whatever you need to do while I shower and I run out, because when I come back, you're mine for the next twenty-four hours. And you're going to get it if I catch you sneaking any work after that."

Her heart leapt when she noticed the hard glint in his eyes. She shook her head and rolled her eyes, trying to discount his threat. He arched his eyebrows, giving her a pointed glance that told her loud and clear he hadn't been teasing. Her eyes widened.

"That's right. I meant it, *mon petit chaton*," he assured quietly. "For the next twenty-four hours, *I'm* your boss. If you test me by focusing on anything but relaxation, fun, or pleasure, I'll have to prove it to you with a punishment." She blinked. He grinned suddenly, a brilliant flash of good humor. She laughed when he swooped down to give her one last kiss. He started to back out of the room but pointed at her foot.

"Shoe size?" he demanded.

"Seven," she replied breathlessly. He nodded, turned and headed toward his shower.

For several seconds, she just stood there, dazed. Despite that charming smile that radiated sex appeal like a beacon, Lin was left with a sneaking suspicion accompanied by an illicit thrill that Kam had been dead serious about what he'd said.

Cocky and *incorrigible,* she thought with wry amusement as she retrieved the towel. She refastened it around her breasts and met her own gaze in the mirror. Her smile faded.

You've never been more irresponsible and foolish in your life.

Nor have you ever been more dishonest.

Didn't Kam deserve to know about her secret infatuation for his brother for the past eleven years of her life?

But when she and Kam were together, like they'd been last night, the only man in the room was Kam . . . the only man in her mind . . . her world. Just because she had some past unresolved—and *unresolvable* feelings for Ian—didn't mean she should go around making dramatic confessions about it to Kam. That was ridiculous. Besides, maybe Richard had been right when she'd said her unrequited feelings for Ian had kept her safe from commitment. Safe from hurt. Safe from rejection. Between Ian and her work, Lin was lucky she wasn't still an untouched virgin. Even so, dipping her toe in the water now and then hardly equated to swimming.

If Richard's analysis was right, what was she doing with Kam? He was no stellar specimen when it came to being an ideal mate, was he? Quirky, commitment-phobic geniuses who also just happened to be drop-dead sexy and could get almost any woman to fall into bed with them were hardly the hallmarks of a perfect partner. Kam had told her point-blank yesterday that his relationship with Phoebe Cane was agreeable to him because it was just about sex, no strings attached. Yes, he'd insinuated that he didn't plan to hurt her and hinted that he had a deeper interest in her than casual sex. Hadn't he?

Why did it feel in retrospect that he hadn't *really* said anything all that substantial last night? She closed her eyes, trying to re-create the intensity of emotion she'd experienced. It'd felt overwhelmingly intimate and beautiful and special while she'd been under his influence. In the morning light, her logical brain tried to re-create the magic of letting go, of trusting . . . but it eluded her.

No, she hardly felt *safe* carrying on this way with Kam.

Yet here she was.

What Kam *did* make her feel, she realized as she opened her eyes and stared at herself honestly in the mirror, was *good*, and more alive than she remembered feeling in her entire life.

Maybe this wasn't wise and maybe it wasn't safe, Lin acknowledged as she opened up a drawer and found a comb. But it *was* wonderful.

Didn't she deserve the spotlight for a precious moment, no matter how short that time was? Didn't she deserve to bask in the euphoria of great sex, risk, and romance instead of always being the efficient, careful, reliable understudy hovering in the wings?

Kam's eyes grew warm when he entered the apartment a little less than an hour later and saw her on the floor next to Angus, a computer in her lap and a cup of coffee steaming on the table not far away. Sunlight flooded through the floor-to-ceiling windows and turned Lake Michigan a sparkling teal in the distance. Angus had succumbed to the warm sedative of the sun a few minutes before, when Lin had scratched her behind the ears.

She smiled as he stalked toward her, his gaze lowering over her appreciatively and lingering on her bare, outstretched legs. "You look a hell of a lot better in that shirt than I do," he said, referring to his gray button-down, which fell on her at midthigh.

"I disagree. I happen to like this shirt on you a lot," she said, taking a sip of coffee.

He tossed a shopping bag on the couch behind her. "You should, since you're the one who picked it out." Lin's hand jerked, splashing some coffee on her upper lip. "Now we're trading off. I'm the one buying clothes for you."

"What . . . do you mean?" she said looking up at him.

He smirked. "You didn't really believe that I thought Ian picked out all those clothes for me, did you? Or chose the new curtains for Aurore, or all that bedding and linens and the new dishes for the kitchen? Give me *some* credit for reading him. Everyone knows he relies on you for stuff like that. Everyone knows you have impeccable taste."

She blushed. "I hadn't realized you knew."

"Your mark was all over that stuff. Your reputation precedes you. Ian, Francesca, Lucien, and Elise talk about you as if you could do no wrong. You transformed Aurore. Only you could make that ancient pile start to look not only elegant, but also comfortable," he said matter-of-factly, kneeling on the carpet and sitting next to her, his back leaning against the couch, one long, jean-covered leg bent, the other one sprawled out in front of him, his hip pressed against hers.

"I'm glad you liked the things. It was hard to choose, never having been to Aurore. Never having met you," she admitted.

For a few seconds, they didn't speak. The sunlight brought out the russet highlights in his dark hair. Before she could second-guess herself, she touched the thick waves. He smelled good, like soap and the outdoor air. "Ian described your character a little to me. It guided what I bought for clothing. Rugged. Independent. Nonconformist." She met his sun-gleaming eyes. "Utterly male."

His eyebrows went up. "Ian described me that way?"

She smiled as she reflected. "No. But somehow, I got that impression."

He caught her stroking hand and pressed his mouth to her palm. Warmth spread in places far away from his lips.

"I like your glasses," he said when he lifted his head slightly, his breath brushing against her skin.

"Thanks. I wear them for reading."

She felt him studying her intently.

"What?" she asked, grinning, sensing he was analyzing her component parts again like he did a machine's.

"This is how you should be all the time," he murmured gruffly. "You can't take the love of work out of the girl, but you should do it more like this. With your hair down. Sitting on the floor in the sunlight. Wearing one of my shirts . . ."

His lips were suddenly moving on hers, warm and sweet as the sunlight. She held her breath during that kiss, as if by doing so, she could hold on to the moment. His arms surrounded her, molding her back muscles in that delicious, bone-melting manner he had. Their kiss became wet and deep, tongues dueling sensually. She slid her hand beneath the blue-and-white plaid cotton shirt he wore, touching his warm, smooth skin. He groaned into her mouth and tightened his hold. He brought her onto his lap with a flex of hard muscle. She landed, straddling his hips, their kiss barely pausing.

Lin wasn't sure how long they kissed and touched, their actions simultaneously languorous and hungry. She was wrapped in a cocoon of sunshine with him and she was melting, her body softening and heating, her flesh yielding in a way it never had before. Maybe he felt the need to stretch the moment, too, because while he touched her, he did so fairly chastely, framing her jaw with his hand or brushing his fingertips against the shell of her ear or her nape. He rubbed her back, coaxing her muscles to yield even more. She touched his neck and shoulders, stroking him through the opening of his shirt. At one point, he leaned back and calmly removed her glasses, placing them on the couch behind him, then resumed his sensual kiss. She felt his arousal beneath her spread pussy, but for once, urgency didn't ride her as it often did with him. Kam trumped all that. His taste and his molding lips and his sleek, masterful tongue.

Inevitably, their arousal swelled untenably, though. She panted softly, helping him to unbuckle his belt and unfasten his button fly. She came up on her knees, granting him room. He worked his clothing down to his thighs, and then she came back over him. He held his erection in place and she lowered, gritting her teeth as his flesh slowly fused with her own. Her core had gone liquid with sweet arousal, but she had to apply a steady pressure to get her flesh to relent. Their gazes held fast until she sat in his lap and his cock pulsed high inside her. A sharp cry escaped her throat and he caught it with his seeking lips, nibbling at her, calming her as he rubbed her back.

"Venez maintenant. Commençons," he coaxed gently against her mouth after a moment. *Come now. Let us begin.* His large hands slipped beneath the shirt and palmed her buttocks. He lifted and brought her back down on him, squeezing her ass when he was fully sheathed, his mouth shaping into a snarl of pleasure. She joined him in the movement, rising and falling onto his cock, their mutual dance creating a divine friction. As they grew more frantic, he took more of her weight, his arms flexing powerfully as he lifted and crashed her down into his lap with increasing speed. The pressure was intense.

"I'm going to come," Lin cried out.

"No," he said sharply. He pushed her down onto his lap with a loud smacking sound. He held her there, his cock throbbing in protest in her deepest flesh.

"Oh . . . I have . . . to," she said in a strangled voice, her hips flexing, straining for the required pressure to come.

"Don't," he said so sharply she opened her eyelids sluggishly. His facial muscles were strained, his eyes fierce. "Make it last." His words went straight to her heart. She wanted it to last, too, but she sat on the launching pad, flaming, straining to ignite. She moaned, her hips struggling against his hold.

He grabbed some of the hair that trailed down her back. He lifted her shirt with his other hand and transferred it to the fist gripping her hair. Gently, he pulled back on her hair, pulling back her head. Chin up in the air, she whimpered when he slapped his palm against her bare buttock in a sharp, rapid rhythm. *Smack, smack, smack.*

"Oh!" she cried out, grimacing. He'd stung her skin, but his cock had jerked viciously inside her at the sound of his palm cracking against her ass. It'd been that which had made her exclaim in a mixture of discomfort and acute arousal. He released her hair and she met his gaze slowly.

"Better?" he asked hoarsely.

She nodded. The absolute necessity to climax had been pushed back temporarily by his spanking hand. They just stared at one another for a moment, both of them breathing heavily. A slight sheen of sweat shone on Kam's upper lip and forehead. The sunlight made his eyes into slits of blazing silver.

"Let's make it last," he repeated.

"I'll try," Lin agreed shakily.

"Don't move," he directed.

Holding her stare, he began to rapidly unbutton the shirt she wore. He pushed back the plackets, baring her breasts to the sunlight and his gaze. His nostrils flared. Again, she grimaced as his cock jumped inside her.

He began to play with her breasts. Lin moaned in rising misery as he plucked at the nipples, stiffening them into aching points. He looked up at her face, watching her reaction. She bit her lip, sweating in a sweet agony.

"I want to move," she whispered tremulously.

"I know. I want it, too," he muttered heatedly. "It feels so good. I want it to last a little longer, though. That's all. Stay still."

He whisked the shirt off her shoulders and down her arms. It was gone. She was naked and quivering, nailed to his lap. She began to unbutton his shirt, but he caught her wrists.

"Not now," he said. "I have something else in mind. I want you to gather all your hair and hold it against your head with both hands. I love your hair, but it's getting in the way of my touching every inch of you."

She quickly gathered the long strands and did as he asked, her breathing erratic. She didn't understand why he wanted her to do this, but following his terse demands excited her for some reason. "That's right," Kam said roughly. "Put out your elbows. Arch your back. Open yourself to me."

So, it wasn't just the restraint of her hair he had in mind. She stared down at him after she'd taken the position. It did make her feel open, her naked body fully exposed, her spine arched, her breasts thrust forward . . . her heart vulnerable.

His gaze ran over her from head to thigh, slow and hot. She was scorched by that stare. She could barely draw breath.

He spread both hands on her hips and whisked them along her sides and over her breasts and down her belly and up her back.

"*Kam,*" she moaned, undone by his worshipful gaze, tormented by his possessive touch. He swept his hands everywhere, his actions somehow both lewd and cherishing at once.

"It's all right," he soothed when she whimpered as he massaged her ass in both hands. "Just a moment longer." He placed his hands on her hips and stretched his thumbs toward her sex. He parted her labia, fully exposing her glistening pink folds and clitoris. Her exposure was complete. A rough groan tore at his throat. His cock swelled. Her shaking amplified. He looked up at her face, his expression tight with rapt wonder.

"God, you're beautiful," he breathed out. Then he leaned forward, his back leaving its rest against the couch, holding her so tightly she could barely draw breath. One of his forearms slipped beneath her ass like a supporting bar, his hand cupping a cheek, his other arm surrounded her waist, hugging her against him. He began to move her. She rose and fell over him like a crashing wave as he took complete control of her weight. Every muscle in his body grew hard and flexed as he strained for relief.

She'd begged for him to unleash the storm, and suddenly she was at the center of it, taking its full wrath. His cheek was pressed against a breast. He gave a low, guttural growl, the sound and vibration in her flesh thrilling her, sending a spark through her. She lowered her arms, her hair falling around them, and grabbed his head.

"Kam . . . oh . . . God," she cried as he pounded her down on him, her voice vibrating with the strength of his short, staccato thrusts inside her. She felt him swell, heard his tortured groan.

He slammed her down on him again, roaring as he climaxed. For a moment, he seemed frozen by pleasure, but then he inhaled roughly and began pounding her up and down on his cock again as he ejaculated. The feeling of him pouring himself inside her sent her over the edge. She cried out sharply, the blast of climax all that much hotter and more powerful for having endured the flames with him.

Chapter Sixteen

She lay draped over him like melted candle wax for long, languorous moments, stroking his strong back muscles, coaxing them to release after their intense contraction during lovemaking. She didn't like that he was still mostly dressed while she was nude, but she felt too weak to undress him, too content to move.

Angus made a muted woofing sound in her dreams, the sound making Lin blink and focus. She saw the bag Kam had left when he'd joined her on the floor and they'd lost themselves to passion.

"You never showed me my dog-walking outfit," she murmured, nuzzling her face in the crook of his neck and shoulder.

"Hmmm?" he muttered lazily as he continued to stroke her naked skin from buttocks to shoulders, his low, resonant hum tickling her ear.

"The clothes you bought me," she reminded him, kissing his neck.

"They won't be as good as the ones you bought for me, but they'll work. Why didn't you tell me you bought me the clothes and the things for Aurore?" he asked gruffly after a few seconds.

"Ian thought you might take offense."

"Why would I take any more offense if you chose things for me versus him or Lucien?"

She brushed her lips against the slowing pulse at his neck and leaned back to look at his face. "I don't know exactly, except to say that I think he worried you'd become irritated if you got the impression he was trying to . . ." She paused, searching for the words. "Make you into something you're not. Change you. He cares about you, Kam. Truly. He just wants the best for you."

"Now that I think on it, I would have taken offense if anyone else had done it," he said after a moment.

"Done what?"

"Bought me things. I know I paid for them, but still . . ." He faded off, his gaze narrowing on her. "Because it was *you*, it didn't bother me. Somehow."

She held her breath. It was an incredibly sweet thing to say. She waited, a prickle of anxiety or anticipation or *something* going through her when he just continued to pin her with his stare.

"Did you ever consider working for someone other than Ian?"

"What?" she asked, taken off guard by the direction of his question.

"I know you told Jason Klinf 'no way' last night—even though from what I heard, he was offering you a pretty interesting opportunity. Others have to have offered you even more lucrative opportunities. I'm just wondering if you ever really considered leaving Noble in the past?"

"Not really, no. I've thought about offers, of course, but never seriously."

"What makes you stay? Why are you so loyal to Ian? Is it because your grandmother worked there and helped him build his company, and it feels like a family endeavor to you?"

Lin looked down from his piercing stare. "Maybe that has something to do with it," she admitted. She hesitated. Kam cradled her jaw and silently bid her to look at him. She saw his questioning glance. "A friend—Richard St. Claire, actually; you know him— recently pointed out to me that I tend to—" She paused, blushing in embarrassment and staring at his collar.

"What?" Kam prompted.

She shrugged. "I tend to cling onto familiar things, like my work, because I'm afraid of change. Of abandonment."

"Abandonment?" Kam asked.

Her blush deepened. "I know, it sounds ridiculous."

"No it doesn't."

She looked up in surprise. "It doesn't?"

He shook his head. "No. Not really. You must have been hit pretty hard when your mother and father left the States, leaving you behind. You were close to your grandmother, right?"

"Very," she said.

"When she passed, and you were all alone in the world. But Noble Enterprises was there. Familiar. Knowable. Comfortable, even, given your history with your grandmother. What's more, you're amazingly good at what you do. That gives a feeling of affirmation all on its own. I can understand how all that would make you want to stay."

"Yeah," she admitted. "I guess you're right."

He stroked her cheek with his thumb. "There's no reason to look sad about it," he said quietly. "It's completely normal. We all want what's familiar. Sometimes I feel like I'm going to jump out of my own skin in this city. I keep longing for home, and the silence of the woods, and my old routine myself."

"You do?" she asked, holding his stare. He nodded. "But you came. You're staying put, despite the fact that you'd rather be home. How come?" she asked.

"Because I realized that unless I stepped out of my comfort zone, I was never going to grow. I'm ready. I'm ready for a change." His thumb brushed her cheek softly.

Her heart began to pound in her ears in the silence that followed.

Angus startled up suddenly, looking around the room. Lin glanced from the golden retriever to Kam with amusement.

"I'd love to know what that dog dreams," Kam muttered dryly. Angus turned at the sound of his voice, her eyelids falling drowsily when he reached and scratched her behind the ears. "One thing I do know, she's going to want a bathroom break now that's she awake. You up for a walk?"

"I'd love one," Lin replied, thinking that the brisk fall air might clear some of the confusion and chaotic thoughts she'd been having lately about work and Ian. What bothered her most was that she never would have been having these feelings if it weren't for Kam.

He'd been the catalyst for everything.

Lin scrambled some eggs, which they ate with toast before they headed out with Angus. They walked south on the lakefront, Kam suggesting they take the path around the museum campus. It was a brilliant, warm fall day with the temperature in the low 60's. They walked hand in hand, talking about anything and everything—comparing notes on favorite spots in London and Paris, architecture, the kind of music they liked. She learned that his full name was Kamryn Patrick Reardon.

"I told you my mother never gave up an inch of her Irishness," Kam said sheepishly when Lin exclaimed over how much she loved the name. "The fact that Trevor Gaines seemed irritated by my Irish-sounding name only seemed to make me like it more."

She recalled what he'd said about how withdrawn and laconic he typically was, and was warmed by the fact that he seemed completely unguarded on that walk. The sunlight sparkling off the great lake seemed to perfectly reflect Lin's effervescent mood. Angus certainly seemed happy in the sunshine, bounding over to every dog and person she encountered on the lakefront path. If the person or pet seemed interested—which they seemed to be more often than not—Kam let the friendly golden retriever socialize for a moment before he pulled on her leash and Angus good-naturedly walked on with them.

Kam pointed to the western cityscape once they'd made a tour of the picturesque museum campus situated on the lakefront.

"Let's go this way. There's a park over here where we can unleash Angus," he said.

"How do you know so much about the city already?" she asked, puzzled.

"Running," he stated simply. "I've been out nearly every day since I've come to Chicago. Gave me a chance to check out the territory. Do you run?"

"Yes," she said smiling, thinking of his extremely muscular, well-toned body. "But I doubt I could keep up with you."

"I know how strong you are," he said, and she thought he referred to having watched her dance. "You could keep up."

They passed Lucien's hotel and kept walking south. By the time they reached Coliseum Park, dark clouds were gathering in the west, although the sun still prevailed in the sky. Kam unhooked Angus's leash in the enclosure, and the golden retriever immediately rushed over to bark and sniff at three other dogs. Lin laughed, watching her.

"If pets are supposed to share their owner's personalities, you must have a social butterfly hidden somewhere inside you," she told Kam amusedly.

He grinned, his expression doubtful. "I'd say Angus and I are complete opposites."

"Oh, I don't know," Lin murmured, her smile widening as she watched Angus bark and bounce around ebulliently with a chocolate Labrador. "You both certainly have the ability to make others happy."

He opened his hand along her neck, his thumb feathering her jaw. She looked up at him and blinked. Until she saw the look on his face, she hadn't fully realized what she'd said. He leaned down and kissed her. Lin knew it was his way of thanking her for telling him he made her happy. She smiled up at him when he lifted his head a few seconds later, knowing her heart was in her eyes. For once, she didn't hide it. He *did* make her happy.

"I might have to take my word back on one thing. I'm just as good a shopper as you are," he said, his hand still cradling her jaw, his gaze trailing down over the jeans, running shoes, and fresh, light green sweater he'd bought her. The sweater clung to her breasts, and his gaze lingered there—not for the first time since she'd donned the garment.

"I agree. You even got the sizes perfect. How did you do it?"

"I pointed out a woman working at the store who looked about your size. Except for there," his brows lifting slightly as he glanced at her breasts. "She was smaller than you, but I didn't say anything. I'm glad I didn't. I like the result."

Lin snorted with laughter. They walked back through the city, pausing to stroll around a bustling Millennium Park before they returned to Kam's new apartment. By the time they returned to Kam's building, it had become cooler and overcast. They'd be getting rain later.

When they'd left the building earlier that morning, Lin had experienced a moment of anxiety. What if they ran into Francesca or Mrs. Hanson? How would she explain what she was doing with Kam when she'd called and told Ian she couldn't make an important business brunch?

On the return trip to the building, she never even thought of it. Her head was too filled with Kam to consider anything else.

Perhaps the realization that she'd so easily forgotten her other life was what was responsible for her temporary relapse into her work mindset when they returned. The promise of a storm cloaked the apartment when they entered. The living room was cast in shadow.

"I'm just going to go wash up," Kam said, pointing toward the bathroom.

"Okay," she said, suddenly feeling shy for some stupid reason. The dim apartment seemed in stark contrast to their former warm, easygoing mood on the walk. There was a hushed quality to the luxurious interior. Expectant. It seemed very intimate. Her awareness of Kam suddenly ratcheted up several degrees, making her feel self-conscious and . . .

. . . excited.

She spotted the computer she'd been using earlier still on the floor. She walked over and picked it up distractedly, sitting on the couch. It wasn't that she really *planned* to check her e-mails, they just popped onto the screen when she touched the mouse pad to turn off the computer. Spotting a new, potentially crucial, subject line, she pulled on her glasses. She was paging down on the e-mail, studying the screen intently when Kam spoke.

"Now you've gone and done it."

She looked up in surprise. Her mouth fell open when she noticed his expression—both grim and amused at once.

"What?"

"I told you what I was going to do if I caught you working," he said matter-of-factly. He stepped forward and grabbed the computer off her lap, setting it on the couch. She was reminded of his piratical side when he lifted his dark eyebrows in a challenging expression. "Are you going to come willingly for your punishment, or should I carry you?"

She smiled, half disbelieving, half anxious because she kind of *did* believe him. "Give me a break."

His brows lifted another fraction of an inch, as if to say, *I'm still waiting for an answer.* His cockiness pricked her pride, but it also excited her. She lifted her chin, daring him with her stare. "I was just checking my e-mail. I'm not going anywhere." She reached for the computer.

"Fine," he said unconcernedly. "So your answer is that you're not coming willingly."

"Kam!" she squawked when he swooped down and lifted her from the couch so rapidly she was taken by surprise. She grabbed his shoulder to steady herself. She was suddenly flying through the living room. Kam gave her a dark glance when she met his stare, but she saw amusement pulling at his mouth. She couldn't help it. She snorted with laughter.

"I told you that you were going to get it if you worked instead of focusing on relaxation and pleasure, buy you just had to go and test me," he said with mock sadness as he carried her down the dim hallway.

"So now I'm going to be punished for the horrible crime of checking e-mail?" she asked, containing her grin. Despite his playfulness, she saw his determination. His single-minded intent to steal her away to the bedroom for what she expected would be more experiments in dominance and submission and smoking-hot sex sent a forbidden thrill through her.

"Somebody's got to cure you of your addiction." He shut the bedroom door with his foot and entered the suite, setting her down next to the four-poster bed, his hands lingering on her hips. "You agree with that, don't you?"

She arched her eyebrows. "It's hardly an addiction. But *maybe* I shouldn't be quite so concerned about work." He continued to watch her expectantly. "Especially on the weekend." He waited. She bit her lip. "Especially on a weekend when I'm supposed to be focusing on fun."

"And?"

"Pleasure," she whispered. Suddenly, all the playfulness faded from his expression. He released his hold on her and sat down at the edge of the bed near the headboard.

"Take off your clothes."

His quiet command kept repeating in her head like an echo. Her mouth suddenly felt very dry. She untied her laces and kicked off her shoes, feeling shy meeting Kam's gaze. Her new sport socks joined her shoes on the carpet and then her jeans. Her fingers felt stiff as she began to unbutton the clinging green knit. The underwear Kam had bought her was in stark contrast to the casual clothing. He'd purchased three pairs of matching bras and panties, each of them silk and lace from a top designer. The set she wore today was a pretty periwinkle blue. When she'd teased him about his purchase of fine lingerie for a day of leisure earlier, he'd merely shrugged, unembarrassed.

"You might wear jeans, but underneath, you're always silk," he'd said.

She gathered the nerve to look up at him as she opened the lightweight sweater and shrugged it off her shoulders and arms. Kam sat unmoving, watching her with an alert focus. From where did these bouts of shyness come, when she'd already shared so many intimacies with him? She dropped the sweater on the floor with her other clothes, realizing that her moments of self-consciousness somehow sharpened her arousal. Her hands hesitated at her waist.

"Take off the bra," Kam said. "I'll remove the panties."

Excitement shot through her at his words. The silence seemed to press on her eardrums as she unfastened the bra and peeled the cups off her breasts. As she tossed the garment onto the floor, she saw his gaze fix on her bare breasts, his nostrils flaring slightly. She stood before him, nude save for her underwear.

Kam blinked, as if coming to back to himself.

"Come here," he said. He reached for a leather cuff on the bedside table. "Lift one foot to my lap," he directed. "Use the table to brace yourself if you need to."

She lifted her foot without hesitation. Her dance training had made her very sure of her balance. Kam opened his hand below her lower calf, sliding his palm along her ankle and heel, squeezing her foot lightly at the arch. He pressed the sole against his crotch. Lin tensed, arousal tingling through her. She could feel the shape of his testicles through his jeans. His cock was trapped in his briefs along his left thigh. She could feel the thick shaft along the left side of her foot.

When he wrapped the thick leather around her ankle and tightened the platinum buckle, she felt herself dampen. She couldn't say precisely why she found the whole procedure intensely erotic, but she knew Kam agreed with her. She felt his cock thicken next to her foot.

"The other one," Kam prompted. His hand caressed her heel deliciously before she removed her foot from his lap. He held out one hand expectantly and she lifted her other leg. He caught it at the ankle and brought it against him. This time, he tucked the captive foot more snugly against his balls, pushing the heel against his root and closing his strong thighs around it. Lin gritted her teeth, her breathing escalating as she watched him slip the black leather around her calf and lower it to her ankle. The feeling of tension only amplified as he tightened the cuff and his blatant arousal resonated into her foot.

After she'd lowered her leg and he'd put a cuff on each of her wrists, he stood from the bed.

"One second," he said. "I'm going to get something from the bathroom." He returned a moment later carrying the clip she'd gotten from her clutch earlier in order to restrain her hair for her shower. He handed it to her. "Can you put your hair up so that it's out of your face?" he asked. Lin nodded, gathering her long hair. He watched her intently as she stretched, her hands over her head, twisting the mass. Her nipples tightened beneath his stare. He liked her in that pose. It was the same one he'd asked her to take earlier when they made love. The memory amplified the intimacy that seemed to be falling over them like a spell.

In the distance, she heard thunder rumble. He turned. She paused in the action of fixing her hair to her head when she saw him remove the bullet vibrator from the drawer. Kam noticed her expression.

"Since checking e-mail is a relatively small infraction, I thought we'd mix a little pleasure with your punishment," he said with a smile. He set down the vibrator on the bedside table and began to unfasten the fly of his jeans. Lin just stood there, her body growing taut with anticipation, her nipples prickling and stiffening as he unbuttoned his shirt. He whipped it off with one brisk twist of lean, defined muscle. He kicked off his tennis shoes and socks rapidly, then jerked his jeans down over hips and legs. His boxer briefs looked starkly white next to the dark skin and hair on his muscular thighs. His erection pressed tightly against the front panel, a flagrantly beautiful package.

He picked up the vibrator. "Come here," he told her. He sat near the bottom corner of the bed at a slightly slanted angle, his knees pointed toward the six-foot mahogany poster. "Crawl up on the bed and kneel next to me here," he told her, patting the thigh toward the center of the bed. His hand opened along her lower back and then her hip, guiding her when she joined him on her hands and knees on the bed, crawling next to this body. "There," he muttered thickly when her head hovered over his lap and she looked down at his cock pressed against stretchy cotton. He took one of her wrists and lifted it, repositioning it between his thighs on the mattress. "Stay still. I'll tell you to move when I want you to."

He twisted slightly, caressing her spine, his touch causing the tingling of her pussy to amplify. What was he going to do? His deliberate manner and orchestration of their positioning was increasing her tension and arousal unbearably. He slipped his hand beneath her panties and caressed her bottom. She bit off a whimper. Outside, thunder rumbled again.

"Shhh," he soothed, pushing her panties down her thighs. "There, that's beautiful," she heard him mutter as he palmed one bare buttock and caressed the other. Heat flooded her pussy. He'd told her to leave on her panties for this simple yet powerful moment of eroticism. He was a devil with his little tricks. She jumped when he lifted his hand and popped first one cheek, then the other, his spanks light as though he was experimenting with the mechanics of the position.

"Oh, Kam," she moaned when he suddenly reached over her ass and probed her pussy with his finger. He penetrated her slit immediately and began pushing his finger in and out. Her elbows gave way slightly, lowering her upper body, as she automatically repositioned herself to take his thrusting finger more ideally.

"You're very wet," he murmured near her ear. "Did you like me putting on your ankle restraints as much as I did?"

"Yes," she gasped. Her muscles tightened in protest when he drew his finger out of her. Panting, she saw him pick up the vibrator and flick on the power. He put his hand beneath her heaving belly and pressed it against her skin, buzzing her. Slowly, he moved downward. Lin clamped her eyes shut, her anticipation almost painful. Her back arched. Her breasts felt heavy and achy.

"Isn't this a nicer way to spend a Sunday than working?" he asked, and she heard the smile in his voice.

"Yes. Oh yes," she muttered as he ran the vibrator over the sensitive patch of skin just above her labia.

"That's right," he growled softly. The vibrator lowered over her sex lips, but his touch was light. "Don't move your hips an inch," he directed sternly. He tingled and teased the flesh until she panted, her muscles coiled tight.

"Feel good?" he murmured.

"Yes." Her eyes clamped shut. "Oh, more. Please," she gasped.

He grunted softly and pushed the vibrator more firmly, buzzing her clit. It felt delicious. She moaned her approval, her hips flexing against his hand. He lowered his hand, depriving her of the exquisite vibrations. "Stay still," he reminded her. She nodded, too breathless to speak, and he pressed the vibrator to her again. Lin stared down covetously at his erection and began to sweat. Kam removed the vibrator, but instantly the ridge of his finger was rubbing her clit.

"Juicy," he murmured his approval. "But I don't want to forget your punishment, do I?" Much to her disappointment, he withdrew his hand from under her and set the vibrator on the bedspread. He grabbed a buttock, squeezing it to his palm. She could feel that his finger was coated with moisture from her pussy. He let go of her, his hand swinging back. *Smack*. He left a tingling patch on the bottom curve of her right buttock. His arm swung back again. He struck her left buttock tautly, then her right again. Lin moaned in excitement. He spanked her prickling bottom again. In her position, she saw his cock jump against the clinging boxer briefs. Without telling herself to move, she instinctively began to lean into his lap, wild to feel his swollen, hard cock press against her lips and tongue.

He halted her with a hand on her shoulder.

"You want that?" he asked, his voice a dark seduction.

"Yes."

"Tell me, Lin."

She licked her lower lip, her gaze never leaving the outline of his cock. "I want you. I want your cock in my mouth," she said, excitement making her sound breathless. He used both hands to jerk at the waistband of the briefs. His cock sprung free, long and heavy. He lowered the briefs to his thighs and then fisted the thick staff at the base. He held his cock up for her. Her mouth watered as she stared at the heavy stalk and succulent, fat cockhead. He tapped her right arm. "Put this hand up on the poster to brace yourself and the other one on my thigh." She followed his directions and lowered, her mouth hovering a bare inch over his cock. "I will have to give you a few more spankings while you suck. Then we will finish with the flogger. I have to convince you somehow that too much work makes for a dull Lin. Am I convincing you that there are better things to be done with your spare time?" he murmured gently

A shudder of excitement went through her as she watched him stroke his cock lazily. She had never craved him more. Distantly she was aware of thunder crashing, sounding closer . . . vaguely ominous.

The hair on her forearms prickled, standing on end. A storm was rushing the city.

"Oh yes," she whispered. She lowered and stretched her lips around his cockhead. Closing her eyes, she gave the crown a firm polishing with her tongue, and then sucked at it. Hard. Kam's rough groan of appreciation emboldened her. She wet the staff above his fingers with her sliding tongue and inserted the thick head again between her lips. His hand opened at the back of her head, gently urging her down over the staff.

"C'est si bon," he groaned as she filled her mouth with him. Her head began to bob in his lap, her intent focused and single-minded. He continued to hold his cock up for her. His other hand drifted down her naked spine onto her ass. He spanked her once, twice, the cracking sounds amplifying her excitement. She bobbed faster. Her actions were fervid and hungry, but he spanked her slowly, taking his time, pausing to rub her buttocks into his palm, seeming to enjoy the warmth he was transferring into her flesh. Lin felt his stare on her as she sucked his cock. It only excited her more. She became fevered, determinedly swallowing more and more of his length. When she ducked down and bumped her lips against his fist, he hissed in pleasure.

"Oh, you get a reward for that, *mon petit chaton*," she heard him say. Then the vibrator was back on her pussy. She screamed, his cock muffling the sound. She ducked down again, taking his cock deep. Her lips tapped against his fist in a rapid rhythm as she crested. She heard Kam's guttural groan of approval as if from a distance. She started to come.

"Oh yeah. Oh yeah, that's so good," she heard Kam say, an edge of wildness to his tone. She realized she was screaming and moaning as orgasm shuddered through her, and the vibrations from her vocal cords were resonating into his appreciative flesh.

He pulled her off his cock. She blinked in disorientation, gasping, staring down at his furious, glistening erection. He pushed the vibrator against her clit, wringing another shiver of pleasure out of her. Lin moaned and panted, shuddering next to his hand, undone by pleasure.

Instinctively, she leaned down again, tempted by his beautiful cock.

"No," he said, halting her, his tone desire-bitten and rough. He dropped his hand from between her thighs. "I was about to come. Your hot little mouth was giving me very little choice in the matter."

He put his hands on her shoulders and encouraged her to straighten. Then he was kissing her sensitized, sore lips, his tongue dipping between them hungrily. "You could make a man forget almost anything with this beautiful mouth," he muttered a moment later, nipping at her moist lips. "But we are not finished yet."

"No?" Lin whispered, still dazed from her thunderous climax.

"No," he said grimly, standing. She watched him as he stepped out of his boxer briefs, her gaze touring his long, muscular body covetously. His cock sprung out from his body in flagrant arousal. He cupped the tumescent flesh in his palm from below, wincing as he stroked himself. The evidence of his sharp arousal sent a fresh jolt of stimulation through her. The dim bedroom suite suddenly flickered with light. Thunder came immediately on its heels. Electricity seemed to flow in her blood, making it race.

"Kneel at the edge of the bed," he said quietly, approaching her. He guided her with his hands, pausing to draw her silk panties down her legs, removing them. She put her knees near the edge of the mattress and braced herself on her arms. She looked behind her at Kam, both anxious and almost unbearably desirous. He grabbed a pillow and put it on the bed in front of her. "Put your cheek on the pillow. Brace yourself on your shoulders," he instructed. "Good. Now put your hands together at your back. I'm going to restrain your wrists," he told her. Her heartbeat throbbed in the ear she had pressed against the soft pillow as he used the hooks and rings on her cuffs to bind her wrists at her back. She pulled gently, testing the restraints. She was bound, and good. A whimper fell past her lips.

"Shhh," Kam murmured, rubbing her hip. He must have thought the small sound signified anxiety, when it was really arousal. He stroked her thigh and hip soothingly. "I'm going to use the flogger on your ass. Not much. Your infraction was minimal," he said, and she heard the warmth and humor in his deep voice.

"I can't imagine what you'd have in store for me if I dared to, say . . . write a memo," she muttered next to the pillow drolly.

"Oh, you wouldn't want to even imagine it," he said, his mock-sinister tone making her laugh. "Well, maybe you would," he admitted. She saw him move from the corner of her vision, and then he was behind her again. She bit off a moan when she felt the soft suede tails slide against her ass. They moved down the crack of her buttocks and between her legs, tickling her sex. She gasped when he pressed up slightly, applying pressure.

"Spread your thighs more. That's right," he muttered thickly when she slid her knees an inch outward in each direction. He lifted the flogger and began to land the tails gently on her ass. It didn't hurt, but the sensation of the tails flicking against her skin and the soft whoosh and tapping sound they made when they made contact struck her as intensely erotic. "How many strokes do you think you deserve for working on a declared day of leisure?" she heard him say.

"Hard strokes?" she asked him shakily.

"Stinging ones. Yes," he said, continuing to flick the tails against her ass.

She bit off a moan of arousal. Why was this such a turn-on? It shocked her, how much his dominance and her submission aroused her, and yes, even the mild bondage and "punishment." In her vulnerable position with her thighs spread wide, she could feel how wet and swollen her sex was. Kam could see it, no doubt.

Heat flooded her face at the thought. She rolled her hot cheek on the pillow.

"Four?" she suggested.

The tails landed lower, flicking against her outer sex. The jolt of excitement that went through her was almost painful it was so sharp. Her pussy clenched tight. The tails landed again on her flushed, swollen sex, and this time she couldn't stop moaning. She heard Kam's low growl and knew he was witnessing her reaction, and that he liked it.

"Four it is, then," he said.

She heard the tails whoosh through the air, her muscles tightening. They landed on her ass with a stinging caress. Almost immediately they were back, this time gently tapping at her exposed outer sex. She whimpered in excitement. Again, she heard the tails whoosh in the air. They landed on her ass with a sharp snap.

"Oh," she muttered, wincing at the sting. Kam rubbed where he'd struck, soothing the burning flesh.

"Too much?" he asked.

"No," she moaned. The fever came upon her again, this time wrought by the sharp sting and his gentle caress. He opened his large hand along her lower buttocks and pushed up the flesh. Lin realized with a rush of excitement that he was making a closer inspection of her pussy. The room flashed and thunder cracked loudly. "God you're wet. Such a sweet, pink pussy," she heard him mumble as if to himself.

"Kam," she pleaded, but for what? The sting of the flogger? The end of this delicious agony? She wasn't sure. She only knew she burned.

The tails whooshed in the air, and again she felt their sting. "Is that what you wanted?" he asked roughly from behind her, his hand rubbing her bottom, easing the prickling nerve endings.

"Yes. No. I want you. I want you inside me," she cried out, not sure what she wanted because need flooded her in all directions.

"You'll have it after one more stroke. You'll have it good and hard," he assured darkly. She tensed in anticipation when she heard the telltale sound of the tails flying.

They struck her ass, the resulting burn making her grit her teeth.

Her muscles coiled tight with tension and arousal. Then the flogger dropped down onto the mattress just inches from her face. She stared at it, panting as she felt Kam grab her hips, adjusting her slightly. The bed was high, ideally suited for this position and his tall body.

"Oh!" She gasped at the sensation of the hard knob of his cock nudging her pussy, forcing her delicate tissues to part for it. He firmed his hold on her, his thumbs digging into her stinging buttocks. He drove his length into her with one hard thrust. Her squeal was nearly drowned out by a boom of thunder. She immediately began bobbing her bottom. It hurt a little, but her hunger far outweighed the slight discomfort of his complete possession. She needed more friction. She required it. He lifted his hand and spanked her.

"Stay still," he demanded in a tight voice. "You're a trial enough as it is without bouncing around like that."

Kam hadn't meant to sound so harsh, but he'd never been strung so tight on a rack of need as he was at that moment. She'd surpassed his expectations yet again, her responsiveness stunning him. It was like she'd been fashioned from his fantasies, so sweet, so giving, so trusting.

He flexed his hips, thrusting into her clinging warmth.

So beautiful.

Her ass blushed pink, but her pussy was a luscious sexual confection, squeezing his cock, sucking at it as he drove into the soft, liquid center again and again. He knew he should stop staring at his cock moving like a well-oiled piston in and out of her—he was going to come faster for it—but the vision was too compellingly erotic. A red haze of lust edged his vision. His pelvis smacked against her buttocks in a hard-driving rhythm. He gathered her plump buttocks in his hands, pushing the flesh together, squeezing his thrusting cock even more.

Lin screamed. He paused, concern fracturing his rabid lust. Was he hurting her? But then he felt the walls of her pussy convulse around him. She was coming. He lost all vestiges of control then, his arm muscles flexing painfully as he crashed her ass against his pelvis, serving her pussy to his raging cock . . .

. . . to his raging need. It was so great, only Lin could quench it.

Climax slammed into him, the spike of pleasure ruthless. He lost the ability to think as he tightened in a rictus of bliss. Something seemed to rip loose inside him. Then he was pouring himself into Lin, giving himself in a way he never had before, giving himself in a way he hadn't known was possible until that moment.

Chapter Seventeen

Kam came back to himself to the sound of rain pounding on the windows. He blinked the sweat out of his eyes and leaned up slightly. He'd been slumped over Lin, trying to recover from his thunderous climax. He straightened, recognizing she was vulnerable, restrained as she was with his upper body weight on her. She moaned softly when he stood and regretfully withdrew from her body.

"You were keeping me warm," she murmured, her voice a throaty, sexy murmur, a result of her screaming while she sucked his cock so deep, no doubt. He unhooked her cuffs and took one of her hands, guiding her. She came off the bed, elegant and fleet in her movements even in a state of satiation. He pulled back the covers and nodded for her to get into the bed first. He came down next to her on his back and pulled the bedding around them. She curled up next to him, her head on his chest. He removed the clip from her hair and stroked the silky tendrils. For several languorous minutes they remained like that, listening to the rain pounding against the windowpane and the rumbling thunder, their bodies slowing. It was sublime. Kam breathed Lin's scent and the fragrance of their combined arousal. She snuggled closer to him, and he was overwhelmed with tenderness for her. Like his former blinding need, it was unexpected and sharp as a newly forged blade. He stroked her naked shoulder, his lips moving in her hair. She felt so small next to him, so feminine, her body seeming to pulse with vibrancy and life.

"Are you warm now, *ma petite minette*?" he rasped.

"Yes. I feel so good," she said so softly he barely heard her above the crash of the rain on the windows.

He ran a hand along the curve of her hip. "I'll say you do."

He felt her smile against his skin. "Did you ever have a kitten?"

"What?" he asked in puzzlement, pausing in stroking her.

"You always call me your little kitten," she murmured. "I just thought . . . from the way you always say it so fondly . . ."

He resumed stroking her, her words making him thoughtful. "How well do you know French?" he asked.

"Not very. I understand it better than I can speak it."

"They are terms of endearment, *mon petit chaton*, *ma petite minette*. Not that I used them regularly. Ever, really," he mused. "It's just that you remind me of a kitten; you're small and sleek and graceful." He cupped her hip and she snuggled closer. "And you curl up to me like one."

She laughed softly. He smiled at the sound. "It's because your body is like a furnace. So you never actually had one?" she added lazily.

He went still. She lifted her head and peered at his face when he didn't respond immediately.

"I had one. Once. A long time ago, when I was a boy," he said slowly. "I'd actually forgotten about it until just now."

She blinked. "What do you mean?"

He shrugged, and she touched his chest, as if to steady him. "I was young. Eight or so, I think."

He saw her elegant throat convulse as she swallowed. "What

happened?" she whispered, and she could tell by the dread that tinged her voice that she'd caught a hint of his disquietude at the unexpected memory that her innocent question had dislodged.

"Nothing. I had just forgotten I ever had a kitten until now."

"A kitten? Not a cat?" she asked, studying him. "Kam?" she prodded gently when he didn't reply. It suddenly struck him that she looked worried, and he wished he had censored himself better. Still, he'd said it now.

"Aurore is in the country," he said thickly after a moment. "There are a lot of outbuildings . . . barns, and gardening sheds. Several cats used to live in them, and the gardener allowed it because they helped control the rodents. One of them had a litter one spring, and I kept one of them for my own. A shiny little brown one. I called her Chocolat. My mother wouldn't let me keep her in our quarters at first, saying we didn't have the money to feed her, but then Chocolat worked her wiles on her, and my mother grew fond of her as well. She was very warm hearted by nature, and she loved animals."

"You get that from her," Lin murmured.

He nodded before resuming. "During that summer, that kitten went everywhere with me . . . except for inside the big house," he added darkly. He fell into silence, his fingers still running through Lin's hair.

"Gaines didn't like cats?" she whispered.

"It wasn't just that. I never showed him that I cared about anything," Kam said. "As a kid, I learned that lesson fast enough. Don't show your weak spots. He'll use them against you. Even my mother . . ." he trailed off, thick regret flooding him. "I never let him know how much she meant to me. I was afraid he'd terminate her employment as a maid and laundress and send her away when he was in one of his tempers over some imagined error he believed I'd made in my work. I led him to believe that I didn't care that much for her, that I looked down on her . . . that I considered her a simple commoner. I never told her I did that," Kam admitted, the truth burning his throat. He'd never told anyone about the ugly fiction he'd enacted.

"Your mother knew you loved her. You let Gaines believe that for a reason, a good one. Of course you would learn early on how to keep things that mattered to you off his radar. He was a sick, twisted man. You were smart and resourceful for protecting your mother that way, especially when you were so young with no one to guide you. Never think otherwise," Lin stated fiercely.

He believed her, but guilt was often not a rational emotion. "Your father did something to the kitten. Didn't he?" Lin asked in a hushed voice after a pause.

"That fall was the first time I went to attend school in the town. Gaines allowed it, but he didn't like it. It was inconvenient for him, to have to do some of the manual labor I usually did for him, assisting him in his workshop. On the first day of school, he grew restless when I didn't immediately report to work in the big house and went looking for me. I'd rushed home so that I had time to see Chocolat. I'd left her that morning with her brothers and sisters and her mother in the barn. She visited them often enough, and her mother continued to treat her as one of her own. Gaines found me there with the kitten. He ordered me to the workshop. After I left, he asked the gardener to round up the stray cats in the barn and drown them. He said they were infected with disease."

He felt Lin shudder next to him. He blinked away the toxic memory and focused on Lin's face. The sadness he saw her in her dark eyes pierced him. He brushed her cheek with his thumb.

"It was a long, long time ago," he said.

"I'm sorry I made you remember."

"I'm not," he said steadfastly before he pulled her higher in his arms and laid her back on the mattress. He came down over her, seeking the sweet benediction of her mouth.

* * *

They spent the entire day in bed, talking and touching and making love. The acute fury of the storm abated, but clouds remained hovering over the city. Rain occasionally pattered on the windowpanes, adding to the sense of delightful relaxation and intimacy.

"You better watch out," Lin told him as she trailed kisses down the side of his rib cage later that afternoon. "This playing hooky business could definitely become my new addiction."

"Then my plan is working," he assured her, cradling the side of her head and praising her gently in French when her mouth lowered still.

Kam got up as dusk fell to take out Angus. Lin rose to call to have food delivered. When the Thai carryout arrived, however, they returned to bed, feasting naked amongst the rumpled bedclothes. Afterward, they roused from lazing about to luxuriate in the large bathtub.

"Where are you going tomorrow?" Kam asked her later when they returned to bed after their sensual soak, Lin's muscles rubbery with the relaxation that came from repeated lovemaking and hot water.

"I have a series of meetings on Tuesday in San Francisco," she said, cuddling closer to him. She really hated the idea of leaving Chicago at that moment . . . of putting distance between her and Kam.

"Do you travel a lot for work?"

She hummed an affirmative, stroking his muscular upper arm. "Usually three or four times a month."

"Do you like it? Traveling?"

"Not as much as I did when I was younger, but I'm used to it. It's not too bad," she said, her eyelids drooping under the weight of drowsiness. Still, she'd begun to wonder about something all afternoon and couldn't resist voicing it now. "Kam?"

"Hmmm?"

"I know that I said I didn't want Ian or anyone to know about this . . . *us*. But if I hadn't said that, would you have been okay with him and Lucien and everyone knowing?"

"Yeah," he said, stroking her shoulder. Her eyes blinked open wider at his firm answer. "I hate faking things."

Of course he would, Lin realized. He'd grown to despise lying and façades from an early age.

"Why would I want to hide the fact that we're involved from anyone?" Kam asked bluntly.

"I don't know. I was just wondering if it would make you . . . you know. Uncomfortable."

"No," he said, and she heard the thread of familiar steel in his voice. "It's you that's uncomfortable with people knowing."

"I'm not," she whispered. His stroking hand on her spine paused. She lifted her head and met his stare. "Not anymore," she said emphatically.

She leaned down to kiss his mouth. His arms slowly closed tight around her.

The next morning, she awoke before dawn, knowing she would have to get up very soon and reenter her normal life, and dreading it. These had been stolen moments with Kam. She was sad they were over. For a while, anyway.

She studied his face as he slept when the pale light of dawn peeked around the closed curtains. The vast, swelling feeling she experienced in her chest cavity amazed her . . . humbled her.

Maybe it was best she was going to be away for a few days. Something had happened to her this weekend. Something earth-shattering. Game changing. She had been a fool to ever think she'd been in love before. She'd never begun to fall until she'd seen Kam, never even knew what the words meant. Her feelings for Ian seemed like a shallow, weak facsimile now, a child's idealistic fantasy.

Kam's eyes were open when she came out of the bathroom several minutes later after washing and dressing.

"What time is your flight?" he asked, his deep, rough voice in the hushed room caressing her sensitive skin. She walked to him and sat at the edge of the bed. He ran his knuckles over her forearm, and Lin wished nothing more than to be back in his arms at that moment. It felt all wrong to be leaving him, even if it was for just two nights.

"It's not until one o'clock, but I need to get into the office this morning."

"Some caveman kept you from catching up on work this weekend," he said with a small smile. "I have something I want to give you before you go to the airport."

"You don't have to give me anything else, Kam."

"It's related to the Gersbach demo on Wednesday. I would have given it to you earlier, but it's not ready until this morning. If I have it delivered to Noble by say . . . ten o'clock, will I get it to you in time?"

"Yes, plenty of time," she said warmly, touching his whiskered cheek. He grasped her wrist and pulled her down to him, his hand opening at the back of her head. "Thank you for this weekend," she whispered against his lips a moment later.

"I expect more of your weekends."

She swallowed thickly, a tingling sensation going through her as she carefully studied his sober expression.

"You'll have them then" she whispered. She started to get up to go, but Kam paused her with a touch on her hip.

"When you get back, there's something important I need to discuss with you," he told her pointedly.

At ten fifteen that morning, Maria tapped on the door of her office.

"The limo will be here at ten forty-five to take you to the airport. And this just arrived."

"Thank you, Maria," Lin said, watching the admin place a pale gray box on her desk. Curious, she broke the tape seal and opened the lid. Inside were two identical jewelry boxes, one of black velvet, the other of red leather. Her heart started to throb in her chest as she opened one of them. She lifted out a message from Kam.

Yours is the perfect wrist for the first prototype of a Reardon watch. Jarvis Cooper, the jeweler from E, put it together for me this weekend. I thought you might like to get used to what it can do while you're out of town. A tutorial will lead you through the instructions when you turn on the device, but call me if you have any questions about how it works.

Just call me period, or I'll call you.

Kam

Lin smiled and set aside the papers, giving an *ooh* of amazement when she saw the specialized timepiece. It was silver and thin, the face of the "watch" a miniature display screen. She pushed a button and activated the device. Immediately the screen lit up. *Welcome, Lin, hope you are having a good time.* She smiled at the greeting and tapped the screen when prompted. When she hit the display that gave the time several minutes later, she realized she'd lost herself in playing with the fascinating device. She'd continue to work with it on the way to the airport.

She removed the Klinf watch that she wore, strapping on Kam's in its place. Unlike most watches, the device went at her inner wrist. Jarvis Cooper, the jeweler, had given the mechanism a trendy, attractive black leather strap—not all that dissimilar from her cuffs. In fact, Lin realized with a small smile, there was a telling platinum loop sewn into the leather. The watchband could be used as a restraint. Despite that prurient purpose, it was a very chic piece. The buckle was a stylized letter *R*, which was made of platinum and worn at the outer wrist, where the face of a traditional watch went. It was really quite eye-catching, Lin decided with a thrill. She loved it. She ran her finger over the *R* in dawning amazement. A thrill of excitement coursed through her.

Kam was going to start his own company in the near future. He was ready *now*. She'd been suspecting it all along. That's what this whole trip to Chicago had been about. He was trying to wet his feet, get experience with the business world. Not because he planned to sell his patent to a different watchmaker, but because he planned to begin his own business.

She'd almost forgotten about the other jewelry box in her mounting excitement. Most women wouldn't have overlooked that famous red leather box. She opened the lid and gasping, staring wide-eyed at the most stunning Tahitian black pearls she'd ever seen. Her fingers ran over the smooth, iridescent jewels of the necklace rope and matching earrings in wonder. Between every third pearl on the necklace was a row of sparkling diamonds. It was a striking combination.

A note was at the top of the box from Kam. It read simply: *They were beautiful, so they must be yours.*

That evening, Kam halted Ian and spoke to him quietly. "May I have a word with you in private before we go up to the deck?"

Mrs. Hanson had just served Ian, Francesca, Lucien, Elise, and Kam in the dining room. It was a mild night, so Francesca had suggested they take coffee up on the deck.

"Of course. Francesca," he called to his wife. "Kam and I will be up in a moment. He needs a word in the library."

Francesca nodded brightly. Ian led Kam down the wide, gallery-like hallway to his library-office.

"Is everything all right?" Ian asked after he'd shut the walnut-paneled door.

"Probably not. For one of us, anyway," Kam replied.

Ian blinked, clearly not having expected that answer.

"Maybe you'd better sit down," Kam said.

"I'm not sure I like the sound of this," Ian said, studying Kam with a sharp gaze.

"Nobody is sick or dying," Kam said wryly.

Ian shrugged slightly. "Then I suppose we'll survive it." He went to sit on one of the two couches that faced each other. He gave Kam a cool, expectant glance. Kam sat across from his brother and wondered for the thousandth time that night where to begin. Never having been much of a wordsmith, he finally just cut to the meat of things.

"I'm going to ask Lin to work for me."

A stunned silence followed.

"Excuse me?" Ian asked, leaning forward, his gaze narrowing dangerously.

"I'm aware that almost every chief executive officer on the planet has tried to poach her from you, so I thought it was only fair to warn you beforehand. I respect you too much to ever consider going behind your back. I didn't come here with the clear intention to offer her a position. I didn't come to Chicago with any intention of undermining you, Ian."

"Have I done something since then to make you want to?" Ian demanded, nostrils flaring.

"Of course not," Kam declared. "You've gone out of your way to try to help me. You and Francesca and Lucien and Elise . . . all of you have been . . . great."

"And this is how you thank me? By trying to steal my top executive?" Ian bellowed in disbelief.

"I'm not 'stealing' her," Kam tried to reason, although he couldn't resist glaring at Ian's accusation. "I'm telling you aboveboard that I'm going to ask her to work for me. With me. It's her decision. She may very well say no."

"Will she?" Ian snapped, blue eyes flashing with anger. He stood, his long body suddenly tense as a coiled spring.

"I have no idea what she'll say," Kam said honestly. "Probably no, just like she says to every other person who tries to hire her."

Ian came to an abrupt halt, swinging around to stare at Kam. "Hire her. *Hire* her? For *what*? You plan to start your own company in the near future instead of waiting to build capital?"

Kam just nodded, holding his brother's stare.

"Using your mechanism as the linchpin product instead of a means of capital for future ones?"

"Yes. But I have a lot of ideas for expanding the uses of the technology."

"Do you think you might have told me this before?"

"I'm telling you now," Kam said, standing. "I wanted to gather some information before I announced it. Figure out whether I could pull it off or not."

"Scope out my prize employee," Ian hissed and cursed under his breath. He started pacing again. "I can't believe this."

"I need her more than you do," Kam said brazenly.

Ian swung around, his eyes wild with disbelief. "You have more balls than anyone I know, and I *don't* mean that as a compliment."

"I'm just telling you the truth," Kam bit out, walking toward Ian aggressively. It was a risk. Ian was furious at that moment, and Kam was irritated himself. No one seemed to rile him more than Ian when he got all arrogant and holier-than-thou. He held Ian's stare. "You sent Lin to work with me because you knew she'd make me look good. She makes everyone and everything look a hundred times better than it is because she's a thousand times the worth of any of us. I suspected she was good before I even met her, but she surpassed by expectations by far. I . . . *need* her more . . . than you do," Kam repeated succinctly.

Ian's incredulous, furious expression seemed to melt slowly.

"You're in love with her," Ian breathed out, stepping toward him.

Kam's heartbeat throbbed in his ears.

"I know I'm a start-up company," he continued levelly, wanting Ian to understand, *needing* him to. He cared about his brother. He and Lucien were all the family he had. "But I have capital, I have the skill to create future technology and I have a fucking *fantastic*, game-changing product. I'm not averse to exploring possible partnerships with companies like Gersbach or Stunde, but I want the control of my technology. If they want it in their watches, they're going to have to pay to use it. I want my product to be available to most consumers, not just the rich and privileged. I didn't know if I could make this work until I met Lin and saw how well we could potentially work together. She's the last piece of the puzzle."

He paused, trying to read Ian's mood. "I wouldn't be surprised if you didn't believe me, Ian, but I am thankful for everything you've done for me. You helped facilitate things for the pharmaceutical deal. It's because of you that I have seed money. You've helped me here in Chicago. I want to show my appreciation by allowing Noble the use of any Reardon product you think you can use."

Ian inhaled slowly. Kam thought he was listening, but he also sensed he was still simmering with anger.

"I'm determined to make this work," Kam continued. "That's why I need Lin. I plan to offer her a full partnership, if she wants it. She can own up to fifty percent of Reardon Technologies stock, if she chooses. The sky is the limit as far as where we could take it . . . where *Lin* could take it, if she decided to. Can you offer her anything equivalent at Noble?" he challenged quietly.

Ian just stared at him, his mouth hanging open. "You fucking little bastard," he said dazedly after a moment.

"I'm a fucking bigger bastard than you," Kam muttered through his teeth.

A bark of mirthless laughter fell past Ian's lips. He set his elbow on the mantel of the fireplace and put his forehead in his hand.

"I'm sorry if you feel that I'm doing this to spite you," Kam said truthfully, feeling the tension ease between them. "I'm not. I don't mean to sound belittling, but it's got nothing to do with you. It's just that . . ."

Ian looked over at him when he faded off. "It's what makes the most sense," Kam continued. "It feels right. Lin is precisely what I need. I think *you* even sense that. And she could use an opportunity like this . . . a place to be in the forefront, where she can shine at her fullest and reap all the benefits. Lin should be with me."

"With Reardon Technologies?" Ian asked pointedly.

"Yes," Kam replied without pause. He knew what Ian was angling at, but he wasn't ready to discuss his personal feelings for Lin, especially when he hadn't even had that discussion with Lin yet. "Of course, Lin might feel differently," he admitted grimly under his breath. "Everyone knows how loyal she is to you and Noble."

"So you haven't spoken to her about any of this yet?"

"No," Kam said. "I plan to talk to her about that when she gets back. She might suspect something. I'm not sure. She's kind of hard to read sometimes."

"She says the same thing about you. I agreed with her. You've certainly gone and proved us right in this case," Ian said, frowning. He turned and faced Kam. "You care about her? You truly do? Because maybe I could start to accept this . . . *maybe* I could maybe even start to feel good about it if it's what Lin wants and you assured me her feelings and her future are a priority for you."

Kam met his stare unwaveringly. "You can feel good about it," he said simply.

Ian held his gaze for several long seconds before he nodded once slowly. "Well, it's not as if I haven't had a sneaking suspicion something volatile was happening between you two. I've sensed something was about to erupt, but I didn't guess this. I won't deny that there have been many times I've regretted not being able to offer Lin more. Not money. She's one of the top-paid executives in the United

States. I mean more of Noble itself. She deserves more for all the work she's done in the past."

"I agree," Kam said.

Ian's eyes flashed in residual anger at Kam's steadfast reply, but then he seemed to calm himself. "You have to understand. It's not the wealth I don't want to share. I don't care about that. I've just never been good about sharing decisions when it comes to my company."

"I'm not blaming you for the way you want to run your business, Ian. Lin wouldn't, either. I heard her defending you to Klinf. She was sincere. That doesn't mean she doesn't deserve more."

Ian blinked and shook his head as if suddenly weary. "You're right. I don't know what I'm going to do without her at work," he said hollowly.

I don't know what I'd do without her. Period, Kam thought.

Kam shrugged and headed over to the sideboard, reaching for two glasses. They both could use a drink. "No reason to panic," he told Ian, pouring some bourbon from a decanter. "The lady hasn't spoken yet." He walked over to Ian and handed him the glass. Ian just studied the golden-brown liquid for several seconds, lost in thought.

"To Lin," Ian said finally, holding up the bourbon.

"To Lin. And her future," Kam replied.

Lin thought a lot about Kam on her trip. She used his innovative device and thought of him and his brilliance. It was amazing, to learn about the rhythms of her own body, to come to understand how certain events, environments, and interactions made her respond. She started to feel more connected to her flesh than she ever had before, the biofeedback mechanism making her consider her physical being in a whole new way.

Lying alone in her hotel room at night, she could think of nothing but Kam and his challenging, intensely pleasurable lovemaking, his devilish smile, the knowing gleam in his silvery-gray eyes. She missed him so much.

They spoke on the phone on Monday night, Lin thanking him profusely for the gorgeous pearls and praising his device almost nonstop. A startling amount of people had noticed and commented on the watch, including many of her business associates in San Francisco. Lin had talked ebulliently about the mechanism, and saw firsthand the fascination and curiosity people immediately had for it. Kam had a future phenomenon on his hands. She asked him point-blank during a phone conversation if he planned to start up his own company sooner rather than later, and he'd admitted that it was his hope to jump right in versus waiting.

By the time she landed at O'Hare on Wednesday morning, she was feeling energized and excited, looking forward to the Gersbach demonstration that afternoon. She'd thought the device was fascinating before, but now that she'd become familiar with it on a firsthand basis, she was enthusiastic in a way she'd never before been about a product.

She was brimming with excitement for the Gersbach meeting because of the product, but she was ten times as thrilled at the idea of seeing Kam again.

Brigit and Otto Gersbach came for the demonstration in Ian's office, but Lucien and, of course, Kam were expected to come as well. Lin was seated in her usual chair at the gleaming cherrywood conference table in Ian's office, casually showing Ian, Brigit, and Otto the Reardon device, singing her praises without a hint of artifice. They were all fascinated. Everyone stood when Kam and Lucien entered the room.

"Hi," Lin said breathlessly to Kam after she'd greeted Lucien.

"Hi," he returned, as Otto Gersbach shook Lucien's hand and they exchanged hellos. He looked wonderful to her, not to mention extremely handsome in a dark gray suit with crisp white dress shirt and black-and-silver striped tie. She met his stare, smiling when she saw that familiar knowing gleam in his silvery eyes as he looked down at her. Her lips brushed against his jaw.

"They already love the watch," she whispered quietly near his ear.

"That's because you're making it look so good," he murmured back before he lightly kissed her lips. It wasn't a professional kiss, technically speaking. For the first time in her life, Lin could have cared less about professional appearances.

The demonstration went well. She explained to the group about her experience wearing the watch, telling them that once she understood what her stress looked like on the display screen, she could take proactive steps to lower the indicators on the bar graph. Her progress in controlling her body's stress response grew exponentially with all the regular feedback. She showed them all in real time how she could control potentially negative stress responses by merely focusing on her breath or doing a brief centering exercise.

"It's like having a constant mirror for your body," Lin explained. "It's hard to learn when things are invisible, but when you see your responses visually or audibly"—she switched the control panel to audio for a series of feedback beeps—"it becomes instinctive to understand and learn from the feedback. I had no idea how my body responded so adversely to landing in an airplane, and don't even *ask* me about my response to two caffè macchiatos after a sleepless night," she said, glancing at Kam fleetingly and repressing a small smile when she saw his knowing look.

Lin had never seen Otto so smitten and enthusiastic about a product. He insisted that Kam come to Geneva sometime soon in order to show the product to the rest of the Gersbach board of directors. After the demonstration was complete, Kam broke the news that he'd decided not to sell his product wholesale, but would consider a royalty use of his product by Gersbach. Otto wasn't pleased about this development, but was starting to come around when he saw how steadfast Kam was on the topic.

Lin's phone began to ring. "Excuse me for just a moment," she said quietly when she saw the caller identification, getting up from the conference table and going to the far side of Ian's extensive office.

The call was from Emile Savaur, Richard's partner. Lin took it because she'd been worried by a conversation she'd had with Richard while she'd been in California. His "flu" was not getting better the way it should have if it were a typical bug.

According to Emile, Richard had gotten worse. Emile had taken him to the hospital, and much to his concern, they'd admitted Richard.

"I'll meet you over at Northwestern Memorial as soon as I finish up with this meeting," she said. Emile had tried to tell her it wasn't necessary, but when she insisted, he'd sounded relieved.

"It was Emile calling about Richard St. Claire," Lin told Lucien when she returned. Lucien was good friends with both Emile and Richard as well, having known the two men since his days in Paris. Everyone seated at the table quieted and listened to Lin. "Emile has taken him to the hospital and they've admitted him. They say he has pneumonia."

"Is it serious?" Lucien asked, his brow creasing in concern.

"It sounds like it," Lin said. "I'm going to head over to the hospital as soon as we're done here. I won't be back. I have class tonight," she reminded Ian. Her gaze transferred to Kam, who nodded in understanding. Had he guessed that she hoped he'd meet her after her dance class like he had last week?

"I'll go with you," Lucien said.

"I'll call you in a little bit," Kam told Lin. She gave him a grateful glance. She hated having to leave when she hadn't seen him for days, but it would just delay their personal reunion a few hours.

The meeting came to an end as Lucien and Lin gathered their things, and the Gersbachs extracted a promise from Kam to go to Geneva for a few days the following week.

* * *

"Do you know Richard St. Claire?" Kam asked Ian once they were alone in his office.

Ian nodded. "He's a nice guy. Young and healthy, too. Seems strange that something like this could happen."

"Some of the newer respiratory viruses can be dangerously virulent," Kam replied.

"The meeting went well. You were right: that device is a linchpin, a flagship product, not a means to an end for building capital. You're going to be able to name your terms with Gersbach and any number of other companies."

"Thanks," Kam said, meaning it. He valued Ian's opinion more than Ian knew. He'd regretted telling him he was going to ask Lin to work with him, even though he was convinced it was the right thing to do. He sat in front of Ian's desk when Ian took his seat behind it. "Does this mean you're not pissed at me anymore?"

Ian leaned back in his leather chair, elbows on the arm rests, fingers forming a bridge near his chin. He considered Kam coolly.

"It means that if I were in your shoes, I'd probably be doing the same thing. I might not like the idea of you taking Lin from Noble, but given what you plan, even I have to agree it's a smart move. She's lit up over that device. She's practically glowing over it, and when that happens, Lin is impossible to resist. You two are going to have trouble keeping up with the demands for that watch."

"You actually think she'll agree to come with me?"

"I've never seen her so excited about a product. She seems even more enthusiastic about you."

Kam cleared his throat in the charged silence that followed.

Ian gave Kam a pointed, steely glance. "That doesn't mean part of me won't be pleased if she turns you down. Still, if she stays with Noble, I hope she does it because it's what she truly wants, not because she's worried about being disloyal to me," Ian conceded.

"She is loyal to you. No doubt about it," Kam mused, feeling a little defeated at the very idea. There was no way he could compete with the years of experience, family ties, and close working relationship Lin shared with Ian.

Ian grimaced slightly and sat forward, bracing his forearms on his desk.

"Are you doing anything in particular to convince her?"

Kam blinked. "I told you how I plan to incentivize her."

"Not like work incentives. I mean anything personal to set the atmosphere. Woo her. Are you taking her out to a nice dinner, at least, in order to broach the topic?" Ian persisted when Kam just stared at him in blank bemusement. "It's a big deal what you're proposing to do. You should do it right."

"Are you giving me *hints* for how to convince Lin to work for me?" Kam asked incredulously.

"It looks like someone has to," Ian muttered under his breath. "Take her out to a nice dinner. Order champagne. Get her some flowers."

"Flowers?" Kam repeated.

"Yes," Ian agreed as if warming to the subject. He picked up his phone and began tapping on the screen. "Get her purple lotuses. They're her favorite. I'll give you the number of the only florist in town that sells them. The owner grows them specifically for me to get for Lin. They're extremely rare flowers. I've texted you the number of the florist," he said, setting down his phone. "Kam?" he asked when Kam just sat there, frozen.

A strange wind seemed to be rushing in his ears. A vision of all those carefully preserved lotus flowers sitting in Lin's bedside table drawer flashed before his eyes.

Lin had said she'd been in love before. When Kam had asked her what had happened she'd said . . .

. . . *Nothing. Absolutely nothing. He was someone else's, never mine.*

He heard her voice as if she'd just spoken. She'd sounded sad. Resigned. If there was one woman he knew who could contain her sadness and pain and face each day with a determined smile, it was Lin. He'd always sensed that trace of sadness to her, a hint of loneliness. He just hadn't fully realized the origins of it until now.

Lin was in love with Ian. Of course she was. She'd never revealed her secret because she'd sensed Ian didn't return her feelings.

She was attracted to him—Kam—because he resembled Ian.

"Kam?" Ian repeated, bringing him out of his analytic trance. "Are you all right? You looked like you'd seen a ghost all of a sudden."

"Yeah. I'm fine. Thanks for the advice," Kam mumbled as he stood. It all seemed so obvious now. Everyone said they'd never witnessed loyalty and devotion like Lin showed Ian. Ian was handsome, powerful, sophisticated, rich, and brilliant—the very epitome of what a woman would find attractive. She'd first met him when she'd been an impressionable teenager. It was no surprise she idolized him from the start. An entire generation of people Ian's age and younger idolized him, not only for all he'd accomplished, but also for his influence in the social media and electronic-gaming sectors.

Ian had given Lin those flowers over the years, and Lin had carefully saved and preserved them near where she'd dreamed night after night. Those dried flowers were the only visible symbol of a passion she'd vowed to keep hidden.

She should have told him. Didn't he have a right to know why she found him attractive? Was the hesitance he sensed in her at times inspired by guilt on her part? Did she know she was wrong in using him as a substitute for another man?

He bid Ian good-bye and left his office. Ian had been right. Kam *had* seen a ghost of sorts. It'd been himself. *He'd* been the phantom in his affair with Lin, a blurry, shadowy facsimile of the man she loved.

Lin's phone began to ring as she walked through the main lobby at Northwestern Memorial. She'd seen Richard and Emile, and both of them were in reasonably good spirits. Much to her relief, she learned that Richard's prognosis was very good.

She suppressed her disappointment when she saw it wasn't Kam calling.

"Ian? Hi," she said into the phone, pausing in front of a floor-to-ceiling window near the lobby exit.

"How's Richard?" he asked.

"He'll be fine. A pretty severe infection had set in, so the doctor recommended a course of IV antibiotics. That was why it necessitated an inpatient stay. They say he's going to recover quickly, though. Lucien just left and I was on my way out."

"Are you coming back to the office?"

"I have my class tonight," Lin reminded him. She was hoping Kam would meet her there.

"Sure, I understand," he said distractedly. "It's just that I wanted to speak to you about something."

"I'll come back then."

"No . . . no, that's not necessary," Ian said. She sensed his preoccupation.

"What is it, Ian?"

"I'd rather not broach the topic on the phone, but I suppose I should bring it up now before Kam mentions it to you."

"What?" Lin asked, puzzled by his manner.

"Kam plans to ask you to work for him. Not just for him. With him. He wants you to be a full partner in Reardon Technologies, his new company."

Lin just stared blindly out the window at a row of cabs waiting at the curb.

"You're surprised?" Ian asked after a pause.

"To put it mildly," she replied hollowly. It suddenly felt very hard to move her lungs. A tingling sensation started on her hands and feet. "How . . . how long has he been planning this?"

"According to him, the idea has been coming on ever since he met you. He has an enormous amount of respect for you, Lin," Ian said quietly. "I think he realized how much he needs you to make this company fly."

Needs you to make his company fly. Is that what all of this had been about? Had her seduction been a means to acquire her for his business dynasty?

"I . . . I don't know what to say," Lin mumbled. She felt numb.

"I can tell it's coming to you as quite a shock," Ian said. "The only reason I mentioned it before Kam had a chance to is that it came to my attention that you might turn him down out of loyalty to me. To Noble Enterprises. I wanted you to know that whatever you decide, I'll be behind you. Kam is willing to offer you things that I can't. He's willing to offer you things most business owners would never consider."

"You make it sound like you want me to leave," Lin said, feeling stung and confused by the news.

"No. That's not it at all. Nothing would make me happier than if you took your time with the decision and came to the conclusion that Noble is where you want to remain. You know how much I value you. At least I hope you do. But the fact remains: Kam's offer is highly generous. I can tell you love the product. With Kam's brilliance and your business savvy, you two would be unstoppable."

The silence roared in her ears.

"Just think about it, Lin," Ian continued, his tone warmer than usual. "More than you've thought about the dozens of other offers you've gotten over the years that you've turned down. You and I were going to discuss this week the relocation of Noble to London, at least for a short time period. That would certainly change up your life as well. If anything, it's another factor you'll need to consider in making your decision."

"Yes. I have a lot to think about. Thank you for telling me your thoughts on the matter, Ian," she said, glad to hear that her voice sounded even.

"I'm available if you need to toss things around. I'm also flexible in regard to making your position at Noble as comfortable for you with the location change as I can. This isn't about me not wanting you, Lin. You're the *best* damn executive I've had, or will ever have. I can say that without a doubt of ever changing my mind. More importantly, you're a good friend. I care about you. I want whatever you want. Do you understand?"

"Yes," Lin managed.

She signed off with Ian and put her phone away. She just stared out the window for a stretched moment.

I want whatever you want.

What if she didn't know what she wanted, though? Just minutes ago, she would have said she wanted what she had with Kam to flourish and grow, but on a personal basis, not a professional one. Or at least primarily on a personal basis. She really hadn't ever considered being *business* partners with him.

The realization that was probably what Kam had in mind all along made her feel like she'd been dropped down a dark, fifty-foot hole with no ladder.

Chapter Eighteen

She went home that night instead of to her dance class, trying to absorb everything that Ian had told her, trying to decode what it all meant. She'd already decided she wasn't going to call Kam until she'd thought things through and gained some perspective.

It surprised her the next morning, however, to discover that he hadn't tried to call her, either. That was odd. He'd said he was going to call her. Before her conversation with Ian, she'd assumed they would be seeing one another.

Not that she relished the idea of seeing him now, but it just seemed strange that he'd avoided her as well.

She spent a highly distracted day at work. At around four o'clock, however, she realized she couldn't keep avoiding Kam. They had the meeting scheduled with two executives from Stunde Watches tonight at the restaurant Festa. Lin had yet to even brief Kam about Stunde.

"Has Kam come into the office to see Ian or called?" Lin asked Maria, poking her head out of her office.

"As a matter of fact, I just got off the phone with him," Maria said, setting down her pen. "He says to tell you he'll meet you at Festa at seven."

Irritation spiked through Lin at his distance handling of the matter, but so did confusion. "That won't do," she murmured. "Can you call him back and ask him to meet me at six thirty at the bar? We should at least touch base about Stunde before we meet with Kyle Preston and Nina Patel."

Maria rang her a few minutes later and told her that Kam had agreed to six thirty. Again, she experienced bemusement that he hadn't asked to speak with her personally.

That night Lin dressed with extreme care for their last meeting with the luxury watchmakers. She still hadn't decided precisely what she wanted to say to Kam, but had already determined they should stick to business before and during the meeting. She'd call him out about his tactics for gaining her trust and interest after everything professional was over and done.

How dare he play with my emotions this way? she fumed silently for the thousandth time. He wanted her for his business and so he'd forced a physical relationship in order to secure his place in her life? Well, not *forced* precisely, she conceded irritably as she zipped up her dress that evening and closely studied her reflection in the bathroom mirror. She'd been more than eager to go to bed with him that first night, and progressively more enthusiastic every time since.

She'd loved every second of his primal, powerful lovemaking.

He just wanted me for his business.

But he could have wanted me for me *as well, couldn't he? A man couldn't fake passion like Kam had shown,* another part of her argued.

Now you are kidding yourself. Of course a man can make lust look like true feeling. Every day women are fooled into thinking sex means caring.

Kam's not most men, though. He's brutally honest.

He didn't tell you what he was planning, though, did he?

Disgusted by her internal battle, she forced herself to focus on the moment. She'd just get tonight over with. After dinner, she had no choice but to confront Kam and try to discern the truth in him. She was admittedly scared of what that truth might be.

Taking a deep breath, she lifted her chin in preparation for battle. She wasn't displeased with her appearance. None of the cracks in her armor were showing on the surface. Her hair was styled in an elegant partial upsweep with loose curls falling down her back. She wore a silk sarong print dress that left one shoulder bare, the feminine ruffles of the skirt tempered with a black leather belt that echoed the Reardon watch. She'd toyed with wearing the stunning pearls Kam had bought her, but no. Those were just another example of his unfair influence on her heart. The watch, she wore because it was business . . .

. . . and this *was* a business dinner, no matter how Kam had tried to alter the playing field to suit him. If there was one thing Lin could rely on, it was her professional persona. Calm. Charming. Polished. She'd rely on that persona tonight, just like she'd depended on it for years to survive.

She arrived at the restaurant bar before him and took a seat in a sleek upholstered chair at a cocktail table. Her anxiety grew as she waited. She sensed his presence before she saw his tall form approaching in the corner of her eye. Several heads turned to admire him as he walked toward her. He may not customarily wear suits, but he looked good in them . . . *extremely* good, wearing them like he did his casual clothing—like a second skin on his toned, athletic frame. His face remained impassive when their gazes locked across the crowded bar. She waited for that gleam of warmth and arousal she'd grown used to seeing, but his glance remained as cool as his expression.

"Thanks for meeting with me early," she said neutrally when he took a seat next to her at the table.

"Ian told me that he spoke to you about the position. I'm furious at him for doing it, although I understand why he did," Kam added grudgingly.

She blinked in surprise. There it was: his ever-present, blunt honesty.

"Don't worry. I know you aren't planning on accepting my offer," Kam said, his eyes flashing.

"How can you know that when I—" she broke off when a waiter approached. They gave their drink orders, both of them tight-lipped.

"I'm not sure this is a good time to discuss it," Lin said evenly once the waiter had left. She sounded calm, but her heartbeat had started to pound in her ears. "I want to tell you a few key things about Stunde, and Nina and Kyle are going to be here any minute."

"Right. The top secret briefing."

She simmered at his sarcasm. "I'm just trying to get through this evening without any major mishaps."

She felt her cheeks heating when he studied her closely for a silent moment.

"Who's going to make a mishap?" he finally queried, leaning forward with his elbows on the table. His eyes were like ice chips. Before she knew what to expect, he reached for her hand, flipping her palm up.

"Don't," she whispered heatedly when she realized what he was doing. He expertly tapped on the tiny screen. He looked up at her with a grim smile when he quickly scanned her vitals, which—*damn it*—indicated a marked escalated stress response like a neon sign.

"What's wrong, Lin, not as cool and collected as you're leading everyone in this snooty restaurant to believe?"

She gritted her teeth in anger and yanked back her wrist. "*That's* none of your business."

"If I were you, I'd take off the device then," Kam replied. "I mean it," he said and gave her a defiant glare, a trace of steel to his voice. "I don't want those people gaping at what's going on inside of you."

"But *you* have that right?" she asked angrily, removing the watch and putting it in her purse. Maybe he was right, as annoyed as that realization made her. They'd gotten through the first meeting with the Gersbachs without the device in evidence, they could do the same with the Stunde representatives. "And if I'm not calm, it's with good reason. You've been messing with me, Kam," she accused, unable to stop herself. "You've had ulterior motives in sleeping with me."

His sharp bark of laughter made her jump slightly. She gaped at him, aghast at his manner. "*I* had ulterior motives in sleeping with *you*? That's rich."

"What's that supposed to mean?" she demanded.

"Lin?"

She blinked dazedly at the sound of the woman's hesitant voice.

"Nina, Kyle. I didn't see you arrive," she said, standing and shaking hands with the Stunde executives. She forced herself into her professional role, difficult as it was, especially with Kam's scowl and surliness fully in evidence when she made introductions.

Fortunately, the dinner was a moderate success, despite Lin's confusion and anger and Kam's inexplicable coolness. At least nothing was ruined, and Kyle and Nina were very interested in the product. Kam's manner during dinner segued from his perplexing anger at her to being aloof and distant, but since Nina and Kyle were unfamiliar with his typical presentation, they seemed not to notice anything unduly remarkable. Like the Gersbachs before them, they seemed to assume he was an idiosyncratic, somewhat withdrawn genius. He answered their questions with his typical succinctness, his incising intelligence impossible to hide despite his preoccupation. By the time the meeting and luxurious meal came to a conclusion, Lin was feeling very raw and abraded, her façade worn thin by

Kam's palpable chill. She didn't think it was her imagination that his coolness was aimed exclusively at her.

Why was he giving *her* the cold shoulder? Wasn't she the one who had a right to be miffed, given the circumstances?

She turned toward him on the sidewalk after Kyle and Nina got into the first cab and it drove away.

"You are such an arrogant ass," she hissed furiously, unable to contain her summation of his character a second longer.

Fury and confusion pulsed through her when she saw the trace of sarcasm cross his handsome face. He glanced down at her contemptuously.

"You really do turn that act on and off like a light switch, don't you?"

"What is *wrong* with you?" she grated out, stunned by his disdain.

His lip curled into a snarl. Suddenly it seemed impossible to Lin that she'd thought he'd been cool since Kyle and Nina had arrived. He wasn't just simmering with emotion. He was about to boil over.

"Wrong with me? Maybe it turns my stomach to watch you smile and charm and look like a beautiful doll all night long. You always have the perfect line on the tip of your tongue, don't you? Does anybody ever see the *real* you, Lin? I wonder if *you* even know who she is."

"You son of a—"

He caught her flying hand in midair. A shock resounded in her flesh. She gasped in disbelief. His blazing eyes burned right through her. She'd never told herself to do it, but she'd been about to slap him before he'd stopped her. Dozens of diners would have witnessed the spectacle she made through the glass windows of the posh restaurant. She'd never lost control in public like this before. She rarely did in private . . .

Kam's nostrils flared in anger. Lin's lungs burned. She couldn't draw air. He jerked her wrist and her body thumped against his.

Electricity seemed to jump from him to her. Against her will, she felt herself respond to his long, hard length.

"So the polished little kitten has claws. Well, that's a *start* at honesty, I guess," Kam muttered through a clenched jaw. His remark bounced off her; she was still momentarily stunned by her actions. He put out his hand to hail the next waiting cab. Lin said nothing when he held open the door for her. She couldn't believe he'd goaded her so easily. Her entire body seemed to vibrate with chaotic emotion.

Kam slid into the seat next to her and tersely gave the driver the address to his apartment before he slid the plastic divider between driver and passenger seats closed. Lin turned to him, her mouth opening to accuse him of being a manipulative bastard. Kam opened his hands along each side of her jaw, holding her in place, and seized her mouth in an angry, searing kiss.

All her confusion about her desires, all the longing she'd felt ever since she left Kam's arms on Monday morning, all the bubbling emotion she'd been feeling since Ian had told her about Kam's plans, all of that and more found a channel in erupting lust and need. It roared to the surface, both a threat and a potent thrill that was impossible to resist.

Still, she was outraged. She wrenched her mouth free after a moment and tore his hands from her face. Their gazes clashed in the city-lit cab. She saw the dangerous glint in his light eyes.

"Do you honestly think I only want you because I want you to work for me? I wish that were true. I haven't had a moment of peace since the first second you walked into that restaurant," he growled ominously, sounding furious at that fact.

"Damn you, Kam," she whispered, affected by his raw admission whether she wanted to be or not.

"Damned is right," he assured her before he bent to her again. This time, his kiss was every bit as dark and dangerous, but it was more controlled. It was the devil's seduction. His tongue claimed her mouth, sweeping it everywhere. He moved his lips in a sensual enticement, sucking at her, pulling her in to him in a way that was impossible to deny. Lin tangled her tongue with his, angry, aroused, overwhelmed. He wrapped a hand at her waist and pulled her closer against his hard body, and Lin knew she was something else.

Lost.

Kam pulled her after him once he'd distractedly handed a pleased cabdriver a twenty for a six-dollar fare. He pulled her through the lobby like he thought he was evacuating a fire, but going in the wrong direction. The doorman behind the desk greeted her by name when they arrived, and Lin gave a breathless, unintelligible reply. She'd been there countless times to Ian's penthouse. Kam immediately swept down on her without waiting for the elevator doors to close. Despite the fact that she was aware of the doorman's eyes watching them curiously as they got onto the mahogany-paneled elevator, she turned her face up and put her arms out to receive Kam's hot, demanding kiss. She melted against his length. The doors closed and she felt herself rising, lifted on the steam of single-minded desire.

Kam's mouth burned her throat. He reached beneath her wrap and began to loosen the single strap of her dress. She arched against him when his hand brushed a prickling nipple, tempting him to touch her. She moaned and nipped at his snarling mouth when he filled his palm with her breast, then plucked at the aching nipple with his fingertips. He bent and ravaged her mouth again.

The elevator doors dinged open. She broke their kiss and whimpered his name when he didn't appear to notice, but just continued to consume her. When the doors started to close, he moved away from her quick as a lightning strike, halting the doors and pulling her after him.

The luxurious, muted hallway was a blur; the snick of the metal lock giving way beneath Kam's key sounding illicit and secretive. The interior of the apartment was dark, the main source of light the rows of high-rise after high-rise glittering like a sparkling necklace along the body of black water. Lin's spell of hazy lust wasn't diminished even when Kam gave a harsh demand to a bounding Angus, telling the excited dog to go into the dining room. Then Kam was pulling her over to the couch and urging her to lie down, her head at the corner. He came down over her, sealing her tight in the cocoon he spun around them of heat and forgetfulness and blind need. His kiss was dark and addictive, his touch on the naked skin of her shoulder, breast, and thigh desired above all else.

The next thing she knew, he was rearing over her, a dark, powerful presence, his arms bracing his body on the back and armrest of the couch, one of his feet on the floor and his knee between her thigh and the cushion. Her dress was rucked up around her waist, her panties evaporated somewhere into the darkness. Her bare breasts rose and fell rapidly, looking pale in the city lights. He lowered one hand to her shin, pushing her bent leg onto the back of the couch, opening her to him. The hard, swollen knob of his cock moved along her labia. She was slick with arousal. She could hear the subtle sound of him moving in her flesh, and it ramped up her excitement. He gave her clit a firm caress, and then he was pushing against her slit, demanding entrance.

"Say my name," he muttered hoarsely from above her.

"Kam." She repeated it, his name on her tongue a pleading endearment. He flexed his hips. Her lips opened into a silent scream as he filled her.

Kam could see her face from the glow of the city lights as he burrowed into her clasping pussy. Hearing her chant his name and watching her lips open into an O of rapture as he slid into her to the hilt left him desperate.

He wanted his name to be the only one seared into this woman's brain. Her heart. The very marrow of her bones. He wanted it in that moment more than he'd ever wanted anything in his life. It was like a fire racing in his blood. He'd burn both of them with it.

He began to fuck her, continuing to brace his upper body at the corner of the couch, his foot on the floor and his hips powering his thrusts. Her cries were sharp. Wild. He couldn't take his eyes off her beautiful face pinched tight with desire.

"Is this what you want from me, Lin?" he rasped, his pelvis smacking in a steady, hard-driving rhythm against the back of her spread thighs and buttocks. He looped his arm around her silky thigh in a snug hold and used his grip to increase the force of his deep thrusts. She was helpless to deny his consumption . . . his total possession. "You need it like this?" he persisted. His blood was boiling. He rode her like a man on fire . . . or with a demon at his back.

"Yes," she grated out, her head coming off the pillow, her face tight with the sweet, harsh agony they shared.

She wanted him, all right. He could feel the inferno building in her. She wanted his cock. She was using him to quench a desire for another. The knowledge was a burr under his skin that he couldn't ignore, despite his rabid lust. His need.

He cursed bitterly and pulled his furious erection out of the heaven of her. She gasped his name, sounding pained. His cock felt like it steamed in the cool air. He kicked off his shoes and jerked his pants and underwear off his legs, followed by his socks. His cock bobbed a furious protest when he glanced back and saw Lin's splayed, pale thighs and her confused expression.

"Come here," he said gruffly, reaching for her. She sat up, and he caught her around her waist. He felt the soft, warm bursts of her panting breath against his neck and the delicious spill of her long hair against the roughened skin of his arm. He grit his teeth in barely leashed restraint as he stalked down the hallway to the bedroom. He had this moment to blaze away all the ghosts, if only for tonight.

He set her on the edge of the bed and found the zipper at the side of her dress. It was the only thing he hadn't taken off of her completely yet. When he'd removed the dress, her long hair spilled around her shoulders and down her arms. She stared at him with large, dark eyes, her mouth trembling slightly.

"It's not fair, how beautiful you are," he told her fiercely.

"Why?" she replied. "My body is yours. All of me is, Kam."

His mouth twisted bitterly at her words. "All of you?"

Puzzlement crossed her face. "Yes," she whispered.

He whipped off his tie and shirt, the only clothing he still wore. He opened the bedside table drawer and found what he wanted. Lin went still when she saw what he placed on the mattress near her: the bullet vibrator and a bottle of lubricant. Her gaze darted to his face.

"Up on your hands and knees," he said quietly.

Up on your hands and knees.

His low, tense dare echoed in her head. She could say no, of course. She'd never once thought Kam would ever do anything to her that she didn't want. But as she met his somber stare and listened to her wild heartbeat, she knew she *did* want it.

Even if this tumultuous, inexplicable night ended her relationship with him, she didn't want to run. All of her life, she'd maintained control, carefully shielding herself from the storm of passion. She wanted to meet this cyclone full on, to take this risk.

It was irrational, but she *wanted* to be branded by him.

Holding his stare, she slowly started to turn on the bed. She saw his breath hitch at her compliance. Like he had the other afternoon, he pulled a pillow down the length of the bed and placed it in front of her. "You know the position," he said from behind her.

Her mouth went dry. She lowered her cheek to the pillow, resting her shoulders on the surface of the bed, her ass elevated in the air. She'd felt vulnerable and excited when she'd taken the position the other night while he flogged and fucked her. Tonight, the feeling of trepidation and arousal was doubled. Her muscles clenched tight.

She swallowed thickly when she saw him pick up the bottle of lubricant and the vibrator.

He wasted no time, immediately turning on the vibrator. Her anticipation grew unbearable when she heard the clicking sound of him opening the bottle of lubrication. She gave a muffled moan when he placed the vibrator next to her clit.

"Try to relax," he said gruffly behind her. "The more you let go, the more you surrender, the more you'll enjoy it." He grunted softly as he found her slit with his thumb and plunged it into her pussy. Lin whimpered in pleasure at the dual stimulation of the vibrator and his finger. "Stretch your hands over your head." He used his free hand to part her ass cheeks. "That's right. God, you're beautiful."

Lin clenched her eyes tight at the sound of wonder in his voice, but also just the hint of anger. Why had the fact that he found her desirable caused that edge to his tone tonight? Her question melted under the delicious buzz of the vibrator on her clit and his fucking finger. It felt *so* good. She bit her lip to subdue a sharp cry when he pressed his other thumb to her asshole, this one lubricated. He circled it over the sensitive ring. She moaned shakily.

"Shhh," he soothed. He penetrated her. She inhaled and held her breath. He grunted softly as he slid his thumb farther into her.

"Have you ever done this before?" he asked thickly.

"No," she mouthed. She was so amazed by the sensation of his finger moving in such an intimate place, in combination with the stimulation on her clit and in her pussy, that she didn't realize right away she hadn't spoken aloud.

"Lin?" Kam prompted, making her eyes fly open.

"No," she said.

He paused, his thumb completely embedded in her ass. Nerves she hadn't known existed seemed to flame to life with the novel penetration. The burn on her clit felt extra sharp.

"Are you sure you want to now?" he asked.

"*Yes.*"

He groaned and began to thrust his thumb in and out of her ass while the other fucked her pussy. He firmed the vibrator on her outer sex. Lin moaned at the indescribable sensations flooding her. Her lips ached, as did her nipples. The stimulation on her pussy and ass at once seemed to cause a fire in her brain. It spread down her spine until it even enflamed the soles of her feet.

"Oh," she moaned, the fever rising in her, prickling the surface of every square inch of her skin. She bobbed her hips subtly, riding his talented hands.

"That's right," Kam murmured, his voice rough with arousal. "Give in to it. Are you about to come?"

"Yes. Oh, yes," she moaned, bouncing her ass more energetically.

"No, *mon petit chaton*." Her lungs deflated when he removed his thick thumb from her ass. "Not until you have taken my cock."

She panted in intense arousal into the charged silence that followed. He kept the vibrator pressed to her clit, making her simmer. She felt him grasp one of her buttocks, opening her, and then the thrilling, forbidden sensation of his cockhead pressing against her ass. He pressed tightly against the muscular ring, but he didn't breach her.

"You have to press back, baby. It will go in easier that way. Take what you can."

She followed his instructions. The pressure was unbearable, but it also somehow relieved the fever building in her. Or did it feed it? She only knew she needed this. His cockhead slipped into her ass. She gasped as pain sliced through her.

"I'm sorry," Kam muttered tensely, but he didn't withdraw. His thick, hard cock remained throbbing in her ass. He ran his hand over her buttock and hip, soothing her. The vibrator continued its delicious buzz. Lin panted for air, and as she did so, the sharp pain she'd experienced faded away, leaving only a wickedly exciting burn.

"Oh," she said, a thread of wonder resonating in her voice. She pushed back experimentally with her hips and more of his shaft entered her. Kam hissed behind her. She'd bumped against his hand. Lin realized he held the stalk of his cock at midshaft while the first several inches pierced her. The realization aroused her. She pushed back again with her hips, gritting her teeth.

"Hold still, Lin," Kam demanded sharply. She froze, holding her breath. "If you had any idea what I want do to you right now, you wouldn't test me."

For a tense moment, both of them remained very still. She sensed Kam gathering himself, but for her part, the excitement was unbearable. Her clit sizzled beneath the vibrator. His cock throbbed in her most intimate flesh.

"I'm going to come," she said shakily.

"No," he ordered, lifting the vibrator.

She keened, feeling the deprivation like a physical pain.

He began to pulse his cock in and out of her, fucking her deliberately, claiming a fraction more of her with each pass. Her keen turned into an incredulous moan. He growled in answer, and suddenly the vibrator was back on her clit. He thrust farther into her.

"Oh my god," she shouted, her head coming off the pillow.

He groaned gutturally. "I'm sorry," he said in a choked voice. "You're very small." He rocked in and out of her gently. Her lungs collapsed. She pressed her hips against the ruthless vibrator, her vision darkening.

"I can't stop it," she cried desperately. "I . . . can't—"

His pelvis smacked against her buttocks. "Then don't," he said harshly. "Burn for me."

Her entire body ignited. She called his name again and again helplessly. Everything evaporated under the onslaught of pleasure. There was only pounding bliss, and she gave herself to it wholly.

There was no room for regret or reluctance. Not in this.

Kam cursed heatedly when he felt the rush of heat around him, and then her tiny convulsions of climax vibrated into his cock, tempting a man already severely tested. Lin called his name, and he gave up. He grabbed her ass with one hand and began to plunge in and out of her, grimacing at the cruelty of the pleasure. She was so hot. Her shouts and moans amplified as he fucked her while she continued to come. He kept the vibrator pressed to her for as long as he could, but then he reached a point of no return. She was burning him from the inside out.

The vibrator fell onto the bed. He grasped her ass with both hands and crashed into her again and again. Her sharp cries penetrated his thick, fevered lust, but he couldn't stop. His pelvis smacked against her ass faster and faster. Honesty carved away all artifice in a moment like this, revealing his true self, savage and raw.

"Who are you giving yourself to, Lin? Who?"

"You," she cried. *"Kam."*

"Don't you ever forget it," he snarled. He thrust, their flesh slapping together. He held her to him, his muscles going rigid. He roared as climax ripped through him, the blast of it feeling like it could have blown a hole straight through his head . . .

. . . his very spirit.

He couldn't catch his breath. His body wasn't calming like it usually did after climax. He groaned, rough and miserable, still clutching Lin to his body like she was a life preserver, and he a drowning man. He began to panic slightly, wondering why the riot in his flesh wouldn't stop.

One burning breath after another, however, and it slowly began to ease. He blinked the sweat out of his eyes, staring down. The image of Lin's delicate rib cage heaving in and out struck him as beautiful. Poignant. With a rush, he recalled how wild he'd been there at the end. How ruthless. How determined to push his way into her body. Her mind. Her heart.

He leaned back his head and gave a muffled howl of rising misery.

"Kam?" Lin asked shakily.

He looked down and saw her lift her head and try to turn to see him. He slowly withdrew from her body, wincing as he did so.

"Come here," he said quietly. He helped turn her on the bed. She whimpered in surprise when he lifted her from the mattress, the front of her body pressed to the front of his. He carried her to the bathroom.

"Kam?" Lin repeated dazedly when he set her next to the steam shower and reached to turn on the water. He pulled her under the hot spray with him, shutting the glass door. He briskly lathered up with soap and gently washed her, avoiding her gaze.

"What is it?" she demanded tremulously. "What's happened to you?"

He looked at her face. She stared up at him, her shattered expression stabbing at him. He shut his eyes and looked away from her when he saw a single tear skip down her cheek. "I'm sorry. I'm sorry I did that . . . tonight of all nights."

"Why *tonight of all nights*? I don't understand what you're talking about. I can't understand you at all ever since Ian told me that you planned to ask me to work for you."

The water pounded on the shower floor in the silence that followed.

"I know that you're in love with Ian."

He met her stare. The water was starting to wet one side of her midnight hair. Water droplets clung to her neck and breasts. Her cheeks were still flushed from arousal. As he watched, her mouth fell open slowly in disbelief.

"What are you talking about?" she asked, her voice flat from shock. When he didn't immediately respond, she searched his face wildly. "Have you spoken with Richard St. Claire? Did you go to the *hospital*?"

A sick feeing swept through him. He hadn't really believed he was wrong in his assumption about her feelings for Ian. Still, proof he'd been correct was a blow for which he hadn't prepared himself.

"No. I guessed it. From something Ian said." Some of the vibrant color washed out of her cheeks. "*He* doesn't know," he assured her, guilt suddenly swamping him. It was unforgivable, the way he'd been acting. He was lashing out at the woman he'd fallen in love with because of something she couldn't help. Love was blind, isn't that what they said? She'd fallen for Ian long before she'd ever known Kam existed. He swept his hand through his damp hair in a frustrated gesture. It seemed ludicrous in the aftermath of his storm of chaotic emotion that he'd convinced himself he was angry at her for not being honest with him. As if he would have ever taken it well, hearing from her lips that she was attracted to him because he resembled his brother, or that while she may enjoy him in bed, her heart belonged to another man.

Yeah, he would have taken that *really* well, he realized simmering in self-deprecation.

"I figured it all out when Ian told me to buy you purple lotus flowers yesterday. He said they were your favorite," Kam explained to her hollowly. "I remembered how you had several pressed ones in your bedside drawer . . . the ones Ian had given you over the years, right?"

She didn't reply. She seemed shell-shocked upon having her secret revealed so unexpectedly. He raised his hand to touch her face—comfort her—but the memory of how he'd treated her earlier made him drop it. He exhaled, suddenly feeling weary.

"That, and a lot of other things I've learned since I've gotten to know you these past few weeks, led me to it. You're so contained. So controlled. I figured if there was anyone on the planet who could take the pain of a broken heart day in and day out, and still be so strong and loyal, it was you." He met her stare. "I just figured it out, Lin."

Her stunned silence was like a shouted condemnation. He stared sightlessly at the tile surround.

"Are you okay? Did I hurt you?" He waved vaguely toward the direction of the bedroom.

"No," she whispered.

He swallowed thickly, relief at her answer barely penetrating the dense weariness that had come over him. "I'll just go and give you some privacy." He reached for the shower door and then turned back. She stood in the exact spot, unmoving.

"I didn't sleep with you to influence you to work at Reardon Technologies. I did that because I can't keep my hands off you. I've fallen for you, Lin. Hard," he added grimly. "I thought it must have been obvious, but what do I know? I don't have much experience with something like this. Any, to be honest."

He stepped out of the shower, shutting the door between them.

Chapter Nineteen

When Lin had finally recovered sufficiently from her shock and got out of the shower to dress, she discovered Kam and Angus were both gone. Had Kam taken Angus for a walk to offer her the opportunity to make a less awkward exit if she chose?

Lin was so overwhelmed by the events of the night, she took that chance. She fled. She was distraught and confused by the things Kam had revealed. Part of her was thrilled that he'd told her he'd fallen for her. She still couldn't believe it, though. But she also felt guilty. She should have told him about Ian. Shouldn't she have?

But there's nothing left to tell, is there?

Lin had recently realized that her romantic fantasy of Ian was nothing, *nothing* compared to the vibrant, amazing, uncontrollable feelings she had for Kam.

Perhaps the main reason she slunk away from Kam's apartment to gather herself that night was that she knew herself to be a fool. She'd spent a good portion of her adult life pining for an insubstantial dream. It'd taken Kam's raw, uncompromising brand of honesty to prove that.

Was it too late for her to admit her true desires? Had she built such a secure façade around herself that she'd never be able to escape the thick walls?

A strange feeling slowly began to rise in Lin that night. It was akin to hearing the wail of a distant alarm come ever closer until that blaring sound filled her consciousness. She'd returned to her condominium, but had never slept that night as that alarming, swelling feeling mounted. It was as if now that she'd discovered the trap she'd made for herself, she could no longer find peace in her confinement.

Why had she left last night? What was she doing wasting time in this bed? She had to speak to Kam. She realized this mounting feeling was all of her emotion bursting through her defenses, all of the unspoken words she wanted to say to Kam crowding into her mind.

Just before dawn, she rose from her mussed bed and rapidly showered. Forsaking any makeup and leaving her hair to dry naturally, she hastened into some jeans, a fitted T-shirt, and an overshirt along with a pair of boots. She snatched her purse and keys and rushed out her front door.

Fifteen minutes and a cab ride later, she waited impatiently at the doorman's station of Kam's building.

"Is Mr. Reardon there?" the doorman asked into the phone. "He has a visitor. Oh, hello Mrs. Noble," the man said deferentially after a moment. He glanced up and gave Lin a pointed glance. What was Francesca doing in Kam's apartment? "Oh, Mr. Reardon isn't there?"

"Can I speak to her?" Lin asked, holding out her hand for the phone.

"Francesca?" she asked a second later.

"Lin, is that you?"

"Yes. I'm looking for Kam. I need to find him. It's important."

"Is everything all right?" Francesca asked worriedly.

"Yes," Lin said, realizing that she hadn't hidden her growing franticness. "Well, not really. I need to speak with him. Do you know where he is?"

"He's at the airport," Francesca said. "He called the penthouse at around midnight last night and said he'd changed his mind about visiting the Gersbachs in Geneva next week. He decided to go now. He booked a flight for this morning, and was calling to ask if I'd take care of Angus while he was gone. I thought it was strange, but—"

"What time was his flight?" Lin interrupted her.

"It's at eight o'clock. He left around ten minutes ago I think. You just missed him. Lin, he said something about possibly not returning to Chicago. He said he might arrange for Angus to be returned to Aurore."

"Airline?" Lin pressed.

"United."

"Thanks. I have to go," she said hurriedly, handing the phone back to the doorman.

"Good luck," she distantly heard Francesca call into the receiver.

"You didn't see Mr. Reardon leaving a little while ago?" Lin asked the doorman in frustration as she started to back away.

"I took a bathroom break a few minutes ago—"

Lin made a sound of irritation and charged through the revolving doors.

"O'Hare. *Fast*," Lin told the cabdriver succinctly as she flew into the backseat and slammed the door.

"Morning traffic. I'll do the best I can."

"I'll pay you ten times the amount of your fare if you do better than that. *Significantly* better."

In the rearview mirror, she saw the driver's eyebrows go up in interest and braced herself against the seat divider when he punched the gas. The alarm amplified to a wailing scream in her head as she hastily dug her cell phone out of her purse. She hit Kam's number. If she begged him to postpone his flight, would he hear her out?

The cabdriver met her challenge, risking about a dozen different tickets to get her to the airport in record time, given traffic. Her sense of alarm became tinged with dread, however, when Kam didn't answer his phone after several tries. Why was she growing so panicked? Surely, even if she missed him, she could fly to Geneva or France or wherever he was to seek him out?

Now that I've stopped playing it safe, I'm tired of wasting time.

She shoved four one-hundred-dollar bills into the cabdriver's hand and rushed out of the taxi, slamming the door behind her, her mind focused ahead on the target of Kam.

Suddenly she was falling. She hit the sidewalk with a jarring lurch.

"You all right?" a nearby skycap called out to her.

Lin grimaced. Her hands stung badly from bracing herself from the fall. She'd tripped over a concrete curb in her haste. Cursing under her breath for her idiocy—she couldn't recall ever taking such a header in her life—she pushed herself up, only to almost fall again when she tried to stand. Her confusion over her sudden unsteady state was replaced by desperate irritation when she saw that the heel of her right boot had broken off.

Kam might be passing through security check any second now, moving out of her reach.

She pushed a mass of wild curls out of her face and limped onto the sidewalk, her gait awkward because of the three-inch disparity of height in her legs due to the missing heel. She staggered through the busy airport, looking for the nearest security check-in.

Security was packed. She searched wildly for Kam's tall form and signature dark, wavy hair, her helplessness and dread mounting until it felt like it'd choke her throat. Nowhere. Not a sight of him. She moved her position anxiously searching, hoping to catch a glimpse of him at the actual security checkpoint.

She checked her watch, and then closed her burning eyelids. It was seven twenty-two. He'd be boarding soon. Even if she pulled the stunt of buying a ticket to get through security, the lines were too long. She'd never make it.

She'd missed him.

Her limbs suddenly felt very heavy. Her heart did. Pain waited until that moment to rush into her awareness. Her knees and palms throbbed with a stinging pain from her fall.

Gone. He was gone. And she was stuck in the sticky web of her own life.

She'd have to catch a cab back to the city on the departure level, she thought dully. She turned around and walked her graceless, defeated walk to the elevators.

"Lin?"

She paused in her progress down the departure level toward the cabstand, her heart leaping into her throat. She turned slowly, her skin prickling, too afraid to believe, and yet . . .

Kam stood behind her, wearing jeans and a long-sleeved, striped button-down, the handle of a rolling suitcase in his hand. He stared at her incredulously. Suddenly he was rushing her.

"What happened?" he demanded, his eyes a little wild. "Why is there blood on you?" He touched her cheek, his brows slanting ominously as he looked down at her. He lifted her hand. Lin realized dazedly for the first time her palm was bloody. She must have brushed her cheek and smeared blood on her face.

"I fell getting out of the cab. I'm *so* glad to see you," she said, her voice shaky with relief.

He looked at her face, amazement dawning on his rugged features. "What are you doing here?"

"I came to ask you not to go. Not now, anyway. I'm sorry I left last night," she said in a pressured rush. "I was . . . overwhelmed by what you said. By everything . . ." she broke off, realizing how inadequate she sounded. She shook her head in frustration. "I'm not in love with Ian, Kam. I thought I was. Once. It's recently been brought to my attention by my friend Richard that my feelings for Ian were an excuse to keep me safe . . . to keep me from taking a risk." She swallowed thickly, the pressure in her chest and throat making speech difficult, even though she'd never wanted to communicate so much in her life. A tear skipped down her face and dampened a tendril of hair that had stuck to her overheated cheeks. She pushed the errant curl out of her face. God, she was a mess. "Even when Richard mentioned that to me recently, though, I was already starting to suspect what he said was true. What I felt for Ian was a girl's infatuation that would have evaporated a long time ago, if I hadn't willfully clung onto it."

"When?"

"When, *what*?" she asked, confused.

Kam stepped closer. She suddenly was inundated by his closeness, by his long, hard body and bold features and piercing light eyes. He was the most beautiful thing she'd ever seen in her life. His scent tickled her nose. She inhaled it deeply, prizing the unexpected gift of it. Of him.

"When did you start to suspect you weren't really in love with Ian?" Kam prompted.

She met his stare and felt all the walls tumbling down.

"I didn't realize it until now, but I think maybe . . . ever since I first saw you," she whispered.

He mouthed something soundlessly, and then he was taking her in his arms. She hugged him tightly against her, clenching her eyes closed in the grip of powerful emotion.

"You said last night that if there was one person you knew who could contain the hurt of a broken heart, it was me," she muttered in a rush against his chest. "But that's not true, Kam. That's how I knew, I really knew for a *fact* I never really could have been in love with Ian. Because when it feels like this," she hugged him tighter, her voice choking, "it's not something you could *ever* contain."

"Shhh. That's a *good* thing, baby. *Such* a good thing," he said warmly near her ear, his hand stroking her back in a soothing motion as she gasped, out of control. "It's going to be all right. It's going to be better than all right. You'll see."

Lin nodded against his chest. She wasn't sure how long they remained like that, clutching at each other desperately while strangers rushed past them in either direction.

She finally removed her pressing cheek from his chest and looked into his face. Despite a veil of blurring tears, she saw his smile, the tenderness of it a poignant contrast to his rugged, masculine aura. He brushed her hair back and cradled her jaw. "You're a wreck, *mon petit chaton*. I've never seen you more beautiful."

She beamed up at him.

"I never thought I'd see the day Lin Soong came undone," he said.

"I didn't, either. But I'm glad it came," she replied earnestly. His smile faded slowly, his expression hardening.

"Je t'aime, mon amour."

Warmth and wonder flooded into her chest, bathing her heart. Her French was good enough to understand *that*, but even if it hadn't been, the message gleaming in Kam's eyes at that moment was unmistakable.

"Yeah. It kind of took me by surprise, too," he mumbled, his handsome mouth tilting in a self-deprecating grin. She laughed and he joined her, the moment effervescent. Golden. He must have recognized her amazement at his declaration of love.

"More like a miracle," she breathed out, awe tingeing her tone.

He brought her wrist to his mouth and kissed her pulse, his passionate gaze seeming to bore straight down into her. How could she ever have even considered forsaking *this* for the safety of her heart? His warm lips lingered for a heart fluttering moment.

"Come on. You should go into the bathroom and wash those cuts on your palm," he said gruffly after a moment.

"I never asked you what you were doing here instead of getting onto your plane," Lin said as they walked to the women's restroom side by side.

"I decided I'd given up too fast. I was coming back to beg for your forgiveness for how I acted last night. I was coming back to put up a fight for you," he said, giving her a hard, glittering sideways glance that caused that all-too-familiar swooping sensation in her lower belly.

"Neither thing was necessary," Lin assured. "But *thank you*, all the same."

Epilogue

Lin knocked on the carved walnut door and entered when she heard the soft "Come in." A smile spread across her face. Francesca lay propped against the pillows in the four-poster bed holding a white-blanketed bundle in her arms. Morning sunlight streamed through the windows. She'd just learned from Ian's grandmother, Anne, that Francesca and Ian had been up much of the night with their new baby. Apparently, the baby had finally succumbed to sleep. Francesca looked very tired, but sublimely happy as she shared Lin's smile.

"Anne told me to come on up," Lin said in a hushed tone. "I saw Ian downstairs. He said he'd be right in with the bassinet so you can rest. He looked *so* happy." She peered down at the bundle and saw the infant's face. His hair was dark, like Ian's, and he was fast asleep.

"Meet James Patrick Noble," Francesca whispered. "He seems to have finally figured out sleep is a good thing."

"He's beautiful, Francesca."

Francesca smiled as she looked down at her son. "He looks like his father. Lucky boy."

"What color are his eyes?"

"Dark blue, but Anne says they might change."

"Kam was struck dumb for I don't know how long when he found out you gave James his middle name," Lin said quietly, stepping back. She glanced around when she saw Ian walking into the room, carrying a white bassinet. He wore jeans and a shadow of whiskers on his jaw. Like his wife, he looked tired but happy.

"We wanted to give him a true family name," Ian murmured, setting down the basket a few feet away from Francesca. "Since Elise and Lucien are his godparents, we thought we'd commemorate Grandfather and Kam by giving him their names."

"Kam is so honored. Seriously," she whispered, giving Francesca a significant glance. "Even though he hardly has said anything about it, I can tell by the sound of his voice whenever we talk about James."

"I know," Francesca said. "I saw his expression when he was at the hospital right after James was born and we told him."

"I'm sorry I couldn't make it for the birth," Lin apologized to both of them. "It was a rotten time to be halfway across the world."

"You're here now. Thank you for coming," Francesca said sincerely.

"Kam says you snagged Reardon another valuable contract with Haru Incorporated," Ian said quietly, sitting on the edge of the bed, stroking Francesca's blanket-covered thigh and peering down at James. Lin recalled how she'd seen a whole new expression on his face when he'd fallen in love with Francesca, and how she'd felt glad for his happiness after so much loneliness and pain in his life. Here was yet another expression as Ian looked at his son, one of deep love and profound contentment.

Lin nodded. "And just in time, with our first shipment of watches going out in two weeks. We needed the extra capital with a royalty contract. It's all happened so fast," she said, referring to the launching of Kam's business. *Their* business, since she'd decided to take Kam up on his offer several months ago and become his business partner as well as his romantic one.

"Kam couldn't have done it without you," Ian said. "Trust me, I know from experience."

Lin laughed softly. "You're doing just fine without me. Don't make me feel guilty."

"Don't you *dare* feel guilty," Francesca whispered, giving Ian a repressive glance. He gave his wife a small smile.

"She knows I'm kidding," Ian rumbled. "I wouldn't have let her go without a fight to anyone but Kam. She's still in the family, so I'll have to settle for that."

"Kam is so happy," Francesca told Lin earnestly. "I've never seen a man so energized and purposeful about his work—especially since you two have undertaken this huge task of starting a company and all that implies—and yet so at peace with his personal life as well. You're the best thing that's ever happened to him."

"He only scowls in his sleep and at dinner parties these days. I actually saw him smile at a waiter while we were in London last week," Ian mused.

Lin smiled, warmed by hearing the couple speak of Kam's happiness. She and Kam had been living together at Aurore Manor for ten weeks now, although both of them were often traveling on business. Lin had to agree with Francesca's assessment of Kam's happiness. She shared in it fully, so who knew better than her?

Francesca shifted James in her arms. "Let's put him down. I'm so tired I can hardly keep my eyes open," she said, transferring the bundle to Ian. Ian took his son and stood.

"Are you sure you don't want Melina to put him to sleep in the nursery?" Ian asked quietly, referring, Lin knew, to their newly hired nanny. "You could sleep uninterrupted that way."

"No, no," Francesca insisted, shaking her head. "It's too soon."

Lin smiled, understanding her. James was only three days old, after all. But if Lin had her guess, it'd be that Francesca had never fully warmed up to the idea of a nanny.

She secured her shoulder bag in preparation to leave. Francesca needed rest, and she was *very* eager to return to Aurore and Kam.

"You shouldn't have made a special trip to Belford Hall, Lin. Kam says you two haven't seen each other for nine days," Francesca said tiredly.

Lin walked over to the bassinet and got another look at James before she departed. "I wanted to come and see James first. I'm glad I did. He's amazing, you guys. Besides," she said, turning to the couple, "this way, Kam and I can settle down at Aurore for the calm before the storm when production begins in two weeks. We have an anniversary tonight."

"Really? Which one?" Francesca asked.

"Four months."

"Four months since . . ."

"We first saw each other," Lin gave a rueful smile. She knew how idiotic these little rituals might seem to a more established couple. "According to Kam, it was all there in that first look, the seeds of everything," she admitted, feeling her cheeks heating.

"He gets that eloquent with you?" Ian asked, looking pleased and amused at once.

"You have no idea," Lin assured with a grin.

Lin drove up the long, wooded drive to Aurore. She'd told Kam she had some errands she wanted to do before returning home, so he reluctantly had agreed not to pick her up at the airport. She'd made good time, though, and was home an hour earlier than she'd told Kam to expect her.

The sun had already set, even though it was only a little after five.

After her flight to France, she'd stopped in the village to pick up some needed supplies at the grocer, and then gone to retrieve her prearranged gift for Kam. Even though the woods were barren with winter cold, Aurore Manor looked warm and inviting when she pulled up in the circular drive before the large house. She'd ordered some greenery for Christmas, and it looked cheerful along with a lush wreath on the front door. Golden light spilled from several windows. She saw the compact car owned by Madame Morisot—their new housekeeper—parked behind Kam's sedan farther down the drive.

Grinning like an idiot, she retrieved her soft little gift, juggling her shoulder bag and the sack of supplies. She'd get her suitcase later. She couldn't wait to give him his gift, but she mostly burned to see him. It'd been *way* too long.

Madame Morisot had on her coat and was walking down the lit hall when Lin entered. Her eyes sprung wide when she saw what Lin carried in her cradled arm.

"Shhh," Lin said, laughing under her breath. "It's a surprise. Where is he?"

"He's upstairs cleaning up for dinner," Madame Morisot said in her thickly accented English. They both were distracted by the sound of Angus's jingling collar as she raced down the hall.

"Hi, girl," Lin greeted the excited dog. When Madame Morisot saw her struggling to be able to pet the golden retriever, she relieved her of her bags. "I have dinner ready and warming in the oven," the housekeeper said, setting down Lin's bags on an entryway table. "I was about ready to go home, I hope that's all right. I think Mr. Reardon wants you to himself tonight," Madame Morisot said with a sly glance.

"Yes, thank you for getting supper ready. We'll be fine."

"I'll see you in the morning."

"Good night," Lin called. She shut the door and locked it behind their housekeeper. Kneeling next to the grocery bag, she extracted a carton of milk, her heart bounding so fast, she was probably off the charts on her Reardon watch.

The thick new carpets muted her footsteps as she rose up the stairs. She opened the door to their bedroom softly, peering into the hushed interior. It was empty, but the bathroom door was slightly ajar.

"Not tonight, girl," she whispered in apology to a panting Angus. She shut the door with the dog on the other side of it. There was a crackling fire in the hearth. She smiled, her excitement mounting, when she tiptoed toward the bathroom and noticed champagne chilling in an ice bucket and two flutes sitting on the bedside table.

Kam walked out of the bathroom wearing a dark blue towel wrapped low around his hips, his taut muscles and skin sheened with moisture from his shower. His dark hair was wet and finger combed back in thick waves. Her body stirred. He looked delicious. Edible. *God*, she'd missed him. He did a double take when he saw her. He went still, a smile starting on his mouth.

"Surprise," she said, holding up the kitten.

He focused on the wriggling, gray fur ball. Lin waited anxiously. She wasn't entirely sure he'd like her gift. His smile slowly spread all the way to his eyes. Without speaking, he walked over to her and took her into his arms. She pressed against his warm, hard body, the kitten and the carton of milk between them. He caught her mouth with his in a kiss that made her feel like a knot had just been tugged tight at her core. She blinked up at him dazedly when he lifted his head a moment later.

"We are *not* going to be apart for this many days again, I don't care how important the business is," he declared with a dark scowl, kneading her shoulders. "Six days, *tops*." She leaned down and pressed her face to his chest, inhaling his delicious scent running her lips over his hard muscle and crisp hair.

"I love you, too," she whispered against his skin.

"No. *Five*," Kam continued. "Four at the absolute most, and then only three or four times a year." She licked at him delicately, starved for his taste. His grip tightened on her shoulders. "Two times a year, if that."

She met his stare and smiled. "I missed you, too."

"Agree to it," he insisted fiercely.

"I agree," she said without hesitation.

His frown faded, that appreciative gleam she cherished so much entering his eyes as his gaze ran over her face. "Business just isn't that important. Never as important as this," he said gruffly, brushing her jaw with his fingertip.

"I told you I agree," she said, going up on her toes and pressing her lips to his. She coaxed them into softening. "I'm a reformed woman these days when it comes to work, you know that."

The kitten meowed loudly. Kam glanced down. His smile dawned to full radiance, brilliant and sexy as hell. He took the squirming kitten from her.

"Do you like him?" she asked hopefully.

Kam held up the little feline in front of his face, examining it intently. He was so big and rugged, and the kitten was so tiny and delicate. The sight caused her heart to squeeze tight in her chest. He lowered the wiggling kitten and cradled it against his broad chest, petting it with two large fingers.

"I do. It's a him?" he asked.

Lin nodded. "I'm sorry I couldn't find a chocolate-colored one, but the good news is that Angus already approves of this little guy," she said, stepping forward to join him in petting and admiring the kitten. She explained how before she had left for Japan, she'd taken the golden retriever for a viewing of the litter at a residence in town. Angus had seemed especially patient with this one, and so she'd based her decision on that.

Kam caught her eye. "You always think of everything, don't you?"

She shrugged.

"Thank you," he said quietly, his gratitude clear. He knew she'd hated what he'd revealed to her about his childhood pet and his father's cruelty. He knew she wished more than anything that she could make it better, even if she couldn't ever erase those hurtful memories completely. This was their home now. Not Trevor Gaines's. Lin would *make* it so.

"We'll call him Marque," Kam said, reaching for the milk she still clutched in the crook of her arm. "It means 'hallmark' in French, and he's a hallmark of a special night. For several reasons, I hope," she heard him say under his breath.

Lin followed him when he walked over to the sitting area before the lazily crackling fire and picked up a shallow, decorative porcelain bowl sitting on the coffee table. When he placed it on the mantel, she helped him open the carton. He poured the milk into it and bent, placing it several feet away from the hearth. Marque immediately began lapping at it when Kam set him gently down next to the bowl. He straightened, his side pressing against hers.

"I thought we could keep him in the back room until he's trained," Lin said quietly as they watched the kitten drink eagerly. "It's nice and warm in there, and it's not carpeted, so cleanups wouldn't be too bad."

"All right. Just leave him to his dinner for now, though," Kam said, standing and taking her hand. "You and I have an overdue appointment over here," he said, leading Lin to the bed.

They made love not once, but twice, in quick succession, their need for one another sharp and swelling after being apart for so many days. Afterward, Lin nestled contentedly in the curve of Kam's encircling arm, her cheek resting on his shoulder, his fingers furrowing through her hair.

"Marque is fast asleep," she murmured after a moment. She could see across the suite in this position. The kitten had curled up at the outer edge of the marble hearth, undoubtedly made drowsy by his milk and the warmth of the fire.

"Are you tired?" he asked, his roughened, quiet voice like a gentle, arousing scratch on her nape. "You've been traveling for twenty-plus hours."

"I'm okay," she said, stroking his strong biceps and squeezing it lightly, enjoying the dense texture. "I don't want to sleep. Not now. I want to be with you."

He kissed the top of her head and scooted into a sitting position. Dislodged from her resting place, Lin flopped back against the pillows. "Good," he said. "Because we've got champagne." Lin stared up at the ceiling dreamily, feeling ridiculously happy to be home. With Kam. He had turned and was opening the bottle of champagne. She sat up in bed, holding the sheet over her breasts, and accepted the filled flute from him several seconds later.

"To our four-month anniversary," she said, grinning and holding up her glass.

"I was hoping today could be another anniversary."

She paused in lifting the glass to her mouth when she heard how sober he sounded. Her gaze leapt to meet his stare. "Of what?" she asked.

He slipped a box into her free hand. She stared at the dark red ring box, frozen.

"Is this . . ."

She trailed off, going dry mouthed at the implication of her unfinished question.

"Yes," Kam said. She met his steady stare. He looked so calm. So solid. So certain. It was an amazing sight. Shivers cascaded down her spine and down her limbs. "Will you?" he asked her quietly.

"God *yes*," she replied fervently, and just like those other times she'd given him important answers, it felt entirely right. "I . . . I doubted at times this would happen to me," she said falteringly.

He caressed her shoulder. "Why wouldn't it happen to such an incredible woman?" he asked, his light eyes gleaming with emotion. "You'll always be number one with me. Always. Nothing and no one will come before you. That's what I promise you. You deserve nothing less."

"I promise you'll always come first, too, Kam," she vowed shakily. He'd known that solemn oath was precisely the one she would hold most dear. Tears of happiness prickled behind her eyelids.

"Open it," he urged in a gravelly voice, taking her champagne glass to free her hands.

A smile spreading on her lips, Lin followed his instructions, opening the lid to their rich, vibrant forever.

Read on for a sizzling extract of

Because You Are Mine

The bestselling ebook serialisation

Don't miss out on this electrifying series:
Because You Are Mine
When I'm With You
Because We Belong
Since I Saw You

Part One
Because You Tempt Me

One

Francesca glanced around when Ian Noble entered the room, mostly because everyone else in the luxurious restaurant bar did the same thing. Her heart jumped. Through the crowd she saw a tall man dressed in an impeccably tailored suit remove his overcoat, revealing a long, lean body. She immediately recognized Ian Noble. Her gaze lingered on the elegant black overcoat draped over his arm. The random thought hit her brain that while the black coat was right, the suit was all wrong. He belonged in jeans, didn't he? Her observation made no sense whatsoever. He looked fantastic in the suit, for one, and for another, according to a recent article she'd read in *GQ*, he was reputed to almost single-handedly keep London's Savile Row thriving. What else would a businessman who was the scion of a minor branch of the British monarchy wear? One of the men who had entered with him reached to take his coat, but he shook his head once.

Apparently, the enigmatic Mr. Noble wasn't planning on doing more than making a cursory appearance at the cocktail party he was hosting in Francesca's honor.

"There's Mr. Noble now. He'll be so pleased to meet you. He loves your work," Lin Soong said. Francesca heard the subtle note of pride in the woman's voice, as if Ian Noble was her lover instead of her employer.

"He looks like he has far more important things to do than meet me," Francesca said, smiling. She took a sip of club soda and watched as Noble spoke tersely on a cell phone while two men stood nearby, his overcoat remaining slung in the crook of his arm in readiness for a quick getaway. The subtle slant of his mouth told her he was irritated. For some reason, this all-too-human display of emotion relaxed her a little. She hadn't revealed it to her roommates—she was known for possessing a *whatever, bring it on attitude*—but she'd been strangely anxious about meeting Ian Noble.

The crowd returned to their conversation, but the energy level of the room had somehow amplified with Noble's arrival. Odd that such a distinctive, sophisticated man would become an icon for a tech-savvy, T-shirt-wearing generation. He looked to be thirtyish. She'd read Noble had earned his first billion with his breakthrough social-media company years ago, before he'd put it up for a public offering, made thirteen billion more, then promptly started another hugely successful Internet retail business.

Everything he touched turned to gold, apparently. Why? Because he was Ian Noble. He could do anything he damn well pleased. Francesca's mouth curved in amusement at the thought. It somehow helped to think he was arrogant and unlikeable. Yes, he was her benefactor, but like artists throughout history, Francesca had a healthy dose of distrust for the patron shelling out the money. Sadly, all starving artists needed their Ian Nobles.

"I'll just go and tell him you're here. As I've mentioned, he was quite taken with your painting. He chose it hands down over the two other finalists," Lin said, referring to the competition Francesca had won. The winner would be granted the prestigious commission to create the centerpiece painting for the grand lobby of Noble's new Chicago skyscraper, which they were in. The cocktail reception in Francesca's honor was being held in a restaurant called Fusion, a trendy, pricey restaurant located inside Noble's high-rise. Most importantly to Francesca, she would be awarded a hundred thousand dollars, something she could sorely use as a struggling master of fine arts graduate student.

Lin magically materialized a young African-American woman named Zoe Charon to converse with Francesca in her absence.

"It's a pleasure to meet you," Zoe said, flashing an orthodontist's dream smile as she shook Francesca's hand. "And congratulations on your commission. Just think: I'll be looking at your painting every time I walk into work."

Francesca suffered an increasingly familiar pang of discomfort over her clothing in comparison to Zoe's suit. Lin, Zoe, and just about every person at the reception in her honor were appareled in the height of sophisticated, sleek fashion. How was she to know that boho chic wouldn't work at a Noble cocktail party? How was she to know that her brand of boho chic wasn't *really* chic at all?

She learned Zoe was an assistant manager for Noble Enterprises, in a department called Imagetronics. *What the hell was that?* Francesca wondered distractedly as she nodded in polite interest, her gaze flickering again toward the front of the restaurant.

Noble's mouth softened slightly when Lin reached him and spoke. A few seconds later, a detached, bored expression settled on his features. He shook his head once and glanced at his watch. Clearly Noble didn't want to go through the ritual of meeting one of the many recipients of his philanthropic efforts any more than Francesca wanted to meet him. This cocktail party in her honor had been one of the onerous activities that accompanied the winning of the commission.

She turned to Zoe and grinned broadly, determined to enjoy herself now that she'd confirmed her anxiety about meeting Noble had been a waste of time.

"So what's the deal with Ian Noble?"

Zoe started at her bald question and glanced toward the front of the bar where Noble stood.

"The deal? He's a god, in a word."

Francesca smirked. "Not much for understatement, are you?"

Zoe broke into laughter. Francesca joined her. For a moment they were just two young women giggling over the most handsome man at the party. Which Ian Noble was, Francesca conceded. Forget the party. He was the most arresting man she'd ever seen in her life.

Her laughter ceased when she noticed Zoe's expression. She turned. Noble's gaze was directly on her. A hot, heavy sensation expanded in her belly. She didn't have time to draw breath before he was stalking across the room toward her, leaving a surprised-looking Lin in his wake.

Francesca experienced a ridiculous urge to run.

"Oh . . . he's headed this way . . . Lin must have told him who you were," Zoe said, sounding as bewildered and caught off guard as Francesca felt. Zoe was more practiced in the art of social elegance than Francesca, however. By the time Noble reached them, all traces of the giggling girl were gone and in its place stood a contained, beautiful woman.

"Mr. Noble, good evening."

His eyes were a piercing cobalt blue. They flicked off Francesca for a split second. She managed to suck some air into her lungs during the reprieve.

"Zoe, isn't it?" he asked.

Zoe couldn't hide her pleasure at the fact that Noble had known her name. "Yes, sir. I work in Imagetronics. May I introduce Francesca Arno, the artist you chose as the winner in the Far Sight Competition."

He took her hand. "It's a pleasure, Ms. Arno."

Francesca just nodded. She couldn't speak. Her brain was temporarily overloaded by the image of him, the warmth of his encompassing hand, the sound of his low, British-accented voice. His skin was pale next to his dark, stylishly coiffed, short hair and gray suit. *Dark Angel.* The words flew into her brain, unbidden.

"I can't tell you how impressed I am with your work," he said. No smile. No softness in his tone, even if there was a sharp curiosity in his stare.

She swallowed uneasily. "Thank you." He released her hand slowly, causing his skin to slide against hers. A horrible moment of silence passed as he just looked at her. She gathered herself and straightened her spine.

"I'm glad to have this opportunity to thank you in person for awarding me the commission. It means more to me than I can convey." She said the rehearsed words in a pressured fashion.

He gave an almost imperceptible shrug and waved his hand negligently. "You earned it." He held her stare. "Or at least you will."

She felt her pulse leap at her throat and hoped he didn't notice.

"I earned it, yes. But you gave me the opportunity. It's *that* I'm trying to express my thanks for. I probably wouldn't have been able to afford the second year of my master's program if you hadn't given me this chance."

He blinked. From the corner of her vision, Francesca noticed Zoe stiffen. Francesca glanced away in embarrassment. Had she sounded sharp?

"My grandmother often says I'm ungracious in the face of gratitude," he said, his voice quieter . . . warmer. "You're right to scold me. And you're also very welcome for the opportunity, Ms. Arno," he said, giving a nod of acknowledgement. "Zoe, would you mind taking a message to Lin for me? I've decided to cancel dinner with Xander LaGrange after all. Please have her reschedule."

"Of course, Mr. Noble," Zoe said before she walked away.

"Would you like to sit down?" he asked, nodding at an unoccupied circular leather booth.

"Sure."

He waited behind her while she scooted into the booth. She wished he wouldn't. She felt awkward and ungainly. After she'd settled, he slid beside her in one graceful, swooping motion. Francesca smoothed the gauzy skirt of the vintage beaded baby-doll dress she'd bought at a secondhand store in Wicker Park. The early September evening had been cooler than she'd expected when planning for the cocktail party. The casual denim jacket she wore had been her only choice, given the thin straps of her dress. It struck her how ridiculous she must appear, seated next to this immaculately dressed, thoroughly masculine male.

She fussed anxiously with her collar, and then sensed his stare on her. She met his eyes. Her chin went up defiantly. A small smile flickered across his mouth, and something clenched in her lower belly.

"So you're in the second year of your master's program?"

"Yes. I'm at the Art Institute."

"A very good school," he murmured. He rested his hands on the table and leaned back in the booth, looking thoroughly comfortable. His body was long, relaxed, and taut, reminding Francesca of a predatory animal whose seeming calmness could leap into full-out action in a split second. Even though his hips were slim, his shoulders were broad, suggesting some serious muscles beneath that starched white shirt. "If I'm remembering your application correctly, you studied both art and architecture at Northwestern University?"

"Yes," Francesca said breathlessly, pulling her gaze off his hands. They were elegant hands, but also large, blunt-tipped, and very capable-looking. The vision of them disturbed her for some reason. She couldn't help but imagine what they would look like against her skin . . . wrapped around her waist . . .

"Why?"

She started from her totally inappropriate thoughts and met his steady stare. "Why did I study both architecture and art?"

He nodded once.

"Architecture for my parents and art for me," she replied, surprising herself by the honesty of her answer. She usually made a show of being coolly disdainful when anyone asked the same question. Why should she have to choose between her talents? "My parents are both architects, and it was their lifetime dream that I become one as well."

"So you granted them half a dream. You earned the qualifications of an architect but don't plan to make it your career."

"I'll always be an architect."

"And I'm glad of it," he said, looking up when a handsome man with dreadlocks and pale gray eyes that contrasted with darker skin approached the table. Noble shook his hand. "Lucien, how is business?"

"Booming," Lucien replied, his gaze shifting to Francesca with interest.

"Ms. Arno, this is Lucien Lenault. He's the manager of Fusion, and the most illustrious restaurateur in Europe. I handpicked him from the finest restaurant in Paris."

Lucien rolled his eyes amusedly at Ian's introduction and grinned. "Hopefully, the same can be said of Fusion very soon. Ms. Arno, it's a pleasure to meet you," Lucien added in a delicious, French-accented voice. "What may I get you?"

Noble looked at her expectantly. His lips were unusually full for such a rugged-featured, masculine man, striking her as sensual yet firm.

Stern.

From where had that strange thought leapt?

"I'm fine," Francesca replied, although her heart started to beat erratically.

"What is that?" he asked, nodding at her half-empty drink.

"Just my usual drink, club soda with lime."

"You should be celebrating, Ms. Arno." Was it his accent that made her ears and neck prickle when he said her name? There was something unique about it, she realized. It was British, but some other influence seemed to slide into his syllables occasionally, something she couldn't quite identify. "Bring us a bottle of the Roederer Brut," Noble told Lucien, who smiled, gave a slight bow and walked away.

Her confusion mounted. Why was he bothering to spend so much time with her? Surely he didn't drink champagne with all of the recipients of his philanthropy. "As I was saying before Lucien arrived, I'm glad about your architecture background. Your skill and knowledge in that field is undoubtedly what gives your artwork so much precision, depth, and style. The painting you submitted for the contest was spectacular. You exactly caught the spirit of what I wanted for my lobby."

Her gaze skimmed across his immaculate suit. Somehow, his apparent love of a perfectly straight line didn't surprise her. True, her artwork was often inspired by her love of form and structure, but precision wasn't what her work was about. Far from it. "I'm glad you were pleased," she said with what she hoped was a neutral tone.

A smile ghosted his lips. "There's something behind your statement. Aren't you happy that you've pleased me?"

Her mouth dropped open at that. She stifled the words that flew to her throat. *I do my art to please no one but myself.* She stopped herself just in time. What was wrong with her? This man was responsible for changing her life.

"I told you earlier, I couldn't be happier about winning the contest. I'm thrilled."

"Ah," he murmured as Lucien arrived with the champagne and ice bucket. Noble didn't glance in Lucien's direction as the other man busied himself opening the bottle, but continued to study her as though she was a particularly interesting science project. "But being glad of your commission isn't the same as being glad you pleased me."

"No, I didn't mean that," she sputtered, looking at Lucien when he uncorked the champagne with a muffled popping sound. Her bewildered gaze returned to Noble. His eyes glinted in an otherwise impassive face. What in the world was he talking about? And why, despite the fact that she didn't have the answer to that, had his question made her so flustered? "I am glad that you liked the painting. Very much so."

Noble didn't reply, just watched detachedly as Lucien poured the sparkling fluid into flutes. He nodded and murmured his thanks before Lucien walked away. Francesca picked up her glass when he reached for his.

"Congratulations."

She managed a smile as their flutes touched ever so fleetingly. She'd never tasted anything like it; the champagne was dry and icy and felt delicious sliding across her tongue and down her throat. She gave Noble a sideways glance. How could he seem so oblivious to the thick tension in the air when she felt as if she'd suffocate from it?

"I guess since you're royalty, a cocktail waitress won't do for serving you," she said, wishing her voice hadn't quavered.

"I beg your pardon?"

"Oh, I just meant—" She cursed silently to herself. "I'm a cocktail waitress—I do it to help pay the bills while I'm in grad school," she added, slightly panicked at how cool, and a little intimidating, he suddenly appeared. She lifted her flute and took a too-large gulp of the icy fluid. Wait until she told Davie how she botched this whole thing. Her good friend would be exasperated with her, even if her other roommates—Caden and Justin—would roll with laughter at her latest incident of apparent social idiocy.

If only Ian Noble wasn't so handsome. Disturbingly so.

"I'm sorry," she mumbled. "I shouldn't have said that. It's just— I'd read that your grandparents belonged to a minor branch of the British royal family—an earl and a countess, no less."

"And you were wondering if I despise being waited on by a mere serving girl, is that it?" he asked. Amusement didn't soften his features, just made them more compelling. She sighed and relaxed a little. She hadn't *completely* offended him.

"I did most of my schooling in the states," he said. "I consider myself to be an American, first and foremost. And I assure you, the only reason Lucien came to wait on us himself is that he chose to. We're fencing partners in addition to being friends. The custom of the English aristocracy preferring the status of a manservant over a maid exists only in Regency English novels in the present day, Ms. Arno. Even if they did still exist, I doubt they'd apply to a bastard. I'm sorry to disappoint you."

Her cheeks felt like they were boiling. When would she learn to keep her big mouth shut? Was he telling her *he* was illegitimate? She'd never read anything regarding that before.

"Where do you waitress?" he asked, seeming color blind to her scarlet cheeks.

"At High Jinks in Bucktown."

"I've never heard of it."

"Somehow that doesn't surprise me," she muttered under her breath before she took another sip of champagne. She blinked in surprise at the sound of his low, rough laughter. Her eyes widened when she looked at his face. He looked so *pleased*. Her heart dipped. Ian Noble was spectacular to behold at any given moment, but when he smiled, he was nothing short of a menace to a female's composure.

"Would you mind coming with me . . . walking a few blocks? There's something crucial I'd like to show you," he said.

Her hand paused in the action of lifting the flute to her lips. What was going on here?

"It directly relates to your commission," he said, suddenly crisp. Authoritative. "I'd like to show you the view I want for the painting."

Anger sliced through her shock. Her chin went up. "I'm expected to paint whatever you want me to?"

"Yes," he said without pause.

She set down the flute with a loud clicking sound, jarring the contents. He'd sounded completely unyielding. He was every bit as arrogant as she'd imagined. Just as she'd expected, winning this prize was going to end up being a nightmare. His nostrils flared as he stared at her unblinkingly, and she glared back.

"I suggest you see the view in question before you take undue offense, Ms. Arno."

"Francesca."

Something flashed in his blue eyes like heat lightning. For a split second, she regretted the edge to her tone. But then he nodded once.

"Francesca it is," he said softly. "If you make it Ian."

She willed herself to ignore the flutter in her belly. *Don't be beguiled*, she warned herself. He was the exact type of domineering patron that would try to dictate, and crush her creative instincts in the process. It was worse than she'd feared.

Without another word, she slid out of the booth and walked toward the entrance of the restaurant, sensing, with every cell of her being, him moving behind her.